Casually Yours

Casually Yours

VIVIAN JIA LAC

SAN FRANCISCO

CASUALLY YOURS
Published by Third State Books
93 Cumberland Street
San Francisco, CA 94110
Visit us at www.thirdstatebooks.com

THIRD
STATE
BOOKS

Edited by Charles Kim and Stephanie Lim
First edition: March 2026
ISBN 979-8-89013-046-4 (trade paperback original)
979-8-89013-047-1 (e-book)
979-8-89013-048-8 (audiobook)

This is a work of fiction. Names, characters, businesses, places, events, locales, and incidents are either the products of the author's imagination or used in a fictitious manner. Any resemblance to actual persons, living or dead, or actual events is purely coincidental.

Cover artwork by Tara Hân-Trần Johnson
Cover and text design by Kathryn E. Campbell

For my sister, Anna,

who has read all my stories

and thinks I'm funny more than half the time.

CHAPTER ONE

Seven years ago

Parker Tran is the last person I want to see waiting for me.

Unfortunately, I don't think he's here for anyone else. I've only made it one foot out the door of Rocky's Diner when I spot the Jeep. A pair of familiar eyes, colder than I remember, bounce from my face to the two extra-large Styrofoam cups in my hands.

"Two-for-one strawberry milkshakes."

I'd spent days envisioning this in preparation for my return to Silverpine. Try as I might, I knew I could only avoid him for so long. In all the simulations I'd run in my head—during lectures, study sessions, at three a.m. when sleep wouldn't come—I'd have the perfect, sardonic remark ready to devastate him. But that wasn't it.

"I didn't get one for you," I add, just so he knows this isn't a happy reunion.

"I'm not here for the milkshake." His grip is already on the door of the black Wrangler, as if standing here with me for a second longer might put him in danger. "Can we go?"

"I don't need a ride," I say automatically, still standing half in, half out of the door of the fifties-themed diner. I glance over my shoulder. The only other patron is smacking the decrepit jukebox, trying to get it to return his quarter. That thing's been out of commission since I was in middle school. "Actually, I'm going to enjoy these here."

A teenager wearing a staff apron saunters over. "We're closing in five." Damn it. Parker is looking at me expectantly, but I won't give in without a challenge.

"What are you even doing here?"

"My mom asked me to pick you up. Demanded, actually." Ah, that's my fault. Cô had called earlier to invite me to dinner, and I'd let my location slip. Since she's sent this harbinger of doom to come collect me, it looks like my attendance isn't up for debate.

"I can walk back."

At this, he throws his head back, and his hand drops from the car. He's going to run it through his hair now.

He does—a show of his irritation. And now he's going to sigh.

"Get in the car, Dani," he says with a loud huff.

I watch thick bangs fall back in place over straight, dark brows. His teammates once bleached his hair blond for freshman initiation. Now that we're well into junior year, his natural color has fully grown out, and I'm reminded, with great vexation, how much I prefer his black hair. Not that the blond looked particularly bad. Even if initiation had entailed shaving his head, I doubt Parker Tran could ever look bad. Has he gotten taller too? He's well over six feet now, and sometimes I think that growth spurt will go on forever.

"Do you want to tell my mom you're going to be late for dinner, or should I?"

I could run, zip right past him, and I doubt he'd make the effort to chase me. But it's not the six-something quarterback I'm afraid of. A dinner invite from Cô is like a royal summons. I've seen her discipline her boys for disrespecting the sanctity of a shared meal, and I don't ever want to be on the receiving end of that straw broom.

"Fine, let's go," I relent, and Parker opens the door of the Jeep for me because I'm holding two milkshakes bigger than my head. Not because he's a gentleman. And definitely not because he likes me. It takes a mighty hop to get in, an ungainly sight as my legs kick at the air before I finally land on the seat. I blame it on the custom monster-truck tires.

"Careful with those." He eyes the milkshakes warily as he settles in next to me with notable ease.

I try to squeeze a shake into the center console, but it's no use. "Why are your cup holders so small?"

He bats my hand away. "They're normal sized. Anything that doesn't fit probably isn't meant for human consumption."

I set the cups on the dashboard while I buckle my seatbelt, and Parker winces. The Jeep is his baby, the apple of his eye. He'd been saving up for it since we turned twelve, painting houses, mowing lawns, and working part-time at a sporting goods store one summer. When he landed his D-1 scholarship, his parents chipped in a sizeable gift, and the motorized eyesore was his. It isn't until the milkshakes are safely in my lap that he finally starts the car.

We drive down roads that we've memorized, past weathered brick shopfronts, the general store run by three generations of Dawsons, and bookstores whose shelves I've devoured to the very last book. If I weren't so conflicted about coming home, I might fall for its nostalgic trap of silver-barked pines shimmering through the fog and air that somehow always smells like fresh bread.

Once we reach the town's center, we're stopped by the first new faces I've seen in years. Parker rolls down the window to give directions to an elderly couple. Travelers lost on their way to Portland make up most of the traffic that comes through here. Just as predictably, the couple erupts in affable laughter, having had the good fortune of encountering this small town's sweetheart. Parker must've said something witty and endearing. I don't know, I'm not paying attention. I stare straight ahead, fixated on skies the same shade of gray as the days when Nathan would drive us into the city. Back then, Nathan was the only Tran brother with a driver's license, and Parker was still someone I called a friend.

From here, only three main roads intersect the center: Pine Street takes us to Green Valley High, our old school; Oak Street leads to the pharmacy that Parker's family owns; and Cedar Street is the way home. The Jeep careens right onto Cedar (again with the monster-truck tires), and I shift all my weight to not lean toward him.

"The milkshakes," he reminds me. "Careful."

I'm already regretting getting into this vehicle. Time seems to slow down in Silverpine, but right now, it's the tension that's making the seconds crawl by. What should be a ten-minute drive feels like a depressing kiddie train looping around a mall—except the mall is Hell, and no matter how hard you cry, the ride never ends.

"You haven't been home for longer than an hour since you came back from New York."

It takes a second to register that he's talking to me.

"And?" *The less time I spend at home, the less likely I'll run into you*. It doesn't require much brainpower to figure that one out. It's the first holiday back from college since we've stopped talking, and living next door to the very person I'm trying to evade means I have to constantly be on the move. Even my oblivious father is beginning to wonder why his homebody daughter is anywhere but home.

"You're avoiding me."

"I've been out catching up with people," I lie. "It's been a while."

"Like, real people?" he asks. "Do you have friends here?"

I can't tell if it's a joke. "How long are you going to stay in town?" I deflect. "Don't you have practice?"

"I don't really want to talk about football."

"Oh my god." I touch my forehead with alarm. "Did I just prove quantum jumping is real?"

"Quantum what? What does that even mean?"

"It means I've jumped into an alternate universe where you don't talk obsessively about football."

Parker clicks his tongue as the car rolls to a stop at a red. "You always have to be a smartass."

The foam cups are icy cold in my hands, and my fingertips feel numb. "Can I put these down? My hands are freezing."

"*Don't*," he warns. "If that shit spills, it'll be impossible to clean, and I'll never get the smell out."

"Your car already smells."

"No, it doesn't."

"You could cool it with the cheap body spray." I know, I'm being petty. "It's hard enough sitting here without the ghost of a teenage boy trying to smother me."

His hand on his face does little to hide his annoyance. "Dani, I'm trying to be patient. I've been waiting around all weekend to talk to you, but if you're going to be like this—"

"You want to talk about what happened last Christmas?"

He stares straight ahead, his jaw clenched. Not a word. I expected as much.

"Don't bother then," I say decisively, and we don't speak for what's left of the ride. Meanwhile, a pit of dread is opening in my stomach. Why did I bring it up? In the quiet, I wonder if he, too, is replaying that day in Grand Central Terminal and how everything changed afterward.

Parker pulls up to his house and cuts the engine, leaving an excruciating silence. The old basketball hoop looms above us, just as durable as the family's old Toyota parked ahead. Like the rest of Silverpine, time has frozen this driveway. It causes a lump in my throat, and I don't climb out of the Jeep just yet.

We met on this small stretch of pavement when we were both seven. We learned to ride bikes here. On Saturday mornings, I'd scurry across from my house to watch cartoons with him. We had driving lessons in the Toyota, and I was there when he backed the car into the hoop stand and for Chú's wrath, entirely in Vietnamese, which was still terrifying even if I didn't understand a word. Some mornings, when I was up early enough, I'd watch him bolt out the door for practice. I can't think of this place without the memory of Parker, like a thorn in my side. As the bright-eyed boy running under the sun or the varsity quarterback, he's there in every imprint with an old football, its leather faded and cracked, tucked under his arm.

But that was a different time. Parker is still the boy who lives next door, but we don't talk anymore.

I stack one milkshake on top of the other and reach for the door.

"Wait," he says suddenly. "How are we going to get through dinner like this? Everyone keeps asking what happened between us."

"I'll just ignore you, and you can do the same." I shrug. "It'll be so awkward they'll have to drop it. You did a really good job at that back then. Pretending I don't exist."

"That's . . . that's not what happened."

"Then why didn't you show up that day, Parker?"

A tense gaze connects us, but once again, radio silence. Another unwanted memory invades my mind. Why now, of all times? I remember being right here when I showed him my welcome packet from Columbia. He said he'd visit me in New York. I promised I'd come watch him play.

Now, I count the days until we're both back at school on opposite sides of the country.

Even if he were to explain, I'm not sure I'd want to stay and hear it. The truth is, there's no excuse that would make a difference now. I've already moved on with my life post-Parker Tran. At some point, everyone leaves, and even he isn't an exception.

I turn to make my exit, but a hand lurches forward with a reaction time that only makes sense for an athlete. I don't realize the Styrofoam tower on my lap is already toppling until Parker's reaching for it. But it's too late. A milkshake collapses at my feet with a *pop*, sending an explosion of sugary pink all over the Jeep's shiny black interior.

For a moment, we're silent again, eyes glued to the creamy pool around my sneakers. Then, Parker's voice cuts through the cold air.

"For fuck's sake, Dani, I told you to be careful!"

"Oh my god, will you relax?" I try to pick up the cup, but it slips from my grasp. My feet twist in the sticky mess, detaching from my brain amid the panic.

"Stop moving, you're getting it everywhere!"

I turn to see hellfire in his eyes.

"I knew this would happen. Who even orders *two* extra-large milkshakes? It's like you're difficult on purpose."

"You make it sound like I'm the unreasonable one, when we

both know you're going to scrub this car down with a toothbrush. Take your time, by the way, we won't miss you at dinner."

I watch his ears go red. "You know what, I didn't miss this. You . . . you were always such a . . . such a—"

"A what?"

"A goddamn smartass," he spits. "You think you're always right. It doesn't matter what I say when you've already made up your mind."

He seethes, and an exasperated hand flies to his hair again. "You know what? I don't care anymore. You can keep avoiding me. I'll do you a solid and stay away from you too. See if I give a shit if we ever talk again."

Parker's words land with a thud. I swallow whatever emotion is gathering in my throat and prickling at the back of my eyes.

"You won't have to worry about seeing me around here again. Or ever, for that matter."

"Just get out of my car."

"Gladly."

I yank at the handle and force the door open. The driveway becomes a blur as anger rushes to my head. I think I see Cô on the porch waving me in, but I'm too focused on the fiery thrum between my ears to be sure.

"On second thought, you can have this."

I whip around and dump the second milkshake on his lap.

CHAPTER TWO

You've got this, Dani Tsai. Today, you become the master of your fate. I repeat this mantra in my head and take a deep, slow breath to calm my nerves. I've been buzzing with excitement all morning, picturing a version of myself three months from now, eating street food in Myeongdong and volcano hiking on Mount Bromo. I hum a tune to myself as I minimize an article on my laptop and run a Google search for popular cafés in Seoul.

Adagio magazine, my daily grind for the last three years, feels brighter than ever. The offices occupy the top floor of a building on Union Square, and the view of the park below looks renewed today. New York in the fall is already a sight to behold, but this morning, even the dead leaves have luster. I find a subdued melody in the keyboard clicks and murmurs of my colleagues. Everything is putting me in a good mood. And I love this place because it's where I met my coworker Charlotte, and Charlotte is about to change my life, potentially.

They say if you can imagine a scenario, it already exists somewhere in the multiverse. I've never been remarkably lucky in my native one, but I think this time, it's finally throwing me a bone. Last week, Charlotte told me about a job opportunity at Modrix, a trendy online publication. They're looking for a correspondent who will globe-trot across Asia and write a dedicated column with features and travel tips. It's a contract position, but I'd get to travel for half a year and write about my adventures in Shanghai, Ho Chi Minh City, or Kuala Lumpur. Charlotte has an in with the editor and set me up with an interview today.

I like my current job as a copy editor. I really do. *Adagio* is a "slow journalism" magazine focused on delivering news at an unrushed, meaningful pace. The content is sincere and thought-provoking, and most importantly for my Asia plans, the publications are quarterly. My boss, Lindsay, has approved the potential contract gig, as long as I can still work remotely to meet deadlines. I promised her I'd manage.

I've never asked the universe for much—I've been careful about that. For all the spoils the hand of fate may bestow, I also know what it's capable of taking. Moving to New York was the one and only selfish act I asked the universe to bless. After ten years in the city with a remarkably quiet life, I don't think it would count as overstepping if I manifested the correspondent position now. I'm allowed to want this.

"Ready for the big interview?" Savannah pops over to my desk like a living exclamation, long-limbed and striking in her red pantsuit. She always looks like she got lost on her way to interview for *Vogue* and ended up with us instead. I'm sure Condé Nast would still take her.

"I think so."

"Don't be modest. You've already started on your itinerary, haven't you?"

With a sheepish smile, I turn my laptop around.

"I'm so excited for you!"

"Let me guess: Dani found a new PBS documentary and is in for a wild weekend!" Tae-woo slumps into the desk chair next to mine. I'm pretty sure his suit is new. And his watch. With a penchant for the finer things, he lives his life with his settings configured to two modes: expensive and unbothered. Tae-woo thought my name was Daniella when I started at *Adagio*, and when I informed him that he was only half correct, he called me Ella for two months.

"Even better. If I play my cards right, I can get two men to fly me around the world." I waggle my brows impishly. He doesn't bite. "I'm kidding, it's a job interview."

"Ah." He gives a cursory nod as he scrolls on his tablet. I can tell he doesn't find me compelling. "Ugh, Lindsay finally got back to me on my Pierre Gagnaire feature. She said bringing it to the editors now would be like 'passing at the one-yard line.' What the hell does that even mean?"

"She's saying it's pointless," I tell him. "The one-yard line is one yard from the end zone, right before the touchdown. I think the Seahawks tried that at the Super Bowl, and it cost them the win."

Savannah cocks her head. "I didn't know you were into football."

"I'm not," I say, resuming my Google search. "Football was a pretty big deal at my high school, that's all."

"Dani!" a singsong voice calls, and I spot Charlotte, my beautiful beacon of hope, rushing over. Her blonde curls bounce like a shampoo ad. "The Modrix guys got us a table at Picotea tonight! I'm so excited. I've been trying to get a res for weeks!"

I tap a finger against my chin. "Is that one owned by an oil heiress, a reality TV star, or an influencer?"

"Knicks player," Tae-woo interjects.

Charlotte puffs air through her nose. "I've had my res canceled *three* times because some athlete with VIP status always gets priority over me."

"Tonight?" Savannah repeats. "What kind of interview is scheduled after work hours?"

"Um, well, since the editor is a friend of mine, he and his associate agreed to meet Dani over dinner. Think of it like a casual business meeting. I'll be there too—you know, to talk you up." Charlotte beams, green eyes flitting over me. "You're going to change, right?"

I glance down at my go-to office fit, a blazer and straight-leg pants. "What's wrong with this?"

She makes a disapproving sound, and I catch Savannah rolling her eyes. Her theory is that because Charlotte shares a name with a character from *Sex and the City*, she believes she's destined to climb New York's social ladder. She's also infinitely more interested in her Instagram feed than the lives of her coworkers, so her enthusiasm does strike me as odd. But I blow past the thought. Even Charlotte must have a yearly quota for acts of good will.

"Fine, I'll change."

"Do something with your hair too. Give some life to that thing," Tae-woo says, like he's tagged in for a jab at me, and a little too eagerly at that.

Savannah purses her lips. "It might help if you curled it."

I pull a face at them and grab for the compact in my purse. I've had the same hair and makeup routine since college: minimal effort, quick enough to get me to morning classes on time. Sure, I immediately fade to the background next to my peers who treat Tuesdays like the Met Gala, but it's never been my desire to stand out anyway. If anything, it's kind of fun to be in the position of admirer, to hear the echoes of *wow* when Savannah steps onto the 6 train—although I do wonder sometimes what it'd be like if once, just once, a man were to look at me and think the same thing.

"And don't wear your reading glasses." Tae-woo is still picking me apart like an article he's been assigned. "I know you think they make you look smart, but they don't."

"He means your eyes are your best feature," Savannah adds mercifully. *Sharp and pretty, like a cat*, Cô used to say.

"Okay, relax, everyone. It's an interview, not a date." I look over to Charlotte. "So, meet at seven?"

She's on her phone, already mentally checked out. "Hm? Oh, yeah."

❧

I have some time after work to get changed before the interview. I'm jittery the entire subway ride to Brooklyn, and once I'm above ground, I sprint to my apartment, expertly weaving among the swarm of bodies on the sidewalk. From the Columbia dorms to a fifth-floor walk-up in Sunset Park, I've seen many a New York rental before landing in a studio in Bed-Stuy. On a day when my legs have the endurance of jelly, I've never been so grateful to live in an elevator building.

As I browse my closet frantically, my phone dings with an email alert. The body is simply a link to an article, "101 Tips for a Successful Job Interview," with the prefilled signature James Tsai, Data Engineer, AWS Certified Data Engineer—Associate. Before I can type a reply, Dad is already calling me.

"I sent you something you should read before your interview."

Do I have the time or mental capacity to read all 101 bullet points before tonight? Definitely not, but I lie. "Sure, Dad."

"Have you eaten yet?"

"Not yet. I'm meeting the editors for dinner."

"Right, you mentioned that." He sounds distracted, and from the rhythmic tapping of a keyboard, I can tell he's in his home office. "Don't get home too late—and don't take a rideshare, they're not safe."

It's the kind of comment you'd expect an Asian parent to make to a twenty-eight-year-old who left the nest a decade ago. It's also never stopped me from ordering an Uber before, but he doesn't need to know that. I've learned to pick my battles by now and don't need to think twice to reply, "Okay, Dad."

"If you get the job, will you go to Taiwan too?"

This question, however, gives me pause. There are two topics my father would rather sidestep forever than talk about directly: my love life, and my mother. From a young age, I learned to read between the lines with him, and right now, that space in between is asking, *Are you planning to see your mom?*

"I don't know yet," I say, truthfully. I tap the speaker icon on the screen so I can open the LINE app on my phone. I downloaded it solely to keep in contact with Mom, since it's the preferred messaging platform in Taiwan. The last time she reached out was a couple of months ago, to show me a mural she'd painted for the Banqiao 435 Art Zone in New Taipei. My limited Mandarin could only produce so many synonyms for *amazing* in reaction to the vivid city skyline and banyan trees.

"If you go . . ." He hesitates.

Is he really going to ask about Mom? I glance at the time on my phone. The restaurant Charlotte mentioned is in SoHo, so it shouldn't take longer than forty-five minutes to get there. I don't have to leave yet, but if Dad starts airing his grievances, this won't be a quick chat.

"If you go, you need to get better at speaking Mandarin. Lots of foreigners get ripped off all the time, and you're going to be an easy target too. You open your mouth, and they'll think, 'Ignorant American.'"

"Gee, thanks for the vote of confidence."

Another master class in the Tsai family art of deflection. This is where I learned to dance around uncomfortable subjects: divert and repress, repress and divert. It's clear to me that as long as Dad keeps his feelings about Mom to himself—does he hate her? Has he moved on?—I should extend the grace of never asking.

That's how it's always been since the divorce. I was six when the papers were signed, and it only took two weeks before Mom packed up her easel and art supplies and flew back to Taiwan. There was no messy custody battle; Dad had job security and wanted me to continue my education here, and Mom wasn't exactly making waves in the art scene stateside anyway. Incidentally, returning home was the move her career needed to flourish, enough to live comfortably in her Taichung condo with the "free-spirited" Jin, a man fifteen years her junior.

It's always been my understanding that what happened to my family is simply off-limits for discussion. Most Asian couples of Mom and Dad's generation don't entertain the idea of divorce and would rather live miserably ever after if it meant saving face. The resulting shame seems to be why we fell out of contact with her side of the family, namely my grandparents. A year after she left, Dad and I moved across the state, from an Oregon cul-de-sac to Silverpine, an even tinier pocket of suburbia. He allowed me to take one box of items she'd left behind—VHS tapes, a few books, and other keepsakes, all buried in a drawer in my room—which was his way of putting the whole thing to rest.

"By the way," Dad starts over the phone, "you remember Parker?"

A coat hanger nearly slips out of my hand. I haven't heard that name in years. Another ghost from my past. Of course I remember Parker. I've been cursed to, until they finally invent a technology that can wipe my memories. Possibilities flood my mind: He got married. He won the lottery. He flew to space—that would be just like him.

"What about him?"

"I heard from his parents that he's in New York."

I try to resist frowning. "People come to New York all the time."

"Maybe you can meet with him."

"Um, no. Why? No, never."

"I will never understand you two." I can almost hear Dad shaking his head from three thousand miles away. "You two used to be so close. Since the day we moved to Silverpine, you spent every second together. I only saw you fight once, over the PlayStation."

The days of Parker and me arguing over who had dibs on *Final Fantasy* don't just feel like a long time ago; they feel like another lifetime. I'd be convinced I'd jumped universes if Dad's memories didn't line up with mine. He was there for that first meeting on the driveway, and I know he saw the immediate spark—a seamless connection between two seven-year-olds, as if they'd known one another in a past life. The beginning of all beginnings.

Having grown up around families who didn't look like us, I did a justifiable double take when the Trans strolled over to introduce themselves. Linh Pham and Hieu Tran—by their insistence, I was to call them Cô and Chú—ran the local pharmacy, they informed us. By their side was Nathan, four years older than me, all lanky limbs and wire-framed glasses, and next to him was Parker.

Parker, with the tan lines on his arms, stark where his T-shirt sleeves ended. That big grin, missing his two front teeth. Scraped knees and hands clutching a football that looked too big for them.

Cô brought it up first: "Parker, you and Dani are the same age! Make friends!"

He asked if I wanted to split an ice cream sandwich and whether I had any Pokémon cards to trade. I said yes, and from that moment on, our childhoods were definitively entwined.

"That was forever ago. You know that I haven't seen or spoken to him in years." Not that I had a choice in the matter. He'd decided that on his own. The milkshake in his lap may have been the nail in the coffin, but Parker already hated me before that. "Anyways, I thought he was in San Francisco."

After moving to New York, I stopped visiting Silverpine as much. It's been nearly two years since my last return. Parker also left town, although he moved just across the state to play for the University of Oregon. I heard—not of my own volition—that he'd eventually relocated to the Bay Area after college. By the grace of higher powers, I have not seen him in seven years. Milkshakegate is my last memory of Parker Tran, and I don't think I'll be crushed if things remain that way.

"Apparently, he's there for work. His mom thought it would be nice if you showed him around."

Guilt seeps in at the mention of Cô, like water under a closed door. "I'm going to be really busy if I get this job. I won't have time to meet with him, and I'm sure he doesn't want to see me either."

"That doesn't sound like the Parker I know."

"Yeah, well, people change." Sometimes they up and leave you. Other times, they become strangers. "I'll call you later, Dad. I've got to head out soon."

After I hang up, I consider texting Mom about the job interview, but I think better of it. I've seen my mother a total of four times since the split: two summertime visits to Taiwan; a brief trip at sixteen to Seattle, where she had an exhibition; and most recently, during a trip to Asia after I graduated college, when I carved out just enough time to drop by and be formally introduced to "Uncle" Jin—he was thirty-five, I was twenty-three. Aside from the birthday greetings over text and occasional video call, we didn't really keep in touch. There's no reason to update her on something that isn't even a certainty.

Before I leave my apartment, I take one last scan in the full-length mirror. With a defeated sigh, and twenty minutes to spare, I get out my curling iron.

CHAPTER THREE

Everybody who is anybody is at Picotea tonight. At least, that's what Charlotte tells me. I don't recognize anyone myself, but every table has a stylish party with portable ring lights, so I guess it's a big deal to be here. The place is buzzing, and the tables are pushed so close together that I could appear in the elaborate video the patron next to me is taking of his tapas. We're seated at the dining end of the restaurant, near the carefree commotion of the bar and lounge.

I can't help but wonder if we're at the wrong place. What did Charlotte call it? A casual business dinner? It certainly doesn't feel like a job interview. To add to my suspicions, the editors from Modrix have been anything but professional since they sat down with us. Charlotte had greeted them both with eager hugs, and the one with dark brown curls, Jerry Rodgers, even cupped her ass. I suppose that's what she meant when she said she had an in.

The man sitting across from me is Ernest Miller. He wears a V-neck so deep, a scraggly patch of chest hair is peeking out with intent, fluttering with the AC as if to wave hello at me. He also winks at me every time he slips an innuendo into conversation, and it makes my skin crawl.

"You guys are crushing it at *Adagio*," says Ernest, and I'm delighted to finally talk shop. "Unlike Jerry, I don't name-drop you guys just to sound smart. I've actually read your stuff."

"*Adagio* is amazing. I'm just a copy editor right now, but I've been lucky to have them publish a few of my pieces." I remind myself to speak with confidence and maintain eye contact. "I've already talked to my boss, and should everything come together, she's agreed to let me work remotely."

"Uh, okay. That's great?"

Uh-oh. That was a tepid response. Would they prefer that I not be overly committed to my current job? "Of course, if there are bigger opportunities, I would be happy to consider them."

"Sounds like you're quite the fireball." He winks at me again.

"Dani is such a hard worker!" Charlotte cuts in so suddenly, I startle and hit my knee against the table. She turns to me with a forced smile, her jaw setting tightly as she whispers, "When are you going to take that thing off your head?"

I hold on to the rim of the bucket hat in case she tries to remove it herself. "I told you, I can't! I literally fried my hair with my curler."

"You did not."

"From one copy editor to another, you know how we feel about misusing that word. I'm telling you, Charlotte, I *literally* burned a chunk of my hair. It's scorched land back there. All because you guys made me self-conscious back at the office." Imagine my horror when the curling iron I hadn't used in four years clamped onto my hair and would not unclamp. Once I'd broken free and the smoke had dissipated, I could do little to salvage the singed mess on the back of my head. "It's so bad, you might even smell the sulfur if I take this off."

Charlotte scrunches her nose. "Fine. Leave it on."

The guys call for another bottle of wine, and the next order of tapas arrives at our table. I'm so nervous that I haven't been able to stomach anything. I sip my sangria in an effort to look natural. "Um, I'm a big fan of Modrix. I think your take on digital journalism is really refreshing." That's one way of putting it. I did check out their website, and in truth, it was all over the place. Without a singular focus, their approach to everything from tech news to lifestyle to personal finance felt, frankly, chaotic. But they seem to be doing well, and if they can afford to send me to another continent, I'll suck up like never before. "I love that you haven't pigeonholed yourselves into one niche."

"Oh, yeah. We call it next-level ideation," Ernest says. "It's not just about clicks; it's about content and conversation. At the end of the day, the algorithm loves genuineness."

"That's our motto at Modrix: Authenticity reaps attention," Jerry inserts. "We're trying to elevate journalism as we know it. Disrupting tradition, shifting the content paradigm. The way I see it, we're creating a movement. A hustle with heart."

"Wow." I fear I'll pull a muscle in my jaw if I smile any harder. That's a whole lot of talking just to say nothing at all. I peek over at Charlotte, who's preoccupied with taking a selfie. She stops to inspect Jerry from behind her phone, grimaces, and then returns to her Instagram account. Well, that makes their relationship clear: The editor is her flavor of the week, to be kicked to the curb once she's exhausted his connections.

Picotea is so packed, anyone trying to make it to the bar has to squeeze past our table. The foot traffic picks up throughout the evening, which means that unfortunately, I have to lean closer to Ernest and his unruly chest hair in order to hear him.

"So, Dani, what do you like to do for fun?"

I can already tell that no one at this table cares to hear about the fantasy trilogy I've been discussing at length on a Discord server. I go with the usual safe reply: "I like to watch movies and read."

"I'd love to catch a movie with you sometime."

Did he just ask me out? If so, isn't that extremely inappropriate? I nudge Charlotte with my foot under the table, but she's busy tuning her antennae to the group of men passing by. The restaurant's lighting is too dim to make out their faces, but I can tell they're exactly her MO: young and expensive-looking in their Tom Ford suits.

She tugs on my sleeve. "The view is *gorgeous* tonight."

I glance over dapper haircuts to the tallest of the pack. He's looking down at his phone, not paying attention to the others. Something about him commands my attention, and my gaze traces his long legs and broad shoulders all the way up to his satiny dark hair.

And then, he looks up, and all the air is sucked out of me.

No way. There is no way. In a city of over eight million people, how could I be here at the same time as Parker Tran?

I duck, snapping my bucket hat lower with reflexes I didn't know I possessed. My knee connects with the table again, sending a fork flying over the edge. I scramble to pick it up, my heart pounding fiercely in my throat. Charlotte pokes me aggressively in my side, but I'm still trying to find my bearings.

My lungs are feeling dangerously deprived. Once I'm certain the party of suits has made it to the other side of the restaurant, I excuse myself to the bathroom. Hunching over the sink, I splash my face with cold water and teach myself to breathe again. *There's. Just. No. Freaking. Way*. Could I be hallucinating from the stress of the interview?

No. I know that face. I know how he walks, the magnetic way he carries himself across a room, his size and intensity. I'd spent years dedicating it all to memory.

Charlotte enters through the door. "What's wrong with you?"

"Nothing," I lie. "It's too crowded out there."

"You've barely spoken, and you're, like, totally distracted. Aren't you having a good time?"

About that. I look at her, puzzled. "I may be imagining things, but I have a feeling Ernest thinks we're on a date right now."

She twists her lips. "You haven't figured it out yet. Dani, that's exactly what this is. There's no interview, I made that up to get you to come out."

"What do you—" It dawns on me then: the restaurant choice, the flirty remarks. "Oh my god! Are you serious? You told Ernest I'm here for a *date*?"

"I was doing a favor for Jerry. He knows everyone in New York, and I'm trying to get a referral to Casa Cipriani before the end of the year. He asked me if I knew someone to set Ernest up with, and I thought you and he might hit it off. But I also knew you'd never say yes if I asked honestly."

"Yeah, because I *hate* being set up!" I throw my hands up for emphasis. A woman steps out of a stall, and Charlotte lowers her voice. "I know, so I had to—"

"Trick me into a double date?" I gasp. "Does the correspondent position even exist?"

"It does, I swear! I heard Jerry mention it last week." She places her manicured hands on my shoulders. "Look, the interview might've been a lie, but if you make a good impression tonight, you can still schmooze your way to your dream job."

"How the fuck am I supposed to do that?"

"The same way we're going to get these guys to pay for dinner—flirt with them! For starters, you can undo a button and let your hair down." She makes a grab at my hat. "Take that stupid thing off!"

I dodge her. "Leave it, Judas!"

Charlotte huffs and takes her disappointment out the door with her. I don't follow yet, reluctant to leave the safe haven that is the women's bathroom. This is quickly shaping up to be one of the worst nights of my life. The half-wits of Modrix I can handle—I just have to keep track of where that single braincell bounces between the two—but Parker? Nothing about this night feels real, as if it were all a vivid nightmare. And yet I should've seen this coming. If everything was meant to go catastrophically wrong tonight, it only makes sense that the universe would throw him at me too.

Should I make a run for it? To where, I haven't decided, but the call of the void is strong. If the interview isn't even real, I should cut my losses and go home. And if I slip out of here fast enough, I might be able to avoid running into my unwelcomed blast from the past.

But then, I think about the untraversed volcanoes in Indonesia, all the adventures still waiting for me. Straightening the protective gear on my head, I let out a groan from the depths of my soul. One crisis at a time. The dudebros might believe they're here for a date, but that doesn't mean I have to be here with the same intentions. I can even play this to my favor. Charlotte flirts with leads all the time if it'll land her a good article. So long as I steer us back to the Asia gig, I won't have to entertain Ernest for too long. I'll charm the chinos off him, let him know what I came for, and he'll have to consider me for the job.

Armed with only my resolve, I fling the door open with force, adrenaline propelling me straight out of the bathroom.

And I head-butt Parker Tran in the chest.

CHAPTER FOUR

The impact is like crashing headfirst into a rock-climbing wall. His chest is a solid barricade of uninterrupted muscle. I nearly lose my balance, but a hand wraps around my wrist to steady me. A big, tanned hand. My breath catches again, but not before I get a whiff of his cologne, and boy, does he smell good.

"Are you okay?" His voice is deep and clear over the restaurant's music, and the familiarity unsettles me. I keep my head down, ignoring the heat on my wrist.

"Sorry," I sputter as I break away to the front of the restaurant. Under the low lights, it's possible he hasn't seen my face, and that would mean there's still a chance he hasn't recognized me. As far as he knows, maybe I'm just a stranger under a bucket hat who exits bathrooms like a raging bull. And while I'll scream profanities at the high heavens once the night is over, it'll be fine as long as he never clues in.

My heartbeat is still alive in my throat, and the adrenaline kick carries me all the way back to the table. I try not to shudder when Ernest sends a smirk in my direction. Returning it with a stiff smile, I take my spot next to Charlotte, who is still eyeing my hat with disdain.

"Have you ever been to Tokyo?" Ernest asks loftily, like he's dropped the smoothest line.

"I have!" I reply. "Something interesting I learned when I was there is that the creamy white topping on sushi isn't a mayonnaise blend. It's actually fish semen."

Charlotte chokes on an orange slice. I know what she's thinking: *That's what you call flirting?* Against my better judgment, I chance a glimpse at the lounge. The suits have converged at the bar, and I pinpoint the top of Parker's head with ease. Looks like the blond thing never made a comeback. His hair is its natural color, bangs parted to reveal his matured face. I can't focus when he's standing there, setting off all my primitive instincts with neon flashing arrows and a sign that reads CAUTION: HOT. To my dismay, he's demolished every suspicion of having peaked in high school by becoming absurdly hotter with age. Genetics are a bitch.

I also note that he's engrossed in conversation, apparently unshaken by our encounter. That's right, in my sudden panic, I'd mistakenly assumed that this would mean something to him. Even if Parker did recognize me, why would he care?

The weight of something I thought I'd buried seven years ago presses inward, but I seal it away once more. My hands curl into fists on my lap as I return to more urgent matters. I don't want to be here, just like I don't want to flirt with Ernest Miller for a second longer. New game plan: I'm going to demand they interview me here and now. I take a deep breath and go for broke. "I graduated with honors from Columbia. I've had my writing featured in the *New Yorker*, and even at the corporate soul-siphons before *Adagio*, I made sure to work my ass off, so I can assure you I have a good work ethic."

Ernest pauses mid-reach for his wine. "Okay. A lot less modest than I took you for."

"You have an open position for an Asia correspondent, right? I'm telling you why I'm right for the job—"

"Oh, we filled that on Monday," Jerry interjects.

I swallow the rest of my words.

Meekly, Charlotte turns to me and whispers, "Dani, I'm so sorry."

I feel like my chair has just been kicked out from under me. All my travel plans—the imagined nights in Beijing, Manila, and Osaka—have definitively disappeared in a puff of sad, gray smoke. I'm gutted. The table has moved on and is talking about something else, but it all sounds like white noise to me.

I guess the universe was never on my side.

"I'm going to go," I mutter, and I stand from the table so abruptly it makes me dizzy.

"Wait." Ernest jumps from his seat too. I let him speak. "If you're interested in traveling to Asia, I do have a proposition for you."

"You do?"

He leans over, and his chest hair beckons me closer. "Well, the thing is, I only date Asian women. You're all so exotically beautiful, so sweet and demure. I'm always looking for a travel companion. And I've been all across the continent, so I'm a wealth of knowledge." He winks at me. "Think of it like having a hot date and a travel guide, all in one."

If I'd eaten anything, I would've thrown it up now. Instead, I gag emphatically in Ernest's face and spin on my heel. "Gross. I'm out of here."

Anger, or mortification, floods my head as I bolt for the exit, not sparing a second look when Charlotte calls out to me. I shove past bodies until I'm safely out in the street. From behind me, I hear the door swing open and hefty footsteps draw near. God, is he really going to try again? Wasn't I clear enough?

"Get lost, creep!" I spin around, and for the third time tonight, the air is knocked out of me. I'm not shouting at the shrub of chest hair I expected. Worse: It's Parker Tran, standing five feet away.

I give his confused look only a second's consideration before I turn back around and take off again.

"Dani!"

Hearing him say my name hits me like a lightning bolt, stopping me dead in my tracks. Don't do it. Don't turn around. I sigh at the sky before turning to face him. He manages to find my eyes under the brim of my bucket hat.

He holds my gaze. I stare back. Now that we're not in the restaurant's dim lighting, I get a better look. In his finely cut suit, Parker Tran is the consummate portrait of a successful young professional. His brown eyes wander over me, and they're just as shining and soul-crushing as ever. His boyhood tan hasn't faded either. In fact, his skin glows under the street lamps.

"When did you realize it was me?" I ask.

"When you attacked me outside the bathroom. Are you okay?" he asks.

"I'm fine," I reply, cringing at how forced the word sounds. For lack of a coherent thought, I say the first thing that springs to mind: "You're wearing a suit." It's weird seeing him in anything other than a football jersey.

"Yeah, there's this thing about going outside where you're sort of required to wear clothing. A formality that's been around for centuries and all."

I let out another exasperated sigh, and Parker acquiesces with a small laugh.

"I met a client here."

I act as if this is news to me. "Since when do you work in New York?"

"I started a week ago. It's only for a few months, though." He holds up both hands as if to assure me he's not encroaching on my turf, as if I'm about to say, *Yeah, I better not catch you on these streets again.*

Parker turns to face the restaurant and rubs the back of his neck. "I left my client at the bar. The other guys from my team too."

That's it? That's what he followed me out here for? It's so tragically underwhelming for something seven years in the making, I almost want to laugh. But if he's giving me an escape, I'd be a fool not to take it. "Well, enjoy your stay, Parker."

I set off at a brisk pace, and so does he—but not toward Picotea. His strides are so long, it's like he teleported next to me.

"Where are you going?" he asks.

"To get food. I had to sit with the dudebros for an hour and didn't even get a proper meal out of it. I'm starving, and we're close to Chinatown."

I walk on autopilot, letting my feet and nose guide the way. I try not to pay any special attention to the fact that Parker is quite literally following me. "Aren't you going back to your client?"

He doesn't answer me. "Have you gone on a lot of dates with the dudebros?"

"It wasn't a date." Not technically a lie; for most of the night, it was a highly offensive job interview. "Okay, if I remember correctly, that one food truck should be right around here—aha!" I've just turned onto Canal Street when I spot it, a small, steamed bao-shaped piece of hope. Charging ahead, I race down the street, noting that I've managed to shake off Parker. Once I fill my stomach, now grumbling ferociously at me, I'll go straight home and let this unfortunate meeting dissolve in time with the rest of our history. Maybe I'll even will myself into another universe where none of this ever happened.

The lady at the order window doesn't acknowledge me. I've been here too often to count, but her apathy is a welcome trademark of every good Chinese takeout spot. This auntie would rather jump into a vat of hot oil than ask me how my day was, but I'll be damned if she doesn't make the best soup dumplings in the city.

Handing my credit card over, I order the set of four bao.

"Cash only."

I gape at her. "I only have card."

"Machine's down."

"Um, I can pay with my phone—"

She lets out a tiny scolding click like I'm wasting her time. "The machine is down."

And just like that, my little bao of hope bursts before my eyes.

I'm not sure how much worse my luck can get. Is it even safe for me to be outside? Do I go home now and risk slipping into a manhole on the way? Maybe that wouldn't be such a bad thing. I could embrace a new life with the underground mole society, where I don't have to think about fake dream jobs or Ernest's stupid chest hair or Parker Tran.

Sadly, I'm above ground, where I realize Parker is still following me like a homing missile. He stands next to me with his hands in his pockets, and I look up at him—way up, because some of us stopped growing at sixteen.

I must be a sorry sight, because he says almost apologetically, "I don't have any cash either."

"I wasn't going to ask," I mutter, suddenly self-conscious. I realize that Parker is watching me, wordlessly, although his jaw flexes like there's something he wants to say.

"What?"

"I've just never seen someone cry over soup dumplings before."

I duck under the safety of my hat again. "I wasn't crying. And they're not just any bao. These are the best in Chinatown." Why am I explaining this? More important, why is he hanging around to hear it?

Parker is grinning for reasons unknown. His smile is as dashing as ever, and I wish I hadn't noticed. As he cranes his neck to look around, I stare at the pronounced vein that runs down to his collarbone because of course I can't be normal right now.

"Why don't I buy you dinner somewhere else?" he offers.

Have I gone delirious from hunger? I don't know what to make of any of this. I've taken measures to avoid ever seeing Parker Tran again—and I was convinced he was doing the same—so the only explanation is that I have, in fact, slipped into another universe.

I watch despondently as the auntie packages four perfectly steamed bao in a container for someone else. My eyes follow the steam drifting past, and I catch a whiff of dumpling heaven while my stomach tries to eat itself.

I hope this is another universe, because that would mean the choice I'm about to make will be inconsequential once I return to my own.

"Fine," I say to Parker, regretting it immediately.

CHAPTER FIVE

Nine years ago

"It's not that bad, is it?"

"Hmm." I slant my head and narrow my eyes at the laptop screen. It's an odd feeling, when a face I know by heart suddenly looks like a stranger. "It's just so . . . *blond*."

Parker's hands fidget endlessly, long fingers running through his newly golden tresses. The rest of him is just as agitated, shifting around in his desk chair. "Tell me I don't look like a Super Saiyan."

"I'm getting K-pop vibes, if I'm being honest."

"That's what my teammates said." He stares intensely, but not at me. He's focused on his own image at the corner of the video call. With a dramatic sigh, he drops his hand onto his lap. "You know what, I'll take it."

"I will never understand the purpose of initiations. How does the color of someone's hair determine their loyalty to a sport?" I roll my eyes. "Men are weird."

"It's not about the color of your hair. It's about what you're willing to give up for the team. Nothing says solidarity like humiliation for the sake of your boys."

"Like I said, men are weird."

There's a knock on the door, and Marisa peeks her head in. I glance at the time on my screen. She's wrapped up her evening classes, but my roommate won't be here for long. When I first moved into the dorm, Marisa warned me that she gets cabin fever and prefers company on her outings. That's how I sometimes find myself on Broadway at two a.m. splitting a burrito.

"Skype?"

"I'll be done in a bit."

She makes kissy faces at me and moans a soft, "*Oh, Parker!*", to which I hurl a pillow in her direction. "Meet later for the usual?"

Marisa's "usual" changes by the day, making it anything but. That said, it's Wednesday, and we both have early classes tomorrow, so she means the dining hall. I give her a thumbs-up and she leaves, but not without blowing me another kiss.

"Was that your roommate?"

"Oh, uh, yeah." I hope he didn't hear her—and I really hope he can't tell my face is burning up. I try to change the subject. "How's practice?"

"Great. I get to use a gym with equipment more expensive than my car. Oh, and on game days, I can travel with the team and pretend to be a member."

The coaching staff have redshirted Parker for his freshman year at U of O. When I asked for layman's terms, he explained that he won't play any games this season, and it won't count toward his four years of NCAA eligibility. They assured him it was a strategic choice to get him in peak shape: He'll gain the size needed to face college-level rushers, learn the team's playbook, and even have time to focus on his studies. Parker agrees with all of that. It's just that, for someone who spends all of his time thinking about football, "no games for one year" is basically a prison sentence.

"It still must be exciting." I try to sound encouraging. "I saw your team on TV! Do you think one year they'll put you in Media Day too?"

"Not if I'm a benchwarmer," he mutters.

Okay, shifting gears again. "How are your classes?"

He shrugs. "If I stayed awake during lectures, I could tell you."

"Parker."

"I'm kidding. They're fine."

I watch as he pulls his hoodie over his head. The dark green sweatshirt with *OREGON* across the chest reveals a T-shirt underneath with the same logo. Since his first day at college, I haven't seen Parker wear anything but the team's apparel. He's even decorated the walls of his dorm with team banners.

He stretches his broad arms and then brings his attention back to me. As if automatically, a smile emerges on his face. "What about you? Bet you love being an English lit major at Columbia."

I nod. "My classes are all really interesting. Postcolonial Lit can be a bit of a snooze, but The Art of Murder is my favorite. Did I mention that before? We literally just talk about fictional murders. There was a whole class on beheadings."

"You did mention it," he laughs.

"I never know if people find this equally fascinating or totally morbid," I muse, hugging my knees to my chest. "I was telling this guy about it—I met him at a mixer—and I couldn't get a read. Like, are beheadings that strange in a fictional context? Did we all just collectively move on from Ned Stark in *Game of Thrones*?"

"A mixer? Like at a frat house?"

"It was cohosted by my roommate's sorority," I tell him. "She invited me as her plus-one."

"Oh." Parker scratches at a spot on his neck. "I've never been to one. Is it like every other college party?"

"Well, there's alcohol and a deejay. Sometimes they're themed."

"Do they actually let you drink?"

"Technically, they're not allowed to," I say. "But you know how these things go. Sometimes the older sisters sneak us drinks. They're very careful, though. They always make sure we're not alone."

"So, you go to sorority parties, and you drink." A crease appears between his brows. "College Dani is different."

I level him with a razor-sharp glare. "College Dani isn't going to miss out like I did in high school. I didn't go to a single house party then! Now that I've moved all the way here, you better believe I'm going to make the most of it."

"No, I get it, I get it. Just—I don't know. Be careful, I guess."

And with that, he disarms me. I know Parker is the last person who would judge; if there was a party within five miles of Silverpine, he was sure to be there. I, on the other hand, spent my most exciting nights at home, in front of the TV. I used to believe I was sparing myself the social anxiety—everyone already knew me as Parker Tran's friend, and I didn't need to draw more attention to that. But I think what I was really afraid of was finding out I didn't fit in with kids my age.

"I thought you'd be proud of me. No one loves a party like you do."

"I can't even think of partying right now," he sighs. "I'm training all the time, and when I'm not, I feel guilty and go to the gym. Yeah, the guys drag me to dorm parties, but I don't drink because I'm so paranoid about getting caught. If you're underage, they take that shit really seriously here. I could get kicked off the team."

I try to decode his expression: a little frustrated, anxious even.

Maybe it's the blond hair washing him out, but when did he start looking so tired?

"It sounds like your entire college life revolves around football."

"Well, yeah. I'm here on a scholarship. This isn't high school varsity anymore; I play for a nationally ranked school now."

"I know, but you're only eighteen. You should be able to act like it sometimes."

He frowns. "Are you telling me to party and get drunk?"

"No, I'm saying you can try to be a regular teenager too," I retort. "A healthy balance might take a little pressure off you."

Parker doesn't respond. He's preoccupied with the wire of his headphones, twisting it between his fingers. I can't help but recall the day the press release went out about his recruitment. Cô threw the closest thing to a block party Silverpine had ever seen. It was early February, but the entire neighborhood dropped by to offer their congratulations and leave with a plate of food and cake. Parker didn't stop smiling once, even when Nathan hosed him down with an entire bottle of champagne.

It's finally happening, he'd said to me. Under the sun, his smile was radiant. As if his joy alone could control the weather, there wasn't a single storm cloud in sight. I remember wishing I'd taken a photo of him; it felt like the kind of moment you're meant to preserve forever. *I'm living the dream, Dani.*

I wonder if this is all still part of that dream.

"Hey, if this doesn't work out, you might have a promising career as a K-pop idol." It's a shot at making light. I can't do much, but maybe I can make him laugh. "How are your dancing skills?"

But Parker is still too fixated on his headphones to look at me. "You don't get it. This *has* to work out, Dani. Football is my whole life."

After we hang up, I sit at my desk recounting the conversation in my head. I pick up my phone and find our chat, hoping it won't irritate him to see my name again so soon. With much trepidation, I type out a text: *Sorry if that joke was in bad taste. You know I'm always rooting for you.*

But I decide against sending it, erasing the message as I leave the dorm to meet up with Marisa.

CHAPTER SIX

I don't make a fuss over picking a spot to eat. It's dinner with the last person on Earth (save for maybe Ernest) that I want to be with. Let's rip the Band-Aid off and get it over with. We've just left Chinatown when I lead him into a diner that does all-day breakfast and bottomless margaritas. Once we're seated at a booth in the corner, I seize the bucket hat from my head and throw it sluggishly onto the table.

"Nice hair."

Shit, I forgot! I scramble to grab the hat again, but my own exhaustion stops me. "You know what? I don't care anymore. The other day, I saw a man on the train wearing a traffic cone like it was a top hat. This is New York—so what if it looks like a pigeon made a nest in my hair!"

Parker's mouth falls open, then shuts. I think his brain is trying to catch up to my meltdown. It doesn't get the chance, because a waitress with deep red lipstick walks over to our booth. She does a double take when she spots Parker, then hums into a smile. "What can I get for you, hon?"

He's quick with his order, but I'm too distracted by my hunger to tune in. I can't remember the last meal I had. My soup dumpling-less stomach is yelling all kinds of curses at me in its native rumbling, and I'm inclined to listen—even if it means sitting across from Parker Tran for the next hour.

"That's all for me, thank you." He motions over to me, and the waitress nearly gets whiplash when she spots my hair.

I scan the menu assiduously. "I'll have the triple grilled cheese with a side of fries, the eggs benedict, and . . . blueberry pancakes, please."

Parker lifts a brow as he collects our menus and hands them over.

"What? I haven't eaten yet."

"This year?"

"Ha-ha. Hilarious. At least I'm not the one footing the bill." I give him a taut smile. Nice try, but I won't let him get under my skin. "What if I said this was all part of an elaborate plan to scam a free meal out of you?"

"I'd say you could've picked somewhere of the Michelin variety if that was your game. Didn't anyone ever tell you to shoot for the stars?"

"I could totally con a man into a reservation at Le Bernardin if I wanted," I mutter, and I know he doesn't believe me. I don't even believe me.

"Maybe on a better hair day."

"Shut up."

Parker rests his crossed arms on the table. The diner's fluorescent lights reflect off the face of his fancy watch, and I'm nearly blinded. I rub my eyes, mascara wiping onto the backs of my hands. I realize how I must look, sitting across from literal perfection in a designer suit. But it can't be as terrible as how I feel. For a moment, I flashback to the not-job interview and sink in my seat.

"I haven't seen you in years," says Parker before I can brace myself for it. "How have you been?"

Are we actually doing this? The last time I left a diner with this same boy—well, man now—it ended with a strawberry milkshake in his lap. I have the urge to throw my hands up and demand, *What the hell are we doing? Didn't we make an unspoken vow to never see or speak to each other again?*

But I swallow that impulse. "Good."

"And how do you like New York?"

"S'great." I don't bother telling him that I like free entry to the Met and the British shorthair cat at my local deli. Grabbing bagels at Zabar's on the Upper West Side and donuts from Peter Pan in Greenpoint. How being in New York always feels like something exciting is about to happen. I doubt he'd care to hear it.

"What do you do for work?"

"I'm a copy editor," I say, annoyed at myself for breaking my monosyllabic streak. "I do some freelance writing on the side, but I've been full-time at an independent magazine for a few years now, and . . . Why are you smiling?"

"Hm? Oh, it's just that fact-checking people and correcting their grammar sounds like something you'd excel at."

He looks so smug with self-satisfaction that I consider quitting my job and becoming a wheat farmer just to prove him wrong.

I glare at him and reply with an edge in my tone, "How's San Francisco?"

For a moment, he seems startled that I've asked. Crap. I hope he doesn't think I went out of my way for that information.

"Not too bad. I moved for work, but I didn't expect to like it so much. It's been . . . Sorry, one sec—"

His phone buzzes loudly as he retrieves it from his pocket.

"I have to take this."

Parker leaves to take the call outside the diner. I have a good view of him through the window but preoccupy myself with my own phone instead. My notifications are dry—only Charlotte has texted—but I pretend like I'm reading the world's most fascinating email.

In the wake of his exit, I'm left wondering what could be so urgent for him to bolt like that. Work? He *is* dressed like a finance bro from Kips Bay. Or maybe someone's waiting for him at home, wondering why he's not back yet. I try to remember if I saw a ring on his finger, but the image of a married Parker Tran doting on a faceless woman assaults my brain, and I shudder.

What's his angle, anyway? Is his plan to dine and dash, leaving me to pick up the bill? Or maybe he's trying to lure me into a false sense of security, and that urgent call was to tell some guy on a rooftop with a laser to my forehead to take the shot. I still don't know what he does for a living. In my paranoid spiral, the suit is looking a lot less *finance* and a lot more *organized crime* now.

Our orders arrive, and it's a couple of minutes before Parker returns from his call. As he walks back to the booth, I take a quick peek at his hands. No ring.

"That was work," he explains, settling in front of a mug of coffee. I realize belatedly that the only food on the table is what I ordered.

I blurt out, "Are you going to tell me what you do for a living?"

He takes a business card out of his wallet and hands it to me. "I'm in sports marketing." He pauses, eyeing me like someone who knows all my tells. "And yeah, I can see it on your face, Dani. You're trying really hard not to call me a *bro* right now."

I blink and make an effort to sound indifferent. "Marketing . . . You didn't go pro?"

"Nah." He waves a dismissive hand. "Wasn't in the cards."

Glancing down at the card, I read his name in simple black text, the accompanying title—Marketing Director—and, in the corner, the company name: Venture Sports Marketing.

"I'm not going to lie—it did occur to me that I hadn't been jumpscared by your face in the middle of Sunday Night Football."

Parker taps a finger on the table. "That sounds like you're saying you were thinking about me."

"Only as a precaution." I take a bite of my grilled cheese. It's greasy beyond belief, but my body cries for sustenance. "What exactly do you do in sports marketing?"

"The short answer? I put athletes in Nike ads and tell every old rich dude who owns a sports team how to get even richer."

I can't tell if his levity comes from a place of self-awareness, which would also be new.

"I've got a few clients in New York, but I'm mainly here to oversee a campaign for the Rangers. It's a whole initiative to boost their digital presence and to connect them with some fresh brand sponsorships. Get more people talking about hockey."

Okay, that explains why he's here, but it doesn't make his arc from *Friday Night Lights* to *Mad Men* any less confusing. I don't know nearly enough about sports or marketing to make a comment of any value, so I move on to my pancakes.

"That's all you're having? A coffee?"

"I had dinner before this. With the client I mentioned earlier."

"So, you're just going to watch me eat? Like some kind of voyeur?"

"A *voyeur*? Seriously, Dani?"

To my surprise, Parker laughs. It catches me off guard, and I realize he hasn't scowled once or muttered something under his breath about me being an insufferable smartass. Aside from the sarcasm, he's been kind of . . . pleasant? It's as if someone hit rewind, and we're right back to a time when I had most of my dinners at his house—when seeing him sitting across from me felt like comfort. The thought creeps in soberly, and I drop my fork with a loud rattle.

He picks it up for me. “You good?”

I make noises that sound like “good” and “fine.” I’m still trying to get my head on straight.

❧

Parker pays the bill as promised. My inner Asian auntie surfaces at the last second to slide in my credit card, but he slides it right back. He even orders an Uber for me so I don’t have to take the train home. I check my phone—it’s already past ten.

“Oh, by the way,” Parker says as we’re waiting for the car. “Are you doing anything this Friday?”

My stomach does a funny little dip. “No. Why?”

“There’s an event at my hotel, and my company is one of the sponsors. You know the St. Regis, right?” He says it like it’s not a city landmark. As if a suite didn’t cost over two grand a night. “Just a gathering of professionals. It’s open to anyone with an invitation. If you want to drop by, I can put you on my guest list.”

I can’t think of anywhere I’d stick out more. “What would I even do there?”

“Meet people. Network.” His dark eyebrows draw together. “I know you spent all of high school doing the exact opposite, but surely you’ve learned how to be around people by now.”

I roll my eyes and go silent.

“Is that a no?”

“It’s not a yes.”

Parker fishes out his phone again. “Do you still have the same number?”

I shake my head, and he flips the screen toward me.

“Give me your number so I can text you the details. You can decide later.”

I hesitate, my face suddenly hot. After a beat, I tap my number onto the screen for him to save.

We're caught in a breeze, and his impeccably styled hair gives in to the wind for only an instant before falling back in place. I remember noticing this as a teenager, and the thought strikes me again: His hair looks so soft, so silky. It never made sense to me why this football-obsessed brute had all the prettiest features, right down to his full lips and offensively long lashes.

When I study him this closely, I can see exactly where my outdated memories of him end and the new Parker begins. The baby fat is gone from his face; now, his jaw is strong and sharp. Around his eyes, I can see how twenty-eight years have mellowed him. And yet, he still carries all the confidence of his quarterback days, when everyone adored him and wanted to be him. And when he smiles or laughs, I catch that same boyish charm from all those years ago.

The more I think about it, the more my head feels fuzzy. This has been the strangest night. I was supposed to be making plans to be in Asia by the winter, not considering a Friday evening with the boy I dumped a milkshake on and swore never to speak to again. College me would be cursing the universe with every known expletive, but right now, I don't know what to feel.

I am very aware, though, that Parker is looking at me. He's been doing that a lot.

"What?" I instinctively hide under the bucket hat.

He shrugs into a wide grin. "It's just kind of wild that I'm talking to you right now."

"Because I haven't flung myself off the Manhattan Bridge yet?"

"No, because I thought I'd have to check *under* the bridge to find you with all the other trolls."

"Oh, were you looking for me? Trying to fulfill a dream of

drowning me in the East River?"

"I see that winning sarcasm is still intact."

"I've always been a smartass. Remember?"

Parker is unfazed by the callback, except for the slightest twitch of his brow. "I did say something like that. A long time ago."

I feign my surprise with a gasp. "And here I thought you'd forgotten all about me."

"That's insane. How could I ever forget about you?"

I could be wrong, but I don't think he meant for it to sound the way it did. He bites his lip, holding my stunned gaze for a second before his eyes dart to his phone. "Your Uber is here."

Once the car slows at the curb, I step to it without another word.

"I'll see you on Friday," he calls out to me.

"I didn't say I was coming."

"I know." A hint of a smile, bordering on a smirk, returns. "But I have a feeling I'm going to see you anyway."

CHAPTER SEVEN

It's alarming to me just how easy it is to find someone online. Parker and I don't have any mutual friends, not even from Green Valley High, but a search of his name on Instagram brings him up as the third result: *parker11tran*. Eleven was his jersey number—it's weird that I remember that.

I scroll through photos of him posing with athletes, attending events, and vacationing on beaches, very suntanned and *very topless*. Unlike mine, his profile is impressive, with a follower count in the thousands. To my knowledge, he has no claim to fame, especially if he didn't go pro. Are these numbers typical for someone in marketing? Who the hell even knows more than a hundred people? Not I. And his photos . . . *dear God*. It's often debated whether real-life hotness translates to photos, but Parker Tran is simply all hot, all the time.

"What are you looking at that requires so much concentration?" Marisa asks from across a quaint wooden table. After the stunt Charlotte pulled, the allure of *Adagio* from yesterday has effectively died, and now I'd rather be anywhere but the office. As soon as I could break for lunch, I called up the ever dependable Marisa Lin, who wasted no time in meeting me at a café in the West Village. "Did your mother text you in Chinese again?"

"As if Beatrice Chen has time to text me," I snort, and she chuckles sympathetically. Marisa knows better than to throw a pity party for me at the mention of my mother. When we first met at Columbia, I didn't think it was necessary to share the story of my family with her just because we lived in the same dorm. Then, sophomore year, when we were roommates by choice, I let it spill during one of those late-night conversations when every secret felt like it belonged in the open. I told her all about how Mom left Taiwan a teen painting prodigy, only to meet a remarkably ordinary fate as a stay-at-home mom in a small town. And if there was one thing Beatrice Chen loathed, it was being ordinary.

"I think she's preparing for a group show at the Taipei Fine Arts Museum," I elaborate. "Which means she's as good as MIA."

"Like you, from this lunch date."

"Sorry." I place my phone face down. "I was on Instagram."

"Oh boy. You going to be okay under that tin foil hat?" Marisa takes a sip of her latte, flips her frazzled ponytail over her shoulder, and brushes a crumb off her jeans.

These days, she wears exhaustion on her face like a battered champion. Her latest graphic design project is her biggest yet: A household name in kitchen appliances has tasked her with rebranding its entire enterprise. Everything from its logo to its packaging is now under her jurisdiction. This means Marisa sleeps four hours a night and spends all her waking hours in Illustrator. Today's lunch is her only respite.

"How long until you spiral over your digital footprint?"

"Avoiding social media doesn't make me a conspiracy theorist."

"Right. Remember when you panicked because your algorithm showed you a croissant?"

"I was literally thinking that I wanted one, and it popped up on my feed."

"Let me tell you a secret about the Internet: If you've ever liked a photo of a croissant, you're gonna see a croissant again."

Marisa is just as much of a smartass as I am, and that's why I like her. I won the roommate lottery when we moved into the same dorm freshman year. She's the one I credit with helping me out of the shell I'd brought with me from high school. While I've always been quiet and jaded, Marisa is outgoing and a little less jaded. Like Daria and Jane, if Jane actually wanted to go to parties and then crush the patriarchy after. A cynical part of me wondered if we'd remain friends after we graduated and no longer had cheap beer and midnight snack runs to keep us close. But Marisa has never let me drift too far from her radar. Even after she got married last year, and I prepared myself to see less of her, she called me the moment she returned from her Maldives honeymoon, complaining about a pizza craving that suddenly became my problem.

"So, who are you stalking on Instagram?"

"I'm not stalking anyone."

"Dani, you open the app twice a year. You're definitely stalking someone."

I shift in my seat and pull the business card out of my purse, sliding it across the table. "Guess who I ran into yesterday."

Marisa picks up the card and her jaw goes slack. "Parker Tran? From the Skype calls?"

I nod an affirmative.

"Remind me what happened to you two. Did you guys date and break up?"

"What? No, of course not."

"Really? But you'd be up at, like, midnight on those video calls."

"Three-hour difference. We had to work around his practice schedule."

"Uh-huh, sure. Anyways, if I remember correctly, you two just stopped talking out of nowhere."

I stir my latte a little with the spoon. "I told you. He stopped talking to me."

"Well, give me the deets. Did you two finally duke it out?" she gasps. "Is that what happened to your hair?"

"No, this is unrelated."

I run my fingers through the remaining, slightly crispier strands. I'd managed to minimize the damage by using a heavy-duty Japanese hair mask and snipping away some of the more hopeless bits.

"It was actually really strange. He was being so *nice* last night—as in, bought-me-dinner-and-an-Uber-home nice!"

"Well, it's been, what? Seven, eight years? The last time you saw him he was still a dumb twenty-year-old."

"Yeah, but do you think people really change that much after college?"

She folds her arms and looks up at the ceiling thoughtfully. "Let's see, you're eighteen when it starts, and you've got a whole system telling you that you can be whatever you want to be. Then your twenties come around, slap you with debt, and destroy your self-esteem."

Something tells me Parker's self-esteem is just fine.

"So, it's possible that he's matured." I stop stirring, letting my spoon fall to the saucer. "He invited me to an event tomorrow night. Something with a bunch of New York hotshots."

Marisa raises her brows. "You think he's trying to make amends? Like he feels bad for everything that happened?"

"That's assuming he has a heart and a conscience."

I take a sip of my latte. It's cold now.

"I just can't figure that guy out. I never could. Whenever I thought about what went wrong with us, I could never pinpoint when things took a turn. Maybe he just got sick of me after spending our whole lives together."

"I was an unwilling third wheel to those Skype calls. That boy thought the world of you."

Then why did he leave me behind? With time and distance, it had become easier not to think about that day. I'd taken for granted the luxury of *almost* forgetting.

As if she can read my thoughts, Marisa reaches out and tousles my hair fondly.

"Stop overthinking it. Go to the event. Have a blast. Show Parker Tran what he missed out on. If you don't leave with him begging to be in your life again, maybe you'll bag a New York Ten and get lucky. The sky's the limit, Dani."

I cast her a wary look, as if I'm half expecting her to unzip her face and reveal an alien underneath. "You're a lot less jaded now that you're married."

"I know. Blame my ever-doting wife," she says with a sigh, handing the business card back to me. "Either way, I think you should go. It'll be good for you. And if it isn't, at least I get to hear about it."

CHAPTER EIGHT

Once I return to the office, my phone lights up rapidly with texts. The first one simply states, *It's Parker*. I save the number, staring at the newly added contact and wondering how far I am from my original universe.

Parker: Here's the info for tomorrow. It's black tie, and if there's anyone you'd like to bring, just let me know.

He sends me an online invitation, complete with the address and time. Monosphere is the official host of the event—one of those conglomerates whose logo is everywhere, even though no one's entirely sure what they do. You just know they've got their claws deep in every corner of the business world. As much as Parker tried to act blasé about it, it looks like it's quite the exclusive event.

Parker: By the way, you were right about the soup dumplings. I stopped by after lunch.

Me: I told you they're the best. But you know how it is with Chinese food trucks, the more hostile the service, the better the food.

Parker: What do you mean? She was so nice. She even gave me an extra bao.

I want to throw my phone out the window and curse this new, ill-fated universe I've stumbled into. What's it like to have the cosmos be forever in your favor? It must be nice to be Parker Tran.

Just as I'm flipping mental middle fingers to the sky, my phone goes off again, but this time it's Dad. He's been worried about me since I told him about the not-interview, but he shows his concern by sending me job postings all day.

Me: Dad, I'm not going to quit Adagio.

Dad: It would still be good for you to have other options.

Me: Actually, I've been invited to a Monosphere event tomorrow. Lots of important people will be there.

Dad: That's great!

Now why did I say that? It's a bit of a white lie—it's not like I have job opportunities lined up—but it might put Dad at ease for the time being. Of course, I didn't mention Parker, because I know Dad will mention it to Cô. And then Parker will get wind of it, and if he's under the impression that I called home to gush about him, I'll have no choice but to move to an island off the coast of nowhere.

Technically, I haven't committed to anything yet. I wonder if Parker would notice if I didn't attend. Would he be disappointed? Even if he was, should that bother me? And now I'm wondering why I'm even wondering about this.

I spin around in my chair to eye the backs of my coworkers, typing away at their desks. Backs that look sturdy, dependable. Designer-clad, with the required disposition for any networking event. Parker did say I could extend the invitation.

"I think I already know the answer, but do any of you want to come to an event at the St. Regis tomorrow night?"

Tae-woo and Savannah practically float over to me. Everyone in the office seems to live for all things grandiose—except me.

"You mean the one hosted by Monosphere?" Tae-woo demands.

I pull up the invitation on my phone for them to see.

"Wait, is this for real?"

I give him a self-assured smile that says, *What do you think?*

"Yes! Yes! I'm in!" Savannah does a happy dance on the spot.

Tae-woo makes a sour face. I can't discern whether or not he hates this. "How did you even get an invitation?"

"I have an acquaintance." Is that the right word? I have no clue. "He works for one of the sponsors—Venture Sports."

"Since when do you know people?"

"Do you want to come or not?"

"*Ugh.* Fine, I'll be there." Tae-woo reacts like I've just invited him to a public flaying, but it's hard to miss the way his face changes.

"What are you going to wear?" Savannah implores.

"Um, a dress?"

"Which dress?"

"I don't know. Whatever I find in my closet."

"Not off the rack, right?" Savannah holds a hand to her chest. The sound her bangle makes when it hits her necklace adds a dramatic *ding* to her horror. "You can't just wear *anything*."

"That's true." Tae-woo chimes in. "You get a room full of New York's biggest egos together, and everyone will be getting a hard-on from judging each other."

I squirm in my seat because I know they're right, but I also know the kind of dress they're hinting at will cost as much as my rent. Or more.

"Hey, Dani." A faint squeak of a voice calls out, and it isn't until I look over that I realize we have company. Charlotte is standing by my desk, looking uncharacteristically diffident.

"I'm not talking to you."

"Dani, I'm so sorry! You were right, I never should've set you up."

Savannah gives her a disapproving sigh. "That was bad, even for you."

"Have you seen her hair?" Tae-woo spins me around in my chair.

I thought I'd done a decent job taming the bird's nest, but Tae-woo has a radar for even your most well-hidden insecurities.

"You did this to her."

I kick his leg. "Technically, *you all* did this. I only tried to curl my hair because you got into my head like the world's worst hype men."

"Guys, I feel terrible. Please believe me." Charlotte clasps her hands together, making herself small. "I had no idea that guy was such a creep! If there's any way I can make it up to you—"

Tae-woo points his tablet pen at her. "Give her one of your dresses."

"Oh!" Savannah claps. "The Valentino crepe gown from last season!"

Charlotte shoots up like a meerkat. Any genuine remorse dwindles immediately. "*Excuse me?* That dress cost me, like, three paychecks. I can't just *give* it to her."

"No, Tae-woo's got the right idea." I nod in his direction. "But I don't want to keep your dress. Just let me borrow it for one night."

"Where are you going that you need a *Valentino*?"

"That's not important."

Charlotte is practically writhing in agony. I know that as much as it will disturb her to see her designer dress on someone else, she's also desperate for everyone in the office to like her again.

"Fine! You can have it for *one* night!" She throws her head back theatrically. Savannah holds back a laugh, but Tae-woo is less courteous, snickering maleficently from his corner. I think they call this schadenfreude. "But I want it dry-cleaned before it's returned."

"Oh, no, honey." Savannah pats her shoulder. "*You're* paying for dry-cleaning."

CHAPTER NINE

Eight years ago

I never had much reason to get excited for the holidays. Since I lived with Dad all year round, the custody agreement gave Mom priority for Christmas, Thanksgiving, birthdays—any celebratory occasion she wished to spend with me. I remember one year, she planned to visit for Christmas, and Dad prepared the guest room for her while I put together an itinerary. I'd never been to the town's Christmas market before and thought it would be perfect to see the lighting of the tree for the first time with her.

She canceled a couple days before her flight, promising she'd "make it next time." But a next time never came, and there was always a reason: She snagged a last-minute spot at a gallery show, or a bout of vertigo made the thought of a fifteen-hour flight unbearable. At some point, I finally visited the Christmas market on my own. I did a lap around the square and grabbed a hot cocoa at the Pine Street Bakehouse before I decided I wasn't missing much.

Holidays at the Trans', however, are a big deal. Chú always closes the pharmacy for the day, sometimes for the weekend. On Christmas, we decorate the tree together, but instead of exchanging gifts, we receive lucky red envelopes. The Fourth of July is

Chú's annual cookout—a chance for him to show off his mastery of Vietnamese grilled pork skewers, while Cô serves her equally perfected chè Thái for dessert. And on Thanksgiving, once all three football games have aired, Chú puts on a Vietnamese direct-to-video entertainment program called *Paris by Night*, blasting it loudly in surround sound. Ever since the first Thanksgiving the Trans invited us over, I haven't wanted to spend my holidays any other way.

This year's *Paris by Night* special starts with an elaborate musical performance that turns into a one-act play that Chú has to translate for Dad. I don't think Dad's following, but they'd cracked open a bottle of Hennessy some time ago, so he's roaring with laughter now. Parker's parents speak mostly Vietnamese at home. Dad's first language is Mandarin; he only uses Hokkien when he's phoning my grandparents. My own Mandarin is conversational at best; I've heard Parker speak Vietnamese only on rare occasions, and Nathan has always been better at it. With this patchwork of languages spoken with varying proficiency, we've always defaulted to English when we're together.

In the kitchen, Parker and I are rolling chả giò for tomorrow's lunch. He's a lot faster, having completed a pyramid of spring rolls that puts mine to shame, but my rolls are cleaner—tightly folded with the optimal amount of filling.

"I can't believe we're already preparing food again," I say. "We had a king's banquet for dinner. I'm so stuffed, I don't think I can eat until Christmas."

"Ha, funny. When has my mom ever accepted *I'm full* as an excuse to stop eating?" Parker uses his forearm to sweep his bangs from his eyes. We'd been talking on video calls for so long that seeing him in 3-D again makes me hyperaware of every little change. For the fifth time that day, I take in the blond streaks, the grown-out roots, and the body that has nearly doubled in size after a year of training and strength programs.

I've been hesitant to bring up football. Parker doesn't seem particularly enthusiastic about his progress, but he doesn't seem too disappointed either. The preseason was a crucial time for him to show the results of his redshirt year and secure a spot on the team's depth chart. While he's not a starter, he now plays backup, which means real game time. The head coach has subbed him in four times since the regular season started, although only in the fourth quarter of blowout games.

"I know she usually makes a whole feast, but does it seem like a *lot* more this year?" I glance around at the kitchen counters. Among the carefully wrapped trays, I can see papaya salad, bánh xèo crepes—some made with prawns, which are my favorite, and a few made with pork, how Parker likes them—grilled lemongrass chicken, and heaps of vermicelli noodles. On the stove sits a large pot of bún bò Huế broth that has been simmering for hours.

He takes half of my egg roll wrappers, his share already depleted. "I think she's just happy that we're all home from school."

Sure enough, Cô is still in high spirits, even after spending half the day prepping dinner. She finds us by the kitchen island, holding a lotion container in her hands. Twisting it open, she reveals hair ties and bobby pins inside.

"Dani, I'll tie back your hair for you. It's too long. You'll get food stuck in there."

"Oh, okay," I say, sitting up straight in my chair. "Thank you."

She starts on a French braid, humming a folk song I'd heard on the TV earlier. "Have you two made plans for New York?"

"We talked about it a bit." Parker shrugs.

"You don't have plans yet? Con, you go next month."

"We have a general idea of what we're doing," I say to Cô.

Unlike Parker, who's too cool to let anyone catch wind of his excitement, I've been grinning from ear to ear at every mention of his upcoming trip. It's hard to plan around the football season without knowing how his team ranks in the Pac-12 yet, so we've decided Christmas is the best time for him to visit me in New York. He's booked a flight to arrive on Christmas Eve.

"We only have a few days, but we can at least check off the must-sees: Fifth Avenue displays, the Rockettes at Radio City."

"You're gonna get bored with all the tourist stuff," mutters Parker. "Didn't you see it all last year?"

"Not all of it. And I don't mind, I think they're traditions for a reason. You should get the full Christmas experience for your first time in New York."

Cô taps on my shoulder. "You have to see the tree! And skating!"

"Rockefeller Center," I say, chuckling. "All on the list."

Parker shakes his head but slides me a teasing grin. "As long as you don't expect me to wear matching *I Love New York* T-shirts and fanny packs with you."

"Matching? Of course not. That's all you."

"Done! Đẹp quá!" Cô tightens the braid and tidies it up with a bobby pin. She's gotten quicker since the last time she practiced on me, taking only half the time.

"Parker, look. How's my braid? Dani looks so pretty, right?"

I focus on my spring roll so as to give the impression that I don't care how he answers.

"Your braid is fine," he says, without addressing the latter question.

"Ugh. I don't know how they drink that." Nathan enters the kitchen, red in the face as he deposits an empty cognac glass in the sink. He takes in the cellophane-wrapped food along the counters and whistles.

"Má, you know we already had Thanksgiving dinner, right?

Unless you were planning to have the entire Pacific Northwest over for an encore."

Cô shakes a finger at him, her jade bracelets dangling. "You! Always so sadistic."

"You mean *sarcastic*. And I don't want to know where you learned that other word."

He pulls up a seat next to us just as Cô steals off to the living room with a plate of dried squid. I wouldn't know, but according to Chú, it pairs perfectly with Hennessy.

"What are you guys up to?"

"Planning Parker's New York trip."

"Christmas, right?" He frowns. "Should I be offended no one has mentioned visiting me in Philly?"

After Nathan moved for school, Parker and his parents had visited a handful of times. But that was when Parker was in high school and Nathan was still an undergrad. Although New York is a lot closer to Philadelphia than it is to Silverpine, visiting Nathan had never come up for discussion. I think I just assumed Nathan had better things to do than babysit his next door neighbor.

"You've got grad school, an internship, and you're working part time," I count on my fingertips. "We would just be a bother to you."

"But you weren't a bother when you were begging me to chauffeur you around every weekend?"

Ages ago, Nathan had cancelled a date in order to drive us to Portland—Parker needed new cleats, and I wanted to take pictures at Washington Park for an art assignment—and now he never lets us forget it.

"Come to Philly. I'll make time for you guys!"

Parker and I exchange a look.

"Oh, sorry. I forgot I'm talking to the two busiest sophomores on this side of the planet," grumbles Nathan, his icy glare cutting through the lens of his glasses. "Should I book an appointment between football practices? Does Miss Dean's List take meetings, or do I have to sit in on one of your study groups?"

"I don't know if I made the dean's list this semester," I tell him. At least, I haven't received official notice yet.

"You made the dean's list last year," Parker points out.

At this, Nathan snaps his fingers. "Hang on. Why don't you ask Dani to tutor you?"

Since the football season started, Parker's talked about nothing but games and practice. I'd almost forgotten he had classes on top of all that too.

"Do you need help catching up?" I ask.

"This is perfect. You two are already on video calls all the time—"

"I don't need a tutor," Parker cuts in, his tone rigid.

"What? You were just asking me if I knew anyone—"

"I was asking for someone else." Parker rolls a spring roll with the final scoop of filling. Wordlessly, he takes the empty bowl to the sink and turns on the faucet. The sound of running water echoes through the room, and I almost don't hear Nathan when he leans closer.

"Do me a favor and check in with him sometimes. You know, if something seems off. I think if he sees you're doing well, it might encourage him too."

I'm not quite tracking, but I nod, waiting for him to elaborate.

"To be honest, my mom was a little worried about you going so far for college. You were so timid in high school. But it's been nice seeing you come into your own. Parker, on the other hand," he casts a quick glance at his younger brother. "I don't think he ever adjusted—to football or the rest of it."

Once he finishes with the dishes, Parker and I go upstairs to his room. He's on his laptop, monitoring game footage. I'm on the bed, flipping through an old manga that I found between his desk and headboard. I can't concentrate on the climactic fight scene because I'm still thinking about what Nathan said. What did he mean, Parker hasn't adjusted? I thought football had taken up all his focus and that things were looking up, but is there more to it? Is Parker falling behind in his classes? If that's the case, why hasn't he told me? Then I note that he hasn't made a sound for the last fifteen minutes, except for the occasional mouse click. I glance to check that he's breathing.

"Nervous about your team ranking?"

"Yes and no. I mean, obviously I want us to be the conference champs, but I also feel like if I don't get to play, then nothing I do will affect the outcome anyway."

"I'm sorry I haven't been to any of your games yet. I know I said I would, but things got really busy after I joined the student newspaper, and then there were final exams." As I try to explain, I'm aware that it sounds like I'm just making excuses. Even Nathan found the time to travel from Philly to watch Parker play. "I did watch a few games on TV, though, whenever I could."

"It's fine. It's not like you can fly in when I don't even have a game schedule. If I was a starter, it'd be different," he sighs and shuts his laptop. "Maybe next year. Then I'll send you an actual invite."

"*Once* you become a starter," I amend. "Promise?"

"I promise." Parker moves to the foot of the bed and lies down. His long legs hang over the side, and he folds his hands over his abdomen. The sumptuous banquet from hours ago must be catching up to him, because he's two slow blinks from falling asleep. Not wanting to disturb, I lean against the headboard, picking up the manga again.

"Hey, Dani."

"Hm?"

"Do you think you'll stay in New York after graduating?"

Where did that come from? I look at him, but he's facing the ceiling. Setting the manga aside, I sprawl out on the bed so we're lying side by side. "I'm not sure. It makes sense to stay if I actually pursue some kind of writing career."

"But you like it there, right? More than Silverpine?"

"Hard to say. They're such different places." I stare up at the ceiling fan, its steadily rotating blades lulling me to calm. Or maybe it's the familiar heat when Parker's shoulder brushes mine. The more pertinent question is where he will end up after graduation. He could get drafted by any NFL team, which means the entire country is his oyster. "Have you ever thought about parallel worlds?"

"Um, can't say that I have."

"It's just that, if the theory's true, and there are multiple universes, then that means within them, there's an infinite number of possibilities too. It's kind of cool, right?"

My fascination with parallel worlds must've started with Alice slipping into the rabbit hole. To my impressionable younger self, the idea of Wonderland opened my imagination to all kinds of hypotheticals.

"Sometimes I think of us in those other worlds, what we're up to. Maybe in one of them, you play for the Jets, and you end up in New York too."

"You think about different universes?"

"I do. After my parents' divorce, I used to imagine other worlds where they stayed married. Like how things would be different if my mom was around."

He's quiet at first. "Do you ever miss her?"

"Sometimes. But I was so young when she left, I can't really remember what it was like when the three of us lived together. I even catch myself forgetting about her, and I feel bad about it afterward."

"Does that mean you don't imagine those universes anymore?"

"Not so much," I admit. "I realized something. If she hadn't left, we wouldn't have sold the old house. And that would mean . . ."

"I wouldn't have met you," he says contemplatively. "Then that means there's a universe where we don't know each other."

For fear of dampening the mood, I clap my hands together and say with authority, "Let's go over the New York plan again."

"Grand Central Terminal, by the information booth in the main concourse," he recites from memory. "Could you have picked a busier meeting spot?"

"It's easier this way. It'll be your first time visiting, and it's a big city, bigger than what you're used to. You won't get lost if you're going where everyone else is going."

He rolls his eyes. "I'm not going to get lost."

"Fine, fine." I nudge his leg with my foot. "But you'll call me as soon as you land?"

He nudges me back. "I'll call you."

❧

As planned, I'm at Grand Central Terminal on Christmas Eve. I've timed my arrival to align with Parker's, provided he follows my detailed directions to take the AirTrain from JFK to Jamaica station and then transfer to the LIRR. Factoring in the holiday rush and buffer time for getting lost, he should still be here soon and hopefully in one piece.

An hour passes. Was his flight delayed? The airline's website shows otherwise. Arrivals are—surprisingly—on time. I shoot him a text, hoping he's got service by now.

Me: Did you get lost?

Two hours pass without a reply, and all I can do is pace nervously around the information booth. My calls go straight to voicemail, and my frantic texts go unanswered. I try his house in Silverpine in case Cô has heard from him, but she tells me what I already know: Parker left his dorm for the airport hours ago. Thousands of faces pass in the main concourse, and I search each one in vain. I wait another hour for a call that never comes. At the four-hour mark, I return to campus alone.

Marisa isn't at the dorm when I get back. She's long gone by now, en route to Houston to spend the holidays with her parents. On my desk is a box of Levain cookies and a note in her handwriting: *For you and your "friend"! Merry Xmas, Marisa.*

I'm reminded of the holiday pastries at Pine Street Bakehouse back in Silverpine and the Christmas market I attended without Mom all those years ago. My chest feels like it's caving in.

Methodically, I pick up my phone to search his flight status again. The text on the page hasn't changed since the first time I checked, a hundred refreshes ago. No cancellation, no delays. He should be in the city by now. Should I call Nathan? Or try Cô again?

A notification lights up the screen, and I nearly drop my phone.

Parker: Sorry. I won't be coming to NY.

Me: Is everything okay? What happened?

Parker: Change of plans.

It feels like a part of me has been torn out and dropped at my feet. That's it? After waiting all afternoon—my calls screened, my texts ignored—he's just had a *change of plans*? I wonder if this is all a dumb prank, and Parker is actually outside my door wearing a stupid grin. I even check, only to feel crestfallen once more when I'm met with an empty hallway. A tightness builds up in my throat. My eyes burn with tears, but I hold them back just long enough to tap the call icon next to his name.

But he's turned off his phone.

I'm not going to reach him, I realize with dread. He's not coming.

Dani: Can you at least tell me why?

I send the text before curling up in bed, and I wait, as I've done all day. Pressing the covers against my face, my head throbs with the kind of pressure that forms when you try not to cry. I set my phone next to my pillow, in case I fall asleep and it rings.

But it doesn't.

CHAPTER TEN

The evening of the Monosphere event, Savannah comes over to my apartment to lend her expertise. With some treatment products and a bit of styling, the bird's nest is officially gone. When I look in the mirror, I hardly recognize the person staring back.

Charlotte's dress is a gorgeous black gown that flows to the floor, with spaghetti straps and a plunging neckline. I've never worn anything like it, and I'm worried my boobs might be too small for the cut.

Savannah's in one of those dresses that has a long, billowy cape. Not many people can pull off that look, but with her five-foot-ten frame, she looks absolutely stunning.

I guess we must've done something right, because when we meet Tae-woo at the hotel, he doesn't tell me I missed the school bus for senior prom. Instead, he gives me his silent approval with a half-smile. Just as Parker promised, we're allowed entry under his list as "Dani Tsai and guest(s)."

Monosphere has booked the St. Regis's Roof Ballroom, the hotel's largest event space. The elegant gilded walls and grand chandeliers suspended from cloud-painted ceilings are not only a spectacle, but also a testament to the building's long history. Staff have strategically arranged standing tables to encourage conversation, and eager beavers are already convening in spirted clusters. As expected, I feel completely out of place. The parties

Adagio throws are lavish in their own right, but this is the kind of event that feels almost too grand to be called a party.

I take a flute of champagne from the first waiter that passes and down half of it in one go. Of course, Savannah and Tae-woo are naturals at this. Someone is already asking Savannah about her dress, and Tae-woo is exchanging cards with a set of brothers who run a tech start-up. I trail behind them, feeling ill at ease and practicing a smile that's more charming and polite and less "robot experiences first emotions."

When I look across the room, I catch sight of Parker right away. A black suit hugs his over-six-foot frame with immaculate precision, tailored to perfection. He's always had the kind of body that only long hours in our school's weight room could sculpt, and it looks like it's held up over time. One look, and you can tell he's a former athlete. But the air of sophistication tonight is new—so unlike the boy from next door that it's almost intimidating.

I think I imagine it at first, but sure enough, he's looking at me too. Already tied up with other attendees, he simply nods in my direction and returns to his conversation.

Just as I'm stalking another waiter for my second glass of champagne, I hear my phone buzzing in my purse.

Parker: Glad to see you got the pigeon nest under control.

Me: Question for you. Do you sleep in suits too?

Parker: Wouldn't you like to know how I sleep.

Me: Hopefully with a pillow smothering you.

I scan the room in all its splendor and pick up my phone again.

Me: This is so awkward. What if someone asks what I do?

Parker: Don't worry, I'm sure people are a lot more accepting of bridge trolls than you think.

Me: I hope you choke.

Parker: Sorry lol. Why can't you tell them you're a copy editor?

Me: Isn't this like a nexus for finance bros? Am I even allowed to be here?

Parker: I told you, it's an event for professionals. You're overthinking it; you'll be fine.

Parker: By the way, that dress looks great on you.

I read the last text more than once, and a tingly warmth rises to my face. Tucking my phone away, the voice in my head reminds me not to slouch. It also tells me I'm a professional who belongs here, but without any alcohol or Savannah to hide behind, I revert to my wallflower roots.

"So, this was your big event." A familiar voice approaches, and I'm actually relieved to see Charlotte's comically large, blonde curls float into view. Even if Jerry is next to her. "Not bad, Tsai—you've managed to make me *not* hate my dress on you."

"Of course you're here." I look over at her armpiece. "I guess you do know everyone in New York."

"How did you get an invite?" Charlotte asks, genuinely curious.

"I went to high school with someone here." That's one way of putting it.

"That explains how Thing One and Thing Two got in." She points a thumb over her shoulder just as Savannah and Tae-woo are traipsing over.

"Oh my god." Tae-woo covers his eyes dramatically. "I thought I was looking at the sun, but it's just your massive head, Charlotte."

"Is this one half of the braincell from the double date?" Savannah asks, then tacks on a quick, "Sorry."

Jerry merely grunts. I doubt he has enough cognitive ability without his other half to understand what's going on.

Speaking of—"He's not here, is he? Ernest?"

"Nope," Jerry finally says. "You know, Dani, Charlotte told me you were a smart girl, but I think your judgment could use a strategic pivot. Ernest is a catch, and you let a good one go."

I stick out my tongue, pretending to retch. "I would rather eat a can of solid farts than ever see that sleazebag again."

"Didn't I tell you to be professional?"

I whip around, and Parker is standing behind me. I cannot believe it only took fifteen minutes for him to walk in on me telling a fart joke. I picture myself climbing out of one of the embellished windows, free-falling from this disaster of a conversation.

"Oh hey, Jerry."

"Wassup, Tran."

Parker takes a cool step forward, and then he's by my side, smirking devilishly down at me. I've never seen his hair styled like this before, with his bangs pushed back. "Hanging in there?"

Charlotte is suddenly right against my ear, hissing, "When did you nab the hottie from Picotea?"

"I didn't nab anything. He's, um, someone I know from back home."

"Parker Tran, from Venture Sports." He shakes hands with everyone in our circle. "Do you all work for *Adagio* too?"

"We do!" Savannah's voice is suddenly loud, very loud.

"Wait, how did you know that?" I don't recall telling him the name of our publication.

"Hm? Oh, I Googled you after the other night." He says it like it's just due diligence. I momentarily panic, thinking of him scrolling through my Instagram but then remember it's a private account.

"How do you know Dani?" Savannah asks.

"I guess you can say we go way back. I was actually in attendance at her first school play. Her role was Villager Three; no lines, and she still messed up. Tripped as she was exiting stage left."

Everyone laughs like a practiced chorus. I've got one foot off the ledge in my head, and I'm this close to jumping.

"So, you're also from Portland? I've always wanted to visit." This is the first time I've heard Charlotte say anything of the sort. "You should *def* give me a list of things to do."

"Portland adjacent," I correct her. "You could say we're honorary Portlanders. Or Portlandian by proximity."

"That is so sad," groans Tae-woo.

I ignore him. "Everyone in our town would make the drive into the city, like, every other week. There wasn't much to do otherwise."

Parker nods, "You should visit. The Pearl District is nice, and you can catch cherry blossoms at the Waterfront too. And this is probably a controversial take to have in New York, but Portland really does have the best pizza."

I hate to agree with him, but he's right. There's a reason *Modernist Pizza* called it the best pizza city in the country.

"If you want the best of the best, go to Ken's Artisan. I've never had better Neapolitan in my life."

"Um, Ken's Artisan is not the best pizza in Portland." I lift my chin and scoff. "It's Apizza Scholls. They're an Oregon institution. No one does a thin crust like they do."

Parker lifts a brow, sizing me up. "I mean, Apizza is a staple, but Ken's does wood-fired, which is arguably better."

"Sure, if you want to argue on the side of unhinged."

"Apizza has a three-topping limit."

"Any more than that and they'll interfere with the crust baking." I glower at him. "You should know better than to question genius!"

"Mm." Parker smiles, but it's an icy one. "Are we going to argue all night? I just want a heads up on how to plan my evening."

I back down, suddenly conscious that there are three and a half people who just witnessed our impassioned debate about pizza.

"Well, now that Dani's done embarrassing us," Tae-woo doesn't spare me the sidelong glance. "Parker, does working at Venture come with any perks?"

"If you're asking if I get to sit courtside for the Knicks, then yes."

It comes as no surprise that everyone from *Adagio* is smitten with Parker within minutes of meeting him. He's captivating and funny, and it's all so effortless. Trying to reconcile this grown-up Parker with the boy who spilled juice on my Pokémon cards is making my head spin. I decide I need another drink. As soon as I find an opening, I slip away to the bar and order a pinot noir.

"It's a lot, isn't it?" A man with a thick beard approaches on my right and leans against the counter.

"Sorry?"

He gestures behind us. "Like, I'm sure your new penthouse on Fifth Avenue is amazing, Karl, but your wife is two martinis away from taking home one of the waiters tonight."

I give him my polite and definitely not robotic smile. "It is pretty overwhelming."

"I'm Isaac Mehta." He shakes my hand. "Venture Sports."

"Dani Tsai," I say. "You must know Parker Tran then."

"Ah, yes, the wunderkind himself. You another fan?"

I nearly spit out my drink. "Me? No. No, we're just

acquaintances." There's that word again.

"You in marketing?"

"Um, no, I'm a copy editor for a publication."

"Oh, wow, that's different. Wait, it's not one of those academic journals that's just gonna go right over my head, is it?"

"It's devoted entirely to Doge, actually." I suck air through my teeth. "Every month we just print Doge memes in various formats. Sometimes it's just one singular page of Doge."

"Wow, I'm sold." Isaac laughs and swirls the liquor in his glass. "You got a card, Dani?"

"Oh, I do." I scramble to take a business card out of my purse. Just as I hand it to Isaac, Parker appears in my periphery like a subtle disturbance in the air. He stops to order a whiskey neat, looking from me to Isaac and then back to me again.

I give him a haughty smile. *Look, I'm networking! I'm not totally hopeless!*

Parker inspects my face for only an instant before turning to Isaac. "Figured I'd find you at the bar."

"I was introducing myself to Dani," Isaac says, standing straight. Not unlike Parker, he's a tower himself. "By the way, I'm head of digital marketing at Venture. Not that you'd need my help marketing Doge, but I'd be happy to be of assistance with anything else."

I take the business card he offers and hold it up. "Look at that subtle off-white coloring. The tasteful thickness of it."

Parker drops his head with a sigh. "*American Psycho*? Really?"

Isaac is a good sport however. "It even has a watermark." We laugh, and he nudges Parker. "She's refreshing. How do you two know each other?"

"Dani and I grew up together."

Isaac blinks at me, and I can read his expression: *Acquaintances, huh?* I pretend not to notice, taking a slow slip of my wine instead.

CHAPTER ELEVEN

He may look the part, but it turns out Isaac is nothing like the guys at Modrix. He only uses buzzwords ironically and seems far more interested in talking about the *Adagio* piece on ghost ships I mention—as a paranormal aficionado, he's stoked to read it. Parker doesn't weigh in much, taking up space like an uninvited observer, waiting for the next stupid thing I'll say. But I'm determined to redeem myself, nearly making it to the end of the conversation—until Isaac brings up the Rangers account and a string of athletes I've never heard of. And just like that, I'm lost.

"I should head back," he declares, nodding to a group on the other side of the room. "It was lovely to meet you, Dani Tsai."

"Surprisingly not terrible for an NFT dude," I say to Parker. "And between you and me, a lot more pleasant than the only other guy I know at Venture Sports."

"I have to ask, do you always travel with an entourage? You know, normally, people stop at a plus-*one*."

"Don't act like you aren't ecstatic to add members to the fan club." I order my second glass of wine and take a spiteful swig of it. "I was expecting Charlotte to fold—she does for every hot guy in a suit—but I thought Savannah was stronger than that."

"Did you just call me hot?"

Shit. "I meant that in an objective way."

Parker's eyes light up with an unabashed smile. Torturously

perfect. "You can just say you find me attractive."

I stay mum. I guess my silence is implicit, because Parker doesn't persist—he just grins, and I think that might be worse. In my mind, I'm winding up to open-hand smack myself. I can't believe I walked right into that one.

"You going back out there anytime soon?"

I draw a lungful of air and look over my shoulder. Shiny dresses, shiny watches, and even shinier people. I don't think I'll ever feel like I belong here—or that I'd want to. I'm sure Savannah and Tae-woo are having the time of their lives. But me? I'm just going through the motions.

"In a second. I need to finish warming up." I gesture to my wine glass. "That's how these things usually go. It's all about finding that equilibrium where you're buzzed and outgoing, but not throwing up in the bushes."

"Spoken like a seasoned pro."

"Not really. I still don't know how I ended up here, and to be honest, I could say the same for you. The only time I imagined you wearing a suit was at the draft." It begs the question, and I let my curiosity get the better of me. "When did you stop playing?"

Almost immediately, I get the troubled sense that I shouldn't have asked because Parker seems to withdraw as soon as I mention it. "Junior year. Think I only played two games that season before I quit."

That's odd. I'd assumed he played all throughout college. "Bad season for the team?"

He grins to himself. "No, they actually made it to the Rose Bowl that year."

My brain scrambles to keep up. I can't fathom what would cause the Parker Tran I grew up with to put a premature end to his football dreams. Then, I do the quick math in my head, and when it hits me, my stomach curls into a knot. "So, when I saw you last time in Silverpine, you'd already quit?"

"Yeah."

"I see," I say, still calibrating. "And then you got into marketing."

"Turns out I'm not too bad at it."

"Did you move to San Francisco because of the 49ers?"

"I moved because the sports market there had more to offer." With a flash of a grin, he adds, "You remembered my favorite team."

"Lucky guess," I lie. When we were kids, Parker used to wear his Joe Montana jersey like it was a second skin. It's hard to forget that. "Is that how you ended up at Venture?"

"Actually, I was doing marketing for a minor league team before I got an offer from them." He rolls his shoulders. "Got any more questions? Or have I passed this round yet?"

I have a million more questions: Do you have amnesia? Or have you conveniently forgotten the time you left me high and dry? What happened to staying out of each other's lives forever? But, to start, I ask, "Why did you invite me here tonight?"

It doesn't throw him off, and instead he returns, "Why did you come?"

Because I lied to Dad that I had a shot at a shiny new job. Because I wanted Savannah and Tae-woo to see that I could hold my own in their world.

No. It's because I was curious about what would happen once I saw Parker tonight.

I hold up my glass. "Free booze."

"That isn't free."

"It is if it's on Jerry Rodgers's tab."

We laugh, but I cut my amusement short because there's no chance we're sharing an amicable moment right now. This alternate-universe Parker Tran has really thrown me for a loop. I almost wish he'd say "Sike!" and tip my wine glass over. At least then I'd know for sure I didn't hit my head back at Picotea and dream all this in a coma.

"There you are, Parker Tran!" Striding over is a petite woman in an eye-catching gold dress, and everyone around us pauses to get a look. Even the busy bartender steals a glance. A corseted bodice hugs her slim figure, and her dark hair is a crown of flawless waves that a curling iron would never have the audacity to fry.

She leans against Parker's arm. "Buy me a drink? You know what I like."

He signals the bartender. "Um, was it a cosmo?"

"Espresso martini," she pouts at him. Lifting a hand to his face, she smooths a strand of hair behind his ear. Parker leans back just enough to slip out of her reach, and I turn to face away. I feel like I've just witnessed a personal exchange I wasn't meant to see.

"Min, this is Dani from *Adagio*, the magazine." Unfortunately, he drags me back into their moment. "Min is in New York for a modeling gig."

I shouldn't be surprised that Parker's already made friends in the city—some of the gorgeous-model variety.

"Hi," I say with an inelegant wave of my hand.

"Love your dress," gushes Min. "Who's your stylist?"

"Oh, this was all the underhanded plotting of one Tae-woo Kang."

"Hmm, I've never heard of him." She scoops up her drink with one dainty hand, and with the other she produces a small piece of plastic. The logo is unmistakable—it's been in my face all evening. A St. Regis key card. With a wink, she slips it into Parker's jacket. "Forgot to return this last week."

Oh. *That* kind of friend.

I watch Min go, noting every head that turns as she crosses the ballroom. Everyone but Parker, who's fixed on his whiskey. "Your plus-one?"

"Nope," he says. "I actually didn't know she'd be here tonight."

"You seem friendly." *Friendly enough for her to have seen the inside of your suite.* I look at his hair where Min tucked it behind his ear—his stupidly divine hair, as soft-looking as ever—and grip my wine glass a little tighter. "I wouldn't want her to get the wrong idea if I keep you preoccupied too long."

"I think you're the one getting the wrong idea." He takes a sip. "Some of the guys from Venture introduced us, but it's nothing serious. I don't exactly do that."

"Don't do what?"

Parker lowers his glass. "I don't date, and I don't do relationships."

"I see," I mumble lowly. That's so very . . . Parker Tran. I remember now that although he went on a lot of dates in high school, Parker never had a serious girlfriend back home. I always figured he'd meet some poor, unsuspecting cheerleader-type in college and then con her into a relationship. They'd have a wedding in Portland—none of the venues in Silverpine would be grand enough—with footballs for centerpieces, and Parker would ride down the aisle in his Jeep.

"I guess some things never change," I muse.

"I was just thinking that about you."

Maybe it's because I've felt at odds with myself all night, being somewhere I clearly don't belong, but it nettles me to hear that from him. "What's that supposed to mean?"

He tilts his head to the scene behind us. "An event full of New York elites and you're talking to the guy you've known since you were seven."

"There has to be another option between feeding myself to

the sharks and—" I press my lips together. "Silverpine's finest export of asshole."

He makes a dry sound, taken aback. "How am I an asshole?"

"You called me a bridge troll!"

"That was a joke!" Parker shakes his head. "I mean, look at you." His eyes scan me at length, and the expression he makes is unfamiliar to me. "You probably haven't noticed it, but every guy has been wondering who you are since you walked in."

I feel my face bloom hot again. "Time out. Don't think for a second that I haven't realized how weird this is." With my finger I point back and forth between us. "We are not friends anymore. Don't you remember how we left things in Silverpine?"

Parker leans forward and seizes my hand midair. I freeze at his touch. His voice is low and husky, and it does something maddening to me. "You don't think I can play nice?"

I can't speak because he's still holding my hand. My heart is a jackhammer in my chest. I look at his lips for a fraction of a second and then look away. What the hell is happening?

Anxiously, I muster my words. "We hated each other."

"I didn't hate you."

Full stop. *What?* That doesn't align with the history that I know.

Time seems to slow until he finally lets go of my hand, and I let it fall awkwardly to my side. Something electric shoots through me, and under my ribcage, it feels stuffy and tight.

I'm still thinking about how Parker's hand felt on mine—big, warm, and alarmingly soft—when Tae-woo arrives at the bar counter. He leans over the corner and orders a boulevardier.

"Tae-woo, let me know when you want to check out that new spot in Koreatown," Parker says breezily. "I'm always up for a few rounds of somaek."

"Yeah, I'll hit you up." No way he broke the impenetrable Tae-woo. We work five feet away from each other but have never even grabbed a coffee together. "Just a heads up: I can drink you under the table, pretty boy."

"I'll try my best to keep up." Parker's laugh is an airy, amazing sound, and I am so very bitter.

Tae-woo steps away with his drink, but he stops to regard us once more. His gaze lingers for an uncomfortable stretch, jumping between our expectant faces.

"What?" I demand.

"Have you two ever fucked?"

Parker chokes on his drink. My heart catapults into my throat.

"No, you debauched gremlin!" I shriek, begging the pits of hell to open up and swallow Tae-woo whole.

"Thought I picked up on a vibe, geez."

"Sorry." I panic, trying and failing to regain some composure once Tae-woo has left. "He likes to make fun of me because I haven't gotten laid in, like, six months." Now why the fuck did I volunteer that information?

Inside my head is a montage of war footage accompanied by a symphony of gunfire and missiles. I want to shrivel up under the bar or drown myself in a fountain somewhere—in a hotel this fancy, there's got to be a fountain, right? Then I remember the key card Min was holding, the one that opens a suite in this very building, where she and Parker have already hooked up.

Now the image of Parker having sex has replaced the warfare in my head. Flashes of muscle, the enormous bare arms of a former quarterback, and oh yes, more muscles. My breathing picks up and warmth runs through me, all the way to my fingertips. Against my better judgment, I chance a glimpse at him. He's gone suspiciously quiet.

The tips of his ears are red—in fact, most of his face is red. His bottom lip is wedged between his teeth, and he seems determined not to look at me. My gut is turning inside out, like I'm dropping from the highest point of a rollercoaster. I'm horrified at the possibility, but if his thoughts are anything like mine, then—

"Oh my god, please don't picture me having sex."

"What? I—I'm not." I can't help but notice the way he loosens his tie and how much redder his ears are. "I wasn't."

I remember, suddenly, that there was once a time when I wanted Parker to kiss me. It was our senior year, on the night of the very last game of his high school football career. My first time riding in the Jeep. When he pulled up to my house, a strange thing occurred. I can still recall his hand on my face and the pulse of anticipation that came with it. Maybe it was because I'd watched *The Spectacular Now* the night before, but I'd convinced myself something was about to happen—and I had secretly wished it would.

He didn't kiss me. But the Parker standing here now feels like the same one from that night.

"Dude, have you been here the whole time?" A man in a navy blue suit throws an arm around Parker's shoulders. Blue eyes take a full inspection of me, with no attempt at being subtle. "Is that Valentino?"

"Don't tell me—the Madison Square Garden guys are here?" Parker grouses.

"If we want to sweeten the Rangers deal, we might as well move while they're hammered."

"Fine, I'll see what I can do." Parker downs the rest of his whiskey and secures his tie as the other man launches off ahead of him. "Looks like I've been tagged back in."

"Do your thing, boy wonder." I cringe after I say it.

Parker is a few steps away before he calls out to me. "Dani."

I turn around.

"In case I wasn't clear . . . you look beautiful."

CHAPTER TWELVE

I hand out my last business card of the night and skirt around the ballroom twice, searching for Savannah. We planned to leave at ten, allowing more than enough time to drain my social battery. I haven't spotted her, so I shoot her a text while I idle by the doors.

"I take it your warm-up was effective." Parker finds me first. He doesn't look nearly as tired as I am—in fact, he looks just as alert and refreshed as he did at the start of the night.

"Rewards for being professional *and* personable." I hold up a couple cards from my new contacts: a prestigious editor-in-chief and a big name from *The New York Times*. Charlotte had introduced us in her efforts to get back in my good graces. "Obtained through the power of alcohol and only mild extortion of a coworker."

"And you were afraid you wouldn't fit in here." He watches as I read Savannah's reply on my phone. "Heading out?"

King Cole Bar. "Yeah, but I've got to meet Savannah downstairs."

"I'll walk you down. I could use a breather."

Perhaps it was the last humble brag about a thirty-foot yacht that did it for me, but I'm burned out. I don't say anything to Parker as we step into the elevator together. Our conversation from earlier cycles through my head, as it has most of the night. When I remember his parting line, my body goes rigid. The nice act is distressing enough, but when he complimented me, it was as if a mental barricade went up, reminding me not to trust the enemy.

From beside me, Parker puts his hands in his pockets. "You're doing that Dani thing where you get all in your head. I can see you filtering through a million thoughts right now."

"Okay, mind reader. What am I thinking about?"

"Hmm." He taps his foot against the floor. "You're either hoping I didn't catch that six-month sex drought comment from earlier, or . . . you still can't figure out why I'm being so nice to you."

I turn my head, and our eyes meet.

"You think I haven't noticed that you've been keeping me at arm's length?"

"I wasn't . . ." The words die in my throat. I know why the entire barside conversation felt so unnatural to me: It's because neither of us wants to mention what happened that Christmas eight years ago or why we stopped talking in the first place.

"To answer your question from before," he says, "I'm not really sure why I invited you, but it seemed like the right thing to do at the time. I wasn't prepared at all the night I ran into you at Picotea. Even if you weren't exactly avoiding me, I had a vague feeling that it might be the last time I would see you. At least for a while."

I respond with silence, and he continues.

"I always thought I'd run into you back home, not that you make it very easy to do so. I, um, heard you don't keep in contact with Nathan or my mom anymore."

I stare down at my feet, afraid that if I face the elevator doors, I'll catch his reflection looking back at me.

He goes on, "And I know that's my fault, after what I did. But a lot has changed in the last seven years; I've changed too. Maybe I was hoping you'd hear me out some time. I don't know if I deserve it, though."

I thought an apology from Parker would make me smug with vindication, or that at the very least, I'd be curious to know why he didn't show up that Christmas Eve. But instead, I feel hollow inside. There remains only a voice, telling me not to ask. I don't know if I can have this conversation yet. If we dredge this up now, it'll feel a lot like suffocating. He's hurt me once before; I don't know that I can piece myself together if it happens again.

Maybe out of mercy, Parker changes track. "How are you getting home?"

"Splitting a cab with Savannah. We're both in Brooklyn."

"I was there the other day, and I thought of that movie you'd watch every Christmas," he says. "*Moonstruck*, was it?"

I don't have many memories of my mother. I remember breakfasts of dan bing with soy milk and dinner spreads of stir-fry and herbal broths. The sweet lilt in her laugh. I also remember movie nights when she and I would wait for Dad to fall asleep to put on *Moonstruck*. Those were the nights I looked forward to the most.

"It was my mom's favorite."

He clears his throat, and his voice comes out a little softer. "Back when you were planning my trip, you put Brooklyn Heights on the list and wrote 'Cher's house' next to it. You were just trying to take me to all your favorite spots, weren't you?"

"I don't remember," I say. "That was a long time ago."

The elevator stops, and Parker walks with me through the lobby, bright and majestic with its gold-overlaid walls. My heels click and echo loudly against the marbled floors. When we reach the Drawing Room, I take in the chandeliers suspended throughout the room and the signature hand-painted clouds on the ceiling.

"Must be nice staying here," I muse.

Parker shrugs, but I see the mirth in his eyes. "It's not bad."

Across the dining area, I spot Savannah at the iconic bar. The whole scene—framed by the *Old King Cole* mural, the wood-paneled walls, and the candlelit ambience—has a dreamy quality. Sitting alone at the counter in her gorgeous, silvery dress, she looks like the star of her own movie.

"Why didn't I think of escaping to the King Cole Bar too?" I pull a face, crossing my arms.

Parker follows my line of sight. "It does seem fitting that you'd find better company with a Maxfield Parrish painting."

"You know who Maxfield Parrish is?"

"Believe it or not, I've been to the Met," he says dryly.

I peek over at him. "Thanks for walking me down here."

"I should probably turn in too," he says, reaching up to rub the crook of his neck.

"So soon? It's not even eleven."

He scrunches his nose and shrugs again. "This stuff gets old quick."

I want to tease him about losing his party-animal roots, but something about the Parker before me seems a little raw and unguarded. I suppose that under the great hair and suit, there's a normal guy who grows weary of nights like these too.

"Anyway, goodnight, Dani."

"Goodnight, Parker."

He smiles that devastating smile. That same boyish charm from the other night. "Maybe I'll see you again."

"Maybe," I say.

Parker turns to leave, his easy strides carrying him across the lobby. A dull ache forms in my chest. His words from the elevator stay fixed in my mind, but it's that brilliant smile that pulls me back to juvenile summers and rainy days huddled by the window.

It's still hard to believe there was a time when my world revolved around that boy. My face is warm from all the wine, and I try to calm the aching feeling, but it only grows heavy and crushing.

Parker Tran was my first friend. He was the first boy to hold my hand, and the first boy to make me cry. Now he's the most breathtaking man I've ever laid eyes on, and when he tells me I look beautiful in a room packed with other people, I forget everyone exists but the two of us.

I was five the first time I watched *Moonstruck* with Mom, too young to form much of an appreciation for it. Nicolas Cage had a wooden hand, and Cher didn't seem to like him when she was slapping him, but she liked him a whole lot when they were kissing. I remember when the credits rolled, Mom was crying. That was the first time I saw her heart breaking, and once I understood that, I couldn't let go of the image. It comes back to me at times like these, when I don't know what to do with my own shattering heart.

I don't realize I'm moving until I'm already running down the gilded halls. When I reach the foyer, I make a sharp turn toward the elevators, and my hand flies between closing doors, willing them open. Parker is the only one inside, and he stares down at me, wide-eyed. I don't spare any room in the chaos of my mind to think, because I know if I do, all the doubt and fear from the last seven years will catch up to me.

Instead, I grab him by the lapels of his jacket, and I kiss him.

CHAPTER THIRTEEN

The moment I step into the elevator, I'm certain nothing will ever be the same.

That's the last coherent thought I have before I kiss Parker. After that, I'm numb to any reasoning as soon as I feel perfectly soft lips parting against mine. He starts slowly, like he's learning how I kiss, and it requires his deliberate care. But then he's all in. Solid hands grab me by the waist, and his velvety warm mouth crashes into mine. The taste of sweet champagne and harsh whiskey makes me dizzy, and I lean into him, as close as I can get. Still holding onto his suit like it's meant to anchor me, I give into everything that is Parker Tran.

With a single gasp, I break away from him. Parker doesn't say a word, but his dark brown eyes sweep over my face, my chest, and our bodies pressed together.

"How much did you drink?"

"I'm not drunk," I insist. It's not a lie. I may have required liquid courage to spur me on earlier in the evening, but I'm painfully aware of how sober I am now. "Equilibrium, remember?"

"Okay," Parker says, though it sounds like he's talking to himself. He bites his lip and takes another hard look at me before his entire demeanor changes, the ambivalence in his eyes giving way to something I can't quite read. Leaning over to the elevator panel, he presses a button. "Just so you know, Dani, once this elevator stops, I'm going to take you to my suite."

I swallow the lump in my throat. "I know."

It isn't long before the elevator glides to a stop with a soft chime. As soon as the doors open, Parker's hand takes hold of mine, leading me down an empty, brightly lit hallway. We stop, and I watch the door of his suite fly open faster than I can see the key card leave his pocket. Strong arms spin me around, and my back hits the wall as his lips find mine for the second time. He cups my face with both hands, and our tongues collide in eager, feverish strokes. There's an urgency in the kiss this time, and I can hardly catch my breath.

Parker lifts me with ease, carrying me to the next room, where I land on a spread of plush pillows. I steal a glance at my surroundings: matte shades of gray and purple and antique charm coming together in elegant luxury. "What the hell is this suite? It's bigger than my apartment."

"Is that important right now?" Parker asks, a little winded.

He has a point. The distance from the bed to where he stands feels endless, and I pull him to my level, letting his sturdy frame drape over me. Feathery kisses land along my jaw, trailing down to my neck, where he sucks gently at the skin. Instinctively, I reach for his hair and—*wow, fucking finally*—it's just as silky as I'd always suspected.

"Get this off already." I urge him out of his jacket, and he obliges, generously losing his shirt, too, and *holy hell*. I really tried to be indifferent every time I'd meet Parker after football practice, but that didn't mean I could keep my teenage hormones in check. When he'd lift his T-shirt to sponge the sweat off of his face, my eyes would drop to his exposed torso, though I'd always pretend not to notice. Now that I can feel that same hard flesh flexing under my fingertips, it's like a drought ending in a sudden, torrential downpour.

"Like what you see?"

"Don't make me say it."

I catch a glimpse of a smirk before he pins me down with another kiss, his tongue slipping into my mouth, drawing a moan from the back of my throat. A hand travels under the hem of my dress, just ghosting along my inner thigh, and I tense with anticipation.

"You're not acting like someone who hates me."

"Parker, I swear to god—"

"Actually, I think you kind of like when I touch you." His hand continues up my leg until his thumb reaches my panties, gently grazing the cloth. "Looks like I'm right."

He teases me where I'm wet, throbbing, impatient. I suck in a sharp breath.

"No smart remark? That's new." Parker's mouth is back on my neck, his lips brushing under my ear as he speaks. "You can tell me if you like it. You've always been good with words."

"I think it's best if we don't talk." I reach for where he's hard and palm him over his pants. He groans, and it comes out raspy, intense—I've never heard him sound like that before. It's as bizarre as it is satisfying. Parker Tran wants *me* so badly he's practically coming apart at the seams.

"So that's how I get you to shut up," I snipe back, and like fanning a flame, my words bring out a wildfire in his eyes.

As he unzips my dress, I can't help but wonder if it's crossed his mind—the absurdity of all this, after everything we've been through, the times together, and the times apart. In no possible universe does it feel real for us to be kissing. Undressing one another. Moments away from crossing an unthinkable line.

And yet, all of it fades once Parker strips me down to nothing and whispers, "God, Dani, you're so pretty." His voice comes out honey-thick. A chill runs down my spine.

He removes the last of his clothing, and I momentarily adjust to the reality that I now know what a nude Parker looks like—and that yes, I *do* like what I see. When he climbs back onto the bed, his hands are hot against my skin, on every curve and dip of my figure, as he makes himself familiar with my body. He arrives at my breasts, taking one into his mouth, and my heart beats so loudly I can hear it drumming in my head.

I kiss him roughly when he pulls away, leaving a taunting bite on his bottom lip, coaxing him to give me more, touch me more. He's quick on the uptake, his fingers traveling south and dipping between my legs. It's all I can do to keep from spiraling under his touch. The act is so intimate, and yet so foreign, it carves out an impossible closeness between us. But I don't let myself dwell, not when it feels *this good*.

He checks in with me one more time. "Are you sure about this?"

I nod, positive that my voice will give out if I speak, and Parker presses a single kiss to my forehead. His lips then work their way down my body, nipping along my stomach, until my thighs are on either side of his head. I watch his toned arms hook under my legs as he props himself in place, and I nearly gasp from the sensation of his tongue against me. His mouth is a marvel of focus and skill, and an ache within me builds up in crushing tides, a coil inside me tensing, tightening, and finally snapping with hot release.

I lose my mind to the rush of my orgasm, still reeling when he moves to the nightstand, and I hear him unwrap a condom. I don't know what feeling has lodged itself in my chest—whether it's nerves or something else entirely—but between the touches, the kisses, and Parker climbing over me, I'm convinced none of that matters.

CHAPTER FOURTEEN

Four years ago

Oak & Orchard is the only store in Silverpine that carries miso paste. I'd been here with Nathan years ago, when we first discovered it, and he'd shared his miso scrambled eggs recipe with me. That's why I'm not surprised to find him in the international foods aisle—two whole shelves long—holding the last tub of miso paste.

It doesn't make it any less awkward though.

"Hey," he says first.

"Hey."

"When did you get back?"

"Thursday night," I answer. "I'm only here for a few days."

He puts the tub in his shopping basket. "I got in yesterday. Didn't know you were here. My mom didn't mention anything."

"I'm not sure she even knows I'm back," I admit, thinking back on the last two days spent holed up in my room. I'd told Dad not to advertise my return, explaining that I'd be busy trying to meet a deadline. "I haven't had time to drop by."

"Busy?"

"Work," I say. "Well, it's freelance stuff, but I've got an article to turn in."

"You should come over for dinner if you've got time. We'd love to have you." When I don't immediately respond, Nathan says in a low voice, "He's not here. He moved to San Francisco."

"Ah," I manage. A new city means new victims of the Parker Tran charm. Bet he's doing numbers over in the Bay Area. I grab a bottle of sriracha and pretend to read every ingredient.

Nathan doesn't budge. He stands stiltedly in the aisle, picking up items from the shelf, only to put them down again. Then, he takes a deep breath.

"Dani, I'm only saying this because I care. Whether or not we keep in touch, I'm always going to look out for you. The three of us grew up together, you know? So, I'm sorry if this seems like overstepping—"

If someone warns you they *might* overstep, they're about to plant a big, fat footprint in a forbidden zone—and drop a landmine while they're at it.

"I think you should reach out to Parker. I can give you his number."

Boom.

"What if I told you that's a terrible idea?"

"You two have been friends since you were seven."

"And it's been three years since we last spoke."

"That's exactly why," he persists. "A little communication could go a long way."

At this, a flare of indignation rises in my chest. "Your brother is the one who should learn to communicate. Whatever grudge he had against me, he could've talked to me about it, instead of bailing on our New York plans and ghosting me after."

I never did learn Parker's reasons for what happened. He left my last text unanswered, and I didn't hear from him again. It used to eat at me, and for a long time I thought I'd done something wrong. I probably could've been more supportive of his football career. Maybe Parker had the impression that because I didn't attend any games, it meant I didn't care, and that's why he iced me out. Nevertheless, I was still frustrated that he'd taken away my right to closure.

When we ran into each other in front of Rocky's three years ago, I gave him an opening to explain, and he gave me nothing. That's when I came to the conclusion that closure is overrated. I changed my number and started spacing out my visits to Silverpine, making them fewer and farther between. I told Dad that if he wanted, he could come see me in New York, and now he sometimes flies out for holidays. I suppose that since we've never been close, it makes it easier not to feel obligated to see each other.

It doesn't matter why Parker disappeared from my life; what matters is that he didn't want to stay. And as it turns out, I'm done wondering why the people around me don't want to stick around.

I expect my accusatory tone to bring out Nathan's defensiveness, but he just stands there, openmouthed, his brows drawn together.

"Did you say Parker didn't show up in New York?"

Now I'm just as confused as he looks. "He didn't tell you?"

"I always assumed something happened on that trip. Like you two had a huge fight or something. But if he didn't show up—" He stops, the implications of this missing piece of information clearly hitting him. "Why didn't you say anything to us?"

"I thought you knew."

"You thought we knew and that we were all okay with it?"

I nod slowly.

"Dani, it was never about taking sides." Nathan looks at me

as if he can't bear to believe I'd thought otherwise. "If anything, my stance is that there's been a communication breakdown on both ends. That's why I feel so strongly about you reaching out to him. Parker, he—he had a lot going on, too, with his situation and, well, it's not my place to get into it. Those are things he has to explain to you."

I return the sriracha bottle to its shelf before it explodes in my grip. "I'm sorry, Nathan, but it just sounds like you're trying to cover for him."

He frowns, adjusting his glasses. "I think him bailing on you wasn't that simple. He probably struggled with it a lot too."

Struggled? The Parker Tran who has done just fine without me? Before I blacklisted "football," his school, and his name on every search portal and social media site, I did come across a post on his team's page. There on the gridiron was the number 11 jersey in the middle of a celebratory huddle, exalted fists in the air. Living the dream, right?

"Can I ask you something?" I say. "Did Parker ever start in a game?"

"He did. In his junior year."

Just as I thought. "Why wasn't I invited?"

"I wish I had an answer for you." He sighs and moves his basket from one hand to the other. "I asked him the same thing. He just said you were no longer speaking."

So much for promises. How do you go from talking to someone every day to removing them from the biggest moments of your life? I guess at some point, Parker decided there wasn't any room for me in his big dreams. It doesn't come as a shock to me, but it still feels like a belated sucker punch to the gut.

"I'm assuming you stopped following college football," Nathan says.

I shoot him a look that says, *Isn't it obvious?*

"It's just that—I don't know, maybe if you heard it from him—"

"I appreciate what you're trying to do, Nathan. But if Parker wanted me in his life again, don't you think he would've tried by now?" My voice comes out firm, steeled with resolve, and I hope he notices. "You may not believe me, but I'm really fine if I never hear from him again. I've had to learn this the hard way, but if someone abandons you, it'll only hurt you more if you keep holding on. I can't keep getting burned by the people I thought would be around forever. In the end, there's nothing I could've done differently to make them stay, so why try now?"

To my surprise, Nathan doesn't challenge this. He lets me withdraw from the conversation, watching as I pick up a bottle of mirin and two instant ramen packets, tossing them in my basket. Before I leave the aisle, I give him one last meaningful look.

"Can you do me a favor? Don't tell Parker you ran into me or that we talked about him. And please, if you can help it, don't let him know how I'm doing. I don't want to know about him, and I don't want him knowing about me."

He hesitates but eventually promises me his discretion. "And what about my mom? What if she asks about you?"

My gut takes a second punch. This one feels a lot more like guilt. "Does she ask about me?"

"Of course she does. She still thinks you and Parker are going to make up. That you drifted apart because of the distance, but you'll reconnect someday."

Why does it feel worse knowing Cô is still gracing me with the benefit of the doubt? If she hated me like her son does, I wouldn't feel so rotten for letting her get caught in the crossfire.

"She misses you, you know," Nathan continues. "But she figured you love your big New York life so much, you don't have time for us small-town folk anymore. Not that she blames you for it. According to her, it's all part of growing up."

How do I explain this to her—that I can't go over there, answer questions about Parker, and stand in the same rooms we grew up in without the memories haunting me? I know it makes me a coward, because I can't tell her the truth: I need to avoid her so I won't have to hear how amazing Parker's life is after leaving me in the dust.

"Tell her I'm well," I say, swallowing the lump in my throat, "and that I hope she's good too."

I part ways with Nathan to browse another aisle, while he pays at the checkout counter. When he reaches the door, he looks back and gives me a perfunctory wave.

CHAPTER FIFTEEN

I've been home for all of three hours and have been screaming into my pillow for two and a half.

When I woke up at the St. Regis, in the enormous expanse that was Parker's bed, he was still sound asleep. As much as I would've liked to appreciate the sight of his abs peeking out from under the covers or the way his hair looked adorably tousled against his forehead, I was also dreadfully aware that the naked man next to me was Parker freaking Tran.

After releasing a silent scream from the chasm of my soul, my body kicked into flight mode. A siren blared in my brain, and I'd entered a code-red emergency state with one option: evacuate. I jumped into my dress and scurried out of the massive suite before Parker could wake up.

Now that I'm home, I'm determined to stay holed up in my apartment, face down in a pillow, until my spirit ascends to another plane of existence. It all comes back in waves, and I'm forced to relive our night of sin—pure, carnal sin. Every time I remember the taste of Parker's lips, his big hands running up and down my body, the heat of his skin against mine, my heart performs a full gymnastic routine in my chest and forces a ghoulish cry out of me.

How could this have happened? Did I hop universes again? Or maybe I've branched into another timeline—a very dark, very sexy, deeply horrifying timeline.

I curl up into a ball and draw a deep breath. Let's think about this rationally, Dani. I had a few glasses of wine and some champagne in me, but I wasn't drunk. There was also that almost apology in the elevator, but that left me stumped, rather than having the effect of sweeping me off my feet. Regardless, the confusing truth is that I did, in fact, want to hook up with Parker. I mean, *I* was the one who kissed *him* in the elevator.

I unroll from the safety of my little ball and stare blankly at the wall.

Why did I kiss Parker?

Last night, I learned three world-shattering truths:

One: Parker thinks I'm pretty. Beautiful, even.

Two: Parker didn't hate me back in college.

Three: Parker is really, *really* good in bed.

My skin burns, radiating warmth under the covers. A montage of our night in the suite plays again in my head, this time like a thrilling football highlight reel. But honestly, the whole night felt like one long highlight, with Parker expertly taking me to a winning touchdown. Once, twice, and okay—four times, to be exact. All thanks to the honed proficiency of his hands and mouth, hitting every pleasure point and unraveling me by the end of our . . . well, I'm not sure what to call it. Crimes against humanity feels about right.

He'd single-handedly eclipsed every sexual experience I've ever had—and that's not even counting his endurance. Even if Parker doesn't play football anymore, he could've fooled me. But the most impressive feat? What he brought out of *me*. It was like I was so game to keep up with him, I became a version of myself that was more confident, sexier, and wilder.

I've never had sex like that before.

Is all his prowess owing to years of experience as a hot, eligible bachelor? I'm suddenly reminded of our conversation by the bar: Parker doesn't do relationships. And he's only in New York for a few months. Also worth noting: He keeps a box of condoms in his hotel suite. Who knows how many key cards he's handed out to women in Manhattan alone? There's a sharp jab under my breastbone when it occurs to me that Parker might not be freaking out about last night the way that I am. Maybe he hasn't spared it a second thought. Maybe he's already moved on.

I pat around the duvet without lifting my head until I locate my phone. It's a little past eleven. Parker is probably awake by now. Shoving the thought aside, I pull up my chat with Savannah.

Me: I'm so sorry I left you! Did you get home safely?

Savannah: Don't worry girl, Tae-woo and I split an Uber. But what I need right now is the tea!!! What, or WHO, did you do last night?

I let out a small, anguished whine and throw a pillow over my face. A few minutes pass, then my phone vibrates again. Expecting it to be Savannah, I scream and drop the device when I see Parker's name on the screen instead.

Parker: Can we talk?

No three words have ever struck greater fear in me. The idea of packing up everything, joining a convent, and turning away from my life of sin crosses my mind. But I stare at the text, and with a shaky breath, I type in my reply.

Me: Now?

I wedge my thumb between my teeth. He's not going to call, is he? I'm not sure if I can speak to him right now. I wouldn't even know what to say.

Parker: I'll come to you. Are you at home?

I think about it, then send him the address of a café a few blocks away. My apartment isn't the place to do this, as I'm certain this won't be a conversation I want to relive every day that I wake up here. After willing my soul back into my body and with a farewell to my days of sanity, I head out to the café.

❧

My leg is shaking violently against the foot of a cold metal chair as I wait for Parker to arrive. Why did I think it would be a good idea to take a seat on the patio? Every time a cab pulls up next to me, I expect Parker to appear, and it sends my heart into chaos. I haven't even touched the Americano I ordered, which was another poor decision, because the last thing I need is for the caffeine to give my heart a beat down too. Although, if being sent to the ER means I can avoid facing Parker right now, this could work to my advantage.

Another cab pulls up to the curb, flooring the gas pedal on my heart. I'm just about to get up and find a seat inside when Parker steps out of the vehicle. I sit my butt down in one swift movement, my spine instantly ramrod straight.

The first thing I notice is that he isn't wearing a suit. It shouldn't come as a surprise, since it's a Saturday, and I'm sure that even if bro-juice runs through his veins, he still has his casual days. The second thing I notice—*are you fucking kidding?*—is that he's wearing gray sweatpants. After the night we just had, did he really have to wear *gray sweatpants* now? It's like he's flaunting that thing at me. With the combined strength of my ancestors, I force myself not to stare at his crotch as he takes a seat across the table. But now my libido has been kick-started, and I'm imagining myself ripping those sweats off him and mounting him in his chair.

Only once I've hauled my mind out of the gutter do I notice that Parker is frowning.

"I can't believe you ran away. You just left before we could even talk about what happened."

It feels like being blindsided, and it takes a few beats before I can pull together any kind of response. "Are you seriously giving me shit about running away? After what you did?"

"I knew you were going to throw that in my face." He closes his eyes and exhales. "So, what was this? Some big revenge plot? Were you going to sleep with me and never see me again?"

"Of course not!" I exclaim. "I left because I didn't know what to say to you. I panicked and needed some time to figure out what the fuck is going on."

"And what did you figure out?"

I review everything from my earlier meltdown: I still don't know why I kissed Parker, but I do know we had mind-blowing sex. I think, maybe, I've mastered quantum jumping between universes. Oh, and Parker doesn't do relationships. *Parker doesn't do relationships.*

"I think we both got caught up in a moment, in the nostalgia. But it was . . ." I swallow, shifting my gaze to the view over his shoulder. I can't tell if my heart is racing anymore because all I feel is a wrenching constriction in my chest. "It was just a one-time thing, right? You said yourself that you don't do relationships."

Parker doesn't respond right away. I can see his face change, his brows pulling together, but I can't decipher any of it. He pockets his hands in his hoodie and looks at the space between us—like he's not really focusing on anything, just looking.

"That's what I wanted to talk about. I'm only here for three months, and I don't know what expectations you might have, but like I said, I'm not a relationship kind of guy—"

"I'm not expecting a relationship," I cut in. Actually, I'm not sure what I'm expecting, but I know that sentence was going to end with a rejection. I don't think I could survive Parker Tran rejecting me again.

Silence brings us to a standstill, and I begin to feel the gravity of the situation. Maybe I shouldn't have kissed him. We were finally starting to get along again. I can't see us ever recovering from this. I mean, we've seen each other naked now—not to mention all the fun parts that came after. Even if we try to pretend it didn't happen, we'll just be awkward around each other, until one day, we stop speaking and become strangers all over again.

"I knew it." I put a hand over my forehead and mumble to myself. "I've slipped into the darkest timeline."

"What are you talking about?"

"Have you ever watched *Community*? You know, 'Remedial Chaos Theory'?" Parker stares at me, but his expression is giving me nothing. "Never mind. The whole idea is that when you roll a die, you create six different timelines, and they all have the potential to yield unexpected results. Last night, after you said goodnight to me at the hotel, it was like I rolled a metaphorical die that led to six diverging timelines in our world."

I see his confused blinks, but I barrel on. "There could've been one timeline where I went home or one where I tripped on my dress and never reached the elevator in time or even a timeline where I grew robotic parts and flew over the city. Anyway, it looks like we ended up in the timeline where . . . I kissed you."

Parker props his elbows on his lap, and for a moment, he holds his head in his hands. I wait for him to say something, my breath stilled.

"So, you're saying the darkest timeline is the one where you slept with me?"

My mouth drops. "I didn't mean it like that."

"Then what did you mean?"

He's got me. Sometimes I don't think before I speak, and other times I think way too much. This time, I wish I had thought a little more.

"God, Dani, are you seriously trying to blame the universe, or a die, or some stupid theory? *You* were the one who kissed *me*. Why can't you take accountability for that?"

I wince at his tone, my face growing hot. "I don't want to hear about accountability from you. You disappeared on me first. I *waited* for you for four fucking hours that day."

"I get it. I fucked up eight years ago. But I'm trying, okay. I told you I've changed—"

"You've changed? You mean, by being nice to me for one night? You've changed because you called me beautiful and said all those confusing things in the elevator? How do I know this wasn't your angle the entire time?"

"Trust me, Dani, this is the last thing I expected to happen between us." His eyes are wide with alarm, telling me he's disturbed by the implication. "Do you really think I would trick you into sleeping with me? That was never my intention. Everything that's happened, from the diner to the hotel, I thought . . ." He takes a deep breath, raking a hand through his hair. "I thought maybe we could be friends again."

I look down at my sneakers. My leg is still shaking. The chilly autumn air bites at my face, but it doesn't relieve the burning inside me. "I don't know how to be friends with you anymore, Parker."

"And that's why it was okay to sleep with me?"

"What about this seems okay to you?" My lips curl, and I pull back in my chair. "If you've got it all figured out, then why don't you tell me what last night meant to you?"

His jaw tenses. "It's not that simple."

"So then, what is there to talk about?"

Parker clasps his hands together and leans his forehead against them, quiet in his thoughts. I was afraid that he'd be breezy about last night, but now I almost wish he'd brushed it off as just a fling. In my head, I see a die rolling, landing on the version of me who stayed at the hotel this morning—the one who didn't run away. But truthfully, I'm not convinced this conversation would've gone any better had I stayed. I get the eerie sense that either way, we're doomed.

"You're right." Parker gives me one last unreadable look before he stands. "I'm not sure why I came here."

CHAPTER SIXTEEN

I'm at the St. Regis again.

Sometime after returning to my apartment and trying to drown myself in the shower, I decided I couldn't leave things with Parker the way I had. Sometimes, when I shut my brain off long enough, my body takes the wheel, and so far, it's led me to this exact lobby twice.

I pace back and forth for a good ten minutes before I whip out my phone.

Me: Where are you?

Parker: Out.

Me: I'm at the St. Regis.

It takes another ten minutes before I see Parker emerge from the revolving doors, still wearing those cursed sweatpants. He takes heavy steps toward me, and suddenly, I'm very conscious that this might not have been a good idea. I can't tell if he's annoyed that I'm here, but the stiffness in his face doesn't suggest he's pleased to see me.

"What part of our conversation did you take as an invitation to stake out my hotel?"

"Where did you go?"

"I went for a walk."

"You go on walks?"

He rolls his eyes. "Yes, Dani, I go on walks." As he speaks, a drove of tourists cuts in from the elevators, wheeling suitcases between us. "Can we not do this here?"

Parker leads me to a corridor with less foot traffic. He extends a hand behind my back to herd me over, but I jerk away, careful to maintain distance.

"What are you doing here? Do you have another multiverse theory to run by me?"

"Actually, one might argue that alternate timelines aren't the same as the multiverse, since multiple timelines can exist within one universe and—"

"I'm going to my suite." Parker turns on his heel.

"Wait, Parker!" I reach out and grab his arm, and then I realize what I've done. This is the first time we've touched since last night. I feel the way Parker tenses under my hand, and I immediately let go. "Can you just hear me out?"

He shifts to face me again. When I glance up at him, he's still frowning. And in the absence of his smile, I recall just how great it is.

My hands clench into fists at my sides. I'm nervous, and I can't tell if I'm shaking, because I can't really feel my legs anymore. "I'm sorry I said you had an angle. I don't actually think that. And I know I've had my guard up, but it's been nice, seeing you again. After this week, I don't want us to go back to being strangers."

Then, a shred of hope: "I don't want that either."

"I'm not sure if we fucked this up by, you know, sleeping together. But it's not like we can pretend it never happened—"

"Dani, if, for some reason, you're having regrets now—"

"No, that's not it," I clarify, hastily adding, "I don't regret it."

"Okay," he says, and his face softens just a bit. "Neither do I."

I let out a deep-rooted sigh. When I arrived at the hotel, it wasn't as if I'd come prepared with a quick fix. I just wanted to let Parker know I was trying. "How do we move on from this?"

He's quiet, letting my words settle. I see the way his face strains with concentration.

"To be honest, I don't have an answer for you. I'm still trying to figure this out too. I thought that finally talking to you again would clear the air, but I feel like having sex made things infinitely more complicated. We'd just barely scratched the surface of being friends again."

"Right? It might be even worse if we dated."

I don't mean it as a dig—I'm just laying out the facts. Parker doesn't have any interest in relationships, and if our conversation at the café is any indication, we're not compatible enough to make it work. We would never be on similar wavelengths, given our history. In fact, the only time I've felt like we were in sync with one another again was when we were having sex.

I run a distressed hand through my hair. "I hate to say it, but last night was really fucking good."

Parker coughs out a chuckle, then quickly smothers it behind his hand.

"Stop laughing. It's not funny."

"Dani, I'm not going to lie. I'm at a loss right now. You tell me we're in the darkest timeline, and then you say the sex was good." He's still trying to hold in his laugh. "I don't know what you want from me."

I don't need to see my face to know it's bright red. "I don't want a relationship."

"I know."

"And I'm sure for you it was just like any other fling—"

"It wasn't." He says it so sternly, the humor of the moment dies instantly. His heated gaze drops to my mouth, then to my chest. "It was . . . really fucking good for me too. And if it were up to me, that wouldn't be the last time."

My breath catches in my throat, and I break eye contact. How can he drop a line like that and expect me not to react? Like every instinct in my body isn't telling me to jump in his arms and wrap my legs around him?

"See? It's already happening. I don't think we can ever be normal around each other again."

"Still better than when we didn't talk."

"Is it? At least then I wasn't picturing you naked all the time." I clamp my hand to my mouth as soon as I say it. Why do I do this? Why do I let my intrusive thoughts win every time?

Mortified, I look up, expecting Parker to laugh again, but he doesn't. His jaw ticks, and I catch the twitch of his brow, the subtle bite of his lip. "Hm, I guess I'm not the only one then."

It's my turn to laugh, because the whole thing is just so bizarre. This is the same boy who couldn't finish an ice cream cone without getting half of it on his face—I'd have to hose him off in my backyard to get the sticky chocolate off. And now all I can think about is pressing that gorgeous face to mine.

"So? What now?" He leans against the wall and folds his arms. Those heart-stopping brown eyes wait expectantly for my answer. There's a brightness to them that's hard to miss, but when it's just the two of us, and he's taking my clothes off, they're dark with an intensity that makes me throw my inhibitions away. My gaze moves to his lips—lips I'd been kissing less than twenty-four hours ago, that had been on my body, taking me so skillfully to the best orgasms of my life—and I swallow.

Whatever happens from this point on will be no more than a blip in the timeline.

I'll be fine.

It'll all be fine.

"Give me a key card," I say. A rush surges through my chest.

"What?"

"Give me your spare key card so I don't have to wait in the lobby next time."

I can see the way my words are bouncing around in his head. A part of me relishes the fact that I'm the one making Parker Tran lose his cool. He pushes away from the wall and straightens to his full height. Then he speaks, and it sends my heart into a flurry that I can't ignore any longer. "Do you want to come up now?"

Yes. "Yes."

We take the elevator up to his suite. Parker doesn't have anything more to say. I don't either, and it seems to be working in our favor. Once he closes the door behind us, he pulls me in by the waist and kisses me hard. His hands are quick to remove my coat, fingertips warm as they slide under my shirt. I tug the hoodie off him, throwing it to the carpet before he covers my mouth with his again.

"I still think you're a dick," I say between kisses.

"And I still find you insufferable," he counters, but I can feel him smiling against my lips.

❧

We don't cuddle or kiss when it's over. That evening, once I've regained sensation in my legs, I lift myself from the bed to get dressed. Parker comes out of the bathroom at the same time, wearing a robe that's barely tied. What a prick.

He walks to the dresser and fetches a key card. Before he hands it over, he studies me with caution. A corner of his mouth turns downward, and his eyes narrow just the slightest.

"I've done casual before; this isn't new for me. But are you going to be okay with this?"

He's giving me a chance to back out. He doesn't think I'm capable of having a casual relationship without getting hurt. To him, I'm still that timid girl from next door who's never stepped out of her bubble long enough to do something as wild as this.

"You're not the only one who's changed, Parker."

I take the key card and leave the suite.

CHAPTER SEVENTEEN

I'm in way over my head. But I can't let Parker know that.

I've always been a long-term relationship kind of girl. I met my first boyfriend at Columbia. He was the only man I've ever known to unironically fill in the "occupation" field with "lyric poet." Graham and I only made it to graduation. And although the relationships that followed were just as unremarkable, I stuck them out for at least two years before calling it quits. Suffice it to say, a casual relationship is uncharted territory—and with the boy next door, whose puberty I had a front-row seat to? There's no playbook in the world that could've prepared me for this.

I still haven't figured out where we stand. Can you be friends with benefits if you're not really friends anymore? At no point has friendship come up again since our talk at the café, and we don't hang out apart from when we hook up. From our limited texting, I know that he spends most of his time dining with clients and attending sports games. Occasionally, Parker will ask me for restaurant recommendations, and I'll reply with something from my Excel spreadsheet of Manhattan eateries, because I once sent him the entire file, and he replied, "I'm not reading all that." But we haven't met anywhere outside of his hotel room since this arrangement started. We do, however, have something of a system down: One of us will shoot a text—*You free tonight?*—and within an hour I'll be at the St. Regis.

All I know is that in the last two weeks, I've been having the best sex of my life. What is it about being with Parker Tran? I feel like I've unlocked a sixth sense devoted solely to pleasure. I feel like a woman possessed, an alternate-universe Dani who doesn't think twice before shoving a man onto a bed and riding him into the sunset. I've never been with someone who knew exactly what I wanted, and at the same time, I've never been so in tune with another person to know exactly what *they* wanted. It's as if everything that had been chaotic and confusing about us falls into perfect balance when we're naked and horny.

Emerging from the bathroom of Parker's suite, I observe him sitting upright in bed, shirtless and scrolling on his phone. I wonder what the inner dialogue in his head is like after coming down from the high of orgasm. I suspect that, unlike me, he isn't overanalyzing every last detail. It must be all mental fist bumps up there.

I reach for my clothes at the foot of the bed, and Parker looks up at me. "How are you still wearing clothes from high school?"

I gaze down at the Green Valley insignia emblazoned over my chest. "It's still a perfectly good shirt. Would've been a waste to throw it out."

"I don't know if it's your hoarding that's more concerning or the fact that you haven't outgrown your teenage wardrobe."

"You're talking, but all I hear is *fee-fi-fo-fum*."

"Giant jokes? Really? When I've thrown footballs bigger than you?"

"I'm actually average height. But I guess anyone would look small when you're a descendant of Ents."

Parker looks like he's trying to recall what an Ent is, and I use the pause to slip out of the bedroom, through the marble foyer, and into the living room. The square footage of this suite is still so disorienting. My MacBook sits on the corner desk, and I wake it to an abandoned article where my last note reads: *Important! Check with source re: cost of . . .* Cost of what? I can't recall what was so important, because Parker had returned from the gym at that moment and lured me into the bedroom with a kiss that had me seeing the curvature of space-time.

He arrives behind me, looking over my shoulder. "Why'd you bring your laptop on a Sunday? Do you take your job with you everywhere?"

"Coming from you—the guy who has every meal with a client?" I retort. "The last time I was here, I ended up waiting an hour for you. I figured I could use the time to get ahead on work."

He lifts an incredulous brow, and I know he's going to tell me to be a normal person and turn on Netflix instead, but his eyes travel back to my screen. He grins to himself as he reads out loud, "How much does a marketing director make."

I shut the laptop with lightning speed. "Just research for work."

A sly tilt of his head is all it takes to challenge me. He's so annoying.

"Fine. I was curious," I relent, rolling my eyes. "I mean, Venture set you up with a hotel that has complimentary butler service! By the way, Anton dropped off your freshly pressed shirts." I point woodenly in the direction of the closet. "It seems like you're a pretty big deal."

"Most of it is performative." He ruffles his hair, smooth strands weaving between his long fingers. "We work with a lot of high-profile clients—professional athletes with huge price tags attached to their names. I'm their point of contact, so Venture wants me to look a lot flashier than I really am."

"In other words, you're a big deal."

He simply shakes his head as he retrieves his own MacBook from the desk drawer, pulling up his emails. In a blink, the unread messages triple in number. As I watch his forehead crease with focus, I look for the boy who'd once been convinced we could communicate from our bedroom windows through a string and two cups.

The memory stows itself away as I slip into my coat. "So, about the hotel's free luxury car drop-offs—what's the sitch?"

"It won't take you far and definitely not all the way to Brooklyn." Parker glances at his phone. "Service also ended three hours ago."

"It was worth a shot." Collecting my laptop, I make a swift exit toward the foyer. Parker is close behind, leaning against the doorframe as I open the double doors to his suite. He's still shirtless, wearing only a pair of black sweatpants. Thanks to him, I've just realized at the age of twenty-eight that I apparently have a thing for guys in sweats.

"You don't have to leave every time," he says as I'm opening the Uber app. "It's late, and I don't mind if you spend the night."

"Um, you know that if you rolled on top of me in your sleep, I could die."

He doesn't laugh. "The actual reason?"

I frown at him. "I feel like the morning after would be too weird."

"And everything else we're doing isn't weird?"

"That's the thing. It's weird enough. And waking up to your face would make it even weirder. I wouldn't know how to act or what to say."

"I'm sorry that you find my face so unsettling," he deadpans. "You can just act normally around me."

Nothing about our arrangement is normal, and for him to suggest that it is makes me wonder if his brain has turned into postcoital goo. "I can't find anything normal about waking up to you spooning me."

"First off, I would never spoon you." Parker grimaces, but with a renounced sigh, he drops it. "Forget it. Have a good night, Dani."

CHAPTER EIGHTEEN

There's something about being at Parker's workplace that fills me with apprehension the second I step into the Venture Sports building in Midtown Manhattan. Maybe it's because, since our arrangement began, I haven't seen him anywhere outside his hotel room. I'm not sure I've fully rewired my brain to be in a professional setting with him where we're both fully clothed.

As soon as I reach his floor, a receptionist lets me know she's been expecting me and guides me to a corner office to wait for Parker, who's still in a meeting. Of course they gave him an office. With a door that closes. I pace around stiffly in the meantime, inspecting what little touches of decor he's added to the space. There's not much, as expected for his three-month stay: an autographed 49ers helmet next to a signed basketball, a carry bag filled with golf clubs, an expensive espresso machine, and surprisingly, philodendrons that look sufficiently watered.

I don't have to wait long until Parker strolls into the room in a gray suit I haven't seen before. Everyone at Venture dresses as if they've got a booking for a Hugo Boss ad after work, and it makes me wish I hadn't worn my old kitten heels today.

Parker's face is a haughty gibe—like a bold-font *I told you so.* "Maybe if you weren't in such a rush to leave my hotel all the time, you wouldn't have switched our laptops."

The bag in my hand does not contain my MacBook, as I'd

come to learn in a panic when I'd arrived at *Adagio* an hour ago. Instead, I'm holding onto Parker's laptop with an outstretched arm. "I'd like to see the goods first, before we make our exchange."

"Movie-villain dialogue. How fitting." His chuckle is humorless as he unlocks the bottom drawer of his desk and reveals my MacBook. "I was planning to review my notes before my meeting. Imagine my surprise when I couldn't get past a lock screen of cats photoshopped as bread loaves."

"They're all *pure bread*," I say around a giggle as I complete our swap. "Get it?"

He blinks at me. "Is that the content *Adagio* pays you to write?"

Parker Tran doesn't appreciate a good pun. I guess there's no accounting for taste.

"You know, you didn't have to come all the way here; I could've gone to your office."

"Your presence would draw too much attention. Charlotte and the others would eat me alive with their questions." I recall my earlier hysteria, when Parker's mug was suddenly smirking at me from my screen. I'd slammed it shut before anyone could notice. "By the way, your lock screen? Shirtless on a yacht? Are you for real?"

"It's actually a sailboat." I don't know the difference, and I don't ask.

The door behind me opens with a click as I'm stuffing my MacBook into its bag. Two more suits stroll in, just as polished as Parker's, and a familiar face greets me with a wide smile.

"Dani Tsai! I was wondering if I'd see you again."

"Hey, Isaac."

Parker looks up from typing on his recovered laptop. "Sorry, man. I'm sending you the Rangers data now. Had a bit of a mix-up this morning." He doesn't spare me the side-eye.

Next to Isaac is an unmissable head of dark, curly hair. I recognize the man as the blue-eyed gent who dragged Parker away from the bar. He takes his turn examining me.

"I remember you. St. Regis, Valentino dress, never spotted without a wine glass."

"This is Dani Tsai, an old friend," Parker inserts. "Dani, this is Reggie Cruz. He's also—"

"Let me guess. On the Rangers deal?"

"Old friend?" Reggie echoes, his interest piqued. "How far back? Did you watch this guy play QB?"

Isaac wags a finger between us. "Right, didn't you say you grew up together?"

"Damn, okay, you're like an OG then." Reggie nods at me. "I'm still catching up on the lore myself. I've heard all about U of O, and the blond era too. Scoured the Internet for that, by the way. Honestly, not your best look. It was giving boy band, but also—"

"Like a lemon made a wish to be human," I say under my breath.

Isaac snorts as Parker cuts me a sharp glare. Reggie clasps his hands together. "Good one. Heather is going to love that."

"Who's Heather?"

"Parker's work wife."

"She's not my work wife," he says flatly.

"That's not what I heard from the boys on your turf."

"We were assigned to the Warriors last year. A deal that big requires a lot of teamwork. At one point, we were practically sharing an office for three months."

That certainly sounds like a work wife. The closest thing I have to a work husband is Tae-woo, and he still tells the cafeteria staff that I'm his assistant.

"I've been trying to get her to fly out, but she said the East Coast air is bad for her skin. Whatever that means." Reggie closes in on Parker and nudges his shoulder. "A work husband would probably have more pull."

"I doubt it." Parker casts him a weary look. "I told her she could take my boat out of the marina sometime, and now she practically lives out on the Central Bay."

I arch a brow. "The boat in that photo belongs to you?"

"Yeah, I got it for day sailing."

"You sail?"

"Just a hobby I picked up."

"I guess there's something about moving to Cali that makes you want to catch some rad waves, right dude?" Reggie emphasizes the end of his sentence with a bad surfer accent.

"Okay, well, to clarify: I'm from *Northern* California, so you can stop with the SoCal stereotypes."

I watch as Parker explains how there are more parks than beaches in the Bay Area, feeling mystified. He's lived a whole life on the other side of the country that I don't know anything about. He's Parker from NorCal now, not Silverpine. He has a boat and does water sports. He doesn't just throw a football all day. He has a work wife—Heather, who's probably a sexy, tanned beach goddess.

I shake off that train of thought just as Reggie gives Parker a pat on his chest. "Before I forget, can you call Kaufman about the soft launch on the ticketing app? He said he'd touch base with you first."

"Yeah, no problem."

"You're a real one." Reggie jabs away at his phone then points two fingers at the room. "While I have you here, can I count you in for my New Year's party? I know it's early, but this thing is a whole production, so I'd like to nail down a head count ASAP."

"I'll let you know if I'm not back in San Francisco by then," Parker says.

"Count me in." Isaac turns to me. "Dani?"

My New Year's tradition involves melting into a couch with a bottle of wine, but rather than admit that to the present company, I say, "Can I get back to you on that?"

"I'll send you an invite later. Be sure to répondez s'il vous plaît."

"Just say RSVP like everyone else," Isaac groans.

"Alright, I'm gonna head out. Gotta make final tweaks on the merch drop before game time." Reggie puts away his phone and makes a quick exit, forging a new path with his bro-nado of cologne and hair gel.

"Actually, I'm glad I ran into you, Dani. That article on ghost ships was a fantastic read," Isaac says. "I was hoping I'd get a chance to pick your brain about it."

"That reminds me, we did a piece on abandoned mining towns that you might like," I tell him. "I can send it to you."

"That'd be awesome. You can keep the articles coming." He smiles down at me, one hand adjusting his tie. "Are you free tonight? We could talk over drinks."

Drinks on a Monday night? Is this spring break in Tijuana?

"I know this great speakeasy in Murray Hill. Kind of an old-timey place—real JFK vibe, if you know what I mean."

To an introvert, making plans without at least twenty-four-hour notice is insanity. But I worry it'll be horrendously awkward for me to turn down the invitation, and then I'll spend the rest of the day cringing and kicking the air at another social blunder. I look over to Parker for help, but he's merely watching the interaction with pointed interest. Silent and useless.

With excellent timing, Isaac's phone vibrates in his pocket. He steps one foot out of the office, device in hand. "I have to take this, but definitely let me know about tonight, okay?"

Once the door closes, Parker gives me a loaded glance. "He's into you."

"He is not." I try to hold back a laugh, but it escapes as a snort through my nose. "He's just being friendly. And I know you're a boat guy—weird, by the way—but don't tell me you're in the boat that believes men and women can't be friends."

"No, they can, but are you sure *that's* the argument you want to go with?" Parker closes his laptop. "We've been friends again for two weeks, and look how that's going for us."

I'm tempted to say that he and I aren't the best example of friendship. "Asking someone out for drinks doesn't mean there are . . . intentions."

"Okay then, you can show up to what is very clearly a date and prove me wrong."

I lean against a cabinet opposite where Parker sits. "Are you really giving me the go-ahead to date one of your Venture bros?"

"I don't exactly have any right to say who you can or can't see."

I know that. That's the whole point of being casual. But it takes me by surprise, nonetheless.

"Unless you want me to give you a reason to back out? Because you know I'm right?"

"That's not—no." I swat a hand at the air. "He just wants to geek out on nerdy ghost stuff. You heard him, he even asked for more articles."

"Are you going to let him read your features?" Parker asks, reclining in his seat. "I liked the one where you used sci-fi classics to project the future of AI. It's just like you to turn *The Jetsons* into a much darker show than I remember."

I stare at him for a beat too long. "When did you read my articles?"

"Remember when I said I Googled you? Well, it brought me to the *Adagio* website. Wasn't hard to find your work from there."

I stop to consider what he's said. Some of those articles belong to sections of our site that are locked behind a paywall. "You paid for a subscription?"

He lifts a shoulder like it's nothing to get worked up about. I watch him rise from his seat and circle around his desk until we're facing each other. Crossing his arms, he looks at me meaningfully. "Look, Isaac is a good guy, but you should know that, like me, he isn't really the committed type."

"You think that's what he's after? A good ol' smash and dash?"

"Well—"

"Like, hit it and quit it? Just another pump and dump?"

"Dani—"

"Wham, bam, thank you, ma'am?"

Parker draws a deep breath. "Are you done? Did you get it out of your system?"

"Sorry."

"If you admit I'm right, I can help you get out of your little date." His voice grows increasingly smug, like sandpaper to my patience.

"I don't need your help," I say. "Who knows, I might even have a good time. And it's *not* a date."

It's not meeting Isaac for drinks that bothers me. It's that Parker isn't making an actual attempt to stop me. He even pointed out that he wouldn't intervene if I started seeing other people. Should I take that to mean he's seeing other people too? I know—that's the point of an arrangement without commitment. But until now, the thought of being with other men hadn't even crossed my mind. Parker's done all this before. He said so himself.

Is this what Isaac meant when he asked me if I was another fan? It shouldn't surprise me that women line up wherever Parker goes. It was like that even when we were kids—all those nights at the local roller rink, girls giggling and trailing behind him on the floor, angling for a perfectly timed run-in. Back then, I thought of myself as just an unfortunate bystander. Now, I'm just another girl catching crumbs of Parker's attention in the proverbial roller rink, and I'm up against models like Min and California babes like Heather. I mean, is a work wife ever really *just* a work wife?

"So, if I were seeing other people," I hedge, "you'd really be okay with that?"

Parker takes his time as he studies my face. "Like I said, it's not up to me."

The truth is, I have no plans to see other people. But I'm trying to prove that I can do casual—even if there's no part of me that desires multiple sexual companions. I don't know if Parker feels the same. I consider asking if he's been seeing other people, but immediately shut that idea down. I don't think I want to know the answer, and it might even weird him out if I ask. Maybe being kept in the dark is its own blessing. Ignorance is bliss, as they say.

"Got it. I just wanted to be clear on the ground rules."

"I wasn't aware we had rules."

"Every arrangement needs some kind of guideline, or we'd just be running amok," I insist. "I don't show up during football games expecting you to drop everything. That'd be like trying to booty call me when I'm watching *House of the Dragon*—and you wouldn't dare. Without some kind of code, it'd be madness. Chaos, even."

"Wow, I had no idea the stakes were so high." Parker whistles. "Let me guess—these rules also say you're not allowed to spend the night at my hotel?"

"In a way, yes." I do my best to sound aloof. "You're free to add your own rules too." I brace myself for a witty remark meant to make me feel ridiculous, but Parker only unfolds his arms. "I just want you to do what makes you comfortable, Dani."

The hint of authenticity throws me off, but I'm still trying to play it cool. "Should we shake on it?"

"I don't think that's necessary."

"Okay, then. Good talk," I say, peeking over at the clock above his desk. "I should give Isaac an answer before I head back to work."

Parker leads the way to the door, but just as he turns the handle, he stops short and lets go. I stare at the view of his broad shoulders until he turns back around, eyes dropping to me. "One more thing."

Then he presses his lips to mine, and I don't have time to react before I'm swept up in the momentum of the kiss. He surges forward, and I take clumsy steps backward until I'm pinned between him and the desk. Parker's tongue pushes into my mouth, deep and hungry as it rolls over mine. His large hands grip my thighs, sliding up to hike my skirt as far as it'll go. His palms are warm, heat oozing across my bare skin. He moves with such authority that every muscle of my body yields, giving him whatever he wants. The laptop bag slips from my grasp, and my arms fly around his neck as Parker kisses me more intensely, more aggressively than he ever has before.

Even without the theatrics of words, I know this kiss is meant to be possessive. It's meant to ensure that even if I spent the evening with another man, I'd be thinking of Parker the entire time.

And it's the best kiss I've ever had.

I've just about come undone when we break apart. All I can

do is hold onto him, listening to his breath falling into rapid rhythm with mine. I have half a mind to tell him to bend me over the desk and have his way with me, but that would place me right in the palm of his hand.

"If I'm being honest—" Parker's low voice carries into the lull. "I don't love the thought of sharing you with someone else in this office."

I don't have the chance to respond before he lets go of me, stepping away to smooth out his collar. I pull my skirt back down and stutter breathlessly, "I—I have to go."

When he opens the door for me, his tone is back to blithesome and light. "See you tonight, Dani."

I pause, confusion settling in as I watch him retreat to his desk. We didn't make plans to meet tonight.

"Dani, you've got my number, right?" Isaac's voice is a distant murmur as I take a stilted walk back to the elevators.

"Uh-huh," I mumble absently, touching a finger to my puffy lips.

That night, I text Isaac and lie that I've caught a stomach bug and won't be able to meet him. Instead, I go to the St. Regis, just as Parker anticipated. When I enter the suite, he's already grinning up at me from his bed.

It's enough to make me curse. But still, I climb right in with him.

CHAPTER NINETEEN

Sexual chemistry between two people is a powerful thing. It's that all-consuming feeling of attraction that seeps into every exchange, every look. The desire is unshakable, as if forces beyond your control are drawing you together. When you feel it, it's electric, almost palpable, and all you can think about is their body against yours.

I sit cross-legged on my couch, gritting my teeth and staring at the text on my laptop. Of all the articles to be assigned this week, I have the ill fortune of editing Charlotte's piece on sexual chemistry. As soon as the document popped up in my inbox, I begged Tae-woo to take it off my hands.

"A sex column by Charlotte? I'd rather rewrite an illustrated manual for a catheter," was his gracious way of shooting me down.

The article hangs over me like a gloomy rain cloud, soaking me in dread. It's taken me longer than usual to get through the assignment, which is why I'm spending a Saturday afternoon trying desperately to finish it. It's not because of Charlotte, and I'm not such a prude that the subject matter would have me clutching my metaphorical pearls. It's because every line about physical attraction or sexual gratification activates some memory of me and Parker in his St. Regis suite. I hate to admit it, but this is hitting a little too close to home.

But sexual chemistry isn't simply "just a feeling." There's a science to it, as well, and as the term itself implies, it has to do with the chemistry of our brains. When you're attracted to someone, the brain releases high levels of dopamine and norepinephrine . . .

I groan with my entire body. How dare you bring science into this, Charlotte? Now she's got me staring down the barrel of the cold, hard facts. I don't need a reminder of how my brain's hypothalamus sends my sex drive into pandemonium whenever Parker is around.

Does having sexual chemistry with someone also mean you'll hit it off outside the bedroom? Not always. Have you ever found yourself attracted to that one Wall Street guy, that bad boy who stands for everything you're against? We're all familiar with the idea of wanting something you can't—or shouldn't—have. Attraction happens subconsciously, and sometimes telling yourself that it'll never happen is what makes it all the more enticing. And if the attraction is mutual, it can lead to explosive, mind-numbingly great sex.

I shut my laptop. That's enough for today.

Flopping onto my back, I make an effort to think of anything unsexy: soup splatter on the ceiling of the microwave, energy prices and crippling inflation, a podcast on alpha male energy. It's no use, so I snatch my phone from the coffee table and bring up my chat with Parker. Maybe I'd been reluctant to give a name to it, but it's evident that what we have is sexual chemistry. I know that I'm attracted to him. And I assume the feeling is mutual. But attraction is just the surface of it. It doesn't explain why hooking up with him is so different from anything I've experienced before.

The last time I saw Parker was three nights ago. As I start typing, my gut twists just like it does in the elevator ride up to his suite.

Me: What are you doing today?

Parker: Miss me already?

Me: Never mind. Have a nice day.

Parker: I'm with a client at Barclays Center. Can I text you when I get back to the hotel?

Me: You're in Brooklyn?

I pause, lifting my head to glance around my apartment. I could probably do a quick lap with the vacuum, but otherwise, it's in an orderly state. Once I was old enough, Dad assigned cleaning duties to me, while he took care of the cooking. I was consistent with the habit even after moving out, right down to following Marisa around with a coaster.

Me: Do you want to come over?

❧

As I wait for Parker to arrive, I suddenly become aware that, after spending the whole Saturday sprawled on the couch getting nothing done, I now *look* like someone who did just that. I pace around nervously, debating whether I should change. Would that seem like I'm trying too hard? I mean, who actually wears jeans at home, anyway?

By the time Parker texts that he's arrived, I only have time to throw my tangled hair into a ponytail.

"I didn't know you work weekends too," I say when he reaches my door.

"I don't, but sometimes you have to work around the client's schedule." He blinks the fatigue from his eyes. "The building's nice. You have an elevator."

"Have you ever seen a New York apartment that wasn't in a TV show?"

"It's just that I always pictured you in one of those classic New York setups. Someplace with too much exposed brick. Lugging your laundry up an unreasonable number of stairs."

"I'm a survivor of a fifth-floor walk-up," I say. "Would not recommend. I was always afraid they'd find me passed out with a pizza box before I made it to my door."

"Oh, you've got stamina. I would know."

Parker is too preoccupied with taking off his sneakers to see my cheeks go red. I stand by gawkishly, debating whether I should offer to take his jacket. This is all new to me. I've never invited a man over solely to climb him like a tree. Is there a protocol for this? Do I bother to give him a tour of the place, or do we make a beeline for the bed?

But he seems to know exactly what he's doing as he steps past me, absorbing his surroundings. It shouldn't take more than a glance or two to scan the studio, but he moves slowly, careful not to miss a detail.

My bed sits on the other side of a rustic bookshelf that doubles as a divider, but he doesn't head straight for it. Instead, I follow his gaze from the weathered spines of old books and the Marble Queen pothos on top to the boho geometric rug anchoring the center of the room. I'm suddenly seeing my apartment as if for the first time too.

Then he peeks over to the windows, and I see him recoil.

"What in the R2-D2 is *that*?"

"It's an air purifier." I walk over so that I'm next to the device in question. It's big and boxy, and probably overkill, but after reading an article on volatile organic compounds in the household, I was all too eager to splurge.

Parker looks around at my compact apartment. "For you and a small town? It looks like the Millennium Falcon's trash compactor."

"You show some respect to Gilbert."

"It has a name." He rubs his forehead, a barb of disbelief in his tone. "Do I want to know how much that thing cost?"

"You can't put a price on air quality. This thing is as silent as a stone. It uses a high-end filtration system that captures 99.99 percent of particles and contaminants as small as 0.1 microns. And with fifteen pounds of activated carbon with potassium permanganate, any trace of odor is virtually nonexistent. You smell that?" I lift a finger and sniff.

"I don't smell anything."

"Exactly."

Parker is speechless. If we were in a cartoon, a singular question mark would be emerging from his head right now.

"I didn't know you had such an aversion to . . . smelling things." He lifts the collar of his jacket to his face. "I picked this up from dry cleaning today, but now you've made me self-conscious."

I know Parker's scent by now—it's practically ingrained in my cerebrum. His cologne is Creed Aventus, and his natural smell reminds me of fresh laundry and driving by the coast at daybreak.

"You smell better than you did in high school."

"Um, what?"

"The AXE body spray was a bit . . ." I crinkle my nose.

He rubs the back of his neck. "Wow, now I'm definitely self-conscious."

"You're fine. I like how you smell," I say mercifully. I can't help but notice that he always manages to shower before we meet—and what that does to my libido.

"Thanks, I think." His ears are curiously red as he moves on to his next point of interest: a framed poster of the film *Chungking*

Express hanging by the TV. "Hey, I remember this. You were obsessed with this movie."

I was ten the first time I watched *Chungking Express*, and to be honest, I didn't understand most of it. But that didn't stop me from falling in love with the aesthetics of 1990s Hong Kong. Now that I'm older, it's still my favorite movie but for different reasons. There's something about the characters being so unapologetically lovestruck that resonates with me. Also worth noting: the dreamy twosome of Tony Leung and Takeshi Kaneshiro, responsible for stirring an entirely different kind of awakening.

Parker's lips form a tight line. "I don't know how I'd feel about a girl breaking into my place to clean. Even if she was as cute as Faye Wong."

My socks stop short of being blown off. "You've watched *Chungking Express*?"

"Yeah."

I wait for the punchline. "Because you lost a bet?"

"What? No. Because it's on HBO Max, and I was looking for something to watch." The expression he makes is contemplative, and I pay close attention to his next words, knowing very well the power they'll have over me. "I think I get it now. Hong Kong in the nineties was a vibe."

I can't hold myself back. I grab Parker by his collar and pull him to my height, kissing him with a force I didn't know I was capable of. I've never been more attracted to him.

"Whoa," he breathes, eyes lighting up with surprise. "I'm not done looking around!"

"Seriously? That can wait. Get undressed, Parker."

"Hold on, you have a Switch?" To my dismay, he frees himself from my grip and drops to the couch, picking up a controller I'd left on the coffee table. "What other consoles do you have?"

I'm equal parts mortified and humbled to have my advances turned down for a *game console*. I stagger into the seat next to Parker, a little dazed. "Um, I have a PS5."

He takes his jacket off and throws it over the arm of the couch. "Let's play something. For old times' sake."

"Not what I meant when I said get undressed," I mumble under my breath. Parker looks at me with muted excitement, and it reminds me of the fifth-grade boy who'd come over just to play *Tekken*. Or the time Dad bought *Madden NFL* for him, and he spent every day at our place for a week.

"You're serious right now?"

"What? Afraid I'm going to school you?"

I level a glare at him and go over my options. I didn't bring any of those relics from our childhood with me to New York. First-person shooter games are probably not a wise choice or anything that involves a fourteen-year-old calling us names over voice chat.

I pass him a Pro Controller for the Switch. "*Mario Kart*?"

❧

I remember now: Parker sucks at games. I started with the intention of wiping the floor with him, but after he finishes dead last in three straight races, I begin to take pity. I intentionally miss the boost at the start and abandon my drifting skills, but Parker is so inept, it doesn't make a difference. He can't dodge a banana peel to save his life, and he drives off the course at every sharp turn. All the NPCs lap him, and with minimal effort, I still manage to edge him out too.

"I thought athletes are supposed to have amazing hand-eye coordination." I drop my controller to my lap. "How are you still this terrible at gaming?"

He ignores me and rolls each wrist, one at a time. "One more race."

"Parker, this is getting embarrassing," I say with pained patience. "And that was the last one of the Grand Prix."

"Let's start another one," he presses, undeterred. Outside of sex and playing football, I've never seen him this focused. His determination is commendable, if anything, so with a sigh I pull up the main menu and set up another tournament.

Parker takes his time picking a character—not that it'll matter, but I indulge him anyway. As I watch him toggle between Luigi and *Baby* Luigi, my frustration starts to give way to the tiniest sprout of enjoyment. It's refreshing to see the perfect Parker Tran be the amateur for once. And despite the absolute disgrace of his racing skills, he's not being a sore loser. I think he's actually having fun.

Somewhere between the old knowledge that Parker is still adorably terrible at video games and the new knowledge that he's watched my favorite movie and didn't hate it, comes the startling realization that spending time with him in a nonsexual capacity is . . . not that weird. I wonder, though, if this is breaking some unspoken ground rule. It's been three weeks since our casual relationship began, and at present, our only mutual interest is sex. As long as we both understand that, it should be fine for us to have a little fun with clothes on, too, right?

After he returns to San Francisco, we'll be able to go back to our original timelines. I can't imagine us keeping in contact once this is over; friends or not, how are we supposed to carry on as normal after a three-month sex arrangement? What would we even talk about? A year from now, this moment probably won't even cross my mind.

It'll be like none of this ever happened.

I lean over and take the controller from Parker's hand, setting it on the coffee table. I kiss his soft, parted lips before he can react. The tension leaves his body almost instantly. Inching closer, I trail a hand under his shirt and over his taut stomach before moving beneath the waistband of his boxers. A sound slips past his lips, and a part of me wishes I could eat each and every one of his delicious moans.

Mario Kart is long forgotten when I climb off the couch and lower myself between his legs. I pull him free from his pants and wet my lips, thanking my earlier self for the ponytail. When I take him into my mouth, Parker sinks against the couch cushions. His head falls back, his heavy breaths filling the air. I have some confidence that I know by now how he likes to be touched and exactly what to do with my tongue to set him off like a live wire.

He grabs me by the back of my head, blunt nails applying pressure. With a muffled groan, Parker bucks his hips, and I meet him with the same fervor.

"Fuck, *Dani*. Fuck, you're so good."

I wonder if he noticed it too—how his breath hitched around my name, like he'd been holding it in, until it finally broke. It stirs the desire in me to unravel the layers of composure that guard him, to remove his mask of perfection. I want to chip away at his cool exterior until the playing field is level. To see Parker Tran at the mercy of his instincts, no better than any ordinary man.

My lips drag over him greedily, moving in tandem with my hands. When he's close, his grip tightens in my hair. "I'm going to come."

Hot spurts hit the back of my throat. He twitches in my mouth, and I meet his gaze when I swallow thickly. I notice the way it makes his eyes cloud over.

It tells me that I have him right where I want him.

CHAPTER TWENTY

Marisa sits up straight in our booth like she's had a big lightbulb moment. "What about Silverpine?"

I lift a mango habanero wing to my mouth. "What about it?"

"For me and Shay," she says. "Small-town life could be kind of cute. Shay loves community projects, so I'm sure she'd find some local initiative to hyperfixate on. We'd have farmers' market days and drive-in movie nights."

"Okay, slow down, Hallmark. We didn't have any of that stuff in Silverpine. The closest thing to a local initiative was the grumpy old lady in the park who yelled at you to recycle." I take a hefty bite of the wing and say, "You wouldn't last a month. You know we don't have a Trader Joe's, right?"

Marisa slumps back against the booth and sighs into her cocktail glass, a fog appearing around the rim. I'm getting a little buzzed, and I can tell she's starting to feel it too. How did the night get away from us? She had come to Bed-Stuy with the intention of grabbing a couple drinks, but now I'm three beers in, and she has that glossy, five-margarita look in her eyes that takes me back to our college days.

I point the lip of my beer bottle at her. "How about Portland?"

"Oh, I can see it. Just a couple of coffee snobs with our matching umbrellas."

I balk at her and throw a cautionary glance over my shoulder as if the entire Pacific Northwest is listening. "No one uses umbrellas there. You'll look silly to the locals."

"Then how are we supposed to keep our matching flannel dry?"

I giggle at her. "Umbrellas in Portland. That's a good one. Next thing you know, we'll be using them in the grocery store when they mist the produce."

Marisa is laughing, too, but I can see her crossing off another item in her mental list. The first time she mentioned the idea of moving was six months ago, in the very same sentence where she revealed that she and Shay were thinking about having kids. Both had been bombshells to me because neither children nor white picket fences had ever been on her radar. But I knew that if there's one person she'd imagine that life with, it's Shay. From the day she answered a "Roommate Wanted" ad and met her future wife on the stoop of their Greenpoint brownstone, she's been madly in love.

"I still think you should stick to Upstate." I say, picking at the label of the bottle.

"Aww, you don't want me going too far," she coos. "Trust me, if I could pack you up and have you live in the room under my stairs, I would."

I crinkle my nose. "I'm good."

"Seriously, I don't want you to be lonely without me. Did you really give up on the apps? You know you don't have to find something long-term."

Here we go. She's still disappointed that my trial run at online dating didn't inspire a Samantha Jones-style era of sexual liberation. I've reminded her that even if my only goal had been to get laid, there was still no way I could sit through a first date with a man whose opening line was, "Are you a domme or a sub?"

I make an X with my arms, signaling a firm no, and she

makes her disappointment known. "Your vibrator is probably working overtime these days."

More like collecting dust, now that I have an absolute stallion to take care of my needs. The quip is on the edge of my tongue, but I hold back. I haven't told Marisa about my casual relationship with Parker, even if this is the closest I'll get to Carrie Bradshaw writing a column about me. One of the reasons why hooking up with Parker is so much fun is because we're the only ones in on the secret. It's the first time in my life that I'm doing the opposite of what everyone expects, and there's a thrilling freedom that comes with that.

I make a silent promise to tell her everything once it's all over, and Parker is on the other side of the country. "I don't really have time to think about dating right now."

"Sure, because you're *so* busy." The way her lip stiffens tells me she doesn't believe me for a second. But she polishes off the last of her cocktail and changes course. "You never told me what happened between you and Parker."

I nearly drop my beer. "Did something happen between us?"

"The event he invited you to?"

My panic subsides, and I say, "Nothing really. We talked. We were civil."

Marisa reaches for a wing. "What does he look like now? Is he still blond?"

Reluctantly, I pull up Parker's Instagram on my phone. I still haven't followed him, and since the last time I stalked his profile, he's added three new posts. In one of the photos, I recognize his outfit from the first time he visited my apartment. He's standing next to a basketball player whom I've seen on the news, throwing up peace signs. So, when he said he was meeting a client, what he actually meant was that he was kicking it with one of the Brooklyn Nets.

"Holy shit." Marisa snatches my phone from me. "If women went to war over men, *that's* what they'd be fighting over."

"Right?" I wish I didn't readily agree with the idea of Parker as a modern-day Helen of Troy, but alas. "Doesn't it make you want to smash your head in?"

"Is he single?"

"Yeah."

"Hm, hard to believe someone wouldn't try to lock that down. I wonder what his deal is." She hands my phone back to me. "What if he's terrible in bed? You said he drove a big Jeep right? Smells like overcompensating to me."

I laugh without humor.

❧

I'd forgotten that drunk Marisa has a tell: calling up her wife with cloyingly sweet declarations of love. Not long after, Shay comes to pick her up. I don't ask about the house search, because I still can't visualize Marisa holding a baby instead of two pints of Guinness.

As soon as I reach my apartment, I wash my face and put on a sheet mask, relaxing on the couch with a lazy leg over the backrest. When I unlock my phone, the screen is still on Parker's Instagram page. I lift my thumb to exit, but the slick from the sheet mask causes the phone to slip in my hand, and I hit the big, blue Follow button instead.

Color drains from my face, and I scream, launching my phone into the air. It collides with the kitchen counter and plummets to the floor.

What have I done what have I done what have I done. I'll have to go off the grid now. Move to a cabin in the middle of the woods and train a courier pigeon to bring me news of the outside world now that I've decided I'll never own a phone again.

My heart rate is turbulence under my ribcage as I slide off the couch, staring at the device. One, two, three minutes pass. I crawl my way over and pick it up.

parker11tran wants to follow you.

The screen changes in a flash, just as I read the notification. Parker is calling me. I answer just as a hiccup rises in my throat.

"Are you stalking my Instagram?"

"I . . . *hic*—" Fuck it, there's no saving me now. "Yes."

I can hear him stifling a laugh. "What's going on with your voice?"

"I—*hic*—have the hiccups. *Hic*—hold on." I peel the mask off my face and myself off the floor, gulping down a glass of water until my diaphragm calms.

"You could've used a finsta if you were going to stalk me."

"What's a finsta?"

"Uh . . . never mind. Explaining that to you will make us both feel old." From his end of the line, I can pick up faint chatter and the muffled sound of a Top 40 song. A familiar voice shouts for Parker to take a shot amid the commotion.

"Is that Reggie?"

"Yeah, we came out for drinks after work."

Sounds like a typical Friday night for the folks at Venture. "You're probably busy. We can just table this discussion—"

"It's fine. Hold on, let me step outside." It's a few seconds before a door shuts, and the noise dispels into the distant sounds of New York traffic.

"Just so you know, I was only on your Instagram because Marisa—my roommate from Columbia—was curious."

"Mm-hmm, and did you mean to follow me too?"

"See, that's where I fucked up."

"I knew it." I can almost hear him grinning. I understand now why he's called me: Not one to ease my suffering, he's trying to catch me in the act. "Accept my follow request already. It's a little unnerving that you get to stalk my page when I can't even see yours."

I tap at the notification. Though reluctance brews, I accept his request. Parker is quiet, and I know he's going through my feed in the silence. My tiny online existence has just gained a new audience member, and I don't anticipate rave reviews. I wait for him to speak, drumming nervous fingers against the cool granite of my kitchen counter.

"Dani, you have, like, twenty posts. How am I supposed to tease you when you're giving me nothing to work with?"

"Not all of us get to post our sexy sailing sessions."

"Did you intentionally find all the photos where I don't have a shirt on?"

"Ha! Pfft," is the sound I choose to make.

"I'm gonna be real: This suspiciously unused account isn't helping to fight the stalker allegations."

I groan miserably. "This is why I hate social media. Everyone thinks they can deduce a personality based on a collection of heavily curated photos. What people conveniently forget is that no one in their right mind is going to propagate a version of themselves they don't want the Internet to see. Frank from Wall Street isn't going to post about his foot fetish or that he steals his neighbor's Postmates. He's got dope pictures of himself in the Hamptons and at Coachella, so he has to be a stand-up guy. But Dani? Dani's a stalker because she only has three selfies!"

"Who's Frank?"

I throw a hand up in the air. "Frank is hypothetical. But that's not the point. The point is that most of it is false advertising. You should know this—you're the one with a marketing degree."

"I specialize in sports, not foot fetishes. That's a whole other market," says Parker. "I'm kidding, Dani. I don't think you're a stalker. Keeping a low profile can be a good thing. I deleted a bunch of my older posts too."

I hadn't noticed. Though I've been lurking, I also made a conscious effort not to scroll too far, afraid of what I might find. "Bad breakup?"

"Just some things I don't care to remember."

I catch the soft bell of a door opening and closing, the hum of lively chatter, but Parker remains outside. "I remember you being chronically offline back then too," he adds. "I was surprised when I looked you up one day and found your account. To be honest, I thought of sending a friend request, but I figured you'd ignore it."

"You looked me up?"

"I was curious. Doesn't everyone look up their old high school classmates now and then?"

"Is that what we are? Old high school classmates?" My voice betrays me, and I hope the disappointment isn't obvious to him. "I've been trying to figure out what to say when people ask how we know each other."

"That was me being sarcastic. I don't really know if there's a label for what you and I are to each other."

I wonder how many drinks he's had tonight. I almost wish he was drunk, because this level of transparency is still foreign to me, and I don't want to assign greater meaning to it.

"Would it be too late to ask you to come to my hotel?" he asks suddenly. I think I hear him swallow. Now I'm sure he's at least tipsy.

It's nearly midnight. Nine times out of ten, if I were asked to leave my place at this hour, the answer would be a hard no. But my body is already responding favorably, so I guess that puts us in the ten percent margin for an exception.

"Wait, fuck. Don't answer that." He takes a controlled breath, and the frenzy in my chest—and loins—is immediately smothered. "I told Reggie I'd hang around to meet his contact from the Nets. If I think about you waiting for me at the hotel, I'll never make it through the night."

A giggle slips out of me. Parker getting turned on over this phone call is not what I'd expected, but it is an interesting development. "What's your schedule like?"

"I have some time off for Thanksgiving, so I'm going back to San Francisco next week," he replies. "What are your plans?"

"My dad is visiting, so I'll be here." This means that by next week, we'll be in different states, and our arrangement will have to take a hiatus for the holidays. I'm suddenly aware of how quickly the last month has gone by. It won't be long before I return to the humdrum life of my original timeline.

As though he's read my mind, Parker says, "If I don't see you before I leave, then we'll have to wait until I get back. Think you can last that long without me?"

"You're the one picturing me naked in your suite right now," I counter, and it makes him groan out of frustration. Amusement bubbles up from inside me, and I'm laughing again before I know it. But the ruckus from the bar cuts me off, trickling in like a sudden stream. Reggie must've stepped outside, because when he calls for Parker, it's a lot clearer this time.

"By the way," he says into the phone. "If you really need a label, you can just tell people we're friends."

A smile spreads across my face. "The unconventional kind of friends."

"Friends who have *really* good sex," he amends, "but they don't need to know that."

He says it like an offhand comment, like it wasn't meant to launch my heart from a cannon into the stratosphere. I know what we have is electric and that it consumes us so completely that we spend hours tangled up in each other. But hearing him say it is another thing entirely.

I wonder if Parker has this with anyone else. He might have a casual relationship in San Francisco, too—someone he feels that same soul-evacuating passion with. It could be Heather, or it could be some other woman. It could even be better than what we have.

"I should go to bed." I decide now is a good time to end the call, before he says anything else that'll keep me from sleeping tonight. "Enjoy your night, Parker."

When I'm half-asleep and bundled under covers pulled up to my neck, my phone buzzes next to my pillow.

parker11tran commented on your post.

With tired eyes, I type in my passcode, and the notification brings me to a photo on my page. I don't remember who took it—Dad, a cousin, or maybe the ex, Graham—but it was posted six years ago, after a visit to Apizza Scholls in Portland. In the shot I'm holding a pizza box with both arms, turning to the camera in a candid moment, a laid-back smile on my face. I try not to post too many photos of myself, but I always liked this one for how natural the moment was. The caption is simply a pizza emoji.

I scroll down to Parker's comment.

Ken's is still better.

CHAPTER TWENTY-ONE

Fourteen years ago

My fingertips graze over smooth leather, the football feeling clumsy in my grip. I can't comprehend how a fourteen-year-old is supposed to have hands big enough to do anything skillful with this, but Parker makes it look effortless.

"You don't need to be rough with it. Pretend it's an egg: Be firm, but careful not to crush it." Parker looks up from his spot on the carpet over to where I'm seated at the foot of my bed. "Okay, for starters, you're holding it all wrong."

I slide off the bed and sit cross-legged next to him. With patient focus, he places my hand over the ball so that my fingers rest across the laces and my thumb anchors underneath in an L shape. "Here you go. Don't squeeze it flat against your hand either, leave some space."

I can only hold on a few seconds before I feel my hand cramping. Letting the ball fall into my lap, I sigh, "I'll never throw a spiral."

"Not here, you won't." His eyes sweep over the academic awards on the dresser to the desk cluttered with schoolwork. "Let's try in the backyard after."

Returning to the pile of VHS tapes by his side, Parker lifts each one to inspect the faded covers. The bottom drawer of my dresser has been pulled open to its full length, with half its contents displaced onto the carpet.

"We have DVDs downstairs," I remind him. "We don't have to watch something from my mom's collection."

"Why not? This is cool. My house doesn't even have a working VHS player anymore." He picks up a battered copy of *Moonstruck* and shows it to me. "What's this about?"

"It's an old rom-com. A woman from Brooklyn falls in love with her fiancé's brother, and he's this super intense guy with a wooden hand. Chaos ensues, there's lots of yelling. Cher is amazing."

"Want to watch it?"

"I save it for Christmas. One of my last memories with my mom before she went back to Taiwan is the two of us watching *Moonstruck* on Christmas Eve. It's her favorite movie," I tell him. Whenever the holidays came around and I knew Mom wouldn't be coming to celebrate, I'd put on *Moonstruck* in lieu of her company. Over the years, it's become something of a tradition.

Parker sets the tape aside for another one. He grins. "*Remember the Titans*. Your mom has good taste."

"That one might actually be my dad's." I reach over him to grab *West Side Story* and the copy of *Breakfast at Tiffany's* underneath. "These are more my mom's tempo. I remember her watching them religiously."

"Everything she likes is set in New York." He reads the covers over my shoulder. "Is that why you want to go to school there?"

"Two of the best English programs are at Columbia and NYU," I say pointedly. "It's just a coincidence."

His brow lifts in that familiar way that I've come to recognize as skepticism. Before he can dig any deeper, I catch the sound of tires against pavement and rush to the window. From my view of the driveway, I see Dad's Honda Civic rolling up to the house.

"My dad is home early," I mutter, kneeling by the dresser so I can load everything back in. "Let's put these away before he sees them."

"I don't get why you have to hide her stuff," Parker says as he hands me a stack of tapes. "He knows you kept these."

"Yeah, but I'd rather avoid the awkwardness. He doesn't like to be reminded of my mom."

"How do you know that?"

"Because we never talk about her," I reply.

"Ever? That can't be healthy."

"It's just the way things have always been." When I hear the front door open downstairs, I jump to my feet and crack my door an inch, rolling my eyes as Parker looks at me curiously. "'Doors open' rule."

He frowns at me as he shuts the drawer. "So, they still haven't told you why they split?"

Leaning against the bed, I pull my legs close to my chest. "I remember them fighting a lot. Dad would skip meals and hole up in his office. I didn't understand what was happening. When I was older, I overheard him talking to my aunt about it. Apparently, Mom's art wasn't selling, and it made things really tense when Dad tried to push her into finding other work."

Parker's sweater brushes against my arm as he shifts to get a little closer to me. "Have you ever tried to ask your mom about it?"

"I wouldn't know how. Our Skype calls are really just small talk now. Mom's forgotten a lot of her English, and my Mandarin isn't fluent. We always reach this awkward point where there's nothing left to say."

He nods thoughtfully. "Can I ask you something? Why do you still hold onto her stuff?"

I stare at the closed drawer for a long moment before saying, "I guess I don't want to forget that there was a time when it was the three of us and we were happy. As long as I have those tapes, they're like a record of my life before the divorce."

My hand is suddenly wrapped in warmth, and it takes me by surprise when I see Parker's long fingers over it.

"You're allowed to talk about her," he says. "You don't have to keep it all to yourself."

"My dad doesn't want to hear it."

"Then talk to me." He gives my hand a gentle squeeze. "Whenever you're upset, or if you just want to vent about your parents, come and find me. Or you can just say, 'Parker, get your ass over here,' and I'll come running."

I laugh, but at the same time, pressure builds behind my eyes. When I glance over at him, there's an ache in my ribs, as if they can't contain the emotion within. Like I'm filled with something that has nowhere to go.

If I were to mark my life as before and after Mom left, I could also see it as before and after I met Parker. I can't say this to him, but that record is just as important to me. In my mind, they are both solid, for me to hold in my hands forever. I collect every football game, sleepover, and inside joke like sacred mementos. Before him, I didn't know I could carve a conversation into my memory, or that all the little things I learned about him would stay with me like engravings: He doesn't like green bell peppers, but red and yellow are fine. His ears turn red when he's embarrassed. Don't bring up the time Nathan beat him in *Mario Party*; he can be a sore loser sometimes.

He turns my palm over and folds his fingers into mine. We

used to do this when we were kids. It's different now, but it also feels like the most natural thing, holding Parker's hand.

He told me once that I was his favorite person. He's mine too.

CHAPTER TWENTY-TWO

I didn't have a chance to see Parker before he left for San Francisco. Between my deadline for *Adagio* and his launch parties for the Rangers campaign, neither of us could find the time to meet. According to his Instagram, he seems to be having a blast in California—even stopping to show his boat some love. I didn't think that November on San Francisco Bay would be prime time for sailing, but with sheer will and weather-proof gear, apparently there's nothing Parker Tran can't do.

I, on the other hand, am not on glistening water, but I am on the West Coast. After a last-minute change of plans, I've ended up in Silverpine on Thanksgiving morning. Dad strained his back while moving a new couch, and since he couldn't make the trip to New York anymore, I hopped on the first flight out. Now, normally, I'd never risk being in my hometown for a major holiday, but since I don't have to avoid Parker, I can breathe easy. Besides, he isn't here. He's probably hitting the golf course with some pro athlete again. Or on another bike trail along the Golden Gate with the NorCal friends he's always posting to his stories, all of whom look like they take wheatgrass shots without gagging and wake up smiling at five a.m. for sunrise yoga.

The Uber I'd taken from the Portland International Airport rolls up to my house a little past ten a.m. Still groggy from the unplanned flight, I haul my luggage out of the trunk and slam it shut. As the Uber drives off, I yelp at the face that suddenly appears before me.

"Welcome home, Dani!" Cô flings her arms wide, her fresh perm catching the wind. I hadn't heard her approach, thanks to the spongy hot pink Crocs on her feet. I let her pull me in for a long hug. It's been over two years since I was last home, and I hadn't exactly gone out of my way to see her then. A pang of remorse hits me in the gut.

"Good to see you, Cô!"

She squeezes my arms. "Trời ơi, you're so skinny now! Do you eat enough in New York?"

"All three meals. Sometimes four." I wipe the sleep from my eyes and try to muster a smile. "How have you been?"

"Oh, you know, same old! Open the store, close the store. I come home and watch K-dramas. Sometimes I even watch at the pharmacy too." She places a finger to her lips as she lets me in on her little secret. "Chú says I'm getting lazy, so I signed up for Jumba class. I go every Friday!"

I think she means Zumba.

"I can tell. You look great," I say, and she brightens with a modest giggle.

Parker looks like both of his parents—he definitely got his height from his dad, but he has his mother's smile.

Cô holds my face with both hands. Her rings are ice cold, zapping the sleep out of my system. "I can't believe it! All the kids are home for Thanksgiving! When was the last time? Almost seven years ago?"

My arms tense at my sides. My mouth falls open, and I hesitate before asking, "I'm sorry—did you say *all* the kids?"

She swiftly turns without answering and scampers over to her front door. Whipping it open, she calls out, "Nathan! Biểu!

Come say hi to Dani!" Cô beckons me over, and I take reluctant strides, wheeling my luggage up the driveway as my mind scrambles to make sense of how Parker isn't in San Francisco right now. Surely, she didn't mean *all* the kids.

It's a moment before I hear footsteps, and sure enough, Parker steps out of the house, looking just as confused as I am.

We lock eyes, and he makes a beeline towards me.

"I thought you were in San Francisco," I say, a hand shooting to my hair. I attempt to flatten the strays into some kind of order.

"I was, for a couple days. But then I thought I should come home for Thanksgiving." He glances at my luggage. "Aren't you supposed to be in New York?"

"I had to come here because my dad couldn't fly. Didn't you see him?"

He shakes his head. "I got in pretty late last night. Is he okay?"

"He's fine. He just strained his back." I watch Parker's face change as we register in unison what this means. "I can't believe we're both in Silverpine at the same time."

I look over at Cô. She stands a short distance away, observing this unforeseen reunion and holding a hand gingerly over her mouth. Her face suggests that this is not the son she was expecting to come running down the stairs. "You two are talking again."

Parker scratches his head. "Má, did you know Dani was coming back home?"

"Of course! Her dad told me yesterday."

"Why didn't you mention it?"

"You never ask about Dani! You two just ignore each other, you're always like that," she spouts, pointing brashly at us. "What happened, con? Did you see each other in New York?"

"Yeah, we've sort of . . . made peace."

"Oh my god, why didn't you tell me?" Cô slaps Parker's arm,

and her shock gives way to a different kind of outburst. She looks positively elated. "You've made peace? Cái gì? What does that mean?"

"We've been hanging out," I say at the same time that Parker answers, "We're just hanging."

The smile on Cô's face stretches to her eyes, and she makes a small noise of buzzing excitement.

My conscience doesn't allow me to prolong eye contact, and I drop my gaze to my sneakers. I can't face her right now—not when I know that the things her son and I do behind closed doors would make her weep. A memory sneaks up on me—Parker behind me, a fistful of my hair in his hand, while I'm on all fours. He had lowered himself until his mouth was at my ear and whispered, *You feel fucking amazing.*

Just as I'm forcing the thought out of my head with an imaginary freight train, Nathan emerges from the house and joins us in the driveway. I haven't seen him since our visits overlapped four years ago. After grad school, Nathan settled permanently in Philadelphia, where he's been working as an architect. It looks like he's ditched the glasses now, and he's grown his hair out into a wavy mane that nearly reaches his shoulders.

He stoops for a hug. "Dani! It's been forever!"

"When did you get back from Philly?" I take in his features from up close. I guess it's true that men peak in their thirties. Does that mean Parker is going to get better looking too? I'm annoyed just thinking about it.

"A couple days ago. The firm let me off early this year."

"Nathan! It's unbelievable!" Cô taps his side frantically, small bursts that nearly jostle his large frame. "Parker and Dani are friends again!"

"Wait, seriously?"

Parker just sighs. "Were you expecting us to fight forever?"

Nathan casts a skeptical look at me, his suspicion lingering long enough for me to clock it. I return a tight-lipped smile—*let's not get into it now*—and he nods in understanding.

Cô is still beside herself with joy, her smile never waning. "Dani, we have so much catching up to do. I want to hear everything. But first, go home! See your father. Parker! Take her bag! Dani flew all the way from New York, so she's tired."

"Oh, he doesn't need to do that—"

"Sure," Parker cuts me off, grabbing my travel bag and slinging it over his shoulder. He doesn't look back as he passes by me, and I trail behind him with my luggage.

"Why didn't you tell me you were coming to Silverpine?" he asks as we step up to the porch of my house.

"It happened so suddenly, I literally bought my ticket last night," I say. "Why didn't you tell me *you* were coming back?"

"I figured you weren't going to be here, so it wasn't worth mentioning," Parker responds. "You usually spend the holidays in New York, right?"

I nod. I guess after years of carefully scheduled visits and avoiding all peak-season stretches, he was bound to notice.

Parker angles his head to look me square in the eyes. "You don't seem too bothered by all this. Don't tell me you're actually happy to run into me."

I sneer at him, "You're about to look my dad in the eye after fucking his only daughter on top of a dresser last week. If I were you, I'd wipe that smug look off your face."

His complacent grin fades, dying quietly on the porch.

I unlock the door and step past the foyer, breathing in the unchanging scent of my childhood home, now layered with a faint whiff of new leather. Dad gets the urge to redecorate every so often, but I always put up a fight to keep things as they are. I'm the type to leave an old high school raincoat on the coatrack, while he swaps out the rug according to his mood. (It's fluffy and creamy white now.) The current state of the house is clearly a blend of our preferences. Along with the couch, I spot a brand-new lamp too. But I know that if I opened the bottom drawers in my room, I'd still find all of Mom's keepsakes—her VHS collection arranged in tidy piles and the little music box that plays "Moon River."

"I haven't been here in years," Parker says.

I shout into the space, "Dad, I'm home!"

"I'll get the tea started. How's oolong?" Dad strolls in from the kitchen with a hand on his back, but he comes to a halt once he sees Parker next to me. The splatter of grays in his hair is more obvious than it was the last time I saw him. He looks a little worse for wear, and it makes my chest tighten, but I chalk it up to the back injury.

"Parker! What a surprise!"

"Hey, Mr. Tsai. How's your back?"

"Better, thanks to the heating pad your dad lent me," he says, his wary eyes darting between us. "What are you doing here?"

"I was just bringing this in for Dani." Parker gestures to the bag on his shoulder. "Do you want this in your room?"

"No," I'm quick to say, because I can't think of anything more horrifying than Parker setting foot in my teenage bedroom. "You can leave it here, thanks."

"Sorry, I'm confused," Dad inserts. "You two are talking again?"

I suppose we'll be explaining this all weekend. I can't really blame them. It's as if Professor X and Magneto showed up on their front lawns, denounced the mutant war, and declared they were best friends again. Only that would actually make more sense; at least everyone knew what they were fighting about. To my knowledge, only Nathan knows what went down eight years ago. Whenever Dad asks about that Christmas, I just say I don't want to talk about it.

"Dani!" Cô exclaims as she rushes through the doorway behind us. When she eyes Dad bending at the waist, she gives him a disapproving shake of her head. "Next time ask for help, and I'll send Nathan or Parker. You're old now; you're not invincible anymore."

Dad waves a finger at the scene by his front door. "Did you know about these two?"

"I just found out, too! It's a Thanksgiving miracle!" She shakes me by the shoulders. Cô is two inches shorter than me, but her strong hands makes me feel like a limp noodle. "Dani, I have a perfect idea. Your dad can't cook with his back in so much pain. You two should come over. I'll make your favorite chả giò, and we'll celebrate everyone finally being home. It'll be one big reunion!"

My mouth drops slowly, and I look to Parker for help. I'm not sure I can sit at a table for two hours with our parents, all eager to know what happened in New York. I'm tense just thinking about having to lie on the spot while simultaneously trying to swat away every inappropriate thought about Parker. Even with all the commotion, I haven't been able to ignore how tasty he looks with a bit of bed head.

He reads my panic—and thankfully nothing else—and says, "Má, they probably already have plans—"

"Actually, that sounds great!" Dad exclaims as he hobbles over. "I was planning to order in, but nothing off a menu can top your cooking. Thank you, Linh!"

Cô mutters something to Parker in Vietnamese and slaps his

arm again before darting out the door.

I lean towards him. "Hi, um, can you stop this from happening?"

"You know how much my mom loves a dinner party." He flinches, rubbing his upper arm. "I'm as powerless as you are."

CHAPTER TWENTY-THREE

Being in Parker's house feels like stepping into an old memory, like the time he and I sat on the staircase, waiting for Nathan to come home from his first-ever date. He told us that Chloe Sinclair kissed him in the movie theater—his first kiss—and that he probably did it wrong. Parker plugged his ears and begged him to stop talking, while I laughed until my sides ached.

It all comes back to me like being wrapped up in an old blanket from the attic, but I can't shake the guilt from having folded it up and stored it away in the first place. When was the last time we all gathered under this roof? It has to have been almost a decade ago.

The house has seen some obvious renovations since those days. Newly installed white counters gleam from the kitchen, and the floorboards have been freshly restored. But Cô still hasn't replaced the tea set that Parker chipped—the white-and-blue porcelain remains in its rightful spot on the dining table, beside a fruit bowl that's somehow filled with mangoes year round. Framed photos of Parker are displayed throughout the house like milestones: Parker in varsity games and Oregon Ducks uniforms and in later phases of life I don't recognize, with people I don't know.

While the brothers are in the living room watching the second Thanksgiving NFL game, I'm mashing a steaming pot of potatoes in the kitchen. Cô put the turkey in the oven a couple hours ago, but she still checks on it every ten minutes. Across from me,

Dad and Chú assemble rice paper rolls. When Chú saw me enter the house earlier, he seemed taken aback and was even more so when Parker told me I was on mashed potatoes duty.

The house is just as lively as it was when we'd gather for holidays. Dad and Chú are comparing their stock portfolios over the low strains of Vietnamese songs on a phone with a looping playlist. Cô shouts for Nathan to grab her good china from the top shelf. He yells back, "After this quarter!"

"It's looking like a good time to sell," I can hear Dad say from his end of the island.

Chú shakes his head, tutting, "The market's too unpredictable."

"But houses here are going fast. That's a good sign." He lifts his chin at me. "Dani, did you read that article I sent you?"

I drop a slab of butter into the pot. "Which one?"

"The one on the housing market in Oregon. It's good to keep up with these things."

"Oh, um," I run through my usual canned responses but can't think of anything to autofill. "I've been kind of busy."

"Busy? Are you actually being productive or just playing video games until 3 a.m.?"

Before I can roll my eyes to the back of my skull, Cô hands me a glass of water. "Parker told me you two went to a big party in Manhattan."

I take a sip from the glass. "We did. He was the one who invited me."

"See? I knew it! I always said one day you two would make up and be friends again. Back then, you kids always stuck together, running around the house, making everyone nuts!" She clasps her hands together and sighs, "I was so, so sad that you and Parker drifted apart in college."

Drifted apart is certainly an understatement. It confirms that she still didn't know about the events that led to our friendship ending.

She lays a hand on my arm. "I think Parker really likes New York. He was always so tired before, constantly working in San Francisco. But now when I call him, he sounds relaxed. Easygoing. I'm always surprised that he actually wants to talk to me!"

I can't come up with an unambiguous response, and I also don't know what to make of this information, so I focus instead on squashing every potato clump in the pot. Once I finish in the kitchen, I wipe my hands dry and roam into the living room, where Nathan and Parker are yelling at the TV over a fumble.

I throw them a glare. "I see the patriarchy is still thriving."

"I was literally wrapping spring rolls all morning before you got here," Parker mutters back from the couch. "All I asked for was a break to watch the game, and then I'll jump back into the fray."

"Stop acting noble," Nathan cuts in from the armchair. "We're only eating at four because you said you have to catch the Niners game at five."

Parker shoots him a look but doesn't bother denying it. I take the far-left seat on the couch, careful to leave a respectful amount of space between us—just enough for two people who are definitely not sleeping together.

Trying to follow the game forces me to dust off the football-designated part of my brain. "A QB sneak on the fourth and 3? Isn't that a bit unconventional?"

"Yeah, it was a weird call." Parker blinks over at me. "If it were me, I would've gone for the handoff. The distance is one thing, but they don't have the best O-line to push for a sneak either."

"Man, with the right personnel, the QB sneak is like a cheat code," Nathan adds. "You've got the biggest dudes just scrumming through to the first down."

"Aren't they risking their QB getting injured, going up the middle like that?" I ask.

"They are, but the play's got potential if it's done right," Parker says. "The ideal QB can read the defense to carry out the sneak: Should he go over, go under, or find a gap? That's how Brady did it. What Nathan's talking about, though, is kind of a new formation, and it's basically unstoppable with the right team."

Nathan nods sagely. "The good ol' Tush Push."

I laugh. "Is it actually called that?"

"Not on paper, but that's the gist of it. You push the QB from behind, and he has the momentum to gain a yard."

"I think I get it," I bob my head thoughtfully. "It's quick and aggressive, so it's hard to block if the linebackers can't get into position in time. If you're facing, say, a fourth and one, and you've got a physical advantage, it's the most effective short-yardage play. Theoretically, of course."

"Theoretically. Right." I could be imagining it, but when Parker turns his head to me, his gaze softens. "I forgot that you know a thing or two about football."

Football is the only sport I have even a passable understanding of, and I'm looking at the reason why right now.

"That's the extent of my sports knowledge," I say, shifting in my seat. "Please don't ask me anything about the Rangers."

We watch the game from our strategically spaced positions, with Parker filling me in on who the players are and which ones are on his fantasy team. Nathan chimes in to let me know who's dating an actress or a model. I can't remember the last time the three of us sat in this room watching TV, but somehow, it feels like no time has passed.

"Oh, wow, I can't believe they squeezed the tight end in there,"

I say and then snort into my hand.

"What?" asks Parker.

"*Tight end* always makes me laugh."

"Can you be mature for once?" Parker says, but he flashes me a heart-stopping smile.

"Okay, I have to address this before it drives me insane." Nathan leans forward. "How are you guys suddenly fine? Did something happen in New York?"

"Nothing in particular," Parker says nonchalantly. "The more time we spent together, the easier it was to be friends again than to stay mad at each other."

That's a surprisingly sensible way of explaining that we boned a near decade of hostility out of each other.

Unlike me, Parker is having a much easier time fielding questions. When Chú asked me in the kitchen if I'd taken Parker to any of my favorite spots, I nearly replied, *He doesn't need my help hitting the spot that matters most.*

"Don't get me wrong, I'm grateful you two idiots worked things out, but I still want a play-by-play. How did you even get in touch? You've never come back to Silverpine at the same time; you two always manage to miss each other. Who reached out to whom?"

"No one. We randomly ran into each other."

"In New York City?" Nathan guffaws. "You're telling me that because the stars aligned, you two are friends again?"

A grin spreads across Parker's face, and he crosses his arms. "Something like that."

Thankfully, the game cuts to commercial, and Nathan heads to the kitchen. I take the opportunity to scoot over to Parker, speaking low enough that my voice won't carry.

"I'm surprised you cut your tour of the California coast short for this. Thought you'd want more quality time with your boat."

"Were you stalking me again?"

"Every time I open that app, my eyes are assaulted with photos of you on that thing. I'm sure the ladies were thrilled to celebrate the return of their nautical god, though."

With his arms still folded across his chest, he regards me through the corner of his eye. "Is there a reason you think women are throwing themselves at me?"

"Seriously, Parker? You've reaped the benefits of *looking like you* your entire life. You don't need me to spell it out."

I can tell he loves this. His goading smile says, *Go on, spell it out*, but I'm not taking the bait. I flip him off in my mind and return to my side of the couch.

"If you want me to take you on my boat, you can just ask." The corner of his mouth twitches as he tries to contain his shit-eating grin. "Since you bring it up so much."

"No thanks. I'm not fond of open water; never have been. The ocean is basically a death trap, and lakes are kind of eerie. Who knows what creature might creep up and nip at my foot? I mean, I suppose it'd be fine if I stay on the boat, and it's not like I *hate* them, but there's a reason every horror movie involves a lake. Honestly, I'm not even a fan of water in general. Oh, but infinity pools? Those I can get behind."

Parker clicks his tongue and turns back to the TV. "Sometimes I think you just like to hear yourself talk."

My brain falters at his condescension, so I let my body retaliate for me and launch a pitiful kick in his direction. Something about this house brings out my inner child. Parker is caught off guard at first, but then his athlete reflexes kick in, and he grabs my leg before it lands. I try to wiggle myself free, but he catches my ankle and pins me down with his other arm. He's laughing, and I'm smiling in spite of myself. A strange emotion churns inside me, and the closest thing I can pin it to is nostalgia. But when Nathan's voice cuts through—"Is the game back on?"—it's like a cleaver to a stump. Parker immediately drops my leg, and we break apart before anyone can see us.

CHAPTER TWENTY-FOUR

At halftime, Parker goes upstairs to take a call from Venture. As soon as he's out of earshot, Nathan moves to my side so quickly it's like he was beamed over by an alien ray gun. I don't need to ask, as he's already immobilized me with the same unsettled look he wore this morning.

"Nathan—"

"You could've done it out of some loyalty to me," he grouses, "but no, it took *divine intervention* for you two to talk again. I don't even know if I can call this a win."

"Isn't the important thing that Parker and I are on good terms again?"

"You were so against it the last time I saw you. What changed?"

I pause to think of the night at Picotea. I still don't know why I let him buy me dinner. I've stopped questioning a lot of my choices around Parker the moment I first let him strip me naked in his hotel suite.

"To be honest, when I saw him, I did consider running away—but it didn't seem right. And then we talked, and it was like all that anger I'd been holding onto since I was twenty wasn't consuming me anymore. It helped that he wasn't being an ass, either."

"Did you guys talk about—you know—what happened that Christmas?"

Just because we're hooking up now doesn't mean I've written

off all that unresolved history. It looms like a rickety bridge in the distance—we'll cross it when we get there. *If* we get there. Maybe I've avoided it because I know we'll be out of each other's lives soon. I haven't been eager to dig up those skeletons.

"I haven't asked. He hasn't mentioned it either."

Nathan nods, and, perhaps sensing my apprehension, changes tack. "Well, this is great. Now that you two are getting along again, it means I can have you both at the wedding—"

"Wedding?"

"Not yet," he replies quickly. "Still have to buy the ring. But there's a girl—"

"*There's a girl*," I echo with a teasing lilt. "Pray tell, Nathan Tran, who is this girl that's made an honest man out of you? And why didn't you bring her home for Thanksgiving?"

"Irene is general counsel for a huge Shanghai corporation. She works remotely from Philly, but she doesn't get US holidays off."

"She's a lawyer?"

"A big-shot one at that. Naturally, my parents love her. And she's great, so why wouldn't they? She's the coolest person I've ever met. We're coming up on three years, so . . . yeah, I think maybe it's time." His last words tumble out in a rush, and his face blooms with a deep blush.

"I'm happy for you, Nathan," I say, trying not to dwell on how much can change in three years or what else I might've missed. His phone buzzes in his pocket, and he pulls it out with haste. The caller photo shows a pretty girl with a bob cut nuzzling her nose against a white poodle.

"That's her!" he declares and exits the room, but not quickly enough for me to miss the sugary pitch of his "Hey, babe." I shudder and giggle to myself. We've only just gotten back to the way things were, but if Nathan gets married, that means there will be a seventh person at future dinner parties. It's almost jarring to imagine our small group expanding, and the possibility of adding an eighth, maybe even a ninth seat.

"Where did Nathan and Parker go?" Chú asks as he enters from the kitchen, stamping out the thought that had begun to form. He holds an iPad in one hand and his phone in the other, looking like he has bigger fish to fry than keeping track of his adult sons.

"Parker's upstairs, and Nathan just left," I say, and my eyes fall curiously to the screen in his hands. Images buffer—elegant semi-detached houses shot from various angles. "Oh no. Is my dad making you read his boring articles too?"

He swipes a finger across the iPad. "I'm just browsing."

"You like to browse houses in . . . Philadelphia?" Upon closer inspection, I see that he's scrolling through Zillow listings. "Kind of expensive for window shopping, don't you think?"

He isn't listening to me, instead glaring over his shoulder like he's trying to summon his offspring. "We need the long table and two more chairs. Tell Parker to get them from the basement."

"I can get them."

"No, Parker can do it. He's so big, you know? Might as well make himself useful, otherwise, what's he good for?"

Oh, I know he's big. I also know one thing that's good for—*dammit, Dani! Not this again!* "I'll go find him."

I shuffle upstairs, padding down the familiar hallway until I reach Parker's bedroom. The door is ajar, open just enough that I can poke my head in. But Parker isn't there. I retreat quickly, not wanting to snoop. Contrary to his claims, I'm definitely not a stalker. I'm not even curious about what remnants of his past are still in there. Even if I am leaning in closer. And maybe a little closer still, for one more quick peek—

"What are you doing?"

I practically jump out of my skin, spinning around to find Parker looming vigilantly in the hallway. My soul vacates my body.

"Uh . . . your dad is calling you. Something about a table."

He's got a sixth sense for Dani goof-ups, and he's already caught on. A smirk appears, grating on my nerves, but I'm in no position to provoke.

"You can come in if you want," he says, extending an arm over my shoulder to push the door open. The movement takes minimal force, but his upper body still bumps into my back, and I know it's intentional.

I follow him into the room, and he shuts the door behind us. As soon as I step inside, the nostalgia from earlier returns, heavier than before. It's as if, by some magic, this space has been frozen exactly as I remember it. The framed Joe Montana jersey still hangs on the same gray walls. His football gear is stacked in the corner. An Adidas duffel bag sits untouched at the foot of his closet. The only modification is where the old beanbag used to be: There's now a desk in its place, textbooks piled on top.

I disregard the prickle in my chest. "I thought you were on a call."

"Yeah, I was using Nathan's PC. I forgot to charge my laptop after my flight." He takes a seat by his desk. I was hoping all his old furniture would be too small for him, and he'd have to embarrassingly cram himself into a chair in front of me.

"Was it so urgent that they had to call you on Thanksgiving?"

"It was. Heather was trying to get a hold of me before she flew out for her own plans."

Oh. Of course it was Heather. When the work wife calls, you can't leave her hanging. I take a nonchalant look around the room, feigning disinterest. "Are your parents buying Nathan a house when he gets married?"

His brows rise. "Um, no? I don't think so. Did you hear something?"

"Your dad was looking at listings."

"Well, I don't know how they'd afford it, but if they do, I'll be pissed off." Parker picks up a pen from his desk and spins it in his hand. "Actually, maybe I'll get married if they're just handing out property like that."

I move past the sudden jab somewhere between my stomach and my heart. "You don't think they'd sell this place and leave Silverpine . . . right?"

His eyes move to the window, and he says distractedly, "I can't see why they would. They still have the pharmacy."

"Right, right." I fidget on the spot until I realize I'm still standing awkwardly by the door. But since Parker took the only chair, there isn't anywhere else for me to get comfortable. Except . . . the bed. I used to hop on there without a second thought when we were kids, watching over Parker's shoulder as he played *Pokémon FireRed* on his Game Boy Advance. We'd have sleepovers here, giggling late into the night until Chú came knocking and we pretended to be asleep. Those conversations are lost to the past now, but the laughter remains fresh in my mind.

I take cautious steps until I'm at the foot of the bed and lower myself to a seat. I sit with the demeanor of a schoolteacher about to reprimand her kindergarten class: back straight and knees together, pointed in Parker's direction.

He watches the entire process like it's some agonizing performance. "Why are you so on edge?"

"We won't get in trouble for being here, right?" I chew on my lip. "Didn't your parents have a 'doors open' rule after we turned fourteen?"

"In trouble? Dani, we're not teenagers anymore. No one's going to suspect anything. They haven't even finished processing that we're friends again."

"Speaking of which, we need to come up with a better answer than 'We're just hanging.' We should coordinate our stories. Nathan's already on our case."

"Who cares what Nathan thinks?" He relaxes in his chair, crossing his legs. "They don't need to know all the details. We can say we went to an event and grabbed dinner a couple times. It's called a white lie."

I scrunch my sweater in my hands. "I don't want to keep lying to their faces."

Parker steeples his fingers, like an antagonist in his villain chair. "Relax, Dani. Yes, it'd be awkward as fuck if they found out, but that doesn't mean we've done anything wrong."

"But—"

"Stop overthinking it."

"And how do I do that?"

"You want my help?" He rises from the chair and takes deliberate steps toward me. It's like watching an incoming storm cloud, knowing that I'm in its crosshairs. The mattress sinks under his weight.

"Why did you sit down?"

"Didn't realize you'd commandeered my bed." He curls a long leg between us. "May I?"

Maybe I'm a little intrigued. "You may."

"I happen to know you decompress best when we're on a bed together." A hand, tanner than I remember, floats to my face, and he traces my lower lip before taking it between his forefinger and thumb. Suddenly, my stress is a precarious sandcastle to his tide, ready to crumble just as easily as I melt into his touch. "See?"

Oh god, I really want to kiss him. It's been over a week since the last time we had sex, so I'm a little pent up. But I tether myself with the reminder that this is not the time nor the place.

"Do you know what you're doing to me?" Parker says, and his voice comes out a husky whisper. He lets go of my lip, but his stare remains fixed on that very spot. "Wearing those jeans that hug your ass like a fucking dream while you talk football to me? I'm the one who's on edge here. Do you know how dangerous you are, Dani Tsai?"

No man has ever told me I'm dangerous before. I've always been run-of-the-mill, unexciting Dani who had okay sex. But that's not the case when I'm with Parker. With him, it's not ridiculous for me to think I'm sexy, sensual, and desirable, because he makes it no secret that to him, I *am* all those things.

"You have no idea, do you?" Parker reaches around with one hand and gives my backside a firm squeeze. "You don't know how fucking hot you are."

My heart wreaks havoc under my sternum. He's so close that I can feel his breath fanning over my face. Our lips are but a hairbreadth apart, and the bed suddenly feels too small for the both of us.

"We can't hook up while our parents are downstairs," I say, my lips ghosting his.

"You're right. We can't," he agrees, but his forehead rests against mine, and when I angle my head, our noses touch. We hedge at this impasse, neither of us moving—except for his hand on my butt, long fingers slowly kneading the curve of it.

"Parker," I purr his name when I can't take it any longer. I want him. I want my mouth all over him. My sandcastle has collapsed into carnal disarray. "I think you should kiss me now."

His smile is as cavalier as ever, but he does as he's told,

landing a chaste, closed-mouth kiss on my lips. "Is that okay?"

I nod. "As long as we—" he kisses me again. "Keep it—" and another kiss. "PG."

"PG. Got it." And then Parker is crushing his mouth to mine, and I fall to the bed as he climbs on top of me. He kisses me like he's been thinking of nothing but kissing me all day. His tongue eases past my parted lips and wet heat dips into my mouth before pulling back to stroke my bottom lip. I can't be bothered to worry about who's downstairs when the only thought in my mind is that he's an impossibly good kisser.

Parker's hand moves over my sweater, closing in on my breast and caressing it through the fabric. I wrap my legs around him, and his weight settles between my thighs. That's when he ruts his hips against me, his jeans rubbing harshly against mine. When my body instinctively jerks toward him, he does it again. *Holy shit.* This is the hottest over-the-clothes action I've ever experienced. I feel like I'm a teenager again, living out some freshman groupie's daydream about the most popular boy in school. I'm in Parker Tran's room, on Parker Tran's bed, kissing—and dry humping—Parker Tran.

"You know, I figured out where your sweet spot is," he says when we break for air. His lips, soft and supple, brush against the skin below my left ear. The sudden contact makes me shudder, and it sends a shockwave down to my toes. "Right . . . here."

He kisses my neck—one, two pecks—and then sucks liberally at the skin. When his teeth come down in a gentle bite, I let out a small whine that sounds amplified in my ears, and I'm convinced the entire house has heard me.

"Shhh," he laughs, and then his lips are on mine again.

I don't have it in me to feel embarrassed. My caution is lost to the wind as one hand runs through his hair, and the other snakes between us until I find the rise in his jeans. I rub him over the thick fabric. He takes a sharp breath and grinds against me once more, the tension in his pants bulging beneath my hand. Parker moans into the kiss, and I blame this moment for my lapse in judgment, because in the next second, my fingers are scrambling to undo his pants. *Fuck, fuck, fuck*. This is not a good idea—

"Parker! Dani! Come eat!" Cô's voice from the first floor is like an earthquake, jolting us back to our senses. My eyes fly open, my distress mirrored in the face staring down at me.

"Fuck," Parker growls as he pulls himself off my body.

My blood is racing, and it's a good ten seconds before I can peel myself off the bed. I comb a frantic hand through my hair and adjust my bra. When I turn to check on Parker, buttoning his jeans on the bed, he glances up at me.

His face pales. "Oh, shit."

"What?"

He points to his neck, and I whip around to the standing mirror by the window. I lift my chin for a better look, and that's when I see it: My *sweet spot* is a whopping purple bruise, a dark, glaring planet on the expanse of my skin.

A bomb goes off inside me, shrapnel of hysteria lodging into my bones. I'm mortified at both of us for letting this happen, but more so at Parker because it was his beautiful mouth that did this, and I don't know where else to channel my meltdown.

"You gave me a fucking *hickey*? In your parents' house?" I grab a pillow and lash it at him. "What are we, sixteen?"

"Okay, okay, calm down," Parker catches the pillow before it can hit him and tosses it aside. "You can wear one of my sweaters to hide it."

"Uh, no, that's not going to work." I rub the tender skin, drawing rapid breaths as I pace the length of the room. "If I go down there in your clothes, it's going to look really suspicious. What I need to do is to go back to my house and change. Do you think you can cover me?"

"Yeah," Parker motions to get up, only to sink back to the bed in slow defeat. "I'm going to need a minute."

"What? Oh." My eyes zero in on the tent in his pants, and my mouth snaps shut.

True to his word, a minute is what it takes before Parker and I are slipping out of his room. As if he's a trained defenseman, he keeps me close to his side and out of view as we descend the stairs. Just when I reach the front door and breathe a sigh of relief, Nathan pops his head in from the living room.

"Where were you guys?"

"I was showing Dani something." Parker lies like an inexperienced teenager. I thought he was supposed to be good at this.

"In your room?"

"I, um, think I left the stove on," I say, hand over my neck. I'm pretty bad at this too. "I'm going to check."

The suspicion in Nathan's eyes doesn't let up all night, as we gather for dinner, and Cô tells me she's saved me a seat—next to Parker. When he passes me the cranberry sauce, his arm bumps mine, and he nearly drops the bowl. I sit there, anxious and stuffy in my turtleneck, and excuse myself as soon as dinner's done, so I can run to my bed and scream under the covers.

CHAPTER TWENTY-FIVE

The next morning, my back is pressed against what I think is a woodworking bench, but I can't be certain. In the pitch black, I can't tell a hammer from a saw, and I'm afraid I might lose a finger. But as soon as I'm hoisted onto the tabletop, and Parker's mouth finds mine, the surface of sharp objects is about as threatening as a bed of clouds. Because that's what Parker's kisses feel like—being in the freaking high heavens.

The muffled instrumental of "Careless Whisper" fades through the walls, until someone in the living room hits replay. Feedback from the karaoke mic screeches with a vengeance, and Chú's voice resumes its soulful crooning: "I'm never gonna dance again, guilty feet have got no rhythm."

I'd be impressed that he can muster this much passion for his third straight rendition, if I weren't so desperate to block out his voice. When Parker suggested we meet for a rare moment of privacy, this was not the ambience I'd hoped for.

"I'm sorry. I don't think I can, you know?" He pulls away from the kiss, and I'm yanked out of the clouds, crash-landing back in his family's garage. The sultry saxophone intro taunts us in the distance, for the fourth time. "My dad's singing is kind of killing this for me."

"No, I get it." I hop off the workbench and brush the sawdust off my pants. "He really likes this song."

"Why did I think it was a good idea to buy them a karaoke machine? They make me regret it every time I'm home." Parker's shadowy figure moves to the light switch, and the garage is illuminated with a flicker, along with the hot shame between us. "So much for sneaking around."

"We need a new rule: No hooking up when we're back home," I propose. "Our parents are already on high alert whenever they see us together. It's impossible to get any alone time."

"Looks like we have no choice." He sweeps his bangs out of his eyes and tips his chin at me. "I take it your hickey hasn't faded."

I tug at the collar of my sweater. My skin underneath is warm and a little clammy. "I've had to wear nothing but turtlenecks in my own home because of you. I keep telling my dad that I'm cold, and he cranks up the heat each time. I'm living in a fucking sauna."

Parker finds this hysterical. I refrain from kicking him.

"Welp, we gave it a valiant try. And now I'm going back to roasting in Mount Doom," I say dejectedly, turning toward the garage door.

"Wait." He snags the back of my turtleneck, and I come to a cartoonish stop, arms flopping about. "You don't have to go home. I have a better idea."

❧

Parker sits in the driver's seat of his dad's new Toyota SUV, one hand on the wheel, the other raked through his hair, elbow perched against the door. I must be wired to expect nothing but trouble from him, because I'm genuinely astonished by how harmless his idea is: grab some takeout, take a drive on the I-84 up to the Columbia River Gorge, and be home in time for dinner.

It rained this morning, and now the sky is overcast. Silverpine stretches out before us with an undertone of gray—rows of trees and rooftops shaded under gloomy clouds. The forecast said to expect showers today and tomorrow and the day after. Maybe it's because I grew up here in the Pacific Northwest, but I don't mind the rain. As soon as we get a stretch of sunny days, I'm the first to complain that it's too bright. Parker says his mom tried to send him out with an umbrella, and we laugh about that for a solid minute, because, can you imagine?

"Where's the Jeep?" I ask.

"In a storage unit."

"You didn't take it to San Francisco?"

"Nope," is all he gives me. He's adjusting his mirrors when he skims a look over my outfit. "Why didn't you change? You don't have to hide your hickey around me."

"I don't want the outside world seeing this monstrosity."

"It can't be that bad. Let me see." At the next stop sign, Parker reaches over and lowers the fabric around my neck. Every neighboring muscle tenses when his fingertip meets my skin. "*Damn*, I did that?"

"You've branded me like livestock."

He bites back a grin, wisecrack at the ready, until I terminate it with a glare.

"I hate you."

"No, you don't."

Sighing, I let my gaze fall to the window. "You're right. I don't."

He doesn't respond, but out of the corner of my eye, I see him reach for the dashboard to turn down the heat.

We can't agree on pizza, so we compromise and grab SuperDeluxe. It turns out we share one unanimous opinion: SuperDeluxe makes the best burgers in the state. Before we exit the parking lot, Parker opens his Spotify app. Song titles zip along the screen as he scrolls. “What do you want to listen to? I’ll let you pick.”

“Gotta be ‘Careless Whisper’ then.”

A sigh leaves his lips. “I’m just going to search ‘driving playlist.’”

“So what excuse did you give your parents to get out of the house?” I ask, locating the takeout bag with my Single Deluxe combo. “I told my dad I was going to the bookstore. That usually gives me a few hours.”

“I didn’t have to give them an excuse.” He helps himself to a handful of fries off my lap before I have a chance at them. “I said I was hanging out with you.”

“Doesn’t that defeat the purpose of sneaking out?”

“I don’t think we need to sneak out if we’re going for a drive. Besides, my mom’s too excited about us making up. She’s not going to risk it by meddling now.” He looks over his shoulder as he merges onto the freeway. The vein in his neck distracts me, and I have to force my attention back to unwrapping my burger. “She’s, uh, kind of always wanted us to date, or something.”

“You know, I got that vibe. I’m surprised she wasn’t deterred by the near decade of no contact.”

“It’s been in her head since we were kids. She was convinced we’d end up together and only dropped it when I met my first girlfriend. This weekend has her hopes up again, I can tell.”

Girlfriend? That’s the first time I’ve heard Mr. Commitment-phobia mention anything of the sort. Ever since I learned about his permanently single status, I’ve pictured Parker hightailing it at the first sign of commitment.

“I thought you didn’t do relationships.”

“I’ve had girlfriends before. That’s how I realized I wasn’t cut out for dating,” Parker explains. He signals for me to pass his Double Deluxe combo to him. “I think my mom mentioned you brought someone back to Silverpine before. Must've been serious."

Despite my effort to block out any and all Parker Tran news for the last seven years, it makes sense that it didn't work both ways. I knew Cô had seen me with my college boyfriend a couple of times, even when I was trying to keep a low profile. What I didn't know was that she'd relayed that information to Parker.

"Not really. Just a guy I was seeing in school. I'd met his family already, so he really wanted to tag along and meet my dad."

"And what did your dad think of him?"

What did my dad think of Graham—the guy who thought it would be impressive to speak to him only in haiku? He wasn't exactly a fan.

"Didn't say much. He tends to avoid any discussion that involves my love life." I bite into my burger and wipe the sauce off my mouth with a napkin. "Have you met Irene yet?"

"Nathan's girlfriend? A couple times, yeah. She's nice."

"I thought you'd have more to say about your future sister-in-law."

His brow furrows at this. "What do you think about that?"

"What? Nathan getting married?"

"I worry that he's jumping the gun for the sake of settling down."

"Three years feels like a reasonable amount of time to know if you want to marry someone," I counter.

"I don't know." He pauses to chew on a fry. "Maybe it's because I've never felt that way in a relationship. Of course, mine didn't last even half as long, but I don't believe in a checkpoint that says, hey, if we reach this mark then we're set for life."

I fold the corners of the paper around my burger, pretending I'm far more interested in that task than in what Parker's saying.

"Is this how you found out you're not *cut out* for relationships?"

"Well, they all started the same way: I'd have feelings, until I didn't. Nothing seemed to last longer than the initial spark. I wanted to be all in, but I couldn't force feelings that weren't there. When you have to remind yourself to be affectionate, it doesn't feel authentic anymore." He reaches for another fry, shrugging. "That's just me, though. I'm not saying that what Nathan has isn't real. She's the only one who laughs at his jokes, so that has to count for something."

I let his explanation bounce around in my brain. "Then how would *you* know you've found the person you want to spend the rest of your life with?"

"I don't think it's about time. I think it's about not having doubts. That unshakable certainty that this is the person you want to wake up to everyday, through the good and the bad," he continues. "But like I said, I've just never felt that way with anyone I've dated. The only time I've ever felt that certain about anything was—"

He cuts himself off, and my eyes snap to him instinctively. "What? Football?"

"Yeah." He takes a sip of his pop. "Football."

The sun begins to peek through the clouds as we drive along the freeway, and I take it as another indication that the universe is bending over backward for the man beside me. It's still early enough in the day that we beat the weekend traffic, so the ride is mostly smooth. Parker doesn't say much, but he asks for a sip of my Fizzy Water, and I take one of his nuggets as compensation.

When we turn onto the Historic Columbia River Highway, memories of past trips along this very road come rushing back. First, I spot the Sugarpine Drive-In, where Chú took us for ice cream so many summers ago. Next, we pass the Vista House at

Crown Point, a field trip destination from our elementary school days.

I know this little stretch of Oregon better than I thought. I remember the cliff walls and the seemingly endless span of trees: dense shades of green broken by autumn stripes of yellow and orange. It's a sight I'll never get tired of. I fall into quiet contemplation until Parker pulls into a parking lot and beckons me out of the car.

"We're ahead of schedule," he says when we make it to the Horsetail Falls trailhead. "Let's take a walk. It'll be nice."

"That's a funny way of saying we're going for a hike." I look at him like he's telling a bad joke. "Parker, we don't have any gear." I glance down at my Converse high-tops. I don't know what sneakers Parker has on, but I think they might be the Dior ones that had Tae-woo foaming at the mouth. Either way, they look expensive. "Neither of us are wearing the right shoes."

"If I remember correctly, the first waterfall is less than half a mile away, and the trail isn't anything too challenging. I think it's supposed to be beginner level." He ignores me and starts walking ahead. "We can probably get to it in twenty minutes."

I don't budge, even when Parker stops and faces me.

"Would you like me to carry you, princess?"

"I'm good," I mutter, dragging my feet forward.

CHAPTER TWENTY-SIX

Though my memory of it is vague, the trail isn't new to me. I know I've been here before with Mom and Dad, and we took the very same path to see the waterfalls. I'd never been the biggest fan of hiking—I like skyscrapers and concrete, not bugs or muddy paths—but as I climb the switchbacks behind Parker's unwavering form, I have to admit, this isn't so bad. Although the trail is a little steep, and I brake to find my balance now and then, it's true that it's beginner-friendly, and I likely won't be falling to my death.

I take time to soak in the landscape near Oneonta Gorge, unfolding across the nearby railroad like spawning on a stunning new map in an open-world game. Mossy rocks verge on the footpath, and among the lush ferns are speckles of white—little explosions of snowberries. The bigleaf maples tower overhead in vibrant bursts of gold, their freshly fallen leaves crunching under my shoes and reminding me why autumn has always been my favorite season.

A narrow ravine comes into view as we arrive at Ponytail Falls, where the steady stream of water gushes over a cavern created by centuries of geologic force, a small wonder shaped by basalt lava and time. The trail continues behind the falls and through a low-ceilinged rock chamber where hikers pass behind the cascade. At the water line, a small crowd snaps photos and dips their toes into the swimming hole.

Parker is already taking careful steps toward the waterfall. I survey the damp path and wet rocks ahead, and my heels take root.

"Um, you go ahead. I don't think I can get down there." I point to my sneakers. "I'll just hang back and read."

"Read?"

I take my phone from my back pocket. "I have a couple *Adagio* articles that I can get a head start on."

He lifts a casual shoulder and then descends to the overhang easily. I find a rock nearby that looks dry enough and not too mossy and take a seat. Tapping into my email, I locate an article about the link between *Jurassic Park* and a generational boom in paleontologists.

The scent of the gorge is earthy, with a hint of rain. It's well past noon, but when a breath of wind passes, the air still feels like a brisk morning. It fills my lungs like a subtle, but addictive menthol. I wonder why I don't read outside more.

When I glance at Parker, he's still standing in the cavern, pacing from one side to the other, occasionally stopping to observe the waterfall. His face tightens in concentration every now and then, until his gaze drifts to me, and our eyes meet.

Parker climbs back up the trail to my little refuge on the rock.

"This is nice," I say.

"I told you." He glances at the waterfall, then back at me. "It's nicer once you get close to the water. Come on."

"But my shoes," I persist. "What if I slip and hit my head on a rock? Or what if I step on a slug?"

Parker offers me his hand. "I'll make sure you don't slip."

"Can you make sure there are no slugs?"

"Dani."

I stare at his hand, and my heart takes the tiniest of leaps. "Don't let me fall," I say, reaching for him. His sturdy fingers fold over mine, and my hand suddenly looks so small. Parker's grip feels strong and reliable, and he holds onto me until we make it to the point of the overhang that's directly behind the waterfall.

As soon as I'm confident in my footing, I let go of him. Though the air is muggy down here, there's something calming about standing in the hollow of the half-tunnel and listening to the roar of the coursing water. Somewhere tucked away in my bedroom, I'm sure there's a photo of me with Mom and Dad at this very spot, but why does being here now feel like it's the first time?

The spray of the cascade wets my face, and I take a step back, patting the sleeve of my coat against my forehead. Several hikers huddle beneath the falls and ask Parker to take their photo. He's generous with his angles, even squatting to get the optimal shot. Once they leave, he strides over to me, lingering at my side as we watch the waterfall in comfortable silence.

"When was the last time you were here?"

"I must've been six," I tell him, leaving out the details. "You?"

"I used to come here a lot after I quit the team. Everyone wanted me to talk about it, but I didn't know how. Mostly, I wanted to be alone," he says, and the look he gives me is a tentative one. "I'm guessing Nathan never filled you in."

I see his reservations in the uneasy scrunch of his brows. After it came up at the Monosphere event, I wasn't sure if the topic was off-limits. I still don't have the confidence to pry, so I shake my head and wait for him to continue.

"Sounds about right. Back then, I swore him to secrecy. I made him promise not to tell you anything if he ever ran into you." He slides his hands into his pockets. "I was still too embarrassed."

"Embarrassed?" I repeat. "Of what?"

"I think you know better than anyone that football used to be my life."

"Really? Did you make it obvious or something?"

That makes him grin.

"Remember when I got the recruitment news? I thought I'd made it. I had these big, inflated dreams that once I got into U of O, my career would explode, and I'd be on my way to going pro. Everyone around me said the same—my parents, coaches, teammates. Then I got redshirted my first year and realized how terribly not special I was."

I pick my words carefully. "I'm no expert, but to me, you were like, the best of the best. I couldn't imagine a better player than you."

"Every starting quarterback in a small-town varsity program thinks he's the best of the best—until he ends up on a roster with guys from big-city high schools who had access to better training," he goes on. "It was the talent gap too. My redshirt year was supposed to help me compete on the same level, but even after all the training, I still didn't stand out. The coaches noticed too. I could tell they were second-guessing my recruitment. I was desperate to prove them wrong, so I trained more. That's all I did, every day. It started to feel like I didn't have a life outside of football. I'm sure you picked up on that."

"I thought you were frustrated about not having game time," I say. "We talked on video calls almost every day, but you never mentioned any of this."

He looks ahead at the waterfall, quiet for a beat. "In my debut game, I played a few snaps in the fourth quarter. It wasn't bad, but not very memorable. The rest of my sophomore season went the same way. I didn't get mentioned in any sports articles; I wasn't on anyone's radar. Then between Thanksgiving and the Christmas we were supposed to meet, I tore my rotator cuff. That put me out of commission for the rest of the season. And the worst part? I caused the injury myself by overtraining. Ironic, isn't it?"

There's a sharp sting beneath my ribs, and I have to stop myself from reaching for him. "Why didn't you tell me?"

"I wanted to. But every time I pictured the conversation, I'd see myself admitting that I'd been struggling to keep up the whole time. That my debut was actually a flop. That even if going pro were still an option, I wasn't sure I wanted it anymore."

He sweeps his bangs from his forehead. They're a little damp from the misty air.

"I'd have to tell you that I'd given up on the dreams I'd had since we were seven. And I wasn't sure you'd understand. I was afraid of disappointing you. You know, it wasn't just the coaches. I cared what you thought of me—more than anyone else."

"Why me?" I add, "It's not like I knew much about football."

"Because it's *you*, Dani. Your thoughts, opinions—they all mattered to me. I didn't want you to think I was a failure."

I swallow, needing a moment to sort through the revelations. It's much too heavy to process all at once. "So, that's why you didn't come to New York."

He nods. "I made it all the way to my gate that day. I was lining up to board my flight, and then I thought of you over there."

He allows himself to look at me then, something changing in his eyes. "You had everything figured out. You were doing great in school, meeting new people, making yourself at home in this huge city. I was happy for you, but at the same time, I wondered where I fit into all that. It was my own insecurities, because there I was, failing on all fronts."

He pauses, and I hear the soft shuffle of his jacket, the clearing of his throat somehow magnified.

"Around that time, I received notice that the school had put me on academic probation. If I didn't raise my GPA, I'd lose my scholarship—and my eligibility to play. Basically, everything that could possibly go wrong was starting to feel very real. I knew once I got to New York, I'd either have to pretend everything was fine or admit all of this to you. And I couldn't do either."

"I would never have judged you," I assert.

"I didn't want you feeling sorry for me either," he says in return. "After we stopped talking, I tried to get back on track, thinking that maybe, once I got my shit together, I could face you again. In my junior year, I got another chance when they made me a starter. Unfortunately, I only played two games before my shoulder started acting up again. The team doctor told me I'd have to sit out the season or risk a full tear. It started to feel hopeless all over again, so I finally quit. The thing is, my injury didn't happen during a game, so no media outlets covered it. To the football world, I just disappeared. And no one noticed."

There's a full-on blockage where my lungs should be, and my hands are balled into fists at my sides. The emotion swirling inside has too many facets to name. I'm devastated for the twenty-year-old boy I once knew, helpless as his dreams crumbled around him. But beneath that lies the sting of betrayal, the ache of wishing he had trusted our friendship a little more.

Solemnly I say, "Parker, we were best friends. All I ever wanted to do was support you. There's no world where you could ever have been a failure in my eyes."

"I realized that too late. I knew I'd made things worse by ignoring your messages, but I still didn't know how to explain everything. I thought you might tell me to fuck off and leave you alone—which is basically what you did when I saw you in Silverpine a year later. I was sure you hated me then."

"I thought *you* hated *me*. It's not like you gave me a warm reception either."

"I know. I was being defensive. I was still dealing with my football career ending. I'd been trying all weekend to gather the courage to talk to you, but there you were, avoiding me. When I finally caught you in front of Rocky's, you were so convinced I was a monster, I started to wonder what was the point in trying to convince you otherwise. To be fair, I was also fully committed to being a moody, washed-up athlete who was angry at the world."

I kick at the dirt under my shoe. "And then I dumped a milkshake in your car."

"That wasn't even the worst part." He exhales a laugh, but his eyes lower to the damp earth between us, and I watch his jaw tense. "You said you never wanted to see me again."

"You told me you wanted me to stay out of your life!"

"Guess I'm a liar."

A couple of barefoot kids choose this moment to waddle past us, shrieking with laughter as they make their way to the water. Parker gestures after them. "Want to get a little closer?"

I give a hesitant nod, and we descend the small slope, crouching side by side when we reach the edge of the swimming hole. I dip my hand into the frigid water, letting my fingers glide along the surface, making ripples across it. Next to me, Parker tilts his head, and I can feel the weight of his gaze for a lingering, loaded moment. The roar of the waterfall above our heads is much louder here, but in our little bubble, every word seems to hang in the air, heavy and thick.

"I tried to text you a few years ago. I never got a response."

A lump rises to my throat. "I changed my number."

"I figured as much," he says. "Until I saw you again that night in Manhattan, I thought you were done with me for good."

"You left me no choice but to move on, or it would have crushed me forever. I had to get used to life without you." I draw a bracing breath. "Before that, you—*you and me*—that was all I'd ever known. It was supposed to always be that way."

I fall silent. The wind picks up, carrying a fine mist with it, and I feel it settle on my skin like a cool haze.

Parker lifts a hand to my cheek, wiping it dry. His touch is warm, soothing.

"The years we spent apart felt so long. But now that I get to see you all the time, it feels like time is moving way too fast."

"You're going back to San Francisco soon, right?" I ask, once I make the connection. Until now, neither of us had mentioned his leaving, something I suspect was intentional on both sides. In less than two months, our relationship—our arrangement—will come to an end. Worry sets in as I consider if we've only reached this point because being around each other made us try a little harder. Once he's three thousand miles away, will our friendship fade into obscurity again?

"You should drop by sometime." He pulls his hand away, folding his arms across his knees. "I'll show you around."

It sounds oddly casual, considering we're two people who are *casually* sleeping together. Part of me wants to point out the obvious absurdity, but I'm afraid he'll see what I'm really asking: *What's going to happen to us?*

So instead, I scoff at him. "Fine, you've twisted my arm. I'll ride your boat."

A single droplet of rain lands on my nose. Moments later, a light drizzle begins to fall. Parker rises to his feet, rolling the kinks out of his shoulders. "We should head back before the trail gets too wet."

He looks at me, palm outstretched again. I draw a deep breath and take his hand.

As we retrace our steps to the car, still holding hands, Parker suddenly says, "Remember when you told me about the Danis and Parkers in other universes?"

I'm surprised he even remembers my rambling. "I think so."

"Back when I was in that football slump, I had this thought: If there's already a universe where I went pro, then maybe it just wasn't meant to happen in this one. And if I did make the NFL there—if I were playing in the Super Bowl and my face was everywhere—then you wouldn't be able to ignore me. I'd track you down and make things right."

"You would use your fame to force me to be your friend again?"

"I'd do anything to make that happen." He focuses on leading us down the path as I stare at his back, wishing I could see the expression on his face. "There's also a universe where that Christmas in New York went differently."

I don't speak; my voice clogs with something crushing.

"Dani, I'm sorry," he says, and I almost miss the squeeze of my hand. "I'm always going to regret that I didn't show up that day."

Turns out, eight years still wasn't enough time to prepare me for this apology. I can't find a reaction that matches the enormity of the truth that Parker kept from me. I have a suspicion that dwelling on the lost years would only make me cry, and I'd be powerless stop it. I also have the urge to tell him that everything is okay now, that we'll be fine.

Relief and remorse take hold of me in turns, making it impossible for me to speak as we sit silently in the car.

CHAPTER TWENTY-SEVEN

I sprint up the porch steps next door, my finger finding the doorbell like muscle memory. I hope it's not too early.

When I left the house, Dad was still sleeping off last night's karaoke session. Chú had found the duet partner of his dreams in him, and around midnight, Parker texted, begging me to come drag Dad home.

It's a little past nine now, but even if Chú is also out of commission, I suspect Cô has been bustling around the kitchen since seven, and both Tran brothers are notoriously early risers.

"Dani!" True to form, Nathan answers the door like a human conduit of the sun's energy. "Good morning!"

"Morning, Nathan." My voice is a little gravelly in comparison, and I clear my throat. "Are your parents up yet?"

"Dad's still asleep. Don't think he'll be up until lunch. Mom went on a grocery run." The closest Asian supermarket is nearly an hour's drive out of town. Cô must've left bright and early to get dibs on the freshest produce.

I nod, even as I try to peek over his shoulder.

Nathan chuckles. "I know we're all getting used to this again, but you don't have to hide why you're really here. Want me to grab Parker?"

"Yes, please." I smile at him. "Oh, and if you don't mind, could I also borrow a football?"

Nathan tilts his head as he considers the request, but he doesn't ask questions. "Sure. Do you want to come in and wait?"

"I'm okay out here."

In the chill of late-November air, I zip my windbreaker up to my chin so it conceals what's left of my hickey. Tightening my ponytail, I squint at my reflection in the screen door. I can barely make out my silhouette, but I check myself once, twice, three times, just to be sure I didn't forget to wipe the toothpaste from my mouth.

The door swings open again, and Parker appears at the threshold.

"Hi."

There's a silly flutter in my stomach. "Hi."

He beams at me. "You wore your hair up. It looks nice."

"Thank you," I say, my voice small. "Are you free?"

"I was going to go for a run." He looks me up and down. "Why do you look like you're about to do the same?"

I spend most mornings in Silverpine poring over a book with a cup of coffee, entirely sedentary. But an idea had struck me the night before, after I pulled the (literal) plug on the karaoke party and headed home for bed.

To be honest, it had been weighing on me since Parker drove us back from the gorge. I wanted to show him how much I appreciated him opening up to me, but I was still having trouble giving voice to my thoughts. Then I remembered our old heart-to-hearts in his backyard, and I had my answer. But since we didn't have much time left in Silverpine, I knew I had to act quickly.

Nathan returns just in time to hand me the final piece of my plan. He reaches past Parker to offer me the football. "Here you go."

The younger Tran brother watches the hand-off, his mouth

twisting. "Something is off about this picture."

"Let's play catch," I propose.

His brows raise in what I hope is pleasant surprise. "You want to play football?"

"Nothing fancy."

"Oh, fun. Can I join?" Nathan nudges his brother in his side. "We could run a few pass plays. It's been a while."

Parker plucks the football from my hands. For one silent moment, he lets his fingers glide over the leather, his forehead scrunching. A sudden panic creeps over me. Have I dug up some unresolved trauma? Was this a bad idea? But as he lines his fingers with the laces, a smile passes over his lips, and I finally let out a breath.

"Sure," he says. "Why not?"

The local park is a short walk away, and we make it there in under ten minutes. Douglas firs tower above, casting shade over the winding walking paths, and the grass is lush and green, invigorated by the steady Oregon drizzle. Not much has changed since the last time I was here with these two—except they weren't over six feet tall back then. I take a slow look around, and I can almost reimagine the bike rides, playground mishaps, and long-ago picnics. This is where Parker first taught me how to throw a football.

We appear to be the only visitors at this time of day, aside from the odd jogger dipping in and out of the park. It's not hard for us to find a spot with an appropriate amount of clearance in the vast green space.

Nathan and Parker are stretching next to me, and I get the vague impression that I've ended up on the set of a sports apparel ad. If a billboard of the brothers went up in Times Square tomorrow, I wouldn't even question it. I start to stretch my arms, pretending to know what I'm doing. Parker's attention is on me, and it triggers my self-consciousness. I'm suddenly very mindful that a former Division I football player is watching me pretend I know a thing or two about athleticism. I feel as if I binged the Food Network for a day, and now I have the task of serving a dish to the Iron Chefs.

Nathan lobs the ball to Parker, who frowns slightly, unhappy with his catch. "You're right. It's been a while."

"You think *you're* rusty? I'm about to gravely disappoint you." I back away from them, stopping a few feet out. Then I hold up my hands, forming a triangle. Parker throws me an easy one with little speed. I make the connection—mostly thanks to his aim—but the ball still bounces off my fingertips and falls to the grass.

"A fumble in the red zone!" Nathan shouts dramatically, palms on his head. "And with that, Dani Tsai just cost us the Super Bowl!"

"Shut up, Nathan!"

I pick up the ball as Parker crosses his arms. "Did you forget what I taught you?"

"I know, I know. Soft hands, like catching an egg," I recite from memory.

Drawing from that same vault of football knowledge, I align my fingers on the thread in a way that feels familiar. I *think* I remember how to do this. Feet apart, knees bent—I follow through with some force in my throw.

Parker catches it smoothly, a little over his right shoulder. "Not bad."

For someone who's supposedly out of practice, the former quarterback falls into an effortless rhythm in no time. We spread out as the passes go deeper. Nathan and Parker are getting faster and a little flashier with their throws, and I start to feel bad for disrupting their tempo.

With an effortless windup and release, Parker launches the ball into another breathtaking arc, ripping through the air with a perfectly polished spin. I catch it low in the bucket I make with my arms.

"Nice catch." Parker gives me a high five when I jog up to him.

"Hey, I need a refresher," I say. "I can't seem to throw a spiral like before."

There's a flicker in his eyes, and then his face brightens with a smile that revives the decade-old image of a boy who once dominated the gridiron. He's in his element, thriving off of his love for the game. If this is the payoff for my little plan, then it was totally worth it.

"I got you, Dani."

But Nathan trots over first, passing his brother on the way. He inspects my right hand on the ball and shakes his head, then steps behind me and guides my fingers along the laces.

"You want to leave a gap between your palm and the ball. It should roll off your fingers, and the spiral comes from your index when you release."

"Like this?"

"Yeah, that's good. Now point your left foot at your target and put your weight on the other."

I try to recenter myself as Nathan pokes at me like I'm a mannequin he's setting up in a store display. "God, your posture is terrible."

He squeezes my arms in an effort to straighten me, when Parker raises his voice.

"Nathan." It startles us both. "I can help her."

We stare at him, not moving.

"Show of hands: Who here played football at a D1 college?"

I glance behind me, and I swear Nathan's holding back a laugh. Amusement twitches on his lips, and he nods, stepping aside. "I'll go long. Dani, you can use me as a target."

Parker surveys me. His first order of business is readjusting the football in my hand, though it doesn't look too different from where Nathan had placed it. Then he gets into place in the spot his brother had just occupied.

"Come here," he says, his voice low, and I scoot a little closer.

I swallow. "You know that Nathan is watching, right?"

"He's already halfway down the field and blind without his glasses."

A big, sturdy hand lands on my lower back; the other flattens on my stomach. I instinctively suck in. He makes modifications to my form, straightening my posture and nudging my legs shoulder-width apart. His touch is firm but gentle. I'm hoping he doesn't notice my skyrocketing temperature as his hand slides from my waist to my hip, shifting weight onto my right foot.

"Pull your throwing hand back to your ear, elbow cocked. Off hand close to your body, like this."

His arms come from behind, directing my hold on the ball. We repeat the motion until I become more fluid with the rotation of my shoulder, the swing at release. He's so close that his breath is hot against my neck.

"Good. Now when you throw, bring your power from your back foot to the front. Let go above your head, snapping your wrist like I taught you. Remember, pressure comes from your forefinger."

Okay, I got this. I position myself for the windup just as Parker steps back to give me space. I draw back my arm, then accelerate forward. Just as he taught me, I put my legs into the throw, and my fingers roll off the laces with a sharp flick of my wrist. The arc isn't very pretty and not nearly as clean as Parker's, but it's not terrible. Nathan breaks into a run and catches the football, tucking it cleanly into his body.

I jump up and down, my heart soaring. "Did you see that? I threw a spiral! It totally spun!"

Parker is all smiles, this time high-fiving me with both hands. "Yep. You threw a spiral." He gazes down at me with what I think is pride. It makes my heart take flight again.

On the way back to the house, Nathan makes a call to Philly, and Parker and I fall back once we hear the dutiful "Good morning, babe" and "I miss you." Parker is still holding on to the football, absentmindedly passing it from hand to hand.

"Never thought I'd get the chance to do this with you again."

"I'm not the best practice partner. Thanks for being patient."

"Can I assume this means you've forgiven me?"

I lift my eyes from the pavement and look directly at him. The wind whistles in my ears, but I'm listening to the calm in my heart instead. For the first time in a long while, it doesn't feel so heavy. My mind had been a flurry after his apology yesterday, but now, only one thought remains: *I'm happy to have you back.*

"If you had been honest with me from the beginning, there wouldn't be anything to forgive," I say, truthfully. "But if it means anything, I'm not mad at you anymore."

He retreats into silent rumination, and I peek over at his arms, the muscles flexing with the ball's movement.

"How's your shoulder?"

"Good as new," he reassures me. "Since I stopped before the tendon could tear, I didn't need surgery. Just a lot of physical therapy."

"I'm glad," I say, a smile in my voice. "Not that you asked for my opinion, but I don't think you need to play football to still be in love with the game. I don't think anything, or anyone, can ever take that away from you."

I haven't even made it up the porch steps before Cô is giving her sons an earful for tracking mud through the front door. In silent resignation, the brothers disperse like trained show dogs—Nathan heads off to grab the Swiffer while Parker starts unloading groceries from the car in the driveway.

I head straight for the backyard, find the hose, and start rinsing off my sneakers. As I'm trying to balance on one leg, my phone hums in my pocket.

Marisa: If I eliminate every city where a serial killer was booked, I might run out of options.

Me: If crime is your main concern, have you considered moving to Iceland?

Marisa: I've always wanted to see the northern lights. It'd be a welcome distraction from all the time I spend wondering when Shay and I will be murdered.

It strikes me that in her hunt for the perfect home, Marisa will likely come full circle and realize that she and Shay belong in Brooklyn.

"Oh, good. You haven't left yet." Cô pushes the gate open to enter the backyard, and a smile spreads across her face. "Tell me what you want for dessert. I'll make it for your last night here."

"Hmm." I give it careful consideration. "Oh! How about sticky rice? I haven't had it in ages."

"Xôi! You're in luck! I bought pandan today." She takes the hose from me once I finish with it, coiling it tightly. "What time is your flight tomorrow?"

"Early. I'll be out of the house by six," I tell her.

When I see the frown marring her features, there's a reflexive wrench in my chest—a feeling that's been there all weekend. I should've visited more. I shouldn't have taken her for granted.

Guilt dredges up thoughts I wish I hadn't entertained: What if the next time I visit, Cô and Chú aren't here anymore? It doesn't seem likely they'd move, but then again, I also thought Marisa would never call anywhere but New York home.

"Cô, do you think you'll stay in Silverpine forever?" I think back to the Zillow listings on Chú's iPad.

"Hard to say," she replies after a pause. "All you kids have left already. One day, Nathan will have a family. Parker will have a family. And then they'll never come home. It's the same with all my friends' sons—they always go where their wife goes. Or maybe Parker will marry a girl from here."

She winks at me and heat surges across my skin. "So, you would move to be closer to them?"

"Maybe. I want to be with my grandkids. I have to be their favorite grandma, you know?"

"No contest," I laugh in spite of myself. "You'd be the best."

"Dani, I know you're busy. You have your big city life now." Cô cups my face in her hand, and I freeze, unfamiliar with this level of parental affection. "But you should come home more, con. We miss you."

Emotion swells, and I have to clench my teeth to keep it from spilling over. In a rare moment of clarity, I realize: I don't want to go back to New York.

I don't follow Cô through the back door, instead looping around to the front of the house to find their car already parked in the garage and out of sight. It's strange to see the driveway empty now, when the Jeep had once been a permanent fixture there. I peer around, wondering when they'd replaced the old Toyota with the newer Toyota.

The hoop stand looms over the vacant concrete, its broken netting weathered by time. It's been years since Nathan and Parker last played one-on-one. I used to wonder why they kept the hoop up after it sat untouched once Nathan moved to Philly. But now, I find myself hoping they'll never take it down. I hope that every time I come home, that hoop will still be there, and the house behind it will stay unchanged.

CHAPTER TWENTY-EIGHT

"So, you're saying your bed broke."

"Yup."

"And we're the ones who broke it."

"Yup."

"Because we had so much sex."

"Yup."

"Nice." Parker lifts a hand for a high five.

I meet his hand in the air with a quick slap, but I don't allow myself to be sidetracked for long. "It's not funny, Parker. I had to chuck the old bed frame, and I've been sleeping like a frat boy ever since."

I point to the mattress on the floor of my apartment, pitifully stranded on the hardwood. There'd been a suspicious creak a few nights ago—deep in the bones of the frame, growing louder until it finally cracked down the middle. As it collapsed, I went down with it, letting out a banshee scream loud enough to wake the neighbors.

Parker and I both left Silverpine on Sunday, with my flight from Portland International Airport departing in the morning and his in the afternoon. As soon as he landed in New York, five hours after I'd touched down, he was at my apartment. Since we'd agreed not to hook up under our parents' roofs, we had some lost time to make up for. I wasn't too shocked to see him at my door, and he didn't seem too startled by me jumping into his arms either. After this reunion, he came over on Wednesday, as well as Friday and Saturday. Evidently, we've had more quality time than my second-hand bed frame could endure.

"I can't say I'm surprised. Doing it on that thing sounded like riding the world's oldest rollercoaster." I don't want to agree with him, but that's exactly what it sounded like. "Do you want to stay at my hotel until you get it fixed?"

"Already on it. This is where you come in." I point to the bulky cardboard box in the corner of my studio, half-opened with wooden boards peeking out. Next-day delivery was a blessing, but I'd taken one look at the dismantled frame and decided I'd rather call Parker to help than risk a hernia.

"You want me to assemble your furniture?"

"I need an extra set of hands. I hate to admit it, but I can't do it by myself. The instruction manual insists on two people. See?" I flip open the booklet and point to the two cartoon figures with their thumbs up. "Didn't you read my text?"

"Yeah, it said, *I need help. Come to my apartment.* I thought you got trapped under your air purifier." Parker rolls up his sleeves, providing a criminally enticing view of his forearms. "It's fine. I'll help you. I'm partially responsible, anyway."

Because he's a distant relative of the Green Giant, Parker makes light work of assembling the bed frame. Aside from me handing him tools and reading the instructions aloud, he doesn't require much assistance, and he even considers sending me away when I nearly take his head off trying to pass him a board. It only takes him an hour to have the thing up and ready—half the time the manual recommends.

"Parker Tran, you are a godsend!" I sag onto the bed once my mattress has been fitted to the new frame.

He dusts off his shirt and walks over to the kitchen to pour himself a glass of water. "And you're a fool. You could've been staying in a luxury suite for free instead of sleeping on the floor."

I won't pretend to be sanctimonious—the truth is, I'd rather be at the suite. The chaise longue in the living room is softer than my bed, and the water pressure hits like it's gently power-washing all your worries away. But the St. Regis is where Parker sleeps, which means it won't bode well for me to start feeling at home.

"It wouldn't have been wise," I say to him, adding, "The staff already think I'm an escort."

"Is that why housekeeping is always giggling at me?"

I meet him at the couch, handing him a coaster while he goes over every encounter with the hotel staff in his head. Color rises to his ears, prompting a laugh out of me. Before Thanksgiving, I used to think a casual relationship meant we could only meet if sex was involved. But ever since we returned from Silverpine, it's as if that imaginary clause no longer exists. Now, being in Parker's company feels so natural—and a little too easy.

"We can hang out like this, right?" I pose the question like I'm sliding a contract across the table for his consideration.

"I don't see why not. We're friends, after all."

"Right. No, I know that. And friends hang out. So, this is fine. We're just hanging out, which is what friends do."

"You're in a loop." He flicks my forehead gently.

"I'm trying to figure out the ground rules. I think they need to be updated."

Parker sets his glass on the coaster. "It's true that this isn't the kind of *casual* I'm used to. But you and I are different. We were friends first." He rubs his chin. "And then enemies for a blip, but that's overcomplicating it. Anyway, we can definitely hang out without having sex."

"Hanging out, no sex," I repeat as I mentally revise the terms and conditions I've drafted in my head. "Because we're fully capable of being around each other and keeping our hands to ourselves."

"We're literally doing that right now," Parker says as he makes himself comfortable on the couch. "While we're on the topic, do you have plans this weekend?"

I pick up my copy of *The Survivalists* from the lower shelf of the coffee table, holding it out for him to see.

"Okay, well, is it possible for you to reschedule that?"

"What do you have in mind?"

"Do you want to come to a Nets game? I know it's not really up your alley, but they've hooked me up with courtside seats. I was going to take Reggie, but I think you and I are better friends."

He says the last sentence around an obnoxiously handsome grin, and I don't tell him I'm already convinced. I pretend to ruminate. "Courtside? I've never even been to a basketball game before. Will I get to see a celebrity?"

"It's likely, yeah. Not that I'd advise approaching them. Most of them don't want to be bothered."

"Oh, I wouldn't dream of it. Meeting a celebrity is one of my biggest fears. I'm afraid of being so starstruck that I'll come across as a bumbling, obsessed fan. Then every time I see them in a movie or TV show, I'll have to relive the embarrassment all over again."

Parker looks at me like that was exactly what he was expecting I'd say. "Before I lose you to another dramatic monologue, can I have an answer?"

"Okay, I'll go with you."

"Saturday at six, then." He gives his watch a quick look. "I've got some time before I hit the gym. Do you think we can—*you know*?"

I follow his line of sight and blanch. "Not again."

But he's already got a Switch controller in his hand, and he's booting up the console before I can say no. "One Grand Prix. I'm definitely going to beat you this time."

Parker does not, in fact, beat me in *Mario Kart*.

CHAPTER TWENTY-NINE

"Stop staring at the jumbotron. The action's right in front of you." Parker nudges me, snapping my attention back to the court. I can see the adrenaline in the air as clearly as I can spot the sweat between the athletes' brows. Every squeak of sneakers is amplified from this close. We're five minutes into the first quarter, and I've had half an hour to get used to my courtside seat, but I can't stop fussing.

What I've learned from this evening's events is that sitting courtside isn't as simple as having front-row seats to a game. When we arrived at Barclays Center, Parker guided me to the VIP entrance, which took us through the back tunnels of the arena. We were informed our tickets granted us access to the Nets' practice court, as well as the Crown Club—where no reservation is required to try a Carbone-inspired spicy rigatoni.

"Looks like you really can con a Michelin meal out of a man," Parker remarked, sitting across from me in a plush velvet chair.

The moment we settled into our premium seats, the silver-haired sharks began to circle. Older men in button-down shirts with dollar signs in their eyes swarmed over to check in on Venture deals and drop celebrity names. It had all faded into background noise, however, because I was far more fascinated by the players stopping by during warm-up. I was still trying to comprehend how the boy next door was dapping up an NBA superstar—when Parker turned around and introduced me as his *good friend*.

Once the game's in motion, the twenty-something-foot screens hanging over center court call my attention. "They don't still do kiss cams, do they? I swear to god, if it cuts to us, I'm going to sock you in the face and make a run for it."

Parker just chuckles, composed as ever. "Now, I know that's a lie. You've grown fond of my face, I can tell."

"Doesn't mean I want seventeen thousand people to see it smashed against mine."

He checks behind us to see if anyone's listening. "Right, you'd prefer to be sitting on my face in private."

My stomach does a mighty flip, and suddenly I'm very hot. I slide off my jacket and place it on the seat beside me, which has been vacant since we sat down. It's only added fuel to my anxiety. I'm antsy that some reality TV star will show up late and claim it, and I'll end up snapped in paparazzi photos next to them, immortalized on gossip forums.

Parker buys two beers from a vendor and passes one to me. "Are you following?"

My face is a snarl of focus as I watch the players run up and down the court. The Nets are playing the Toronto Raptors, and so far, they're leading by five. "I think so. But everything I know about basketball is from *Slam Dunk*, and I watched that when I was ten."

I get a rundown on the rules, and Parker gets a recap of the *Slam Dunk* ending. His phone pings once and then again in rapid succession until he finally unlocks it with a pleased laugh.

"Reggie found out I took you the game instead," he explains.

"How?"

"Live stream."

"They can see us?" I ask, looking with mortification over my shoulder.

"Glimpses here and there. You know there are cameras, right?" He taps a reply, and text bubbles flash on the screen in quick bursts. Each message makes his grin widen, and he fires back with speedy thumbs. When he finally sets his phone aside, he says, "Sorry. Venture group chat."

I dither over asking, but my curiosity gets the better of me. "Is that, like, a company-wide chat or . . ."

"Just my friends."

"And your work wife?"

"I told you; Heather's not my work wife."

"Yet you thought of her right away." I reply a little too hastily. "And she has your boat and calls you, like, all the time."

"She's got my boat because I can't leave it sitting at the marina for months without upkeep. Also, Reggie calls me just as much—does that mean I have to work-marry him too?"

"I think Reggie would probably be happy to real-marry you," I say, then steamroll right into my next question without self-restraint. "Does Heather look like she works at Venture too?"

Parker raises a quizzical brow. "What do you mean?"

My expression flattens with the silent energy of *you're kidding right?* "Here at super sexy Venture, we pair your super sexy athlete with our super sexy staff."

"Good one. We should get you to write campaign slogans." He shakes his head. "I mean, the obvious answer is she's good-looking. But she's not my type, and I'm pretty sure I'm not hers."

"Can I see?"

He doesn't question my motives and takes out his phone again. When he hands it to me, an Instagram page is already on the screen. It occurs to me that a girl could text him right now, and I wouldn't be able to avoid seeing it. The thought doesn't persist, though, because I'm immediately distracted by photos of a gorgeous, tanned blonde idling on the beach and sprawled across the hood of an Aston Martin. As I swipe through bikini photos, my jaw drops open at the most amazing pair of knockers I've ever seen.

"*That's* not your type?" I sputter. "Even with the—" I make the universal sign for gargantuan breasts with both hands.

His lips press into a flat line. "My type doesn't correlate with the size of a woman's chest."

I dismiss him with a laugh. "I'm sorry, but you, as a straight man, cannot expect me to believe that."

"Dani, we're not all hardwired to prefer one type of woman. Breasts come in different sizes, so naturally we have preferences too. You have certain traits you like in men, don't you?"

Tall, with arms that look like they can throw seventy yards on the fly. But that's a can of worms I'd rather not open. I glance down at my own chest, coming in at an underwhelming B cup.

"So, what's your preference?"

In what feels like the longest three seconds of my life, Parker's eyes sweep over me, quite literally sizing me up. I chew my lip, skin flushing hot again.

"Some guys prefer big boobs, and that's great. I mean, *all* boobs are fantastic—you can never go wrong. But I like when they sort of . . . fit perfectly in my hands?" As if he's imparting age-old wisdom to me, his delivery is measured and calm. He makes the motion of holding something delicate. "I can't explain the feeling, but it's nice. Snug. Like if dreams were a pillow, cupped in the palm of my hand. It's almost like . . . like . . ."

"Stop. I don't want to hear it." I stuff the phone back into his pocket. So, Parker likes small boobs. I'm going to file this piece of information away into a folder called *Facts I Never Wanted to Learn About the Boy Next Door.*

"Anyway, I like your boobs."

"I don't want to talk to you about boobs anymore."

A time-out is called by the Raptors, and another group of men rallies around Parker—some introducing themselves, others chatting like old pals. Hands are shaken. New contacts saved to phones. This group is younger than the last, more relaxed in their polo shirts. One of them approaches me to ask if I'm enjoying the game.

"This is my good friend, Dani," Parker tells him. It isn't until his visitors disperse that he takes his seat again. "That was the Nets' GM."

"You know the general manager personally?" My eyes widen. "Are you friends with Jay-Z too?"

A glammed-up woman with silky brown hair approaches, and at first, I think she's here for Parker too, but she halts at the seat next to mine. Lifting her sunglasses, she stares down puzzledly.

I grab my jacket in a rush. "Sorry!"

"No worries, love." Her face relaxes as she sits down. "I really should've prepared for the traffic. I'm from London, and we live in permanent congestion over there."

"Oh, wow, you came from London! You must really love basketball. Or the Brooklyn Nets."

She laughs, faint lines appearing at the edges of her eyes. Everything from her smile to her fur vest and thigh-high boots is striking. I wonder if I'm sitting next to someone from *The Real Housewives*.

"Sadly, no. I'm in town for business, and a friend from *Vogue* gifted me a ticket. To be honest, I feel like an impostor being seated this close. I hope you can bear with me for tonight. I take it you two are big fans?"

"Ho, boy, you couldn't keep us away." I don't know what I'm saying, let alone why, but I know I feel intimidated. "We're all about the sports here. Huge fans of the sports."

"Stop saying the word like it's trademarked," Parker mumbles into my ear.

"Shut up," I hiss back with a slap to his leg. Swiveling toward the woman, I drop the ruse. "I'm sorry. I'm an impostor too. Not this guy, though—he practically gets paid to be at games. I'm trying not to feel out of place, but to be honest, the only sport I'm familiar with is football—oh, American football, that is! I don't know as much about soccer."

She's smiling sympathetically so I'm certain she thinks I'm an idiot. But she offers a hand. "Estelle Pearson. I'm chuffed to meet a fellow impostor."

"Dani Tsai," I say, shaking her hand.

"Parker Tran," he says, introducing himself. "And don't listen to her, I'm not getting paid to be here."

"Dani Tsai . . . I think I know that name." Estelle fetches her phone from her designer purse. "Any chance you've written for *Adagio*?"

I gape at her. "You know who I am?"

"I've been reading *Adagio* for years now. I'm an editor for *Dénouement*, a magazine in the UK. We're also a quarterly publication."

"I've read your magazine!" Lindsay almost always has a copy of *Dénouement* on her desk, and I've borrowed an issue here and there. With its emphasis on original artwork and world-renowned experts backing its articles, it's produced some of the most insightful long-form journalism I've had the pleasure of reading. It's where I first learned about the perils of breathing unfiltered air in a Gilbert-less home.

Estelle beams and drapes her long hair to one side. "I started reading your magazine as a means of scoping out the competition, but I've come to properly enjoy it. And your pieces really stood out to me! I loved the one you did on libraries around Europe. Did you really take all those photos yourself?"

"I did!" I sit up straight, hands wrapped around my beer, excitement stirring. "I had a plan to visit the most iconic libraries while I was there. My only regret is that I didn't make enough time in Germany to see the Wiblingen Abbey library. That and the Tianyi Pavilion in China are my holy grails as far as libraries go."

"Wiblingen Abbey is stunning! An absolute masterpiece of the Baroque. You'll fall in love with the frescoes." The crowd erupts into cheers after a three-pointer, and Estelle waits for the applause to die down. "I thought you had such a whimsical approach to your journalism, but when I Googled you, there weren't many results. I couldn't find a website or even an X account."

"I'm not actually a journalist. I'm a copy editor," I say sheepishly. "But I do some freelance writing, mostly for *Adagio*."

"Well, I'd love to read more of your work."

Estelle and I chat through the second quarter, and I tell her all about my trip to London—how much I loved taking the Tube, visiting my favorite galleries in Shoreditch, and walking into an unassuming pub only to join the drunk locals in belting out "Sweet Caroline" by the end of the night.

"I loved Sunday roast too," I prattle on. "I stayed an extra weekend just so I could have it again."

She giggles. "You know you can have a roast any day of the week, right?"

"I know, but there's something cathartic about it being a Sunday-only thing." As I finish off my beer, a hand swoops down to take the empty cup from me.

"Want another one?" Parker asks, standing up from his seat.

"Sure," I respond. "Where are you going?"

"It's halftime. I'm going to head back to the lounge."

My eyes track him as he maneuvers easily through the crowd, exchanging words with players, until he disappears into one of the tunnels.

Estelle leans over and says, with a note of mischief, "I think he's sulking because I've stolen his girlfriend all night."

"We're just friends," I clarify with a polite smile.

"Really?" She looks surprised but doesn't press.

I remember passing by The Pantry earlier—a literal candy room in the VIP section—and ask Estelle if she'd like to secure snacks with me. We return to the court with our hands full of popcorn and sweets just in time for the game to resume. I split a Kit Kat bar with Parker as he goes over the rules of fouls with me. When the game goes into overtime, Estelle lets me know she has to leave for an event on the Upper East Side.

"Dani, you've been lovely. I hope we can stay in touch. What are your socials?"

"Oh, um . . ."

"She has an Instagram." Parker nudges me, and when Estelle passes her phone, I type my username into the search bar.

"Big night for you." He shoots me a quick look once she's gone. "You know there was a basketball game going on, right?"

"I'm paying attention now, I promise." I offer him a smile and a Twizzler. "I'm having a good time, Parker. Thanks for inviting me."

"As long as you're having fun," he says warmly and takes the candy from me. As the players round up under the basket for a free throw, Parker checks his phone again.

"How's the Rangers campaign coming along?" I ask.

"The kickoff was pretty solid. We got the new app running, and I'm hearing good feedback on the player spotlights we've been doing on socials. I'm hoping we'll get the fan zones up at Madison Square Garden soon; it'd be good to launch some giveaways."

I chew my popcorn thoughtfully. "And you oversee all of this?"

"More or less. I'm liking that it's a lot more hands-on this time," he says. "I was on a campaign for the Warriors last season, and we spent most of it buttering up the stakeholders. Even when Venture sent us to Chase Center, we were in the hospitality suites most of the time, so we couldn't enjoy games like this."

The references to *us* and *we* stand out to me like beacons in a stormy ocean, because I remember Parker talking about this campaign before. In his Venture office, with Reggie and Isaac present, he'd said it was a big project that required a lot of teamwork between him and . . . Heather.

I hate that my memory is a perdurable vault for all things Parker Tran.

I want to focus on the rest of the game, but my efforts are futile. Parker is endlessly amused by what's going on in his phone, and when I sneak a peek, I see the text bombs are indeed from the super sexy Venture group chat. Someone's sent a couple photos of a boat in a marina. The last thing I see before forcing myself to look away is a selfie of a blonde in sunglasses.

CHAPTER THIRTY

Ten years ago

Because Cô tells the story at every single one of Parker's games, I can recite it from memory: It was his sixth birthday, a year before I moved to Silverpine. His uncle gifted him a football and put on a recording of the 1989 Super Bowl, the one with Joe Montana's game-winning touchdown pass to John Taylor. Parker went to the park after and asked some of the older kids to practice throwing with him. Once he was old enough, he begged his parents to sign him up for youth football camps, and the rest is history.

It's a Friday night, and although the varsity season is long over, Parker is playing an alumni charity match. The crowd turnout for a friendly scrimmage is incredible: The bleachers are packed with students, faculty, and folks from all over town, who arrived in droves to watch a Division I recruited quarterback play his last home game. Our school has pulled out all the stops, with the band and a cheer squad to mark the team's unofficial send-off.

A few heads in the cheer section turn my way, exchanging whispers. In our eye-catching hues of red and white, I can tell that we stand out. The four of us—Cô, Chú, Nathan, and me—are wearing Parker's old Griffins jerseys. It was Nathan's idea for each of us to wear one from Parker's four years on varsity. His freshman jersey—the smallest of the set—nearly reaches my knees. Parker has always made me feel pocket-sized, but I don't recall him being this big at fourteen. When I breathe in, I recognize the familiar scent of the Costco detergent Cô buys in bulk, along with a faint trace of body spray.

Nathan gestures to the two black stripes under my eyes. "Nice touch."

"Have I ever been one to half-ass anything?"

"Don't say *ass*, Dani," Cô chides.

To no one's surprise, Parker is a burst of unmatched energy on the field. He launches passes with pinpoint accuracy, making easy targets of his receivers. Every time he puts the ball in the air, it's an unstoppable missile. By the end of the first half, he has three touchdown passes and not a single interception. I think everyone has the sense that this is no ordinary game: There's something magical about him tonight, and he has all of us under his spell.

The floodlights turn on in the second half, illuminating the field as Parker scores his own rushing touchdown—faster on his feet than I've ever seen him. Cô is jumping up and down with a cheer that rivals the freshman girls screaming in the front bleachers. I hear the click of a camera and notice that the local press has shown up.

By the fourth quarter, the Griffins are up 32 to 15. The center snaps the ball to Parker, and the tight end explodes down the field. Parker launches a stunning forty-yard laser beam, and it's caught effortlessly in the end zone. As the clock ticks down to the final seconds, the team is already celebrating its victory. A cheerleader jumps into Parker's arms, and the stands are a frenzy of whoops and applause. Every eye is on him. Spectators erupt with joy, fired up as if they'd come off the goal line themselves. I wonder how it feels to have everyone you know rooting for you.

I love watching Parker play football. Something about him lights up from within; he's mesmerizing, and I can't get enough. I watch as he and his teammates lift the Gatorade cooler to dump over the coach's head, and a laugh bubbles out of me. I know one thing for certain: Parker Tran belongs on the field. Friday nights are indisputably his. I think of all the games I'll miss once I leave, and I have this tiny, selfish desire for tonight to last forever.

The players return to the locker room as a crowd assembles around Parker's family, congratulating them with handshakes and hugs. I have an inkling this will take a while, so I tell them goodnight and descend the bleachers. Parker and I have our own plans for tonight—he intentionally withheld the details from me, but I'd been instructed to wait for him in the parking lot following the game.

No sooner have I sat on the curb than I see it: tall and wide, with mud-hungry tires and a hardtop that looks like armor. The jet-black Jeep Wrangler rumbles into the parking lot, rolling to a stop in front of me.

"No way," I gasp as Parker steps out.

He wears his usual postgame attire of jeans and his letterman's jacket. That smile—the one that reaches his eyes—I've only seen a handful of times.

"My parents surprised me with a little recruitment gift."

"*Little*?" My mouth falls open as I circle the vehicle. "Can I touch it?"

"You can," he laughs, and I take my time opening doors, running my hand along upholstery. I don't climb in just yet—this moment feels too big to rush. "Why didn't I see it in the driveway?"

"I drove straight here from the dealership."

"Wait, does that mean—" A grin tugs at the corners of my mouth. "Is that why you told me to meet you here? Am I the first one to get a ride?"

"Wouldn't make sense if it were anyone else."

My heart swells with gratitude. Sometimes I have this silly fear that Parker will outgrow me. Before high school, we used to see each other every day. The longest time we'd spent apart was the three weeks his family spent in Vietnam. But when we entered Green Valley as freshmen, something shifted. Parker found his stride early; people in a small town have a way of sniffing out someone destined to be A Big Deal. He's been popular since day one. I had a modest group of friends from book club whom I sat with during lunch, but we didn't see each other much after school or on weekends. By junior year, Parker was fully focused on recruitment: meeting coaches, attending showcase events, and traveling to camps.

On a smaller scale, I was preparing for my big move to New York, building up my college applications with AP classes and extracurriculars. Every once in a while, I'd picture our futures splitting off in such different directions, I'd wonder how we'd ever find our way back to each other.

Then Parker does something like this and reminds me that even if our paths diverge, he's still saved a spot marked *Dani*. I wipe my hand under my nose, trying to dial back my emotions.

He makes a surprised sound. "Are you going to cry?"

"No. Shut up," I scoff, allowing myself one more lap of the car before meeting Parker where I started. He's got his eyes trained on me, hands in his pockets.

"I saw you in the bleachers," he says. "Wearing that."

"It was Nathan's idea."

He gestures to the number 11 in large, white print. "It looks good on you."

I don't know if it's the compliment or Parker pointing to my chest, but my cheeks are warm, and I imagine just as red as his ears have turned. When his eyes fall to mine, they catch the shine of the floodlights in the distance, and I forget whatever response I'd planned to say.

I only have to be a mute tomato for a second longer, because a pair of boys are gravitating toward the Jeep, whistling loudly. "Damn, Parker! Nice ride."

"Watch your sweaty hands," he chides. "Mike, I know you don't shower after games."

"Shit, all I got was my dad's old Civic."

"Hey, let me test drive it. Just once around the lot."

Parker hovers near his car, trying to form a protective barrier against his grubby teammates. The shorter of the boys—a running back on the team—drifts toward me. "Dani, right?"

I blink at him. "You know my name?"

"Of course. You were in my World History class," he says. "Do you know my name?"

"Caleb Brennan." I didn't need to search my brain too long for it. "You did a presentation on the Defenestrations of Prague. I thought it was hilarious that people were thrown out of windows so often they had to come up with a term for it."

"Right? That makes me feel better. Mr. O'Connell gave me a D because apparently it didn't count as an actual historical conflict," he mutters bitterly. "By the way, why didn't you come to Bend with us?"

A few of the seniors on the football team drove to Bend for a weekend. Someone's older brother helped them rent a cabin, and someone else's cousin supplied the beer. That's the story

Parker told me, anyway. He didn't get into the particulars after he returned.

"Oh, um, I was busy." What was I doing that weekend? Either I was working on my college essays or adding hours to my *Animal Crossing* save file.

"I thought you'd be there, since you and Parker are—" He stops, and I know what's coming.

"We're best friends," I insert before he can speculate.

He merely nods, digesting this information. "Okay, that makes sense. Since Amelia came."

After that weekend away, a rumor spread that Amelia Reyes and her girlfriends had driven down to Bend to join them at the cabin. Word in the hallways was that there were six boys, six girls, and only five bedrooms to split. Again, I didn't have the lowdown.

"I thought he was going to invite you, but she showed up instead," Caleb says. "I didn't even know they were seeing each other."

My fingers curl at my sides, the jersey bunching up beneath my grip. I pause, trying to discern if it's another rumor or if Caleb's just told me a bad joke, until I realize he's posed the sentence as a question and is looking to me for confirmation.

"I didn't know either," I admit.

What I do know is that sometimes Parker goes to parties and doesn't come home until the next day. Every now and then, a girl will show up at his door asking if he wants to catch a movie. Most of what I hear is through the rumor mill—which makes it easy to dismiss—and never from the actual source. Parker doesn't make a point of telling me things like who he has a crush on, and I've never asked.

Until now, I didn't want to know.

I turn to Caleb. "Does Parker have a girlfriend?"

"Shouldn't you know that?" he asks, and I hear the accusation clearly: *What kind of best friends don't talk about this stuff?* I stare down at my sneakers, where I've discovered the single most captivating grass stain.

Before the agonizing silence can go on too long, Mike lets out an undignified yelp as Parker grabs him by the leg. They wrestle by the car, and Caleb can't resist jumping into the action.

"You pulling up to Kyle's party?" he asks Parker as he captures Mike in a headlock.

"After I take Dani home."

"You should come too." Caleb winks at me. "If we're lucky, maybe someone will get drunk enough to be defenestrated."

Once we're alone in the lot again, Parker opens the passenger door for me. I study the gap from the ground to the Jeep, unsure if the car's too big or I'm too small. Either way, this isn't going to be a graceful climb. "Why is it so high off the ground?"

"It's pre-lifted."

"What does that mean?"

"It means there's bigger tires and more ground clearance for off-roading."

"And how often do you, a teenage boy from suburbia, go off-roading?"

Parker's face is telling me to shut up. "Just use the step to get in. And watch your head."

"I'm wearing a skirt under this. Can you look away?"

He silently obeys, closing the door after me and making his own effortless entry into the driver's seat. The engine roars to life as we pull out of the lot. Parker turns the radio on and fiddles with the air conditioning controls, checking with me if it's too cold. I don't mention my conversation with Caleb, opting for silence while Parker recaps his plays from the game. I only understand half of it, but I listen intently like he's telling the most riveting story.

"You were on fire tonight," I say. "I feel so lucky whenever I get to watch you play."

The Jeep pulls up to the curb between my house and his. He kills the engine and leans back in his seat, getting comfortable and signaling to me that I don't have to go yet. I watch him reach for the sleeve of my—his—jersey, and he gives it a gentle tug. "You can keep this if you want."

"I can't. What am I going to do with it? Take it to New York?"

"As long as you don't take it to bed." He cringes, and I slap his arm. "Wait, look at me. You didn't actually put eye black on your face, did you?"

Parker leans forward. He's so close I can smell his shampoo.

"Of course not. It's eyeshadow. Look." I rub one of the stripes and show him the smudge on my fingers.

And that's when it happens. The next few seconds proceed in slow motion as he reaches over and touches my face. I sit there, still as a stone carving, but my heartbeat is loud, like thunder in my bones. He brushes his thumb against the stripe under my eye, and his touch on my skin is hot. Or maybe it's me who's gone ablaze.

"Huh. It is eyeshadow."

"That's what I said," I mumble back.

If it were anyone else, I might dare to think of this as an intimate moment. But this is Parker. And Parker isn't supposed to make my heart feel like it's about to give out.

Hold on. If that's true, then why is my pulse racing faster and faster? This is a lot like one of those scenes in Mom's romance movies. This is when she'd grip my shoulder and gush that something magical was about to happen.

Is he going to kiss me?

I've never been kissed before.

If he kisses me, it might not be so bad.

I might even kiss him back.

But then I blink, and he withdraws his hand, finding his phone instead. He reads a text off the screen. My fingertips land on my cheek, the skin once feverishly warm now chilly and exposed.

"What did Caleb say before he left?" He startles me back to reality. "*Defriendnistrate*?"

"Defenestrate. It means to throw someone out a window." I'm self-conscious when he doesn't laugh, and so I shrug, "It was funny to us."

"Since when do you and Caleb have inside jokes?"

"Since when have you been dating Amelia Reyes?" I blurt out.

In another slow, torturous moment, Parker looks to me with a thousand burning questions in his eyes. The world around us seems to stall—the air too heavy, the wind outside at rest—until he finally speaks up.

"Where would I find the time to date anyone between training and camps?" he says, confounded. "If I'm not in Eugene to see my coaches, I'm always with you."

Something that feels a lot like relief washes over me. "Caleb mentioned your trip to Bend. There were all those rumors, you know, about Amelia and her friends staying with you guys."

He rubs the back of his neck. "Well, they did stay over."

The drop in his voice is all it takes for me to put two and two together. "Did she sleep in your room?"

I might've missed his nod if I wasn't so locked in. "So, the rumors are true? Did you two—"

"No."

"You slept in the same bed and *nothing* happened?"

"We made out." He swallows. "And we fooled around a bit. But not, like, all the way."

"Fooled around how?"

Parker can't sit still; he's shifting in his seat and tapping on the steering wheel. "Do we really have to talk about this?"

"Why do you feel like you can't tell me these things?" It starts as a flicker, then a spark goes off inside, demanding that I dig and prod at this sore spot until it becomes an open wound. Maybe it's defensiveness or frustration at how unfair this feels. Maybe I just want him to know I'm upset. "I'm your best friend. If you can't even tell me that you fooled around with a girl, what else are you going to keep from me? What about when you lose your virginity?"

He draws a deep breath as he drapes one arm over the steering wheel. His mouth is a hard line, and he's insistent on looking anywhere but my face.

"Oh." It lands like a deep cut. The pain of the self-inflicted blow makes my voice shake when I ask, "How did it happen?"

"It wasn't Amelia," he clarifies. "I was at a party, and I'd had a few beers. Honestly, I don't remember much. She was in the year ahead of us, so she's already graduated now, and I never see her anymore—"

"Okay," I cut him off, turning to the window. Maybe I don't need to know after all.

"Dani, if it was you—" he says, barely above a whisper. "Would you tell me?"

"I—" I can't answer that, because I've never been in a situation where it even seemed possible. "I don't know."

"Yeah. That's what I thought."

Of course we wouldn't be able to run from it forever. But I

always thought it'd happen when we were in college, where I wouldn't have to watch someone else become his new favorite person.

It makes me laugh. I can't help it. Right now, there's no bigger joke than our own naïveté. "This is so weird. We've known each other our whole lives, but I'm just now realizing that outside of the bubble of our houses, I don't actually *know* you. The rest of your life—when you're at parties, or from what I hear through rumors—it's like a different you."

"I wish you wouldn't pay attention to the rumors. Most of it isn't even true. People here are so bored with their lives, they have to make up shit to keep themselves entertained."

"Some of it is true," I counter.

"Dani." He takes hold of my wrist, urging me to look at him. "I didn't keep it from you intentionally. I just—I wasn't sure how to bring it up. I'm sorry, okay?"

I bite down on my lip to quell the squeeze of my throat. It makes it hard for me to speak—not that I know what I'm supposed to say to any of this. I shake myself free from him and make a grab for the door handle. "You should get to your party."

"Do you want to come?" he asks, sounding a tiny bit hopeful.

"No, I'm good." I hop out of the car, landing on the pavement with a dull thump. "I'll return your jersey tomorrow."

CHAPTER THIRTY-ONE

Parker's suite at the St. Regis has a bathtub and separate standing shower. On paper, this makes it the ideal setup for two people, unless they both have an aversion to baths. Parker prefers showers because they're quick and efficient. I still have to commute from Union Square in the middle of December, so my first impulse upon arriving at the suite is to duck into a hot shower. Unluckily for me, Parker is just getting back from the gym on a particularly chilly evening, and he stops me on the way to the bathroom.

"Can I go first? You take twice as long."

"I'm about to freeze my toes off," I protest.

"You'll be fine. I'll turn the heat up."

"Surely you can wait half an hour."

"Hmm." He crosses his arms. Something flickers behind his eyes as he glances down at me. "Want to shower together?"

I was afraid it might be awkward, but there's little time to feel self-conscious when being naked in close proximity allows instinct to take over. Parker's hands are exactly the warmth I need as he pins me against the cool porcelain wall. He kisses me, and I open my mouth, taking in water at the same time that I taste his tongue. There are few things in this world that taste better than Parker Tran.

I've had him fold me in every direction by now, but it takes a second to acclimate when he turns me around, bending me at the waist. The cascade of water feels like soft sighs on my back, and I don't have to guess what's next as he spreads my legs from behind. I hear the sound of foil tearing and look down to see the condom wrapper float over the drain. I'm both impressed and embarrassed that he had the foresight to bring a condom into the shower. He'd already expected we'd end up this way, with me bent over in anticipation for him.

My teeth clench, and I let out a sharp gasp as he slides into me. It's so familiar to me now, and yet it still sends a bolt through my system. His grip tightens on my hips, and my hand intuitively wraps around the shower knob for balance. Every muscle in my body is quick to surrender to him, and my mind ascends even faster into the bliss of it all—water at the perfect temperature, pressure like a gentle massage, and the sensation of him moving inside me, deep and intense.

He lifts my leg skillfully, and when my back arches, it lets him hit a spot that sends me into dizzying ecstasy. He moves faster, over and over, until my knees nearly buckle, and a needy moan spills over my lips.

"Come for me," he demands, and I do exactly that. It seems to push him over the edge too, and I can tell he's close when he slumps over me. He lets out a sharp groan, low in his throat, like it's dragged his soul out with it. His breath comes down hot on my skin, but crawls over me like a cold rush. I don't think I'll ever get used to hearing that sound. A few more thrusts, and Parker slips himself out of me, sliding the condom off and finishing on the slick marbled floor.

Before we can deplete the hotel's hot water supply, we leave the shower—now a steam chamber—an hour later. I'm light-headed and searching for water in the minibar when both our phones buzz with a message alert.

"Reginald Cruz's New Year's Eve Bash," I read off the screen in disbelief. The conversation at Parker's office feels like so long ago, I was sure Reggie would've forgotten. "Are you going?"

Parker looks up from his phone, displaying the same event page. "Are *you* going?"

He waits for my answer as I take a long chug of water, considering my options. I could stay in with Marisa and Shay, bingeing *Abbott Elementary* until someone says, *Oh, look, fireworks*, and we mumble, *Happy New Year* before refilling our wine. We've had the same routine the last two years, and I haven't had any reason to shake things up.

Or, I could spend New Year's Eve with Parker before he returns to San Francisco—whenever that is. The timeline he gave me was three months from October, which means we're toeing the finish line now. But he still hasn't booked his flight or indicated when Venture wants him back home. I half expect him to spring the news on me one day, as he has a habit of doing.

"I'm going to go," I say. "Might be fun."

He seems surprised, but only for a moment. Then he taps the screen and updates his status to *Attending*.

❧

"This was a mistake."

I throw cautious glances at the extravaganza before me, uncertain whether the smoke in the air is from a fog machine or if the venue's actually on fire. I can picture the space as a charming, exposed-brick loft in the daytime, but tonight, it's transformed into yet another raging nightclub in Lower Manhattan. Streaks of neon flash in my eyes, and I can feel the bass of a treacherously loud EDM track thudding beneath my breastbone. There are too many people in New York. And why does it feel like they've all gathered here? Every time the crowd erupts in whoops and cheers, I ask Parker what's happening, and he tells me another pro athlete has just walked in.

Tucked away in our small corner booth, I try to make myself inconspicuous—a near impossible feat when Parker Tran is chaperoning you, and everyone wants to rub elbows with the golden boy. "What's the game plan for tonight?"

Parker takes a sip of his whiskey ginger. "Well, I know better than to ask you to dance, and you're avoiding the bar in case someone traps you in conversation. So, my guess is we're not leaving this booth tonight."

"You don't have to stay with me," I proffer. "I'm basically deadweight to you."

Sitting across from me in a designer overshirt, his bangs swept back in that patented trying-without-actually-trying style, he looks like he's exactly where he belongs.

"Strength in numbers. This is your first Reggie Cruz party, and I'd feel bad leaving you on your own."

My phone stirs on the table suddenly, and I snap it up in a flash. A LINE notification appears on the screen from my only contact on the app.

"Is that Estelle?"

I shake my head as I open the message. Mom's New Year's greeting is written in Chinese, a generic message for good health and prosperity. I wonder how many of her relatives she's copied and pasted the very same wishes to. I type a quick reply in English and send it off without too much thought.

Estelle and I have kept in touch since the Nets game. She asked for my portfolio the other week, which has tied me up in a knot of tension—the good kind. I know I shouldn't expect a response so soon—last I heard, she was hopping from Vienna to Lisbon—but every buzz of my phone has me jumping in anticipation.

"She'll get back to you after the holidays," Parker reassures me. "Maybe a drink will help you relax. What do you want?"

"Can I get a hose hooked up to their vodka supply?"

"I'll get you a gin and tonic." He leaves before I can nag him for something stronger. If there's any hope of making it through the night, let alone vacating this booth, I'm going to require more punch to my warm-up.

Like magic, a bottle of Belvedere lands with a clunk in front of me. I look to the ceiling. What the fuck, universe? But there's a hand around the bottle's neck, and it doesn't belong to some phantom interference. It's Reggie's.

"Parker's my boy, so it pains me to see him saddled to a corner booth at my New Year's party." He points squarely at me. "If that means making you drink until you're fun, then so be it."

"Look at that, I'm convinced." I lick my lips as he twists the cap off the bottle. "This is why they pay you the big bucks at Venture."

"That's a good sacrificial lamb." He rotates a chair before plonking down, legs on either side, because of course he sits like an edgy cartoon character. "So, what's your deal? You listen to NPR? Still read a physical newspaper?"

"I—Yes, but only because I work in print media—"

"I'm just trying to gauge your vibe." He lines up a row of shot glasses on the table. "Still weird that Parker brought a date."

"Um, I'm not his date."

"Don't drink with him," Parker cautions as he returns, handing me a gin and tonic. "Reggie, whatever you want from her, the answer is *no*."

"I'm hurt, dude. Did you forget our code? Courtside tickets are for bros, not—"

"*Reggie*," he says again, his tone a little sharper. "You made up that code yourself. Dani is my oldest friend; of course I'm going to take her to games."

"*Friend*. Sure." With a tight, polite smile, Reggie turns back to me. "Dani, how was your Christmas?"

"Um, it was fine. Parker came over to hijack my PS5 and played *2K* all afternoon. Then we watched *Moonstruck* because I watch it every Christmas. We couldn't agree on takeout, and neither of us wanted to cook, so we made hot pot with scraps from my fridge, and—"

I stop short, shifting to glance at Parker, who's also gone mum. These days, he's been seeping into my daily life, little by little. We've been seeing more of each other—less for sex and more to spend time together, doing everything and nothing in between. You could call it our new normal, but I know how it all sounds to Reggie. I think Parker does too.

Sure enough, Reggie's smirk is one of vindication—like I've just handed him the incriminating evidence he needed to rest his case. Without a word, he pours the Belvedere into two shot glasses and slides them to me and Parker.

"Don't drink with him." The warning comes from a second towering presence. Silhouetted by the glow of LEDs, the face is unrecognizable until Isaac Mehta is standing right next to our booth. "Parker, have you greeted our guest of honor yet?"

A tall blonde in a slip dress practically glides toward us, and I nearly choke on an ice cube. I know *this* face too. My familiarity is a byproduct of too much Instagram stalking—scrolling through beach selfies and Aston Martin-bikini photoshoots—which is exactly why I can't admit I recognize her.

Suddenly, I miss when every face in the room was a stranger to me. This is *a lot* of Venture for one table.

CHAPTER THIRTY-TWO

"Heather," Parker stands up, and she pulls him into a tight hug. "I didn't know you were in New York."

"I missed you so much I had to fly over!" She grins at him, a megawatt smile that could probably power this loft. I can't believe this stunning bombshell isn't Parker's type. If the stares from all the men around us are any indication, I think Heather might be *everyone's* type.

"It's good to see you again," Isaac says to me, alerting Heather to my presence. Her gaze flits over me, and I instinctively draw into myself.

"Is this . . . ?" She trails off, giving Parker a pointed look. He clears his throat but doesn't answer.

"Dani Tsai," Isaac answers for him. "Dani, this is Heather from Venture San Francisco."

"*Dani Tsai,*" she echoes, but it doesn't sound like an acknowledgment. The venue is dark but not dark enough, and I see her nudge Parker in the side. He elbows her back.

"Sit. Drink," Reggie orders, pulling up an extra chair. Isaac slides into the booth on my left while Parker slides in on my right. Heather takes the seat next to him.

"You look great," Isaac says, eyes falling to my exposed lap. I have exactly two party-appropriate outfits, and between the bedazzled two-piece Savannah once talked me into buying and the red minidress with the cut-out waist, I chose the one that didn't turn me into a disco ball—even if it means tugging at the hemline all night.

"Are you cold?" Parker hovers. He looks at my bare legs, too, then over at Isaac. "I can get my jacket for you."

"I'm okay," I tell him.

"Isaac, how do you know Dani?" Heather asks.

"We met at a Monosphere event. And since Dani knows I'm a big fan of the paranormal, she just had to ghost me."

I wince. "I was supposed to get back to you."

He waves a hand. "Take a shot with me, and we'll call it even."

Reggie wastes no time filling three more glasses with vodka. "Why don't we give Heather a warm New York welcome?"

"No, thank you." Heather lifts the shot glass and sets it back down in front of him.

"She doesn't drink," Parker explains, and Reggie throws up his hands in defeat.

"Juice cleanse."

"You've been on a juice cleanse since I met you." Parker laughs, and Heather sticks her tongue out at him before breaking into her own giggle, and now the two are in their own world.

I finish off my gin and tonic in one fell swoop. Of course Heather doesn't drink. Unlike me, she doesn't require liquid courage. Why am I not surprised that Parker's work wife is perfect in every conceivable way?

"Dani, I hear you and Parker are *good friends*," Heather remarks.

What is it about hearing the word *friends* that is particularly grating tonight? Even at the Nets game, that's how Parker introduced me to everyone. It makes me wonder if he's ever mentioned me to anyone without that classification.

"We were neighbors back in our hometown."

"Acquaintances who grew up together," Isaac says wryly, and Parker lifts a brow at him.

I try to sound flippant. Unbothered. "Parker says you've been looking after his boat."

"Oh, he's been such a sweetheart, lending it to me all this time," she gushes, squeezing his shoulder. "Most guys get so uptight about these things, but not him. Just ask, and he'll let you take his Aston Martin for a weekend to Lake Tahoe, no questions asked."

"That's your car?" I gape at Parker, then double down. "You drive a convertible?"

"Before you judge me," he says, giving me an all-knowing look, "being in a profession with my kind of clientele means I have to drive cars they want to talk about."

"I think I prefer the Jeep," I mumble back.

Isaac drapes his arm along the back of the booth. "Are you into cars, Dani?"

"She isn't," Parker cuts in. "Dani would rather take the subway than sit in traffic."

"That's what I thought until I got the Porsche. Man, those German engines are so *clean*."

"Oh, boo." Reggie blows a raspberry. "I'm so over driving in the city. You all look like morons sitting in gridlock. This is why we have a traffic problem."

"Please, Reginald, get off your high horse. You fly BLADE to the Hamptons." Heather purses her lips. "And I don't know how you can afford it, so either it's Daddy's money, or you've got a sugar mama."

The booth bursts into laughter as Reggie flips them off. I try to find the humor myself, but I can't fake a laugh without looking painfully out of place. Just then, Heather leans in to whisper something to Parker. Her eyes meet mine, but I look away.

"When are you taking this guy back to San Francisco?" Isaac tilts his head at the pair.

"That depends on if he ever wants to leave New York."

"The Rangers campaign is still going on," Parker says.

"Did they ask you to stay for the whole season?"

"Well, no. Reggie is taking over starting All-Star Weekend."

I look at him. "When is that?"

"Next month," he answers. Our eyes lock, and I feel the silent thread stretch between us—a countdown I hadn't realized had already started.

"I don't have to leave right away," he adds, with reassurance in his voice. "Venture hasn't assigned me to anything back home yet."

My insides clench with familiar dread. Dropping my volume, I say to him, "I feel like we should've talked about this."

"It'll be fine."

"Will it?"

"Yes, Dani. It will." And just like that he's back to breezy, unaffected Parker. He reaches for the bottle. "Another round?"

"It's the Venture squad! Aww, you guys are so cute!"

A petite woman in a satin cami dress swoops in between Parker and Heather, forcing herself into the booth. She's wearing those New Year's glasses where the frame forms the shape of the year. I really wish they'd stop trying to make every number work, because I can't locate her eyes.

"Hey, Min," Isaac greets her first. "Thought you'd be back in Singapore by now."

"Are you kidding? I'm booked here for the next six months. Going viral on TikTok was the best thing to happen to my modeling career." She helps herself to a shot and loops an arm with Parker's. "Happy New Year, handsome."

Then she removes her glasses, revealing dramatic white eyeliner and a splatter of rhinestones. As she flutters her long lashes, the dread inside me takes another form—something heavy and cold, like a stone dropped into water. A sudden awareness creeps up my spine.

I've seen her before: at the St. Regis, the night of the Monosphere event.

She had the key card to Parker's suite.

The music that was ear-splitting moments ago fades out, the timing so precise it almost feels like a kick in the shin. I hear her clear as day as she whispers in his ear, "You're still staying at the St. Regis, right?"

Next to me, Parker goes tense, shifting in his seat. He slips his arm out of Min's grasp just as Heather's brows shoot skyward, and for a split second, her eyes flick to me again.

"Damn, Parker," Reggie whistles. "In front of Dani is just cold."

"I'm confused." Isaac points between Parker and me. "Aren't you two seeing each other?"

Min looks at me like she's just realized I've been here the whole time. She straightens up, horror registering on her face.

"What exactly *is* your relationship?" Heather implores, crossing her arms.

The table waits for Parker to say something, each second ticking by as if in slow motion. He's searching my eyes like he'll find the answer there, but all I can do is blink back my uncertainty.

We were best friends once. There was a time when I couldn't imagine my life without you. Then you disappeared. But now you're back, and we're figuring out how to be friends again. But also, we're fucking.

The longer I wait for his response, the tighter my chest gets. It's like my heart is shrinking to make room for the ache.

Deciding that I can put us both out of our misery, I rally my nerves long enough to say what he won't. "We're friends."

Min breathes a sigh of relief, while Heather squints at us like she's entirely unconvinced. My explanation seems to diffuse some of the tension anyway, and the table moves on to talking about an exciting Venture deal. It all sounds like faraway murmurs to me, and the music in my ears is a garbled hum. But when Min leaves the booth with a final word for Parker, I hear it with excruciating clarity.

"Stay next to me when the ball drops so I can steal your New Year's kiss."

I reach for one of the abandoned glasses and down the shot. Then I throw back another one.

"Slow down," Parker whispers to me. "Do you want water?"

I wish he wasn't so nice to me. Then I wouldn't be wondering if he's like this with all the other girls.

"Bathroom," is all I say, and I flee to the back of the loft.

Locking myself in the single-stall room, I turn on the tap and take a series of deep, controlled breaths. I frown at the chunky platform heels that I'd dug out specifically for tonight. How long have my feet been numb? I stopped feeling my legs around the time Heather joined us.

Then it hits me like an anvil falling on my head: Has Parker been bringing Min back to the St. Regis this whole time? Has he been with her in the very same bed where he undressed me for the first time?

I don't want to jump to conclusions, but because I apparently *love* to suffer, I'm already conjuring the mental image of the two of them together. It shakes me like having my heart punted the full hundred yards.

Dani, you colossal idiot. Why did you assume you'd be different from the other girls? Because you used to share toys as kids? Idiot. Idiot. Idiot.

Sweat beads on my forehead, and the Belvedere surges like a wave from the pit of my stomach. I swallow a handful of water to keep from throwing up. I need to get out of here before anyone can see me like this.

When I shove the door open, Heather is standing against the wall across from me.

"You okay?"

"Did Parker send you?"

She shakes her head. "I wanted to check on you. I feel like we kind of ambushed you back there. I would've freaked out too."

Is that what it looked like to everyone? Heat creeps up my neck, and maybe it's the alcohol in my bloodstream, but the words come tumbling out before my thoughts can fully form. "Are you Parker's work wife?"

"Oh, god. Who said that? Was it Reginald?" Her eyes widen, then she lifts a hand to rub her temple. "It's just dumb water cooler talk. Unfortunately, being a woman in this field means I'm apparently banging everyone I work with." She sighs, then adds, "Trust me, Parker is, like, everyone's little brother at the San Francisco office."

"But you have his boat. He lets you borrow his car too."

"Okay, *favorite* little brother," she amends.

"He takes all your calls too."

"Who do you think got dumped with his San Francisco clients when he came to New York? That's why he's been so gracious about the boat. But I'm not special. Parker would do that for any of his friends."

I look down at my feet, feeling warm all over my face. "When we were in high school, Parker got his dream car, a black Jeep Wrangler. He would've never let anyone else behind the wheel."

"I think they call that a sign of maturing."

So, it's possible Parker and Heather have a genuinely platonic relationship, and he wasn't lying when he said she wasn't his type. I'd been hyperaware of every whisper and small touch, but could it all just have been innocent gestures between friends?

Parker and I are friends, and we've been far more intimate.

"But, even if that's all true," I start slowly, "Parker is still going to go *back home* to San Francisco with you, where he won't think of me anymore, because he'll just find another Min to entertain him—"

A hand flies to my mouth, and I hold back the urge to throw up again.

"Honey," Heather says gently, and she places a hand on my arm. "Have you talked to Parker about any of this?"

How can I? I was the one who suggested we keep things casual. He'd even checked with me—asked if I was okay with the arrangement. I thought I was. But that was back when I was guarding my heart from the possibility of his seeing other women. Of course, the fear was always there in the backroom of my mind, but I locked it away and distracted myself with the happier thought of our rebuilding our friendship. But how am I supposed to be casual when the truth is, the idea of him with another woman is making me sick to my stomach?

He's been clear from the beginning: He doesn't do relationships. We established the ground rules early on, and he's free to see whomever he wants. If there wasn't a Heather, there was going to be a Min.

In other words, this has all been a setup to get hurt, and I laid the trap myself.

"I'm sorry. I need to leave," I tell her. "Can you please let Parker know?"

Heather studies me for a long moment, lips parting like she's about to say something, then pressing shut again. Finally, she gives a reluctant nod and steps aside.

CHAPTER THIRTY-THREE

A white Audi pulls up in front of my apartment building a little after two a.m., long after the Uber dropped me off. I wasn't keen on going to bed after making my escape from Reggie's party, finding consolation in a bottle of red wine I had stored for special occasions. After chugging two glasses, I was in the middle of wondering—dreading—who Parker might've kissed at midnight, when Heather called and asked for my address. She said she had a special delivery to make and apologized in advance.

"I hate to agree with Reginald, but driving here really does suck," she says as she climbs out of the sedan with a huff, flipping blonde curls over her shoulder. Her makeup and hair are still magnificently intact at this late hour.

"The subway runs 24-7," I say, then immediately cringe. "And you had to lug a six-three former quarterback across the city, so I'll just shut up."

I hug my coat tighter around my pajamas, glancing over her shoulder at the tinted windows. I can make out a shadow in the passenger seat. Slumped against the glass is one Parker Tran, and I don't detect any movement.

"Is he okay?"

"Yeah, he just fell asleep," she assures me. "After you left, he went straight to the bar and spent the rest of the night there. He was three drinks in when he insisted he had to talk to you."

Should I prepare for a conversation that ends with, *We should stop seeing each other*? With the way I left things, I wouldn't blame Parker for backing out of our arrangement now. He'll remind me what *casual* means—of course he would see other people—and that I have no right to be upset. Now he has every reason to cut me loose. Start the new year with a clean, Dani-less slate.

"I got your number from Parker, hope you don't mind," Heather explains. "I told him if you were still up, I'd take him to see you."

"How very work big sister of you," I say with a small smile.

She grins at this. "Hey, so, I got the deets from the other guys for you. Turns out Isaac was the one who introduced Min to Parker. It was the first week he came to New York, and they haven't been in contact since then. They all thought she'd left the city until tonight—even Parker."

Oh. So that's how it feels to breathe again.

"Heather, Parker and I aren't together," I frown at her. "So it really shouldn't matter to me if he were seeing Min or any other girl."

The look on Heather's face hovers somewhere between wanting to spill a secret and holding back. She props an arm on the open car door and sighs.

"I don't know the whole story. I tried to pry the details out of him over Thanksgiving, but Parker's not the oversharing type. All I know is, he's in no rush to go back to San Francisco, and I think that has a lot to do with you. Did he tell you about the Nets thing?"

I shake my head.

"It's just interesting that he's so keen to land a deal that would keep him here a few more months." Heather gives me a coy shrug before she opens the passenger door, helping Parker to his feet. Plastered and fighting a losing battle against gravity, he can hardly stand up straight.

"I'm going to need your help, girl. It's like moving two hundred pounds of muscle."

I scurry over and sling one of his arms over my shoulders. He begins to show signs of life, the grogginess evaporating from his eyes.

"Dani," he says with a crooked smile. "Is that you?"

Without warning, strong arms wrap around me, pulling me tight against his body. He smells of whiskey, just like the first time we kissed, and my heart squeezes in my chest. I can't remember the last time Parker held me like this. Holding someone during sex isn't the same as a hug. It is tender, affectionate, like a Band-Aid for your soul.

"I missed you," he says, and just like that, he quiets all my nerves. I think I hear Heather giggling, but Parker's giant arms around me shut out the rest of the world. I can't see past him.

"Friends, right?"

I poke my head out over his shoulder. "I'm sorry for all the trouble tonight."

"Don't be. It's nice to see him like this. Reminds me that he's human too." She slides back into the driver's seat. "Hey, so I'll be here for a couple weeks. I feel like we didn't get a proper chance to talk tonight. We should do lunch—without the boys."

"Okay. You have my number."

I wave goodbye to Heather as the Audi peels away, then lead Parker into the apartment lobby, one clunky step at a time. The difference in our builds humbles me immediately. For a grueling three seconds, he leans too much of his weight on me, and I try not to crumble beneath him.

"How much did you drink?" I blurt as we wait for the elevator.

He's not listening. His head hangs low, his hair far from its usual pristine state. With a husky drawl he mumbles, "Why did you leave?"

"Turns out I'm not cut out for a Reggie Cruz party. Sensory overload and all." I hope that sounds convincing.

"You were upset. If you weren't, you would've said something to me before you left."

"Is that why you were drinking?"

"You get me all anxious. Like I'm going to mess this up again."

"What does that mean?"

"The last time I messed up, I didn't get to see you for seven years."

A dense, aching weight sits in my stomach. The elevator door opens, and I shuffle us inside.

"Isaac was hitting on you all night," he says. "He thinks you're cute."

"You had a *model* throw herself at you," I mutter back. "And even if Heather isn't your work wife, at some point you must've noticed there were three women vying for your attention at that table."

He keeps going, ignoring me. "You brought a guy home to Silverpine. I've never brought anyone home to meet my parents."

It's the last thing I expect to hear from someone who doesn't even want a girlfriend. A single overhead light buzzes faintly in the small lift, reflecting in Parker's glassy eyes. His cheeks are rosy with a soft blush that creeps up to his ears.

"Are you actually jealous?"

"Shit, what am I even saying? All of this is confusing as fuck to me." He drags a hand over his face. The elevator comes to a stop, and he eases some of his weight off me. We walk with a little less difficulty to my front door.

Confusing is putting it mildly. Parker's feelings were ambiguous enough when he wasn't talking about them—now his drunken admissions have only complicated things further. What's clear is that this doesn't feel so casual anymore. If we're not careful, one of us is going to slip, and then there won't be any going back.

I don't unlock the door right away. Parker leans against the frame, gazing down at me with a myriad of emotions on his face. I reach for him, sweeping his bangs out of his eyes. My hand lingers against his heated skin, and he smiles, resting his cheek against my palm.

I sigh at the throb in my chest. "How much of this are you going to remember?"

"Why? Plan on getting some dirt out of me?"

Maybe I'm the one who's going to slip. And maybe I don't really mind. "Can I ask you something?"

He arches a brow, prompting me.

"Did you think about me? When we were apart all those years."

When he answers, it takes a minute for me to swallow down my heart.

"All the time."

❧

The first thing Parker does when he enters my apartment is down a mug of coffee and jump in the shower to sober up. I listen at the door for movement, knocking every five minutes to make sure he's still alive. Each time, he croaks back an unconvincing, "Not dead."

When he finally steps out, I hand him a glass of water and an Advil. He's still in the same clothes because he doesn't keep any spares here. There's no point in giving him a drawer when he's never spent the night.

"How are you feeling now? Sobered up yet?"

He floods his mouth with water to avoid answering. I pretend not to notice that his ears are still glowing bright red. Fighting the urge to tease him, I take a seat at the kitchen counter and start slowly swiveling in place, waiting for him to find his voice again.

"Stop," he finally says.

"Stop what?"

"Whatever you're doing. Sitting there. Watching me." He threads a frustrated hand into his hair, pushing against damp locks. "I'd rather you make fun of me, so go ahead."

I bite down on a grin. It's no use. The corners of my mouth are so taut, my cheeks start to ache. "There's just *so* much material. Do I start with how alcohol turns you into a hugger? Or with why Heather thought the best place to dump your drunk ass was at my doorstep?"

"Heather dropped me off here because apparently, when I'm drunk, I don't stop talking about you." He sets the glass down in the sink and levels a look at me. His face says that this has been the longest night. "Is that clear enough for you?"

I chew on my lip, avoiding his gaze. That doesn't clear anything up. None of this lines up with the reality I was living four hours ago: *I* was the one losing it over the thought of him with another woman. He was supposed to be the sensible one, casual and cool, not hitting the bottle because I left him at a party without saying goodbye.

"About Min," he says suddenly. "I want you to know, I met her before I ran into you at Picotea. It was one night, and there was never any overlap. The last time I spoke to her was when she returned my key card."

"Heather alluded to something like that." I speak directly to my hands resting on the counter. "I guess you didn't give her your

New Year's kiss, then."

"What? Of course not."

"Stupid question: *Did* you kiss anyone at midnight?"

"Who would I kiss? You left the party," he asks, searching for correlation. "Why would I kiss anyone else?"

"Because it's an age-old tradition. It's also a good excuse if you want to make a move on someone. Like hey, everyone else is kissing and here we are, in close proximity." I spin in my chair, shying away from him. The wall seems like a better place to look. "And those are the ground rules, right? You can see other people, and I can too?"

"Dani, I'm not seeing anyone other than you," he says, his voice stony. "I haven't, since this started between us."

I pause then whirl back around to face him. "Since the first night?"

"Since the first night."

It hits me like the loud, gritty screech of brakes on pavement when I realize what this means: I've been spiraling all this time for no reason. I'm so horrified at my own thickness that I can't even take comfort in the relief washing over me. It doesn't help that Parker is staring at me, stupefied. But then his expression softens.

"Have you been worried about that this whole time?"

I let my head fall to the counter. "Yes," I mumble into the granite.

Curling inward, I silently plead in my half-cocoon shape that Parker won't prolong this humiliation. But then a small chuckle breaks the silence, and not long after, he's laughing.

"What's so funny?"

"We meet three, sometimes four times a week. How much sex did you think I was having?"

Reluctantly, I lift my head. My skin is scorching. "I'm new to this, okay? I've never been casual with anyone before. And for the record, I also haven't, you know—" I clear my throat and amend, "I haven't been seeing anyone else, either."

"That's what I figured. I wasn't sure at first, when you asked me about seeing other people in my office, but like I said, we meet so often," he says, calm and assured. "Look, I think I know what's happening."

"You do?"

"Dani, it was naïve to think that this—me and you—would ever be straightforward. Before we even learned how to be friends again, we introduced sex into our relationship, and that meant neither of us was thinking clearly. And now . . . well, we're more than just friends."

He hits the nail on the head without any pretense, voicing everything I'd been too afraid to say out loud.

"But if I'm being honest . . ." He rubs a hand on his neck, still curiously flushed with color. "After the first night, I knew I didn't want to see anyone but you."

A soft *boom* echoes in my ears, and I'm pretty sure my heart just exploded. I grapple for words. "You're not still drunk, are you?"

"Believe me, I wish I was. It'd make this night a lot less embarrassing."

A long breath fills my chest as I hop off the stool and make my way around the counter until we're face to face.

"You're right. We're more than friends now. We crossed a line, and it happened so quickly, we didn't have time to figure out what crossing it actually meant. But now . . . we're kind of stuck on this side."

He stares down at me, his features relaxing into a smile. "I think I prefer being on this side with you."

As expected, Parker Tran says all the right things.

"Hey, so, I know the ball dropped like—" He reaches over to the counter and wakes his phone. "Three hours ago."

Then he ducks his head and kisses me, a soft landing on my lips.

"Happy New Year, Dani."

Suddenly, my legs are in danger of giving out. As if he hasn't just jumpstarted every muscle in my body, Parker starts moving around the apartment, collecting his belongings. "I should get going."

In just one night, he's overhauled everything I thought I knew about our relationship. Parker has only been seeing me. He only *wants* to see me. We're in this gray area, where I can be as honest as I want about my feelings, without ever saying what those feelings are. How did we clear up so much, only to land in an even more ambiguous place?

We're more than friends. We've crossed a line with no possibility of going back. But he's made it resolutely clear that as long as we're on this side, it's just me for him, and him for me. And he's said it with such certainty that I have to rein in every impulse to push him onto my bed and kiss him, just to show him how much it means to me.

Then again, I haven't had much self-control lately.

"Wait." I steel my stomach. "You can stay here tonight. If you want."

Parker stalls at the door. "Like, sleep over?"

"If we're crossing lines, we might as well get them all out of the way."

CHAPTER THIRTY-FOUR

Parker runs a hand through my hair, eyes flickering over me. Leaning in for a kiss, he whispers as our lips meet, and I feel it like a soft tickle. "Are you really okay with breaking our ground rules?"

"I don't think they ever held up," I say, as my hands move over his bare chest, feeling the rise and fall of it with every deep breath.

"Imagine my shock: Dani Tsai is breaking a rule." A playful bite comes down on my lip. "*And* you made me complicit. Talk about a bad influence."

"You have a way of bringing that out of me." I kiss him a little harder, just the way he likes it. He pulls my pajama top over my head and drops it in a pile with the rest of our clothes. Because this night has gone on long enough without our hands all over each other, I'm hoisted off my feet and tossed on the bed in no time.

And he's right there with me, climbing on top of me and grinning down at my red-hot face. His mouth trails the curve of my neck until he finds my sweet spot. A tender nip, and then he sucks on the skin like it's a habit now. It still brings out a quiet gasp from me, and I weave my hands into his hair to keep myself from falling apart too soon.

When he speaks again, the teasing edge is replaced with a

hushed, sultry tone. "I can't take you anywhere without some guy trying to undress you with his eyes."

"Does it matter, so long as you're the one I go home with?"

"You're right. It doesn't." He leaves a searing trail of kisses down my neck to my breasts, where his tongue laves over a nipple, sparking a flutter in my stomach. "But just once, I'd like them to know this is all mine."

It still catches me off guard to hear him say these things about me, about my body. No matter how many times I've been naked in front of him, my heart is rendered useless whenever he reacts like this. Like he can't believe I'm here. Like he's stunned to be the one allowed to put his hands on me.

His fingers slip between my legs, and I shudder as the sensation rockets through me, stirring my bones. He's patient as he works to elicit a colorful moan out of me. I shut my eyes, but I know he's watching intently. He always does. It's like he's proud of his work; he basks in what his touch does to me, the way I come alive in his hands.

I don't need to tell him what I want next—his intuition does that for him. He drops his head between my legs, his mouth taking over.

"Mm, *god*," I breathe, arching into him.

He knows my body so well, knows exactly how to make me lose my mind a little more each time. In just three months, he's come to understand my body better than anyone else ever has. And I can see what it does to him, the thrill that radiates when he gets me close—

Close—

So close.

The tension snaps across my body as his tongue drives me to an orgasm. It lights a fire in me, and I lift myself to mount him, legs straddling his sides. Our eyes lock, and my breath catches when I see his long lashes, the shine in his dusky brown eyes when the light from my window hits them at just the right angle. He's so gorgeous, it's unfair.

Parker holds my face like it's a delicate thing, his thumb tracing my swollen mouth. When he pauses at the parting, I take him between my lips, tongue curling around his balmy skin. I pucker, giving his thumb a tender suck, eyes never leaving his. For an incandescent moment, he stares at me like he can't believe this is real.

And then a flare ignites somewhere behind his eyes. "What is it about you? Every little thing you do. You drive me wild."

He's hard against my thigh, and I decide I can't wait any longer. I take all of him inside me, and he reacts with a sharp inhale. His touch sears my skin, scorching a path to my waist. He guides me into motion, and I grind onto him. With every roll of my hips, I meet the hard press of his body against mine, and it's an immaculate feeling. My mind clouds with rapture, and I forget everything that came before this moment: the worry, the doubt—all of it fades to nothing.

I look to his lips—lips that are begging to be kissed—and I give him what he wants. His kiss is pure heat and energy, an unbridling of something I'd try to dissect if I were capable of a single unified thought. But all I can feel is the euphoric rush that hits when he thrusts up into me. Our movements quicken, and I sink my fingers into his shoulders for support, my knees going weak beneath me.

"*Parker*." Tension builds up once more, pleasure crashing down on me as I come a second time. His name is a shaky cry on my tongue, and my pulse is a wild throb. With his chest flush against me, I feel his heart pounding just as fast. I want to believe that he feels it too—that tonight is different from all the other nights. This doesn't feel like just hooking up. It's more intimate than that. So much more.

With his hand on the small of my back, he lowers me so I'm under him again. I hook my legs around him and draw him near, something hardwired in me needing him as close as possible, like it's written in my genetic code. His thrusts are harder and faster now, as he chases sweet release.

I catch his mouth for another kiss, and with it, his raspy, broken voice: "*Fuck*, Dani. Nothing feels better than you."

I feel wave after wave ripple through him as he comes. His eyes glaze over, and his breath is hot and heavy against my ear, revving my heartbeat. Parker kisses my forehead, just like the first night, and the world around me narrows to a single point where nothing exists but us.

CHAPTER THIRTY-FIVE

It turns out sleepovers are quite agreeable for two people who are looking for any excuse to be in each other's company. Two weeks into our new arrangement, Parker's cooking dinners at my place and bringing over a gym bag with extra clothes and his laptop. In the mornings, I wake up to him spooning me before we get up to brush our teeth side by side. It's so easy to be with each other. It was like this when we were kids too. But at the same time, there's this itch to hit pause and demand, *What's going on between us? What are we?*

Somewhere in the back of my mind, I'm hoping—anticipating even—that Parker will turn to me and tell me he's all in. We're already exclusive, and if Heather's right about the Nets deal, then maybe he wants to stay in New York. All signs seem to point to go—a serious relationship is on the horizon, and we're moving full steam ahead.

But there's no way I can ask him about any of this. Not when defining our relationship might knock out the foundation from underneath it. Neither of us seems to want to acknowledge just how far we've drifted from *casual* into . . . whatever this is.

Parker is leaning against the bookshelf, watching me wrestle a fitted sheet over my mattress. "Why did we stop having sleepovers when we were kids?"

"Probably because we were entering high school, and it was

weird enough with our parents enforcing the 'doors open' rule," I say, tugging on a stubborn corner. "Plus, you were so busy with football, it wasn't like you were inviting me over for slumber parties at that point."

He walks over and tucks the sheet in for me. It takes little effort on his part. "That had more to do with how hard it was to act normal around you."

"Normal? Like how?"

"Like pretending my hormones weren't raging just from being near you," he says. "Remember that time our families carpooled to Portland, and we sat in the backseat together? You wore a skirt and your thigh kept bumping into mine. I was hard as a brick the entire ride."

I blink at him, and when I don't have an immediate response, he crosses his arms. "You really couldn't tell?"

"You dated cheerleaders who filled up bras better than I could ever dream," I tell him. "I'd always assumed that if we hadn't been best friends, I wouldn't have even been on your radar."

"That's exactly why it was so confusing to be around you and talk about the things teenagers usually talk about. I mean, I was a teenage boy in hormonal overdrive, and the one girl I wanted to do all those . . . physical things with was basically off-limits." He stretches his neck to one side, the motion a bit awkward. "Because you were my best friend, and best friends don't do those things."

The confession trips me up, and suddenly I'm sixteen again, in front of the cutest boy in school and nursing a hopeless crush. I swallow and let the words slip out. "Your cousin Kevin's pool party."

"What about it?"

"You had just come back from youth camp, and it was like you got your six-pack overnight. I couldn't stop staring," I say, my face aflame. "And then I had a sex dream about you that night."

He pauses for a loaded second before erupting into a laugh. "Do I get to hear the details of this dream?"

"Not in this lifetime." It feels like someone has lit a match under my skin. I look up at him, noticing that at some point he'd closed the distance between us. As his laughter fades, leaving behind a crooked, playful grin, he reaches out to tuck a strand of hair behind my ear. My back instantly goes rigid. I'm still trying to adjust to the small, intimate gestures of someone who isn't officially my boyfriend.

Just then, my phone dings from my nightstand, startling me out of that thought. A glimpse at the notification makes my stomach bottom out. "Estelle emailed me."

"About your portfolio?"

"I don't know. Maybe. I'm too scared to open it."

He reaches over and tousles my hair. "It's going to be good news."

I pull up the email and immediately flip the phone to him. "You read it."

He laughs. "No, Dani. *You* read it."

Before I can protest, Parker's own phone is buzzing in his pocket, piercing the tension with a second jolt to my heart. He looks down at the caller ID and frowns.

"Sorry. I'll take this in the kitchen."

I'm left alone with Estelle's email, with no one to help me stall. I take a seat at the foot of the bed, count to three, and unlock my phone.

Dani,

Happy New Year, love! I know this email's a bit late coming through, so I do apologize. I've only returned to London a couple nights ago. A friend of mine in Madeira insisted I make the trip to see the New Year's fireworks, and once I stopped at the Azores, there was no sending me home! I'm tempted to say that I'll be taking every meeting from a hot spring in Furnas from now on.

I managed to have a proper look at your portfolio upon my return. I know I've been stingy with the details, but now that we've laid the groundwork, I can give you the gist of it: My colleague from *Vogue* and I are starting a new publication in New York—a slow journalism magazine for women, by women. I want ladies from all walks of life on this project sharing their experiences, championing one another.

There's a position open for associate editor that I'd love you to interview for. We're still a small team, so you would be contributing as a staff writer as well. From what I've read, I think your writing is exactly what we're looking for. You have a way with prose that reads as clever and erudite while still being charmingly personal.

We'll be starting interviews this Thursday, and I have an opening for you at 3 p.m. I do hope you will give some thought to the position.

Cheers, Estelle

I read the email three times before I finally allow the knot inside me to unfurl. This is good news. It's not a job offer, but I'd be delusional to think Estelle would be handing those out like free samples. Once I collect myself, I scurry over to update Parker.

"Got it. Okay," he says into his phone, eyes flying over to me. "Yeah, I can do that."

I take a seat at the counter across from him, catching the indistinct murmur of a man's voice on the line. As soon as he ends the call, Parker sets his phone down and smiles at me. "Well?"

"Estelle is starting a new publication and wants me to interview for an editor position."

"I told you! And she reached out to you personally, so that's a good sign."

"Yeah, and it's in New York, so that's even better."

At this, Parker gives a stiff nod, and for a sliver of a second, his smile falters. He looks down at his phone, absorbed in contemplation while I search his face.

"Was that Venture?" I ask him.

"Yeah, the San Francisco branch," he says quietly, brows pulling down.

Sometimes, I wish I weren't so tuned into every shift in the air around him. I've learned to read every pause, blink, and twitch of his face. All of it speaks volumes to me, and I've already picked up on what that call was about.

"You have to go back, don't you."

He runs a hand despondently through his hair and cuts me a grim look that makes the knot inside me resurface.

"When?"

"By next week," he answers slowly. "The Super Bowl is coming up, and San Francisco takes the lead on that every year. There are ad campaigns, sponsorship deals, just a shit ton to do. And if I'm being honest, they needed me there weeks ago."

"And they didn't ask until now?"

"I was working on something with the Nets. They were waiting to see whether we landed the deal, but it looks like we got passed over for another firm."

"Even if you'd gotten it," I say quietly, trying to navigate around the growing ache within my chest, "you would've just been postponing the inevitable, right? Your job—your life—is in

San Francisco."

He avoids my eyes, mumbling down at his phone. "And yours is here."

There's no reason for me to feel blindsided. This was never his home. When Parker gave me the key card to his suite, it was with the understanding that all this would come to an end once he left New York. That was the arrangement. We could break every ground rule in the book, but it would never buy us more time.

Why did I let myself get hopeful over sleepovers? This was never a serious relationship. And without that commitment, there are no expectations for what comes once we part ways. After all, Parker never asked me to be his girlfriend.

But . . .

I don't want to go back to life without you.

I don't want to be with anyone else.

Does this really have to end?

I can't say it out loud, instead leaving the words to sit in my throat, strangling me.

CHAPTER THIRTY-SIX

Across a small table lined with bamboo steamers, Marisa has been gawking at me for the last five minutes. She fails to acknowledge the older woman who rolls up with a cart, so I tell her in Mandarin that we'll pass on the beef tripe. After some time, Marisa finally lifts her chopsticks, but immediately sets them back down before blurting, "*You and Parker?*"

I pick up a shumai and bite into it. "Remember the Monosphere event? That was the first night."

"First? There have been *multiple* instances?"

"We were sleeping together for three months." I'd been nervous about having this conversation, but once I stammered through the initial confession, I realized the rest of it didn't have to be as torturous. Marisa's perception of me has already been flipped upside down. Giving up the details now is basically just housekeeping.

Frenzied eyes dart around the table. Then, a pair of chopsticks is pointed at me. "So, whenever you said you were working overtime at the office . . ."

"Sneaking off to his hotel."

"This is a lot to dump on me over Saturday dim sum." She props her elbows on the satiny white tablecloth and holds her head as if it were in danger of caving in.

"You take as long as you need to process this."

The agreement I'd made with myself was that I'd tell her everything once Parker left New York. It would also benefit me by putting the whole thing to rest. But now, I'm not so sure what coming clean means.

"I noticed you didn't use the word dating."

I take a gulp of steaming pu'er tea. "It was casual."

"That doesn't make this any less messy." There's a pause, long and heavy, and I know she's trying to determine whether to mince her words. "I mean, sure, I'm proud of you. I've been saying forever that a little mindless sex would do you some good. But I worry that you and Parker have too much history for you to come out of this unscathed."

How do I tell her it's already too late for that?

It's been three weeks since Parker left New York. When I met him at the St. Regis for the last time, he was checking out of the hotel and returning his key cards. A sobering moment for me to see the last three months packed up in a single suitcase and two bags. All I could do was watch as Parker swept out of my life just as abruptly as he'd crash-landed in it. It left me feeling numb.

"Have you two talked since he left?"

"Of course. We're still friends. He FaceTimed me the other day to show me the new air purifier he bought for his apartment. Apparently, my air quality propaganda actually works."

Marisa blinks up from the feng zhao between her chopsticks. The chicken foot hangs dejectedly in the air, and I read her mind instantly: *That's not what I meant.*

"We haven't had a chance to have that kind of talk," I frown at her. "We've both been busy with work."

"In other words, neither of you wants to acknowledge that you can't get your freak on when you're three thousand miles apart."

"You have such an elegant way with words."

My phone lights up on the table, and I careen to take an anxious peek, but it's a spam email. I deflate back in my chair. It's eight a.m. in California. Parker must be at the gym getting his morning workout in.

Marisa glances between me and my phone. "You can't be okay with not knowing. Maybe if this was some nobody off an app, but this is Parker we're talking about. If you just leave things up in the air, then what does that mean for your relationship?"

"There's no relationship," I correct her. "Look, I don't even know when I'll see him again. We didn't exactly make plans. But if this was never meant to be more than a three-month fling, then so be it. Somehow, someway, this was always going to come to an end." The only variable was whether or not I'd be ready when it did.

Turns out I was not.

But I clench my teeth and chase that bad feeling away. I'd planned on telling Marisa the truth today, but it didn't mean I was looking to be consoled just yet. I'd only recently accepted the reality check that three months of pseudo-dating wasn't enough to change Parker's stance on relationships.

"You're not even going to ask him what he thinks?"

"I . . . hang on, sorry." I take the obvious diversion as it's handed to me—a plate of perfectly toasted egg tarts. "I've had my eye on this dan tat for a while now."

Marisa spares me a disapproving sigh, but after a long sip of tea she says charitably, "Fine. Dropping it. But you know I have to ask how the sex was."

Another cart lady chooses this moment to pull up by our table. She tries to entice us with a plate of tofu-skin rolls, and after going back and forth with Marisa, she gives up and moves along.

I wait for her to be out of earshot and lean forward. "It was like every man I'd been with before him was amateur hour, prepping me for the real thing. He showed me how they do it in the big leagues."

Marisa grimaces. "On second thought, maybe I don't really want to hear this."

"I didn't even know I could bend that way."

"Moving on. Please." A shudder wends through her body. "Have you heard from the new magazine yet?"

A sinking sensation pools in my gut. I suppose I have Parker to thank for sidetracking me. Otherwise, I'd certainly be spiraling over the editor job. When I showed up for the interview, only Alfreda from *Vogue* was there to receive me. Unlike Estelle, she didn't seem too charmed by my nervous blathering, and I couldn't get a read on her. It's been a couple weeks now, and I haven't received any news.

I poke at the abandoned dumpling in my bowl. "Nope. Moving on, please. Tell me all about the house hunt. You've narrowed it down by now, right?"

Success. Deflection completed. Marisa is suddenly much too excited about her own news to keep up her prying. "Binghamton! It was right under our noses all this time. A gorgeous detached Victorian. And the best part is, I can do weekend trips to see you. Granted, it's a three-hour drive, but that's totally doable."

"Surely that's not the best part of your future home."

"You're right, it's the third bathroom." She slides the last egg tart toward me. "I just wanted you to feel special."

CHAPTER THIRTY-SEVEN

Me: Mario Kart?

Parker: Sorry, not tonight. Gotta get these press releases for SB in ASAP.

Parker: Can you do tomorrow?

Me: Can't, Marisa is starting to pack up her place, and I promised to help.

Me: Friday?

Parker: Meeting with the Warriors team, but I'll lyk if something changes.

I set my phone down on the kitchen counter and flip open my laptop twenty minutes after powering it down. It wasn't an exaggeration when I told Marisa there was no good time to have a talk with Parker. From the second he set foot back on the West Coast, Venture had thrown him straight into the Super Bowl rush. His name was already attached to several ad campaigns, and he was spending the better part of his days in meetings with brand executives. I thought it'd be wise to make use of all the free time I suddenly had to ask Lindsay for more assignments. Spending long hours editing someone else's writing has the advantage of distracting me from writing something of my own, namely, a long and revealing text message that I'd most certainly regret.

The time-zone difference hasn't been forgiving either; more than once, I've knocked out on the couch with my laptop open, only to wake the next morning to a missed call from Parker. But sometimes, if time permits, I'll boot up *Mario Kart* and find an invitation from him to meet in a lobby. Not the gilded, marble-floored one of the St. Regis, but online.

In our last phone call, Parker had mentioned offhandedly that Venture wanted him back on the Warriors campaign now that he's built a repertoire. If it runs the duration of the NBA postseason, it will have him committed until summer. And if, by some miracle, I get the editor position at Estelle's new publication, then I'll have to stay in New York for the launch, at the very least.

I want to be optimistic, but my programmed cynicism doesn't make it easy. It's not as if I could ask him to give long distance a try. If I bring it up and he doesn't feel the same, then that'll put a decisive end to any shot at a relationship. Contrary to what Marisa believes, talking about it might not be the fix to all this. The way things are now, all I have to worry about is ambiguity.

Well, at least we'll always have *Mario Kart*.

As I'm checking my phone for the time—nine p.m. here, six in California—the screen flashes with an incoming call, and I accept right away.

"Hey," comes Parker's low and gruff voice. "I have some time before I have to jump on another call and wanted to check in."

Now, three weeks isn't a life-altering amount of time to be apart, but when you're used to talking to someone every day, you become sharp to even the tiniest change. The first thing I notice is how tired he sounds. It tugs at my heart, but I make myself say, "Hey."

"Have you heard from Estelle?"

"Two weeks without word." I let out a long breath. "I think it's safe to call it?"

"Don't put that into the universe. You're going to get the job."

"So, I'm leaving it up to kismet now?"

"Don't have to. Like I said, you're going to get it."

There's that unshakable confidence again. It's enough to tide me over, and for once, I don't have that gut drop when I think about my interview with Alfreda. Over the line, I can hear Parker typing, but he pauses to stifle a yawn.

"Are you still at the office?"

"I am," he says. "You'll be pleased to know I got an air purifier here too."

"Ah, a Gilbert Jr."

"Let's not call it that," he returns, flatly. "Shit, sorry, Dani. I gotta go. My boss is already calling, and he needs to approve these press releases by tonight."

Before Parker hangs up, he makes me swear to a *Mario Kart* session next weekend. I remind him to sleep at a reasonable hour, aware that he'll do exactly the opposite and that I won't be taking my own advice either. I finish the article Lindsay assigned me last Monday and open my emails to locate a fresh assignment. It's nearly two a.m. when I finally wash up and take my laptop to bed with me. Waking the device, I type my password into the lock screen.

A single unread email is sitting in my inbox.

Dani,

Hope you've been keeping well. It's seven in the morning in London, and I can't stop thinking about the carne asada I had last time I was in New York. Once I'm back over there (won't be long now), I'll have to take another gander at your Excel sheet (you ought to get that copyrighted).

Alfreda had a chance to read your portfolio, and we had a proper chat about you. She was especially touched by your article about being brought up by TV mums. I didn't think it was possible, but you managed to squeeze a tear out of her soulless puppet shell! Well done, love. You've absolutely smashed it!

With that said, I'd like to formally offer you the role of Associate Editor at *From Venus*. That's the name we've settled on—you know how it goes, men are from Mars and all that. Let's touch base next week. We'd love to have you on board by February so we can start putting our heads together for the debut issue.

Cheers, Estelle

The words don't immediately sink in, but when they do, my heart races with excitement. I fumble around the bed for my phone, pulling up my call log to find the first person I want to share the good news with.

It rings and rings, but he doesn't pick up.

Right, he said he'd be busy all night. I can wait until the morning to tell him.

I try not to feel disheartened as my eyes trace the empty space next to me. Our sleepovers hadn't lasted very long, but I'd grown used to Parker's presence beside me in the middle of the night. It's strange that I hadn't realized it before, but being with him felt a lot like being in his house in Silverpine. It felt like home.

Now I have to get used to life without him all over again.

Aware that I won't be falling asleep soon, I swipe to the LINE app. Taiwan is thirteen hours ahead, so it's not an inconvenient time to try calling. Plus, I'm still buzzing from Estelle's email and need to talk to someone about it.

It rings twice before Mom's face fills up the screen. "Dani!"

Her eyes glimmer under the sun. They're still sharp and watchful like a cat's, but time has etched fine lines at the corners, softening what I'd once found intimidating about her. When I was a kid, everyone would tell me I had my mom's eyes. I used to think I resembled her, but looking at her now, I see someone I don't really recognize. "Hi, Mom."

"How is New York?" she asks in Mandarin.

"Good. Cold." I'd say more, but my Chinese is rusty. Mom turns to speak to someone out of frame, and when she shifts the camera, I notice the terrain around her: jagged rock faces and dramatic cliffs, with endless blue ocean beyond them. "Where are you?"

"Amalfi!" Bursting into a spiel about beaches and fishes, she tells me animatedly about her desire to paint it all. I can't understand much but draw context from the words I can pick out. Then, with a steadying breath, she shouts back in English, "I'm on my honeymoon!"

A lump forms in my throat. "You got married?"

She seems to read my shock and adds mercifully, "It was very sudden. We didn't even have a real ceremony! Just dinner with friends after we signed the papers."

"Wow. Even so, congratulations, Mom."

"It's no big deal. I didn't want you to feel like you had to come all the way here," she replies, waving a hand in the air. A diamond sparkles where the sun hits her ring finger. "Anyways, what did you call for?"

"It's nothing," I mutter so quietly, I can hardly hear myself. "It's just been a while since we talked."

"I miss you too, honey." Joy breaks across her face in a wide, radiant smile just as the wind sweeps through her dark hair. It's not a smile I've seen on her before, and all of it feels so foreign to me—the woman on my screen a familiar stranger.

I try to smile back, but it falters halfway. "I'll let you go, then. Enjoy your honeymoon, Mom."

CHAPTER THIRTY-EIGHT

Three months later

"Estelle, I'm sending you another round of pitches. We should narrow down our contributors by next week at the very latest." My fingers move over the trackpad, clicking out of my inbox and back to the ongoing Zoom call. The face on full screen makes me nearly jump out of my seat once I register that my boss is quite obviously glaring at me. "Is now not a good time?"

"You're on holiday," says Estelle sharply. She leans back into her leather upholstered chair, giving me room to breathe again. "You're not supposed to be working."

"I didn't take PTO, so technically, I'm still on the clock, just three hours behind you."

"When you asked to go home, I assumed you were taking time off. That's why I approved it." Red coffin nails tap irritably against the edge of her desk. "It certainly wasn't an invitation to move your mad twelve-hour shifts from the office to your childhood bedroom."

I throw an abashed glance at the *Slam Dunk* poster in plain view and the stuffed bear—a prize from the town fair eons ago—sitting prominently at the foot of my bed. Perhaps not the most professional setup, but I can't use Dad's home office while he's also working.

"We just dropped our debut last week," I remind Estelle. "We have momentum that we should be carrying into the next issue."

"Do you know what I did after the launch party? I went home and spent two days catching up on *Love Island* and drinking a criminal amount of wine." With a pensive look, she adds, "Working during leave is a violation of company policy. Must I write you up with HR?"

"Sure, you can address that to me, and I'll handle it this afternoon," I return with a grin. "Until you hire an HR department, Estelle, *I'm* your HR."

For the last three months, I've devoted every conscious moment to the *From Venus* launch. The team Estelle put together consisted of the two of us, Alfreda, a couple of staff writers, an art director, and an intern. This meant I was editing and writing articles during the day and chasing down contributors at night, all while wearing the hats of an underqualified ad rep and office manager. At some point, the days began to blur as I drifted from task to task. I spent mornings in and out of meetings, skipped lunches to write in my office, and went to bed with my laptop fused to my wrists. The next day, I'd wake up and start the same routine all over again.

Being busy is good, I've learned. It's my preferred state. Once I lose myself in a creative flow, I don't have time to waste refreshing my Instagram feed or wondering what's going on in San Francisco. I'm far too occupied to spare a thought for all the things that lie beyond my control.

Not to mention, I like my job. I'm good at it. Being thrust into a high-pressure, fast-paced role forced me to grow alongside the chaos. Once our first issue went to the printer, I knew all the late nights had paid off and we had something to be proud of. Hard to believe that half a year ago, I was almost willing to work for a pair of douchebags if it meant they'd fly me around Asia. The other day, I picked up a copy of *From Venus* at a newsstand on Union Square just so I could see my name on the masthead. That was far more rewarding than any paid vacation.

"I know you're invaluable to the team. I'm not sure that *Venus* would've launched on time without you. But I draw the line at working on holiday." Estelle is still glowering, eyes locking on the camera as if daring me to respond. "I'm not a monster. I'm not Alfreda."

"But—"

"I won't hear it." She brushes me off with a flick off her wrist. "Before I forget, your friends from *Adagio* had a launch gift delivered to your office, a curious-looking plant, like a little palm tree with a braided trunk."

"Must be a Pachira plant. They're called money trees. They're supposed to be lucky." Tae-woo had one on his work desk. It makes me wonder if he had any part in picking out the gift, and the thought instantly makes my forehead crease. Maybe absence really does make the heart grow fonder.

"This as well." Estelle reaches into the bottom drawer of her desk. An elegant, dark green bottle with a ribbon around its neck comes into frame, supported by both her hands. "Didn't think it wise to leave a bottle of vintage Dom Pérignon unattended in your office, lest a sneaky intern or Alfreda find it."

I scratch at my chin. "Who would send me five-hundred-dollar champagne?"

She flips the card attached to the ribbon. "Parker Tran. Isn't that your friend from the basketball game? Why would he send this here and not directly to you?"

"It's been a couple weeks since we last spoke," I admit. "He doesn't know I'm not in New York."

Something shifts in Estelle's expression, a thought aligning.

The corner of her mouth dips ever so slightly. "You know, Dani, I had my most productive year at *Dénouement* around the time I got divorced. I was promoted to senior editor by the spring and wrote an award-winning piece on gender politics." She pauses and then says gently, "It won't make you feel better to drown yourself in work."

I see where she's going with this but refuse to bite. "Is it really drowning if you enjoy what you do?"

"Darling, it's drowning if you don't come up for air." She lets that one marinate for a beat. "Right, then, you're taking the rest of the week off. That's an order."

"You can't do that."

"I can do what I like. I'm your boss."

"Alright, let me ask what HR thinks of that." I suck in a breath, pretending to think. "They say no."

"Dani, much as I adore you, you're going to burn out at this rate, and I need you in one piece for the next issue," she warns, her voice clipped, leaving no room for compromise. "Be a dear and take a proper holiday, would you? I don't know what one does in the Pacific Northwest, but having a good cry would be a start. God knows it helped me."

Estelle crosses her arms, waiting for me to agree with her. If I've learned anything from every heated exchange that ended with Alfreda storming out the office, it's that Estelle Pearson gets what she wants. I concede with a promise that I won't touch work as long as I'm in Silverpine. After I end the call, I make a list of all the tasks I'll have to jump on next Monday and then find my phone underneath a stack of Post-it notes.

One missed call while I was talking to Estelle. From Parker. I quickly tap his name to call back, but my attempt goes to voicemail.

"Hey, you've reached Parker. Sorry I missed your call . . ."

The last time I caught him between meetings, he'd said April would be particularly packed, with the NBA playoffs starting and the NFL draft at the end of the month. I thought he'd finally get some downtime with the Super Bowl out of the way, but he hasn't shown any signs of slowing down.

Either way, this game of phone tag has been going on for some time. Since when did it become so hard to check in with one another? Why are we so out of sync? We'd established such an easy rhythm in New York. Making time for one another felt so effortless because we both wanted it so badly.

Suddenly, I recall the conversation on our drive to the gorge, the methodical way Parker explained his past relationships: *They all started the same way: I'd have feelings, until I didn't. Nothing seemed to last longer than the initial spark.* My pragmatic side is telling me that if the pattern remains true, then Parker's feelings are already fading. How long can you keep a spark alive when you can't see and touch each other?

Does that mean when Parker left for San Francisco, he'd already accepted this would end?

I hang up without leaving a message. Instead, I text him a quick thank-you for the champagne and toss my phone on the bed, where it's out of sight.

CHAPTER THIRTY-NINE

When I initially asked Estelle if I could go to Silverpine, it was with the intention of working, but with a much-needed change of scenery. Being alone in my apartment with only my laptop as company was making me feel unhinged. As soon as she signed off on the request, I booked the first flight out to Portland.

I'd spent so many years avoiding home that I forgot the kind of peace that comes with being here. Silverpine is the only place I seem to feel any normalcy these days. New York doesn't offer the same comfort as finding Dad quietly reading the news in his office or going next door to see what spring vegetables Cô has planted in her garden. Sometimes, when I let myself detach from work, I hear the pad of footsteps climbing the stairs, and a tiny bud of hope ignites in me. I hold my breath each time, in case I meet a familiar face coaxing me out for a game of catch or a ride around town in the Jeep.

Curiously, Dad isn't in his office when I go downstairs. Even stranger is the trail of cardboard boxes that's been strewn around the house sometime between my morning coffee and my call with Estelle. I peek into each one for a clue, but they're empty. I suspect it's a belated New Year's purge, or the damage after another furniture haul. Which would also be odd, because I didn't hear any delivery trucks pull up on our driveway.

"What are you doing?" I ask once I find Dad in the garage.

He's too distracted with opening old paint cans to register my question. Once he confirms they're dried up, he places them in another cardboard box and finally looks over at me. "How was your call?"

"Good. My boss asked me to stop working."

At this, his brows come together, eyes narrowing with suspicion.

"She didn't fire me," I clarify. "She says I'm overworking myself and wants me to take a break. All paid time off, of course."

"You have a good boss," he says, but his face is still tight with doubt. Ever since I showed up in Silverpine unannounced, my father seems to think I'm on the brink of a meltdown. And yet, he hasn't hit me with the obvious *But why here?* when I told him I needed a breather from New York. It probably hasn't helped that I've been stingy with details, and Dad has never been the type to pry.

Silence closes in on us. Dad and I have always been terse with our conversations, but it isn't typical for us to be this awkward.

"If you're not working—"

"So, what are you doing—"

Our words overlap, and Dad gestures with his hand for me to speak first.

"What's with the boxes?" I ask.

"I was just clearing things out. Your room could use a purge too, now that you're here." His face is noticeably stony as he says this. "You've been hoarding things forever. All those clothes from high school, and there's your drawers too."

He means one drawer in particular, the one packed full of Mom's discarded VHS tapes. Truth be told, moving out and leaving it behind meant that the drawer didn't occupy my mind the way it once had. But it's been different for Dad. He has to be here all the time, coexisting with it, like an unavoidable sore spot.

"I'll get to it," I say unconvincingly.

"Dani." I can hear the sigh in his voice. "How long are you going to be staying here?"

"Just a week. I'll be gone by Saturday." A humorless laugh rises to my throat. "Do you want me out of your hair that badly?"

"It's not that. It's just . . . well, your timing is not so great."

He turns back to the paint cans, allowing the silence to stretch between us once more. Though his hands are busy with prying the lids open, his absent gaze suggests he's anything but focused.

A cold sensation settles over my skin once I realize I might not like what I'm about to hear. I don't think there's anything in the world that can prepare me for bad news from Dad. Not since the morning he told me Mom wouldn't be living with us anymore. "What is it?"

"A realtor is dropping by at the end of the week."

"Wait, why?"

He lifts a hand and gestures to the boxes around us. "I'm thinking of selling the house."

I know I've heard him correctly, but my brain scrambles to catch up. That chill sinks from my skin into my bones, and for a disorienting moment, all I can do is let my mouth hang. "*What*? Are you serious? Why now, all of a sudden?"

"It's been on my mind to downsize for a while."

"I—I don't understand," I sputter. "Where are you going to live?"

"I'm not sure yet," he shrugs, like he hasn't just dropped earthshattering news on me. "Maybe Jersey. Philadelphia is an option too."

"You're moving east?" I gasp, completely flummoxed now. But at the mention of it, my thoughts snap back to Thanksgiving.

"Then when I caught Chú looking at listings . . . they were for you?"

"He's really trying to sell me on Philly. He has a great time whenever he visits Nathan there, apparently. Now he's always finding listings to send to me."

"Hold on, back up a bit." I press my hand against my forehead. This entire conversation feels a lot like hallucinating. "Aren't you supposed to run this stuff by me first? This is my house too!"

"Dani, you've come home four times in the last five years."

"I'm here now, aren't I?" I shoot back. "If I hadn't come back home this time, would you have even told me?"

"Of course I would've," he says. "I was trying to figure out how, but it hasn't been easy. I knew you wouldn't take it well."

"Understandably! You made this huge decision without consulting me first! What if I don't want to sell the house?"

"I didn't bring it up to negotiate with you—"

"Right, because you can't have a real conversation with me." My jaw clenches, and I exhale sharply though gritted teeth. I can feel my hands trembling. "You do this, Dad! It's like you're so afraid of talking about anything uncomfortable or difficult or *painful*, you'll do anything you can to avoid it! That's why we never talk about Mom, isn't it?"

I wince as soon as I say it. *Shit.* I've gone and dropped the M word.

Dad looks like he's miles away. I watch with a sinking feeling in my stomach as his hand pauses on the lid of a can and slides the container out of reach. I don't know what kind of reaction to expect. We've never had this fight before, and I was beginning to think we never would.

But he doesn't sound defensive when he finally speaks. Instead, his voice comes out small and a little somber. "Dani, do you know why I want to move out east?"

I stare at him, waiting for him to answer his own question.

"When you told me about the Asia correspondent job, I wasn't so crazy about you going so far away. If I'm being honest, I was relieved you didn't leave. It made me realize what a shame it is that we live so far apart."

"You want to move to be closer to me?"

"Would that be the worst thing?"

"No, of course not." I take a couple steps to the Civic in the middle of the garage, leaning against it. I'm surprised I've managed to stay on my feet this long. "But I really wish you'd talk to me first."

Dad stands next to me, crossing his arms as he rests on the car. The seconds pass in this shared stillness, our eyes trained on the wall as if the right words to say will materialize there.

"Your mother got remarried."

"I know," I say. He glances at me, surprised. "I happened to call her during her honeymoon. How did you find out?"

"One of her cousins reached out," he replies. "I'm sorry I didn't tell you. I wasn't sure if you wanted to know."

"She looked like she was having the time of her life. Now that I think about it, the Italian coast really suits her," I try to sound casual but end up frowning at the floor. "Can I ask you something?"

He nods after a beat.

"I barely hear from her anymore. She doesn't seem to care how I'm doing. It's been years, and she hasn't tried to see me again." Emotion clogs my throat, but I swallow it down. "Was it always like that? I mean, I have these memories from when I was a kid, and it seemed like she wanted to be around then. What happened to her?"

Dad sorts carefully through his thoughts. When his jaw finally relaxes, he speaks in a quiet and measured tone. "No, it wasn't always like that. Our marriage started happily enough, although in hindsight, we did rush into it. Your mother's visa was about to expire, and we were two lovesick students who thought being together was all that mattered. We didn't stop to consider we might want different things."

"You mean like having me?"

His face crumples slightly at this, marred with hesitation. "She knew how much I wanted a child. I asked her to settle down in a small town, and she was worried about how that would affect her art career. But she *did* try, for the first few years, because she loved you. Until one day . . . one day, she started picturing a life that didn't include you or me, and she made her choice. Your mother brought the divorce papers to me, and by then, I was sick of fighting. I was just so tired."

Dad tilts his head back and lets out a long sigh. I'm almost too scared to see what face he's making. I don't think I could handle watching his heart break again.

"I'm sorry, Dani." It's barely a whisper, but it's enough to knock the wind out of me. "I didn't want you to feel like you had to carry the divorce around with you. You've never been one to ask questions either, so I guess over the years, it got easier to just ignore it. To pretend we were fine. And I thought we were. But I realize that was the easy way out for me. It wasn't fair to you."

"I didn't want to hurt you by mentioning her," I respond. "I was always so confused about what I was allowed to say or feel."

"I know—I know, and that's my fault." He shakes his head but then looks at me intently. "If you'd like, I can get in touch with her. It's not too late to set something up. Maybe she can go to New York and stay with you a while."

I can see the apology weighing down his eyes. The shadow of

remorse is unmistakable. My gut feels at odds with itself as guilt and grief press against each other. Ever since I was a kid, I've had the sense that the more I love something, the harder it is to hold. That's why I can't get rid of Mom's tapes, not when they are among my last remaining connections to her. I've thought that if I don't let go, maybe the universe will eventually reward me for my stubbornness. Every so often that childish hope pops up, like whenever I miss my mom, or even now, when I think of saying goodbye to our house. It's the same part of me that wishes Parker would tell me he wanted a serious relationship.

But I'm tired of holding on. When it hurts this much, perhaps the only option is to let go.

"I'm okay, Dad," I assure him. "If that was something she wanted, we wouldn't have to persuade her. I'll keep that door open in the future, but I've had twenty-two years to learn how to live without her."

Reaching out, I take his hand in mine and give it a light squeeze. The unfamiliar gesture elicits the slightest twitch, but his gaze is warm and full of affection. He doesn't say anything but gives my hand a small tug back.

As I'm heading to the door, he asks, "You'll really be okay if I sell the house?"

"I don't know," I answer honestly. With my feet paused on the stairs, I take a lingering look around the garage. "It's hard to imagine anywhere else as home."

This might be the one thing I'll never learn to let go of.

CHAPTER FORTY

I think Dad can sense how desperate I am for a distraction. He doesn't nudge me to open up again, but as soon as I get that lost, dejected look in my eye, he gives me another moving box to fill or sends me on a sudden grocery run. When he asked me to drop off his dry cleaning, I could tell he was tapped out of ideas. Dad almost never gets anything dry-cleaned.

It's just as well. After leaving the cleaners, my quest for diversion takes me to the pharmacy, where Cô is all too delighted to have my company. She also has no objections to me following her around Silverpine all day. In the afternoon, we deliver medications to some of the town's seniors, then swing by the hardware store to pick up fertilizer before returning to close up the pharmacy. Time seems to fly as we finish up at the local supermarket for Cô's weekly restock.

"So nice you are home, con." She puts the car in park after pulling into the driveway. "How about you stay at Cô's house tonight? We can have girls' night!"

"Great! It's a good thing I grabbed popcorn." Exiting from the passenger side, I circle around to open the trunk, but Cô hurries after me.

"What are you doing? Put that down!"

I pause with my arms clasped around a fertilizer bag. "I was going to take this to the garden."

She swats me away. "It's too heavy, you will hurt yourself. I will tell Chú to come help."

"But—"

She shoves a tote bag full of food in my face. "Take this to the kitchen."

I'm pretty sure her grocery haul is more of a threat to my back, but I decide not to tell her this as I lug it into the house. Once inside, I kick off my sneakers for a pair of slippers and make a beeline for the kitchen. Setting the bag on the counter, I stack the frozen items in the freezer first. Flour and oats go straight to the pantry, and soy sauce goes in the cabinet closest to the stove for easy access. I'm all too familiar with the snack drawer and make quick work of replenishing it. It's only the dried vermicelli noodles that are stumping me, and I scan the kitchen trying to figure out where they fit in Cô's meticulous system.

"Cabinet by the fridge, top shelf."

My body reacts before my mind does, but it locks up so I can't move. When my thoughts catch up, they collapse in on themselves like dominos. I'd never mistake that voice for anyone else's. It's the only one that sounds different when he calls my name. It's etched in me like a secret spilled beneath my skin, from intimate whispers in the dead of night.

I whip around to face Parker—or a Parker-like figment of my imagination—and nearly drop the bag of noodles.

"Here." He plucks it from me and reaches over my head, placing the noodles on the highest shelf with ease.

All the air leaves my lungs in a rush. I can't believe any of this is real, that he's really here. Am I dreaming? I blink hard, expecting him to disappear the second I wake from this trance. But he doesn't. "What . . . why are you—"

"Why am I in Silverpine?" He takes a step back to give me a

long scan. "What do you think? I came back for you."

"What does that even mean?"

"Well, I heard from my mom you were back in town. Next thing I knew I was booking a flight." The mask of calm nearly slips as he adds, "It's really good to see you. I missed you, Dani."

His hair isn't styled; it looks messy even, like he hasn't had the time to give it the usual attention. Did he race here from the airport?

"What about Venture?"

He offers a shrug and nothing more. "I have to admit, I'm surprised you let yourself take a break. You've been in full grind mode since you started your editor job. For a while, I thought you'd disappeared on me."

"I've barely heard from you since the Super Bowl. You've been just as busy."

"I've tried calling you."

"So have I," I say back, a little too pointedly.

The words hang in the air, and the room falls into a brief hush. I'm still trying to process what his sudden appearance means, but it's impossible not to feel slighted by the past three months of communication deadlock. I can't help but be a little guarded.

Parker's eyes search mine. Whatever he's feeling, he keeps it well hidden. Or perhaps the separation has dulled my senses, and I can't quite read him. Just when it seems like the quiet has gone on for too long, he leans against the counter and speaks. "I know there's the distance, and I've had a lot going on at work, but that doesn't mean I stopped thinking about us. But I can't tell if it's the same for you. Ever since I left, I've gotten the sense that something's been . . . off between us. Am I imagining it?"

"No, you're not wrong," I sigh, my shoulders dropping. "I guess it was easier for me to throw myself into work than think about things ending between us."

"I wasn't aware that we had ended."

I fold my arms over my chest. "Parker, you left without mentioning anything about the future. I assumed that meant it was over."

"What was I supposed to say? I couldn't ask you to drop everything and leave New York for me. I knew you wouldn't ask the same of me either."

"Exactly. You're not going to quit Venture or leave San Francisco, and I'm not going to walk out on my new job. I suppose if we had some kind of arrangement, then you could still visit and stay a couple weeks at a time. And I'd go to San Francisco, but—"

I stop myself.

But all it'll ever be is casual.

He stares at me, and I take in his anxious face, the pinched brows and the tight line of his mouth. I finally start to feel the heaviness of how much I've missed him. A week ago, we were on opposite sides of the country, but now, if I were to reach my hand out, I could lay it on his chest and feel the same heartbeat that had once lulled me to sleep.

"Parker? Why are you here?"

I flinch as a stunned Cô steps into the kitchen, her voice piercing the stillness and scattering everything left unsaid. Parker must not have alerted anyone to his return.

"I came back for Dani." He's said that twice now, and I'm still not any closer to an explanation that makes sense.

Her eyes fly to me, but my face is just as baffled as hers.

"That means . . ." She brandishes a finger between us with a gleeful spark. "You two are finally . . . ?"

"No, it's not what you think." I hold up a hand reflexively. I need to get ahead of the misunderstanding before it can make the tension any worse. "Parker was just telling me he needed a break from work, and when he heard I was here, he thought what a great idea it would be to also come home. Right?"

He raises a brow in my direction and opens his mouth, but closes it without a word.

"That's it?" Cô says sullenly. "You come home to slack off and bother Dani on her vacation?"

Parker makes a noise of disapproval. "Why is it vacation for Dani, but I'm the one slacking off?"

I almost feel bad for throwing him under the bus because Cô isn't subtle about her disappointment. "Má ơi! Why did they give me a windhead for a son?"

"Airhead, you mean," Parker grumbles. "And don't call me that."

"Airhead, groundhead, whatever." His mother throws an arm up in resignation, but an idea strikes her, signaled by her widening grin and the spark in her eye. "Wait. You're here, so you take Dani out tomorrow."

"Oh, no," I insert swiftly. "That's not necessary—"

"You want to go to Portland, yeah? You talk all day about that fancy pizza, 'the best in the city!'"

"We're not going to go all the way to the city for pizza."

"Why not? Your dad told me you do nothing all day! Just stay at home, sleep on the couch, watch the same movie over and over again. He is so worried about you!"

My face burns as I realize Dad must be keeping her updated on my pathetic sulking, and those updates include how many times I've rewatched *Chungking Express*. But that embarrassment is short-lived, squashed by my looming dread of what the next few days with Parker might look like. This can't end well, right? Even if he's told me he misses me and came all the way to Silverpine to see me, I'm still going back to New York at the end of the week. Aren't we headed down the same road to disappointment once we go our separate ways?

But Cô is not one to be deterred. "Parker will drive you! You kids have fun. But not too much pizza. Eat dinner at home, okay?"

"Sure, I can take you to Ken's tomorrow," Parker offers, pushing off the counter.

I shake my head. "I was referring to Apizza Scholls."

"Oh, I'm sorry. I thought she said best pizza in Portland."

If his mother wasn't in the room with us, I would deck him right then and there.

CHAPTER FORTY-ONE

Parker is helping himself to his third slice with what might be the most impressive poker face I've ever seen on someone devouring pizza. Balanced on the armrest between us, the takeout box wobbles every time I shift in the passenger seat and accidentally nudge it with my arm. After waiting in line at Apizza Scholls for nearly an hour, it wasn't much of a surprise that we couldn't secure a table. Our only option was to take the pizza back to the car and eat it while parked on a nearby block. Currently, a bed of napkins is the last line of defense between pizza grease and the interior of Chú's Toyota, and I have a momentary flashback to the two strawberry milkshakes in Parker's Jeep.

I sigh at him. "Just say it."

"Nope." He bites into crust. "I decided I'm going to be pleasant today."

I lift the box lid to help myself to a second slice. I don't care what Parker thinks; this is still the best pizza in Portland—nay, in all of Oregon. And I made a good call ordering the classic margherita. "I know you're dying to tell me that Ken's is better."

"This is good pizza, there's no denying that," he says diplomatically, peeking at me from under his SF Giants baseball cap. "We're both enjoying it, so why sour the mood?"

"And if I said the wood-fired hype was just food podcast propaganda?"

His fingers twitch around a balled up napkin, but he seems to think better of it and changes tack. "Hey, you should ask Apizza if you can write a piece on the restaurant."

"I don't know that I could sell it to Alfreda. Our intern tried to pitch a food-crawl piece, and she shut it down. 'Too lowbrow,' apparently." I air-quote the words and roll my eyes.

"She'd be crazy to say that about your work. I don't know why they can't give you more freedom to write what you want. I read the first issue cover to cover, and your pieces were the most interesting ones."

A warm tingle starts in my chest and works its way up to create a soft flush on my face. "That's your bias speaking."

"Maybe a little. But you know I'm right." Wiping his hands clean, he smirks over at me. "What should we do next? Do you want to stay in the city?"

I check my watch. We hadn't anticipated such a long wait in line. "I'd like to stop by Powell's since we're here, but we should head back soon if we're going to make it in time for dinner."

I move the pizza box onto my lap, and Parker starts the car. When I reach for the display screen and navigate to Music, the system syncs automatically to Android Auto instead of Parker's iPhone. Without warning, smooth and sultry saxophone notes float through the car's cabin, the familiar melody making us jump in our seats.

"What the . . ." Parker looks around, puzzled, finally lifting the armrest to check inside the storage compartment. "Oh my god. My dad left his phone in the car."

"Careless Whisper" is on full blast, and I can hardly hear my own thoughts over it. My head falls into my hands, shoulders shaking with laughter. "Does he listen to any other song?"

"I can't. Not today, George Michael." Parker turns off the music with a quick tap of the screen. "Every time I hear that song, I think of us in the garage and my dad killing any shot I had at hooking up with you."

"It was for the best," I say around a grin. "There was no way we weren't gonna get caught. The hickey was risky enough. That's why we have rules. No funny business when we're at home."

I glance over in time to see his jaw set, his eyes trained on the road ahead. "That rule still exists?"

"Yes. Which means nothing can happen this week."

"I know, but I'm just saying, if the rules are still in force, then doesn't that mean that we're not over?"

Parker takes a glimpse at me, and his gaze falls on my mouth for a fraction of a second. My body freezes in that fleeting moment. What am I supposed to do when instinctually, every muscle in me still craves him? How do I pretend I don't still think about all those nights at the hotel?

But I tamp down that urge by reminding myself that what I want doesn't align with our rules anymore. And although nothing leads me to believe Parker is here to ask me for a serious relationship, I've already made up my mind: If he doesn't want to be my boyfriend, I'm not going to wait around for our schedules to line up to be his *casual* friend.

"Maybe I'm breaking every ground rule by saying this," I harden my voice, summoning every ounce of my courage. "But the thing is, I just can't go back to casual now."

"Dani, I'm not asking that of you."

"Then why did you come back to Silverpine? To drive me around and wait in line for pizza?"

"Do I really need a reason? I miss you. I spent the best three months of my life in New York with you, after seven whole years thinking I might never see you again," he says. "Of course, I would come back when I hear you're in our hometown."

But is that really enough for you? Because I'm always going to want more than this. I know I should be honest, but what am I so afraid of? That the only other option is to move on with our lives? My throat closes up as I watch the streets slip by in smears of color—painted walls, cyclists in their bright gear. There's a faint haze in the air from the earlier drizzle. I can't seem to focus on anything but the ticking of the turn signal when the car stops at a light. My mind has been in its own haze of uncertainty for days. I came to Silverpine for some clarity; why do I feel even more confused than before?

"Are you all right?"

Pulling in a long and deep breath, I blurt out, "My dad is planning to sell our house."

Parker's eyes go wide. The initial flash of shock settles into a blank expression. Did I look just as stunned when Dad broke the news to me? "Your house next door to us?"

"That's the one." My answer comes out more dryly than I intended. "He wants to move out east to be closer to me."

"Your dad's going to leave Silverpine?"

"Yes, and I can't tell him not to do it, especially now that he's making an effort to build a relationship with me."

"But what about you? You don't want to sell, right?"

"Of course not. It's been my home since I was seven." I look down at the pizza box resting on my lap and suddenly notice how tightly my hands are clutching the sides. "The worst part is, I spent so many years avoiding this place. Now that I can come back, I thought . . . I don't know, that it would last a little longer?"

"You can always come back," he reassures me.

"But it'll be different," I say. "We won't be neighbors anymore."

I try not to think of the times I wheeled my luggage up the

front porch and found Dad waiting for me in the foyer with a cup of oolong tea. I try even harder not to recall all the Thanksgivings and Christmases spent next door. I don't want to start crying. I've done a good job of holding it back for so long now.

After we leave Powell's, the ride home is quiet, and I don't think either of us knows what to say. In the silence, I let myself absorb the sight of our hometown as it rolls into view. Towering evergreens make room for the cobbled paths leading up to the town center, where mist clings to the cedar shingles of the storefronts. A pair of older men are sitting with mismatched mugs outside the Pine Street Bakehouse. As we pass it, the chime bell above Dawsons tinkles sharp and clear with a swing of the door.

"It's too bad we couldn't take the Jeep out again," I say, facing the window. "You know, for old time's sake."

"Next time," Parker promises me.

CHAPTER FORTY-TWO

I suppose Estelle was onto something. A few days of bumming around without any work to do, and my bed has quickly become my favorite place on Earth. I can't fathom being anywhere else at ten a.m. on a Friday. It almost seems audacious of the universe to expect me to go back to an existence in which I am away from my home, saddled with real-life responsibilities.

I look over at the curled issue of *From Venus* on my nightstand and blow out a resigned sigh before peeling myself off the bed. I leave for New York tomorrow; I'd better make use of the time I have left. After washing up, I head downstairs, where the door to Dad's office is closed. I don't want to bother him, so I go straight to the garage, where he's left a pile of flattened cardboard boxes. I take one with me, send a quick text to Parker, and make my way back upstairs.

Standing at the center of my room and tapping my foot against the carpet, I take a long, hard look at the old birch dresser. Then, I sit down and pull open the bottom drawer. The copy of *Moonstruck* catches my eye, and I pick it up to run my hand over the creased cover. The image of an enamored Cher, arms thrown up, has long been burned into my mind. Here is a woman struck by love, and for all the trouble it's caused her, she's never been more liberated.

Just like the night I first kissed Parker, I think of Mom

crying as the end credits rolled across the screen. Was it only *Moonstruck*, or did all the movies she loved so much bring out the hopeless romantic in her? For a long time, that was the version of her I chose to remember. I'm sure that whimsical woman in my memory would kick her feet up and squeal if I told her all the little things Parker did to make my heart race. And when it came down to it, I'd ask her if letting him go again is the right choice, or if I'm making a mistake. If she were still that version of my mother today, perhaps she'd know exactly what I'm supposed to do.

Reaching into the drawer again, my hand bumps a wooden case in the corner, knocking the lid slightly ajar. I lift the music box with careful hands and wind it up using the small metal turn key. The drum rotates within, its pins intricately plucked to produce the melody. I listen to the chime of the first notes and a familiar warmth spreads through me down to my fingertips, which have gone still.

A knock on the door snaps me out of my reverie. I call out, "Come in."

The door clicks open, and Parker pokes his head in. When he spots me by the open drawer, he doesn't speak a word and waits for the song to come to its end. "I've never seen that before."

"I stored it away because I was afraid of wearing it out," I explain. "It plays 'Moon River.' I didn't know the title at first, and for the longest time, it was simply the song from Mom's music box. Then I found an old cassette mixtape that she had made herself, and Audrey Hepburn's version was the first track."

"*Breakfast at Tiffany's*, right? You mentioned it's one of her favorites." He steps inside, closing the door behind him. "I got your text. Lucky for you, bubble wrap is yet another thing my mom hoards."

"Perfect." I grab the roll he extends to me, tearing off enough to wrap around the music box.

"Are you packing already?"

"I'm sending these back to my mom," I reply, meeting Parker's troubled gaze. He studies my face, concern written in his features. "A belated wedding gift."

"Your mom got married?"

"Yes, and I wasn't invited. I think she didn't want me to feel obligated to attend."

He takes the spot next to me on the carpet and says softly, "I'm sorry, Dani."

"I should've expected it. She's been worlds away, living her own life since she left. It just so happens there isn't any room for me there." I try to crack a smile, but it doesn't do much to ease his worry.

"That doesn't mean you have to be fine with it," he says. "Are you sure you want to give up all this? I know how important it is to you."

"My dad is very likely going to sell this place. It seems kind of silly, trying to take her from house to house when she never wanted to come along."

When I used to picture this moment, I was afraid it'd be too painful for me to bear. But thinking of Mom receiving this box now, it doesn't scare me anymore that there might be a future where we can't go back to the way things were. All those memories I'd kept sacred in that drawer, they're like pages I've read too many times, I can flip past them now without flinching.

"It's always going to hurt a little," I admit as I start on a pile of Disney classics, retrieving each tape one by one. "There was a time I thought I was missing out on something by not having her around. I used to look at other families and wonder if mine was incomplete. But if I'm being honest, I stopped feeling her absence a long time ago."

"When did that start?"

"Sometime after my third Christmas with you guys."

Parker watches me attentively as I move the box closer. "What do you need me to do to make this easier for you?"

I purse my lips, thinking. "You can help me bubble wrap."

With a nod, he reaches for the roll. As he lifts a VHS tape from the drawer, he says to me in a gentle whisper, "What you're doing is really brave. I hope you know that."

The box gradually fills up with neat, meticulously padded columns. I hand him the last of the tapes after they've been wrapped, and we place the music box in a secure corner where it won't be jostled around. Once the drawer has been emptied, I seal the cardboard and Parker carries the box downstairs, leaving it by the front door.

"Is that all you're going to pack?" he asks when he returns to my room.

"For now," I say, plopping onto the bed. "There's still time. The listing hasn't even gone up yet."

"It's so weird to think of you moving. I can't picture anyone but you and your dad living here."

"Don't start that," I warn. Once we start getting sentimental over the move, it'll sink in that it's really happening.

"You know how you'd leave your desk lamp on whenever you stayed up late to study? I used to be able to see it from my room." He glances over at the window. "Back then, there were nights when I'd get anxious about recruitment and couldn't sleep. But if I looked over and saw your light on, I knew you were still up. It made me feel less alone."

I follow his gaze to the curtains glowing faintly, sunlight

seeping through the fabric. "I didn't know that."

Parker seats himself at the foot of the bed, and his broad frame makes it hard not to get close. I cross my legs, and my thigh rests against his. "I wish I'd gotten here sooner. You're already leaving, and we barely got to hang out."

"When do you have to go back?"

"Monday. I'm flying straight to Detroit for the draft," he murmurs, reaching over to stretch his left shoulder. "I'm assuming you've already started working on the next issue."

"I'm a week behind because of this little getaway," I groan.

"I hope that doesn't mean you're going to work insane hours again. Seriously, you should be sleeping more."

"Take care of yourself before you worry about my sleep, Parker."

"I can't help but worry about you, though." A smirk lifts the corners of his mouth, but it's a bittersweet one. "Hey, I wanted to ask. There's got to be a universe where we stay in Silverpine, right? What do you think it's like?"

I've thought of this before, another world where Parker and I didn't leave for college and never had that falling out. "Hmm. Do you remember that sporting goods store you worked at for a summer? I imagine you open one just like it."

"Oh, yeah. I liked working there."

"I know." I add, "You also coach a youth league on the weekends."

"You definitely still write," he inserts. "You also revive the local newspaper, because you're always saying it's a pity that no one reads it anymore."

"*The Pinecone Press*," I beam at him. "At the end of the day, we come back to your place for dinner, then movies at mine. Um, but at that rate, we might never leave home, and then my dad will be begging me to move out."

"My mom would love that. I would too." He grins and offers his hand on my lap, open and waiting. I stare down at the quiet invitation before lacing my fingers through his, allowing the warmth of his touch to flow through me.

After Dad moves, we'll be a two-, maybe three-hour drive apart. I won't have to make the journey out here to see him. I'm certain Parker has realized this as well. Without our house, that means fewer occasions to be in Silverpine, fewer holidays spent next door. I've already missed so many Thanksgivings that I won't be able to make up. Will there still be a chance for me to mend those bridges? Or will there come a time when, once again, Parker isn't in my life anymore?

In the past, I was so confident our friendship could make it through anything. But then it was lost without warning, and before I knew it, seven years slipped by. The worst part is, at some point, its absence became normal to me. I learned to live without him.

"What time is your flight tomorrow?"

"Noon. My dad is going to take me early in the morning. Then I guess it's back to real life." I grit my teeth against the slow-burning ache. *Even though nothing about the three months in New York felt real to me.*

His hand tightens around mine. "I don't think I'll ever get used to saying goodbye to you."

Before I can respond, Parker brings me in for a tight embrace. Just like when he held me on New Year's, I feel it in my soul: cozy, soothing, *home*. We sit like this in a tender, unhurried moment, and when he kisses my forehead, I close my eyes against his chest.

I love you.

Then and now, I never stopped loving you.

A sting rises behind my eyes, but I hold it back, laughing to myself. "This is silly. We'll see each other again, even if it's not in Silverpine."

I know this, but why is it so hard? Why is it that every time we say good-bye, it feels like the end? Since I was a child, I've felt like I was chasing something that stayed just beyond my fingertips. But for three magical months in New York, I had a glimpse of what it looked like to have it all: those nights at the hotel when I thought my heart would burst, conversations that made me laugh like a kid again. Not just the heated moments, but the slow afternoons playing video games and falling asleep on the couch. Every time, it was Parker on the other end. It's always been Parker. How could it ever be anyone else?

Maybe in that other universe, I'd tell him all this, and he'd want the same thing. Not casual, but the *real* thing. In all the variations of timelines and parallel worlds out there, there has to be one where we get it right.

Although one thing, I'm sure, is a constant in every universe: I'll fall in love with Parker Tran every time.

CHAPTER FORTY-THREE

After Parker drives me to the post office to drop off Mom's package, I return home on my own. There's no way I can say goodbye to him a second time tonight, not when the urge to cry is still sitting raw in my throat. Rather than spend the rest of the day wallowing in bed, I decide I can watch *Chungking Express* one more time. A whirlwind of neon lights and flickering signs spills from my laptop screen, illuminating the dimmed room. In the restless Hong Kong night, a woman in a flight attendant's uniform walks up to a snack bar where a man is repairing a broken door. It's here that Faye Wong reunites with Tony Leung. She draws a boarding pass on a napkin and asks him where he wants to go. He answers, "Wherever you'll take me."

The credits roll, and I shut the laptop. I don't bother to check my phone; the sun hanging low beyond my window has already informed me I've been here too long. My stomach grumbles under the bed covers, and I realize now that I've forgotten to eat all day.

On my way downstairs, I hear a loud clatter from the kitchen, and I worry that Dad is attempting another recipe from those YouTube channels run by Taiwanese aunties. He's never been much of a cook; that was Mom's role, and after she left, I found myself next door for dinner more often than not. Nevertheless, I have to commend him for trying.

But the smell wafting from the kitchen is much too fragrant

to be Dad's doing, and I know at once who's responsible. I peek in, and sure enough, Cô is stationed by the stove with an apron on. She smiles widely when she spots me.

"You're alive! I'm making dinner."

"Were you here the whole time?" I ask. "Sorry I didn't come down sooner."

"You sleep well?"

"Yes, very well," I lie, but the way she's inspecting my eye bags, I can tell I'm busted.

"Here, go eat." She ladles congee into a bowl and hands it to me. I take a seat at the dining table in the adjacent room, and the screech of the chair leg against the floor is jarringly loud. While next door buzzes with commotion and laughter, our house has always sat in hush and calm. It never bothered me much. Dad and I both find comfort in silence.

Cô arrives with cilantro and finely shredded ginger to add to my congee. I pull out the chair at the head of the table so she can sit next to me.

She sweeps my hair over my shoulder. "You are so busy with your new job. Don't forget to eat. Sleep early too. I asked Chú to pack vitamins for you."

"Thanks, Cô."

"Eat, con, eat," she urges. The first spoonful of congee is like a quiet sigh of relief—familiar flavors taking me back to shared meals on chilly evenings with the scent of simmering broth weaving through the air. I take another hurried bite.

"This cháo recipe is from my mom. She always said cháo can fix anything. If you're sick, it heals you, body, mind, and soul." Her eyes meet mine with a softness that doesn't require words. No flicker of judgment, just a deep compassion. "Even when your heart feels sick."

I set the spoon down on the placemat. "I guess you already know about us moving."

"Your dad told me. And I talked to Parker too." With a crease in her forehead, she looks torn between continuing that thought or holding back. "He told me everything."

"Everything?"

"I know he didn't go to New York back then. He is the one who stopped talking to you." She shakes her head with a sigh. "He made a stupid mistake, but Parker still cares about you so much."

I chew my lip nervously. "Did he give you all the details?"

She nods. "Yes. The hotel. Upstairs in his bedroom."

I hold my breath for an excruciating beat. "I'm sorry, I know that's not exactly the traditional route you wanted for us."

"Dani, you guys are old enough to do what you want," she says, but her mouth is drawn tight into a flat line. "Maybe it's a little shocking. Keep it a secret from Chú, he's still old-fashioned."

"To be honest, I thought you might be happy to hear about us, even if we weren't technically dating. I expected you to shout it from the rooftops or throw a party."

At this, a hand flies to her chest. "How can I celebrate when you have a broken heart now?"

I flinch at this, her motherly instinct pouring over me with sympathy. "How can you tell?"

"You're so quiet, you don't smile, and you watch the same movie every day. It hurts Cô to see you like this." Worry carves itself into deep lines across her face. "I don't understand. Why can't he be with you?"

"It's complicated," I reply. "We live three thousand miles from each other, for one. And if history is any indication, we aren't very good with distance. It was hard enough as friends, how would we make it work as a couple?" *Not to mention, your son has a jaded view on love and doesn't believe in relationships.*

"Then you two move back home."

This actually makes me guffaw. "We're about to sell the house!"

Cô folds her arms over her chest with an indignant huff. I pick up my spoon, but with the weight beneath my ribs pushing up like a tide, the next bite is almost tasteless. I sit back in my chair and meet Cô's watchful gaze.

"I had this tiny hope when Parker showed up here. I thought he was going to tell me he wants to be with me. But I don't think we want the same thing. If we did, then it wouldn't be this hard, right?"

"Give him time. I think he has a good reason to come back here."

"I'm sure you know this, but Parker has always been the type to act on his feelings," I say. "They might've brought him here this time, but what happens when he remembers where his home is? Is he going to choose me then? And I know how selfish that sounds, because he had a whole life in San Francisco before everything happened between us."

"It's not selfish to want people you love to stay," Cô insists. "That's human, Dani."

"Sometimes I feel like Parker and I exist in different worlds. When he popped into mine for those three months, he was just passing by. Taking a detour before going back to where he belongs." My hand curls into a fist on the table. "Even back in college, I had this fear that he'd go somewhere I couldn't reach him. And then one day, he really did disappear."

A tremor in my voice betrays me, but I can't cry now. I've done a good job at keeping myself together. All the late nights at the *Venus* office when I was one email away from breaking down, only to rein it in. I even managed to stay composed when I passed Mom's things to the post office worker. But now, the impulse fights back. My mind dredges up the VHS tapes, and suddenly I regret not watching *Moonstruck* one last time. Every crushing emotion from the last three months is on the verge of spilling over. I have a clawing need to let myself fall apart.

"I love him, Cô." The words slip from me as a sob catches in my chest. "But when has loving someone ever convinced them to stay with me? What good is it if it's never enough?"

She leans over to gather me in a hug. "You have a soft heart; we call that 'dễ mềm long' in Vietnamese. Sometimes you get hurt, but it's not a bad thing, to love with your whole heart. Never change that, Dani."

That's what it takes to finally let the tears go. My face falls into my hands, and I cry over a bowl of congee as Cô holds me. And it's one of those long, exhausting cries.

CHAPTER FORTY-FOUR

"Are you sure I won't go over baggage allowance?" I peer into a second tote bag handed to me after I just managed to squeeze the first one, filled with vitamins and over-the-counter medications, into my luggage. This one contains a random assortment of items: fuzzy socks, snacks from the Asian supermarket, and toothbrushes with the local dentist's address on them. Cô must've done a lap around her house, collecting anything she deemed useful to me. While this level of care isn't uncharacteristic, I get the feeling she's still concerned after watching me cry last night until my congee turned cold.

She scans the luggage on the floor of my bedroom and waves a dismissive hand.

"What if it won't close?"

"Sit on it. Always works for Cô."

"Yes, ma'am," I say back, unzipping my luggage to organize the items inside for the third time. A loud thud from downstairs makes Cô yelp and cluck her tongue in grievance. Dad and Chú have been rearranging furniture all morning, with some of the older pieces getting moved to the curb. When the realtor dropped by a couple days ago, he made suggestions about how to spruce up the place for photos. Dad took these to heart, and now every room is getting a makeover to look its best in the listing. Which means this is really happening. We're selling the house.

Cô moves to the window, drawing the curtains wide as golden sunbeams pour in. It's a remarkably sunny day for April in Silverpine. As she gazes outside to appreciate the light, her face suddenly twists in bewilderment. "Why is that thing here?"

I stand up to get a look, expecting to find the couch or TV stand discarded outside, but I hear it before I reach the window: the low growl of the engine, the off-road tires that hum like a swarm of bees. Staring at the driveway, I watch as Parker's black Jeep Wrangler makes its unmistakable homecoming.

"Is that Parker?" Cô asks, but the car is already so far up the driveway that it slips into a blind spot. We exchange a puzzled look, but I don't immediately move from the window until Cô gives me a gentle push toward the door. Stumbling out of my room, I reach the stairs, where I see Parker making his way through the foyer, stepping over cardboard boxes. He glances up at me from the landing, and I freeze, trying to commit this image to memory. This might be the last time he enters this house looking for me.

"Why is the Jeep here?" I finally manage to ask.

"I took it out of storage," he says, shoving keys into his jacket pocket. "You said you wanted to take it out for a ride."

I descend the last steps to get to him. "I'm leaving soon."

"I know," he says, and he waits for me to reach him. "Can we talk?"

Cô is already behind me, her slippers pattering noisily on her way down. "Why did you bring your old car here?"

"Dani? Have you finished packing yet?" Dad is next to enter from the living room, with Chú in tow. They take turns looking Parker up and down. "We're supposed to leave in an hour."

Parker cuts in, "Actually, if it's all right, I was hoping I could take her to the airport."

"In your Jeep?" Cô scowls. "That thing is safe?"

"I do maintenance on it whenever I'm in town, and if I know I'll be gone for a while, I have a friend from high school do it for me. Trust me, it's safe."

"Really?" Chú scratches his head. "Don't you drive an Aston Martin in San Francisco?"

"It's a sentimental thing. You wouldn't get it." Parker shakes his head before he regains his focus and pivots to me. "Dani, I really need to talk to you."

"About what?" I blink up at him, the urgency in his voice prickling my skin.

"Trời ơi, you want to get dramatic now?" Cô groans as she tosses her hands up in exasperation. "Goodbye is not the end of the world. Even if Dani moves, she will still come here and spend every Thanksgiving with us."

That's the first I'm hearing of this. "I will?"

"Christmas and Fourth of July too," she says resolutely. "This is your home."

She is right. I spent the best years of my life next door. It's another piece of home, just like this house. Why did I ever doubt that? Her reassurance instantly makes me feel lighter, but I steal a peek at Dad to check with him. He simply nods, a hint of a smile on his face.

"I'm not trying to say goodbye," Parker inserts, and his eyes sweep over the four of us, gathered around him in a circle. "Look, I just need a minute with Dani. Without an audience."

His expression wields an impatient intensity, and he shoves a restless hand through his hair. The longer I watch him, the more my chest tightens painfully. What's so urgent that he has to speak to me now, an hour before I leave? I'm afraid that it'll leave me crushed, like so many times before when I allowed myself to get my hopes up.

"Parker, if you've come to tell me it's not over, you should know that this—the coming and going, without any promise of something real—it's not what I want. I want more." Ignoring the stares around me, I push past my nerves to add, "An actual relationship."

Dad coughs and then whispers hoarsely, "Relationship? What is she talking about?"

"Oh, *so* complicated," Cô hisses, making no effort to be discreet. "Dani wants to be with Parker, Parker wants to be with Dani, but they're too afraid."

"Afraid of what?"

"Exactly!"

"Má!" Parker shouts. "Oh my god. This isn't how I wanted to do this."

"Fine." Cô places her hands on her hips. "Go on, con. Say what you want to say."

His jaw unclenches with a slow exhale, and for a brief moment, he seems to be collecting himself. When he gazes down at me, he speaks with a steady calm. "Remember when I said I came back here for you?"

"Starting to sound like a threat, but yes."

"I love you. That's what I came back to Silverpine to say."

The room falls still. It's so quiet, all I can hear is the roaring of my own pulse. Suddenly, my heart is teetering on a cliff, one breath away from falling over.

"I've loved you all my life," he continues. "Since we were kids riding bikes for the first time. Since the night I saw you in my jersey. Every time you worked on an article and didn't realize I was watching you. The scrunch of your face when you're focusing, every tweak of your brow. I have it all saved in my brain.

The moment I met you in New York, I fell in love with you all over again."

Time pauses around me, like the universe is stalling for this one moment. I can't stop the tears welling in my eyes. How long have I waited to hear him say it? That wish has always been there, secretly tucked into every game of catch, every ride in the Jeep, and all those nights in New York when my hand would find his under the bedcovers.

Parker clears his throat, and a fierce blush spreads across his face, all the way to his ears. Cô has her hands over her mouth in stunned silence. Dad and Chú are standing side by side like statues, mouths agape. No one moves an inch. Twenty-two years I've been in love with the boy next door, leading up to this one breathtaking confession, and we can't even get the room alone.

"Let's go outside." Parker takes my hand, and Cô lets out a delighted squeal. I can't seem to catch my breath as he leads me out of the house and onto the front porch. My legs are weak beneath me, but adrenaline is keeping me from falling. That, and the hand that won't let me go.

CHAPTER FORTY-FIVE

My attention flies over to the Jeep, the bulky presence parked in front of the garage doors. He wasn't lying when he mentioned the maintenance; the car looks no different from the first time he picked me up in it. Under the sun, the black paint job still gleams with a luster that time hasn't dared to touch.

Parker stops walking when we reach the driveway but keeps his hand tight around mine. The weight of his confession is preventing me from spiraling out of orbit, but the restless beat in my chest makes me dizzy nonetheless. *He loves me. He's loved me all this time.*

"You know what I did when I went home last night?" he says, his words cutting through the haze in my head. "I watched *Chungking Express*, hoping to find some revelation in your favorite movie that might tell me what to do. But when I got to the end, I was more irked than anything." A frown pulls at the edges of his mouth. "Do you think they end up together?"

"Faye and Tony? I don't know, it's hard to tell." My brows draw together as I try to connect the dots. "She was only stopping by on a layover. He's holding the grand opening for the Express, but she can't attend it. The boarding pass isn't even real, it's just a napkin."

"That's weird. Why did I assume it was a happy ending the first time I watched it? I guess I figured Tony would go after her, if he was in love."

"Parker, where are you going with this?"

He looks down at my hand and gives it a tender squeeze. "When I got back to San Francisco, it was like I hit a wall. I threw myself into work because that seemed to be the only way to get around it. And then I was here with you again, and I realized I don't know how to go back to life without . . . *this*."

I bite down on my lip as a tiny fear casts a shroud of uncertainty. It's all so perfect, it almost seems impossible. "When you left New York, you didn't mention anything about the future or what would happen to us. I assumed that meant you didn't want anything more than casual."

"I've steered clear of relationships for so long, I didn't think I knew how to be a boyfriend to you," he explains. "We had rules too, and it was confusing when I started wanting something real. I wasn't sure if I was even allowed to want those things."

A softness in his eyes reminds me of our conversation at the gorge, under the waterfall. No defenses, no masks, just his unguarded truth. It stirs in me a protective instinct, and I reach out to him, cupping his face in my palm.

"You want to be my boyfriend? You know what that entails, right?"

"I'm familiar with the concept."

"It means cohabitating with three different air purifiers. Waiting in line with me at the next viral restaurant. Staying in to watch movies on a Friday night when I don't feel like going out."

"You mean, like everything we've done since New York?" he counters, and as always, his confidence is unshakable. "I was already your boyfriend before you knew it."

"But how would we do this?" I ask almost reluctantly. "We live on opposite sides of the country."

"About that." A bold grin lifts the corners of his lips. I know that one. It tells me I should prepare myself for what comes next. "I asked Venture to transfer me to New York."

The shock hits me like a wave, and I take a step back. "You can't leave San Francisco for me."

"Well, that's too bad, because I sent them my request this morning."

"Parker, you need to think this through—"

"This is what I want, Dani," he says. "I don't want casual, and I don't want to wait months to see you for two, three weeks at a time. Those aren't options anymore. At least, not for me."

He sounds so assured, so unhesitating, that I want to put all my faith in him. Haven't I waited my whole life for this? This is the first boy I wanted to kiss, ever since I learned what a kiss was. My eyes pool with tears once more. Parker reaches for my face but can't wipe them away in time.

"I don't know if you're doing the right thing, but I know that I want to be with you. Ever since we were kids, it was all I ever wanted." Taking a deep breath, I ready my heart. "I love you, Parker."

It's so easy to say. I've had it on the tip of my tongue for so long. Maybe it's as simple as that. Maybe that's all the reassurance I'll ever need.

I watch the way his face changes. His eyes softening, the slight parting of his lips. Thoughts that I can't read flying through his mind.

"We suck at casual." He smiles at me, and it's as crushingly charming as ever. How is it possible to love someone this much? My heart has never been so full. It's like every second that I'm not kissing him is tragically wasted.

I pull him in and kiss him hard. God, it's a wonder how I lasted three months without this. All at once, my doubts fade to a quieting solace. I can't be worried about the future, or tomorrow, or even the next minute when I lose my mind to the stunning thrill of this kiss.

A muted protest is on my lips when he breaks away too soon, whispering into the space between us, "I should take you to the airport."

I glance over his shoulder at the Jeep before returning to him with a defiant grin. "I'm not catching that flight. I already decided that when I stepped outside with you."

Startled, he asks, "Are you sure?"

"My dad might kill me, but it's fine. I can take a red-eye tomorrow and be back by Monday morning," I say, giving his chest a reassuring pat before circling the car to the other side. "Shall we go for a ride?"

Without missing a beat, he opens the door for me, and this time I don't struggle to climb in. Even after seven long years, it's just as I remember. The very same aux cord hangs forlornly from the center console, and the all-black interior is as pristine as ever, all traces of strawberry milkshake diligently scrubbed away.

"This is so nostalgic," I say in quiet awe as Parker climbs in beside me. "You know, the first time you picked me up in this car, I thought you were finally going to make a move on me."

He winces at this, turning on the engine and fiddling with the controls just like when he was eighteen. "If I'd known I could've kissed you sooner, that night would've gone a lot differently."

"Okay, humor me." I buckle myself in. "What would've happened instead?"

"Well, you would've kissed me back because you were likewise obsessed with me."

I laugh. "And then?"

He thinks about it. "And then I would've said, 'I know you're going to New York for school, and I'm staying in-state. But I don't mind waiting. I'd wait forever for you.' Turns out I'm pretty good at it."

Somewhere off the side of a cliff, my heart beats wildly for this man. I don't know how he keeps doing it, but I hope he never stops. "Not me. I don't think I can wait any longer."

"No, I can't either," he says, and Parker finally kisses me in the front seat of his Jeep.

EPILOGUE

PARKER

Three years later

"Parker, the game's on."

Nathan has come into the kitchen to help himself to a beer, and he stares at me expectantly from the fridge. I glance at Dani, still flipping through her three-inch-thick binder, and Má, who's watching over her shoulder. Her reading glasses slide down her nose as her face twists in concentration. Dani's own expression mirrors that focus, though the undertone of panic is a little more obvious. At the center of our huddle is an impromptu seating plan on the kitchen counter, Post-it notes and red X's scattered all across it.

I shoot him a look, opening both hands in disbelief and mouthing, *Seriously?*

"The Niners are on."

"You've got to be kidding." I throw my head back and gesture to the chart as Dani adds another Post-it, then immediately peels it off. "Can't you see we've got more important things going on?"

Thursday Night Football is the last thing on my mind. We've got a crisis at hand, with the worst possible timing. Dani's aunt just found out that her ex-husband is bringing his new twenty-two-year-old girlfriend as his plus-one to our wedding. Her frenzied phone call ended with a demand to put at least four tables between them, which means we have to rearrange the entire Tsai side now, less than twenty-four hours before the reception.

"Can you put your aunt here?" Má offers, pointing to a circle two away from the head table.

Dani winces. "That's where Dà Gū is sitting, and they can't stand each other. They'll bicker all night."

I start drawing up a new card for the seating board. It's a good thing we opted for handwritten. "Maybe we can retract your uncle's plus-one?"

"No, we can't do that now." She taps her pen against the marble countertop. "Would it be totally awful if I seated the girlfriend at the kids' table?"

Before I can tell her how perfect that idea is, she shakes her head and goes back to scrawling on another Post-it. Her features sharpen with intensity, heightened by her catlike eyes. That happens whenever she's deep in thought. *God, she's so pretty*. No, Parker! Now's not the time!

Dani catches me mid-thought and gives my hand an encouraging pat. "You can watch the game. One of us should get to unwind before the wedding."

"And let you hog all the stress to yourself? No way." I kiss the top of her head and take a moment to stretch in my seat. Since the planning began ten months ago, I've been trying to be as involved as possible. Not just because I want to take the load off Dani, but because I care about the wedding as much as she does. The venue, guest list, catering, and every Post-it attached to each respective heading—I know that binder inside-out by now.

"Are you sure?"

"Yeah. I'll catch the highlights later."

She gives me a sweet smile before returning to the chart. *Oof, my heart.*

"Why can't you send some of them to our side? You can even stick 'em with the Phams for a good time. Má's side is always a party." Nathan attempts to lift a sticky labeled *Tsai #3*. As he invades our space, the beer bottle in his hand spurts a single droplet, landing an inch from Dani's binder. Her face turns white. A terrified gasp leaves my lips. Má shouts, "Chết rồi!" and curses at him in Vietnamese.

"Nathan, go away!" Dani flaps a hand at him, and as her arm flails in the air, the three-carat diamond on her finger catches the light from overhead. Nathan groans, covering his eyes.

"Dani, what did I tell you about waving that thing around? You're going to flag an airplane down on us!"

He hasn't spared us the jokes since we came home last Thanksgiving and broke the news of our engagement. As it turns out, Dani's supposed aversion to water disappeared when the chance arose to take my sailboat out on New York Harbor. One evening, with the sun setting over the Manhattan skyline, I got down on one knee and asked her to be my wife. See, I knew holding onto that boat would reap its benefits: If you can get far enough out on the water, you'll find the perfect moment to be alone. Dani cried, and I did too, but no one shed more tears than my mother as she broadcast our announcement on Facebook Live for relatives in Vietnam I've never met.

Dani's phone buzzes on the counter, and I see the flash of terror in her eyes. What last-minute disaster awaits us now? She taps at it frantically and sighs.

"Tae-woo won't stop texting me," she says through clenched teeth. "Between him, Charlotte, and Reggie, I don't know who's being the biggest pain. They're the only ones who booked hotels in Portland because the Silverpine Inn wasn't bougie enough for them. Now I have to deal with all their questions about which Portland club is popping off or where all the hipster hotties hang."

I hold out my hand, signaling for her phone. "Give me that."

> **Me: This is Parker. Go take a walk. Fall into the Willamette River for all I care. But from now on, you're banned from texting the bride.**

I set the phone down and rub my temples. Great, now it's starting to get to me. We flew in from New York a few days ago to start preparations, and everything has been a blur since we landed. Having the wedding in Silverpine was a given, but that also meant having two-thirds of our guest list fly in. You never really grasp how many people you know until they're all asking you where the best brunch spot is. No matter. I have to keep it together. For Dani.

"You're really not going to watch the game?" Nathan is glaring at me over the lip of his beer. He can't seem to comprehend the urgency here. Ironic, because he was a lot less distracted when he thought he'd be planning his own wedding, back when Irene was still in the picture. "What, did the Giants make you switch your loyalty from the Niners?"

"Hey." I point a stern finger at him. "None of that blasphemy."

New York was the obvious choice for Dani and me. Venture didn't have any transfer openings, but the sting of disappointment didn't last long. In a couple weeks, Reggie lined up an interview for me with the New York Giants' marketing team. As soon as I received an offer from them, I handed Venture my two-week notice and bade farewell to my six years in San Francisco. The fact that Dani didn't have a Giants joke in her arsenal told me she was feeling more guilty than she let on. I had to remind her what a sweet deal my new gig is. Not only do I get to return to my football roots, but I never have to sit through another client dinner again. There are other forms of torture I'd choose over some fossil who's never left the western hemisphere explaining sushi to me.

When all was said and done, we moved to an apartment in Manhattan to make my drive in and out of Jersey a little easier. Now, instead of being forced to appear at launch parties, I get to clock out at five and go straight home to the only person I want to hear ramble about food.

"Con, go to the hotel now, before it gets too late," Má says to me in Vietnamese, adding, "It's unlucky for the bride and groom to spend the night together before the wedding."

"I'll leave once Dani goes to bed."

"I don't think she's going to sleep tonight," Nathan whispers as we watch her flip to the allergy portion of her binder to triple-check it against the menu.

"Then I won't either."

"Everyone here, go to bed before midnight." Má's voice is a rigid warning to the room. "Don't forget, tomorrow morning is the tea ceremony."

Asian weddings have an excess of traditions, most of which Dani and I decided to forgo to keep the celebration as low-key as possible. But we agreed to do a tea ceremony. It's a good thing there's so much overlap in Vietnamese and Taiwanese traditions, because with this, we've managed to placate both sides. Which reminds me, I have to go over the Tsai family tree again tonight. Imagine the horror of calling an auntie by the wrong title after she's just handed me a bulky red pocket stuffed with cash.

"You kids skipped over so many customs, I'm surprised you

even considered the tea ceremony." Dani's dad strides into the kitchen to offer his input. Because what's family for, if not to backseat-drive your big day? "Do you remember your cousin Jeff's wedding with the traditional Chinese banquet? It was so beautiful! They even included a lion dance!"

Dani throws me a quick glance. I'm well versed in these by now. This one's saying, *Whatever comes next, under no circumstances are you to say yes*. "You guys should add that in! A lion dance is supposed to bring you good fortune."

After selling the house, her father moved into a row home in Philadelphia, not far from Nathan's condo in Fishtown. I hear they actually hang out, which makes me laugh considering how dramatic we were about not being neighbors anymore. Turns out our families are closer than ever. The two-hour commute to Manhattan also means Mr. Tsai (or Dad soon) drops in every few weeks so we can tackle Dani's ultimate foodie spreadsheet. Saying goodbye to her childhood home took some adjusting, but I can tell it means more to Dani to have her father around, and not just for the holidays. Twenty family counseling sessions (and twenty pints of Morgenstern's ice cream) later, the progress is in the small concessions, like how she's about to hold her tongue no matter how ridiculous she thinks it is for him to suggest a lion dance.

"I think it's a little too late for that, Dad," she tells him calmly, but like a flipped switch, she suddenly gasps. My pulse skyrockets. "Oh my god, I forgot!"

"What? What's wrong?" Má demands before I can get a word out.

"I didn't get Aaron's tux pressed!"

"You scared me." Má deflates against her chair. "Don't worry Dani, no one cares about your cat's tuxedo."

"But Aaron Purr—"

"Aaron Purr Tsai-Tran," I sneak in.

Dani nods. "Aaron Purr Tsai-Tran is going to be in the wedding photos too."

"Trời đất ơi. You're joking, right?" Má rolls her eyes. She's still bitter that her introduction to our newest family member started with "We have exciting news," but didn't end with us showing her a sonogram.

"How dare you," I *tsk* at her, feigning outrage. Wrapping my arms around Dani from behind, I make sure to add, "That's our child."

"Give me a real grandchild first, then I let you joke about the cat."

"And that's my cue to leave." Mr. Tsai sighs and makes his exit, but not before giving me a consoling good-luck pat on the shoulder. Within seconds of his departure, my own father has made his appearance in the room, sliding a remote control into my hand.

"Parker, if you're not watching the game, turn on the karaoke for Ba, okay?"

"Right now?" My jaw drops. I can feel blood rising to my neck. "Is it that urgent that you sing 'Careless Whisper' the night before my wedding?"

A hearty wail makes me turn on the spot, and Má is sobbing loudly into a tissue. This is nothing new; she's been a mess of emotions since picking us up at the airport. "What? Why are you crying now?"

She rotates her phone for me to see the email on the screen.

"You're crying over a shipping notification?"

"They finally shipped your engagement photos! They took so long, I waited months! Coi! So beautiful!"

In the preview, Dani and I, in traditional Vietnamese wedding attire, are posing at Pebble Beach with the Brooklyn Bridge as the backdrop. The shoot was done by some famous wedding photographer who Dani claims is a big deal—a gift from her boss, Estelle. In her modern red áo dài, she looks absolutely beautiful. And did anyone really doubt I could pull off royal blue and gold dragons?

"Dani, I was thinking." Those are the last words we want to hear when Mr. Tsai moseys back into the kitchen. "My cousin from Taipei has his own band. Maybe you could squeeze him in for a performance. They do a great rendition of Andy Lau's 'Wedding March.'"

At this, Ba immediately perks up. "You're changing the program? I can sing something for you. Dani, what's your favorite George Michael song?"

Oh my god. There's so much going on. Why did I assume the Tsai-Tran-Pham trifecta would let me marry the woman I love in peace? I peek at Dani, and she's gone hollow-eyed. Her brain has retreated to its safe place. I know that look. My fiancée needs to decompress, and it's up to me to sweep her away from this madness.

"Hey." I take her hand. "Let's go for a drive."

❧

For a blissful moment of time, Dani and I sit in silence in the Jeep, parked in front of Rocky's Diner. Dani was determined to overwrite the trauma from our past, so we made a habit of coming here once we started dating. Now it's simply the spot that makes our favorite strawberry milkshakes.

"We're getting married tomorrow." I still get the urge to vocalize it from time to time. It's like saying it out loud makes it all the more real. *It's finally happening.*

"We're getting married tomorrow," she repeats, and she squeezes my hand. "Are you nervous?"

"Nope." And I mean it. I've never been more sure about anything. Even football doesn't come close. "Are you?"

"I'm nervous about walking down the aisle. I keep having nightmares where I fall on my face before I get to the altar." She takes a long sip of her milkshake. "But I'm not nervous about everything that comes after that."

"I *am* a little concerned that my dad is treating tomorrow like another karaoke night," I say as Dani passes the Styrofoam cup to me. "Do you get the feeling everyone else is making our wedding about them?"

"Yes! God, this was supposed to be chill, stress-free. I mean, flying all the way out here was one thing, but I thought that scheduling a wedding on a Friday would deter people from coming. Everyone—even our sympathy invites—is showing up! And they're all driving me insane! All my single cousins are asking me to introduce them to your athlete friends. Like I won't be too busy getting *married* to play matchmaker! Don't get me started on how everyone's a food connoisseur, all of a sudden. Everyone has an opinion on fried bao for cocktail hour."

Normally, I love listening to Dani fly off the rails on a tangent. She can make anything sound interesting. But there's a difference between a spiel on how *Fallen Angels* both is and isn't the sequel to *Chungking Express* and the kind of rant that happens when she's losing her sense of control.

Suddenly, she whips her head around at me. Her long, dark hair is a pretty flourish under the diner's neon lights. "Should we just elope?"

I care about the wedding. I really do. But if it meant I got to be Dani's husband by tomorrow, I would marry her anywhere. The only thing is, I know how much this wedding means to her. Otherwise, she wouldn't have lugged that binder everywhere for nearly a year. "You don't mean that."

"It's true, I don't. I could never do that to Cô—I mean, Má." She falls back against her seat and grins to herself. "I like the sound of that. *Má*."

Dani ultimately decided not to invite her mother to the wedding. This way, she said, she couldn't be disappointed by the inevitable excuse for her not showing up. I wanted to make sure she wouldn't regret her choice, and for a while I considered trying to change her mind. But her mom caught wind of the engagement anyway and had a bouquet delivered with an offer to paint a Beatrice Chen original for us. She didn't ask about the wedding, and when I saw how this made Dani breathe a sigh of relief, I took it as a private understanding reached between the two. The very next morning, Dani called my mom to see if she'd fly over for dress shopping. As she put it, "The mother of the bride should be there." The answer was obvious.

I hold up her hand and kiss her knuckles. "At least we have Bali after."

Her face relaxes with appreciation. "I'm already picturing myself in that private infinity pool."

"And now I'm picturing you naked in that infinity pool." With that image, I'm taken to my own happy place. I can't help it. The five-foot-four woman next to me in her plaid pajama bottoms drives me wild. In a password-protected album on my phone, there are exactly three nudes of Dani from our short tenure apart, before my move to New York. They might be the most sacred possessions to my name.

I peek over at her in the passenger seat. She pops the lid off the cup and downs the last of the milkshake with gusto. And now with a napkin methodically folded into a square, she's going to wipe the foam off her upper lip. *So cute*. It's a funny thing to feel yourself falling in love with someone over and over again. In my mind, I can pick out all those small instances, saving each one like a snapshot.

I had the same feeling the night Dani showed up at the St. Regis in that black dress with the mercilessly low neckline. My head was a void sucking up any intelligible thought, leaving behind a single, resounding *Wow*. I was trying desperately to keep my composure around her. Whiskey was my lifeline, and I was only getting through our conversation at the bar by the grace of alcohol. I thought about kissing her all night. I didn't expect she'd beat me to it.

Another moment burned in my memory is when she wore my jersey to my last game as a Green Valley Griffin. I'd never seen a prettier girl in my life. And the same was true in that ballroom. I later learned that the black dress belonged to Charlotte. It almost seems like a crime that I'll never see Dani in it again or get to take it off her one more time.

The only thing that's going to top all that is when I see her in her wedding dress.

"I'm going to get one more for the road." Dani motions to the empty cup and hops out of the Jeep. I try not to check out her ass when she walks back to the diner, but it's no use.

My phone buzzes in my pocket, snapping me out of my personal paradise.

"I want to go over my best man speech with you." It's Nathan.

"I told you, whatever you wrote will be fine. You know me and Dani better than anyone else."

"So, I can talk about how my commitment-phobe little brother is getting hitched before me? And the time I caught you two sneaking around on Thanksgiving?"

Nathan clued in to our relationship even before Dani and I knew what we were. I asked him how he figured it out, and he said, "The hickey on her neck after you two disappeared into your bedroom? You're lucky our parents are so oblivious. They still think hooking up only happens when you spend the night. It's like they've never heard of a quickie." A disturbing visual that I could've gone my entire life without. I hate him.

"You two have so much history, and I want my speech to do it justice. It's got to make Dani laugh *and* cry."

"We'll review it at the hotel together," I concede. I should be a little more compassionate with him. I'm sure he's over Irene by now; it's been two years since the engagement fell through. But it can't be easy to watch all the excitement from the sidelines and think about how the centerpieces look like the ones your ex-fiancée picked out. I suppose that's why he booked a two-bedroom suite for us tonight. He said it was to keep me company, but I think he's trying to get away from the wedding hysteria at home.

"If we ever make it to the hotel. You know you can't stay home tonight, right? Why haven't you packed your stuff yet?"

"I still have to make sure Dani is okay—"

"Parker!" I watch my bride-to-be burst through the diner doors, shouting anxiously for me. Instinctively, I spring out of the Jeep to meet her. She latches onto my forearm with a death grip, her bottom lip trembling.

My heart is in my throat. "What is it?"

"M-Marisa just called," she sputters. "They lost Aaron!"

"Sorry, false alarm," Marisa giggles as she hands me a feather wand. "Hey, who needs the fire department when you've got this guy?"

I push a shroud of leaves blocking my view and spot a ball of gray fur nestled on top of a branch. Aaron Purr is just out of reach, in a tree in front of the Silverpine Inn. I wave the teaser toy to get his attention. He blinks his round, golden eyes at me, uninterested.

"The only task I gave you before the wedding was to look after Aaron," scolds Dani next to me. "I can't believe you let him get out."

"I took my eyes off him for a second!"

With a yawn, Aaron finally starts to inch toward me. I grab him as soon as he's close enough and scoop him into my arms. Dani is wearing the expression of a mother whose son has returned from war as I pass him along to her.

"Hey buddy, you gave Mommy and Daddy a scare," I say as I scratch his head.

"Aren't you supposed to be at your hotel?" Marisa asks me.

"I'll go after this," I tell her. "Why is everyone so concerned about what bed we sleep in tonight? Bunch of perverts."

"If you have time to spare, I can bleach your hair before the ceremony."

"Actually, I need your help," Dani says to Marisa. Her frown hasn't let up yet, something I've been all too aware of. "Can we go up to your room?"

I move to follow them into the building, but Marisa stops me at the doors. Aaron Purr meows at me from her arms.

"Ah-ah. Maid-of-honor duties."

❦

Dani left Marisa's room without much to say during the ride home. I check her face every few seconds, but her expression only grows more and more solemn. It makes my gut tense with worry. Is all the pre-ceremony pressure taking its toll on her?

Even when we arrive at my bedroom—hers, for tonight—she still doesn't utter a peep.

"Are you okay?"

"I'm just tired."

"Almost convincing, if you weren't talking to me." I take a long look at her as I tuck her hair behind her ears. "What is it, baby?"

She finally relents with a sigh. "The slideshow."

"I put it on a USB and gave it to Nathan already."

"No, it's not that." Dani pauses, eyes darting from mine. My gut is in all kinds of knots now. "They don't have any photos of us together for a whole seven-year span. I thought I could slip something in at the last minute, so I asked Marisa if I could borrow her Photoshop skills."

I so badly want to breathe a sigh of relief, but the tension on Dani's face only deepens, so I take a different approach. "Was she able to whip something up?"

"Yes." She pouts. "Not her best work."

Dani takes a seat at the foot of the bed and beckons me over, then pulls up an email on her phone. As soon as the photo buffers, my hand flies over my mouth.

Don't laugh, Parker. My jaw tenses. I press the corners of my lips.

I know that Dani's friend Marisa is a professional graphic designer. A fairly good one, at that. I can see it in the seamless blending of two superimposed images and the shadow adjustments that add depth to her creation. So, I'm aware this isn't a matter of skill.

But before me is painfully contrived attempt at merging

Dani's and my college graduation photos. Somehow, Dani had managed to find shots where we're posing close enough to trees, and that gave her a foundation to work on. From there, Marisa had expertly concocted some kind of enchanted, sprite-filled forest of luscious shrubbery and speckled toadstools. A whimsical, fabricated memory of Dani and me celebrating our milestone with all our fairy friends.

"Oh, wow," I say stiffly, brow twitching. "You know, I remember taking this photo. Wasn't this where you unlocked your wizard magic for the first time—"

"This isn't a joke, Parker!" Dani groans and tosses her phone aside. "Everyone's speech is going to mention how we went from childhood friends to husband and wife, but once the slideshow plays, there's going to be a blaringly obvious gap in the years. It'll be a reminder to everyone that we weren't friends."

I can see on her face that she's crushed. It makes my chest ache for my adorably sentimental fiancée. If I could turn back time, I'd give her an album full of happy memories. But I can't, and that's okay. Because everything we've built together in the last three years is far more important than any of the time we lost.

"Come here." I tug her close and hug her tight. She's tense in my arms, and I want nothing more than to melt her worry away. "How long is the slideshow again?"

"Ten minutes, thirty-two seconds."

"And how much of that is everything after high school?"

"Like, four minutes?"

"So, in those four minutes, we have the engagement photos, our trips to London and Mount Bromo, family barbecues, and any impossibly cute selfies. That seven-year span would've realistically been around a minute, give or take. So, sixty seconds, in a ten-minute slideshow, during a five-hour reception, on day one of our lives as husband and wife." She's watching me attentively, and I take the opportunity to press a kiss to her cheek. "In the grand scheme of things, what's one minute to a lifetime of being married to my best friend?"

She's silent for a beat, and then I feel her ease against my chest. "How do you always know what to say?"

"It's simple math," I shrug. "You're the smart one."

I know I've done well because Dani rewards me by peppering kisses all over my face. Something I've learned about having Dani Tsai as my girl is that she's prone to these little explosions of affection. I think it's called cute aggression.

"I love you," she says, her smile returning.

"I love you too, Dani."

There was a time I almost lost my shot at this. In all honesty, I'm actually relieved the seven-year gap isn't in the slideshow. I don't like to remember it. Back then, it felt a lot like living on autopilot. I was emotionally checked out after my football career came to a premature end. I enjoyed my work and directed all my energy there instead. But at some point, even the shine of the all-star games and celebrity events faded. Everything around me was in dull, muted grays.

When I ran into Dani in New York, I was able to see in color again. I didn't know it was possible to feel things with the intensity of the sun until it was happening to me. Nights at my hotel when I was always one breathy moment away from letting myself slip and say too much. All the times we were apart, and I'd stalk her Instagram waiting for her to post (she never did). I wanted all of Dani: her highs, lows, and especially the ordinary middles. If you ask me when this desire began, I probably couldn't tell you. I think I was born with it in my composition. I think that part of me has always belonged to her.

I want to stay a little longer, but a passing glimpse at my watch reminds me I should be leaving for the hotel. Just when I'm about to tell her goodnight, Dani slides onto my lap and dips her mouth below my jaw, landing soft kisses along my neck.

I freeze with my hands on her waist.

"Now?" I ask carefully. "We're not supposed to, you know, before the wedding."

"Why? Because some puritans decided centuries ago that a god would curse us if we saw each other naked before our vows?"

"I happen to recall a time when it was forbidden for us to have sex in this house." I tilt my head. "With our parents downstairs."

"What prude came up with that?"

"You, Dani. That was your ground rule."

At this, she fixes me with a look that's meant to shush me. Her catlike eyes are searing into mine as a hand slips under my waistband. I instantly react with a twitch from inside my pants. "They'll never hear us. They've got the karaoke machine on."

As I give serious consideration to what's about to happen, a laugh rises in my throat. I've known her all my life, but every day with Dani, in all her beautiful, complex designs, feels brand new. Once again, I snapshot the moment, saving it close to my heart. I just keep falling in love.

"What's so funny?"

"I'm just happy." I can't think of what else to say. She's always been better at words. "You do that to me."

At least it makes her blush. "Go lock the door, Parker."

I kiss her on the forehead and do as my wife tells me.

ACKNOWLEDGMENTS

This story took shape, as one does, over hours of maladaptive daydreaming on the train. Now that *Casually Yours* has come to life, its presence in the real world still feels like a wonder. With my deepest appreciation, I would first like to acknowledge the team at Third State Books: Stephanie Lim and Charles Kim, for this extraordinary opportunity and for your belief in me; Prerna Chaudhary, for championing the manuscript in its early days; and Emily Tom, for your role in promoting this work. This debut book was made possible thanks to your guidance and encouragement.

My thanks also to Tara Hân-Trần Johnson, for lending your artistry and talent in creating this stunning cover; to Kathy Campbell, who designed this book; and Jennie Liston, who copyedited it.

To Ma and Ba: I have spent a lot of time writing words, yet I still can't find the right arrangement to express the depth of my gratitude. I could not have done this without all your care and endless worrying. Special thanks to everyone whose support, in any form, carried me through to the very last word: Uncle Ty and Aunt Hung; Victoria Quach; Tori Ly; Alan Li; Amanda; Natalie Chong; Tara Blondeau, who read the first draft; and Thanh Ly, who nudged me to take the first step. I will always be grateful to each and every one of you.

To Nobu, for whom I would do anything, and to little Luna, we miss you every day.

And finally, to my sister, Anna. I mentioned that this book has come to life, but from the first through all the drafts that came after, you know better than anyone how many lives it's lived. (I like to think of these as Dani and Parker's alternate universes, which only you and I know of.) Thank you for your patience through every rewrite and for your unwavering enthusiasm every time I said, "Let me run this by you real quick." It has been an honor to write stories for you.